The Case Against

DIGGER
MOSS

The Case Against Digger Moss

By Dave Sullivan

ISBN: 0-75963-616-8

This book is printed on acid free paper.

Cover Design by Kathy L. Sullivan
Author photo by Grandmaison Studios

1stBooks – rev. 8/30/01

To Ruth and Kath,
my first and most loyal fans

CHAPTER ONE

Digger Moss looked at the large plain manila envelope. He recognized all of the rest of the mail in his basket. He was in a hurry, trying to mentally catalog each piece of mail for later handling when he had time. But the unmarked envelope bothered him.

"Where did this come from?" he asked a nearby clerk.

The clerk looked at the envelope. "It was in the mail that was sorted down on the first floor, Judge. Tina brought it up about a half hour ago."

"Who?"

"Tina. She's a new runner in Room 320."

"Oh." Moss tried to picture Tina but could not. Must be very new, he thought.

"But," the clerk pointed to the upper right corner of the envelope, "it wasn't in the mail. It was delivered. See, no postage."

"I saw that," Digger answered, looking at the envelope that contained no postage or return address. Only a plain white gummed label that proclaimed in large bold capital letters, "HONORABLE JAMES DIGBY MOSS," addressed it to him. Below the label in the lower left corner of the sealed envelope were even larger block letters stamped in red ink warning that the contents were: *"PERSONAL AND CONFIDENTIAL."*

Judges received brown envelopes from the appellate courts marked "Confidential" when opinions affirming or reversing trial judges' decisions were issued, but they had return addresses. Even confidential letters from the Board on Judicial Standards regarding complaints filed against a judge always discreetly showed the return address without identifying the sender. This was not like either of those.

Digger threw the mail back in the basket. He would pick it up later when he got off the bench. He straightened his robe and started into the courtroom.

"All rise!" commanded the bailiff. "District Court is now in session, the Honorable James Digby Moss presiding."

1

Digger ascended the three steps to the platform behind the bench. He wished he didn't have to go through this hearing, just now, however short it would probably be. The unidentified envelope bothered him for some reason he could not understand. Why? What difference could it make? He had no idea how the contents of that strange envelope would change his life.

He struck the gavel on its clapper and announced, "Please be seated." As he seated himself, he read from the file before him on the bench.

"State of Minnesota vs. Jennifer Lynn Nelson." Digger looked over the bench to counsel table and continued, "The record should reflect that the defendant is present in court and with her counsel, Michael Reynolds, and Jordan Swanson is here representing the State." The judge looked at defense counsel. "Mr. Reynolds, this matter has been scheduled for a plea. You may proceed."

"Thank you, your Honor," said Mike Reynolds rising to address the court. "The parties have reached an agreement in this matter. The defendant will plead guilty to an amended charge reducing the gross misdemeanor assault charge to misdemeanor assault. The parties will still request a pre-sentence investigation and later sentencing date. There has been no agreement regarding sentence, the parties both desiring to wait for the PSI result." Reynolds sat down.

"Is that correct Mr. Swanson?" asked Digger looking at the prosecutor. And if it is, let's get on with it, he thought to himself, the envelope still on his mind.

"That's correct, your Honor," said the prosecutor. "We've checked with the victim and believe that under the circumstances it is appropriate for this reduction of the original charge. The other party involved has received a similar sentence. Your Honor, I believe that the police reports, particularly the report of Sgt. Miller, provide the basis for the plea agreement which we have reached."

Digger flipped through the pages of the file. Examining Sergeant Miller's report to which the prosecutor referred him, he said, "I see. Yes, that's sufficient for my purposes." He looked toward the defendant. "Ms. Nelson, in order for the Court to accept your plea of guilty, I must first be satisfied that you understand the rights which you are waiving when you enter a plea of guilty instead of proceeding to trial. Second, you must acknowledge the facts which constitute the crime to which you are entering the plea. In order to accomplish those two purposes I will ask that you come forward and raise your right hand to be sworn and then have a seat here in the witness box." He gestured to the witness chair on his left. The defendant came forward somewhat tentatively raising her right hand to face the clerk. The clerk administered the oath. When the defendant reached the witness stand and seated herself, she stated her full name for the record as requested by the clerk.

"Jennifer Lynn Nelson."

"Ms. Nelson, I'm now going to invite the lawyers to ask you some questions about this case to provide us with information which we need. You understand that you will be answering those questions under oath?"

"I do," she said.

"All right, then," said Digger, "Mr. Reynolds, you may inquire."

"Thank you, your Honor," said Mike Reynolds, remaining seated at counsel table while he began the examination of his client regarding her rights and the written, signed plea petition he would soon be filing with the court.

Digger watched the defendant in the witness box while the two lawyers asked her questions about the case. As the prosecutor went through the facts with her, insuring that she was going to acknowledge the facts of the reduced charge to which she was pleading, Digger mentally checked off the elements of the crime as he made his decision as to whether to accept the plea.

When the lawyers were finished, Digger announced, "The court will accept the plea of guilty, request a pre-sentence investigation, and the clerk will notify you of the sentencing date."

"Anything else, counsel?" asked Digger.

"Nothing more, your Honor," said Reynolds.

"Nothing more, your Honor," echoed prosecutor Swanson.

"Very well, then," said Digger, "Court is adjourned." He rapped the gavel on its clapper and stood to leave the courtroom.

On the way to his chambers, Digger grabbed the envelope and other mail from the wire basket near the clerk's station.

In his chambers, he tossed the mail on his large uncluttered desk and poured a cup of coffee. He sat in the large high-backed leather chair, put the other mail aside and concentrated on the envelope. He glanced at the clock. It was 9:45 a.m. Again he examined the address label. Slitting open the end with his letter opener, he pulled out several documents and a smaller envelope which, he discovered, contained several black and white photographs. With what he assumed to be normal human curiosity, he looked at the photographs first.

"Jesus Christ! What the hell is this?" he said aloud. He glanced at the open door to his chambers and the hallway beyond and studied the pictures again.

"Jesus!" he said again, although this time barely above a whisper.

Quickly, he looked through the pages that accompanied the photographs. He gulped hot coffee from his cup. He pulled a handkerchief from his back pocket and mopped his brow. Among the loose papers was another smaller envelope with another block-lettered label with his name on it. He opened this white, business size envelope. He removed a single white, 8 ½" x 11" sheet which he held in front of him. He did not need his glasses to read its message. Huge black letters centered on the sheet of paper asked a single question:

DID YOU REALLY THINK YOU COULD GET AWAY WITH THIS?

Digger opened the deep file folder-sized desk drawer on the left side of his desk. With both hands he rummaged through the file folders and other papers in the drawer. Finally, he gave up searching.

"God damn!" He rose from his chair and moved to the window. He stared through the glass at the Duluth harbor.

James Digby Moss was a judge of the District Court. At age 59, Digger Moss was neither the oldest nor the youngest judge in the St. Louis County Courthouse in Duluth. Still in good physical condition, the 175 pounds he carried was about the same weight at which he played college football for the University of Minnesota.

As one of the "Golden Gophers" he earned his nickname "Digger." Because of his relatively small size, but muscular build, he was a running back, and a star running back at that. Although, he undoubtedly earned his nickname because of his mother's maiden name, which was his middle name, it was also said of him that he could dig under the pile of players and come out the other side with the ball. Of the four years he played for Minnesota he was named to the All-Big Ten Team three times and was All American his last two years. The last year, he was named MVP of the Rose Bowl for leading the Gophers to a 21-10 victory over U.S.C.

At the time it was believed that he was simply too small for pro football. He thought it and the pro teams thought it. So, he satisfied himself that he had had a wonderful time and a great college career. He chose law school because of the independence he felt he would have by being his own boss, controlling his own destiny, and setting his own ideals for the way he would practice.

After graduation, Digger worked at the Hennepin County Attorney's office in Minneapolis for two years to get litigation experience, then moved to Duluth to begin his private practice with an established firm with a large litigation section. By the time he accepted an appointment to the bench, he had a reputation as one of the area's finest civil trial lawyers and he was the managing partner of his firm then named Jensen, Brand, Moss, & Littler. Jensen, Brand had offices at 1600 Alworth Building which occupied the top two floors of the fifteen story building on the lower side of Superior Street. When the structure was built in the early part of the century, it was the tallest building in Minnesota, and some said the tallest west of Chicago. What they really said was that it was the tallest west of the Mississippi, but since Duluth is east of that river, they really meant there was no building west of the Mississippi at that time which was taller. Following the superstition of the time, the Alworth Building had no thirteenth floor, or at least not one that was so named. Thus the floor above the twelfth was the fourteenth, and the top floor of the fifteen-story building was the sixteenth floor where the lawyers of Jensen, Brand had offered legal services to their clients for most of the firm's nearly one hundred year existence.

From his chambers, Digger could see the Alworth Building rising above the other structures on downtown Duluth's main street. Its higher floors were silhouetted against the backdrop of the blue waters of Lake Superior.

I've got to talk to somebody, thought Digger. He knew that he was in a crisis that he could not handle himself. All his life he had prided himself on his independence, his ability to handle his own problems without outside help. He had managed to get through twenty-five years of litigation practice, dealt with all kinds of partners, clients, and legal problems, and he had not been without a few personal problems of his own. But always he had managed. This was different. This time he had to admit to himself that while he had not done anything wrong, he *had* been stupid. Before he was always dealing with a problem in which he was involved, but one which had been brought about by someone else. For this he had only himself to blame. Sure, he could blame whoever was after him. He could blame them for setting him up and double crossing him, if that is what was happening. In the end, he was in trouble because he had been foolish and not careful enough.

Who? He thought about the persons he knew in whom he could confide. The choice was easy. He knew a lot of people. He had a lot of friends. He commanded a lot of respect among the bench and bar and in the community. But there were really only two people for this degree of confidence. Mike Reynolds and Kate Riley. He would begin tomorrow.

Kathrine Megan Riley was also a District Judge, although without the robe, she didn't look like one. Digger smiled to himself. Who did? What does a judge look like? But, whatever the answer may be, he thought, Kate Riley didn't look like one. Her dark mahogany red hair framed a freckled face and mischievous bright emerald eyes. Her Irish appearance was true to her character. Although she was compassionate and patient, she had a temper that knew few bounds when and if it was finally unleashed. With a vocabulary like a drunken sailor, she was not at all like she was when she donned the judicial robe and ascended the bench.

Digger and Kate had started almost together. Digger was appointed just a few months before Kate. They went to new judges' school in Reno together. As the two new judges in the courthouse, they developed a camaraderie that had lasted up to the present time, long past when they were no longer the newest judges in the courthouse.

Michael Reynolds was one of Duluth's premier criminal defense lawyers. He was a sole practitioner who also officed in the Alworth Building. He had many years' experience as a part-time public defender. Besides his criminal law practice, he occasionally handled civil cases and family matters. Digger and Mike had a few cases together over the years and developed a close friendship. Before Digger was appointed to the bench, he relied on Mike to take referrals of any criminal cases that came into Jensen, Brand.

The next afternoon, Digger Moss appeared at the door to Judge Riley's chambers. Kate Riley smiled as she looked up from the papers on her desk, her bright green eyes shining. "Hi, Digs! What's up?" She observed him leaning casually in the door frame of the entrance to her chambers. He was holding a large plain brown envelope. Noticing Digger's expression, she asked, "What happened to you? Did your best friend die, turn up gay, or your best gay friend turn out to be straight?"

"I'll tell you soon enough," Digger answered. "I saw Mike Reynolds downstairs and asked him to join us. I see you've finished your afternoon calendar. Have you got a few minutes?"

"For you, always." She put down her pen and turned those bright emerald eyes at him and smiled mischievously. "I can't alienate the only judge in this courthouse I ever get to talk to. If it weren't for you and the monthly judges' meetings, I'd think I was working in a one judge courthouse."

"Thanks," Digger sighed as he slowly moved toward her window, studying the view of the steep Duluth hillside beyond.

"But Jesus Christ, Digger, what the hell's wrong with you? You do look like you've lost your best friend."

A gentle tapping sound came from the entrance to her chambers. They both looked to see Mike Reynolds standing in the doorway, one hand raised, knuckles pointing toward the door frame, a large black briefcase in the other.

"Hello, your Honors," said Reynolds, dropping his briefcase to the floor. "If you've summoned me before you to tell me I've been disbarred and neither of you has the courage to tell me by yourself, let me have it. I can take it." He sat down across the desk from Kate Riley.

"Well, I see you're in your usual fine spirits," said Kate. "I wish I could say the same for Judge Moss here."

"Oh?" Reynolds turned to look at Digger. "Problem?"

Digger Moss took a seat next to Mike Reynolds. "You have no idea," he groaned.

Kate Riley looked at the envelope Digger had placed on her desk in front of him. "May we assume it has something to do with the contents of that mysterious envelope you've been hugging since you got here?"

Reynolds looked at the envelope, and then back at his friend Digger, who actually looked scared. "You got me worried, my friend. What's going on?"

Digger opened the envelope.

Kate cleared her desk. The envelope's contents were spread out for them all to study. Kate and Mike read and looked at pictures in stunned silence. Digger waited, nervously tapping the letter size envelope on the desk. He withheld the message to show them last.

Three of the pictures clearly showed Judge Digger Moss standing in the parking lot of the Pickwick restaurant on East Superior Street exchanging money for a package. Two more pictures were close-ups of the package. Three more showed the package opened and containing what appeared to be plastic baggies of a white powdery substance. Another picture showed the money fanned out so it could actually be counted in the photograph: $3,500 in one hundred dollar bills. More pictures showed further exchanges at two different locations with additional pictures of money and what appeared to be drugs.

Included in the documents were test reports, presumably of the substances in the photographs, showing that the materials tested were cocaine, methamphetamine, and raw heroin. And there were more documents in the envelope.

"Oh, God," Kate Riley whispered as she read a thirty-nine year old police report about some U of M football players caught using marijuana. Their names included James D. Moss, then a junior on the Minneapolis campus.

Mike Reynolds was reading a criminal complaint. Diagonally across the body of each page was a large, bold type watermark proclaiming the document to be a *"DRAFT,"* so this was not a final complaint, but someone had at least taken the trouble to begin its preparation. The caption stated it was the case of "STATE OF MINNESOTA vs. JAMES DIGBY MOSS." The charge was that the defendant had on more than one occasion unlawfully possessed with intent to sell mixtures with a total weight of more than ten grams that contained cocaine or heroin. He, the complaint alleged, violated Minn. Stat. § 152.021: "Controlled substance crime in the first degree." The maximum sentence was stated as "... imprisonment for not more than 30 years or to payment of a fine of not more than $1,000,000, or both." Because there were three separate counts for three separate offenses, the complaint also noted that if a conviction were in addition to another conviction, the penalty would be, "... not less than four years nor more than 40 years and, in addition may be sentenced to payment of a fine of not more than $1,000,000."

The complaint was not signed by a complainant from the sheriff's office or the police department. It was not signed by a prosecutor from the county attorney's office. Of course, thought Mike, it *is* just a draft. He handed it to Judge Riley.

"Holy shit!" Kate Riley gasped as she saw the caption. Her eyes looking up at Digger. She read quickly in silence.

When they had seen and read everything, they looked at each other and then at Digger.

"No wonder you look worried," said Reynolds.

"Worried? Shit, Digger," Kate lowered her voice, looking at the open door to her chambers, "you're fucked, man!" She rose to shut the door and returned to her desk.

"The complaint isn't signed. It doesn't identify a prosecutor," Mike said. "Where'd you get this stuff, Digger?"

"In that envelope," he pointed, "delivered to my mail basket."

Kate examined the large plain brown envelope with renewed interest.

"There's more," said Digger.

They both looked at him, waiting.

"Here," he said, tossing the white letter size envelope on the desk.

The judge and the lawyer reached for it at the same time. The judge won. She removed the single sheet of paper, glanced at the huge block letters, mumbled something under her breath and turned the page around so Mike Reynolds could see it.

Kate leaned back in her high-backed desk chair and breathed deeply. "What do you make of that?" she asked them.

"When did you get this?" asked Mike.

"Yesterday."

"Have you heard anything from the police or the County Attorney?"

"No."

Kate looked at Mike and asked, "Are you thinking blackmail?"

"Maybe," said Mike.

Kate turned to Digger. "Did you really do drugs in college? When you were on the football team?"

"Yeah, that was a long time ago," Digger acknowledged. "We were young. We smoked a little grass."

"Hell, Digger," said Kate, "it wasn't even the Sixties, yet, when you were in college."

"I would think that would have been huge news," said Mike. "Big Ten Champions Using Dope!' I can see the headline now."

"It was covered up," Digger answered. "They were too worried about their football team. The cops never pursued it."

Kate got up and walked to a small closet, which contained a small refrigerator from which she took three cans of Diet Coke. Handing one to each of the two men and pulling the tab on her own, she said, "I don't give a happy shit if you toked up once in a while forty years ago. I want to know why you're doing hard drugs now, and, for Christ's sake, why you're selling the God damned stuff!" She took a long drink, obviously waiting for an answer.

Digger stood and moved back to the window. He stared at the hillside as if deep in thought. His two friends watched him, waiting.

"I didn't," he said, finally.

Kate Riley looked relieved, at first, but then looked back at the photographs strewn across her desk. "Bullshit! Here you are buying $3500 worth of drugs in the Pickwick parking lot, for Christ's sake! You don't buy that amount without selling to other people. Digger, the evidence here is slightly stronger than ironclad. Wouldn't you say so, Mike? How would you advise a client with this kind of shit against him?"

"Negotiate like hell," Mike answered.

"Of course!" She pointed a long slender finger at him. "You'd do your best to cop a plea; and if you got much of a deal with this evidence against you, I'd be demanding a damned good explanation from the prosecutor before I'd approve anything but a straight up guilty plea and at least a guidelines sentence. Right, Digger? Hell, Digger would be tougher than I would be."

"I didn't do it," repeated Digger.

Kate rolled her emerald green eyes under long dark lashes. "We're listening," she declared.

"Sit down, please, Kate," Digger said as he resumed his seat across the desk from her. She sat.

Digger Moss began his story.

CHAPTER TWO

Judge Kathrine Megan Riley and Michael J. Reynolds, Attorney at Law, listened intently as Judge Digger Moss told his story.

"About three months ago," he began, "Greg Larson from Duluth P. D. came to me. He asked for my help and, God help me, I gave it to him."

"What did he ..." Kate was interrupted by Mike who held a finger to his lips.

"He was working undercover, he said, on a drug investigation that involved members of the police administration and some other government officials suspected of dealing in illegal drugs, possibly including drugs seized by law enforcement in other investigations." Digger looked up at the ceiling, recalling that first meeting with Sergeant Larson.

"The reason he said he wanted my help was to set up a 'sting' operation. I was to participate in purchases of confiscated drugs from a known drug dealer. Greg Larson was looking for confiscated drugs from the police evidence locker that he believed were getting back out on the street instead of being destroyed."

"I smell the Constitution," said Mike. "Boys and girls, can you say E-N-T-R-A-P-M-E-N-T?"

"Shhhh!" Kate glowered at Mike and held one finger up to her lips. "Where did you get the money?" she asked.

"Shhhh!" said Mike. Kate glowered at him again.

Digger continued. "The money I used was police money used for drug buys, I guess. Greg gave me the money and arranged the meetings. I took the money he gave me, exchanged it for the drugs, and returned the drugs to Greg afterwards."

"Who was the 'known drug dealer'?" asked Kate.

"His name is Carmen Diego. His street name is 'Zorro.' You probably have not heard of him before. He is relatively new to Duluth. He has been active in the drug scene and has been under investigation for some time. Larson told me he was chosen because he has no prior record. Larson believed that using him in the sting operation would enable him to make a more effective promise of immunity for information regarding police and other public officials involved."

"And did it work?" asked Mike.

"I don't know," said Digger. "I only made the buys and returned the drugs. I don't know what, if anything more, Larson's investigation revealed."

"That's it?" Kate demanded, shaking her head. "Didn't you have some protection? Something from Greg Larson to show that what you were doing was assisting the police?"

"I did," answered Digger. "I requested and got a note from Larson explaining the sting operation and his request for my assistance."

Kate Riley looked relieved. "Well that's it, then. Where do you have it?"

"I don't," answered Digger sadly.

"What? Why not?" demanded Kate.

"What happened to it?" asked Mike.

Digger looked at both of his friends. Slowly, not knowing whether they would believe him or not, he said, "It was stolen."

"Oh my God!" Kate stood and threw her empty Diet Coke can into the wastebasket several feet from her desk. "You know, Digger, Mike and I are your friends. But can you even expect us to believe all this?"

"I know," said Digger, looking down at the top of the desk. "It sounds hard to believe, doesn't it?"

"As Kate said a minute ago," said Mike, "if you were my client, I'd be pressing hard to cop a plea."

Digger went back to the window. "I came to you because you are my friends. I came to you because my story is so incredible that only true friends who trust me might even begin to believe it. I came to you because the evidence is so strong I cannot possibly handle this by myself." He turned from the window and said to them, "I need your help."

Mike Reynolds rose from his chair, backed away from Kate's desk, and leaned against the wall near the door. "You know, there are canons of ethics which regulate my profession that probably direct me to report this situation to someone. I'm sure there are similar rules for Judge Riley that would require her to report to the Board on

13

Judicial Standards or some other agency." He glanced down at his feet on the rich, thick carpet of Kate Riley's chambers. "I refer to those rules of professional responsibility to which we must both adhere without adding comment about any obligation we may also have to report the commission of a crime."

"Christ, Mike!" cried Kate. "You want to turn in Digger Moss for dealing hard drugs?"

"Of course not," he answered, "but as we consider the fix he's in, we'd better consider what kind of trouble we may be bringing down on ourselves, now that we've heard his story."

"He's right, Kate," said Digger. "I need your help, but I don't want to get either of you in trouble. Because I know I'm innocent, I guess I didn't think about what problems you may have if I don't prove my innocence."

Kate smiled. "You don't have to prove your innocence, remember? Innocent until proven guilty, presumption of innocence and all that."

"Yeah, right," said Digger. "The evidence against me is so strong that, if you weren't my best friends, you'd be calling the police right now. I've got to clear myself."

"I know you don't want to hear this," said Kate, "but sound advice would be for you to contact the police and tell them the story right away, the sooner the better." She glanced at her desk phone.

"I don't dare. The investigation involved government officials, police personnel, and even police administration officials. I can't be sure whom I can trust."

"Isn't the easy and obvious answer to get Greg Larson to confirm your story?" asked Mike.

"I thought so," Digger answered, "but I'm not sure."

"Of course that's the answer," declared Kate. "Why do you have any doubt?"

"Remember I told you my note from him explaining what I was doing was stolen?"

"Yes?"

"He was the only one who knew I had it."

"Oh." Kate looked dejected. "So what do we do? We've got to do something."

"Agreed," said Mike, returning to his chair. "We need a plan. I understand since Greg Larson was the only one who knew about the note from him, you think he must have been involved in its theft, but maybe not. Maybe someone found out. Anyway, if Greg Larson is not involved in some plot against you, he'll confirm. If he is, we still ought to be able to force the truth out of him."

"But, how?" asked Digger. "If he's involved, I don't see how we can force him to say anything that would incriminate him."

"Right," agreed Kate. "If he sees two judges and a lawyer coming after him, he'll clam up tight."

"I agree, Digger has to go alone," said Mike.

"Go? Go where?" asked Kate.

"To see Greg Larson." Digger nodded at Mike.

"I don't like it." Kate held up one of the pictures of Digger. "You told us Larson was the only one who knew what you were doing, but here on my desk is a picture of Judge Digger Moss and somebody named 'Zorro' engaged in a major drug transaction. If Greg Larson is the only one who knew what you were doing, then he sent the pictures or has given them to someone else. Confronting him is too dangerous. Confronting him alone is way too dangerous."

"Don't confront him."

"Then what's the point?" asked Digger, he and Kate both looking at Mike.

"Just go and see him. Talk to him." Mike went on. "Tell him about your envelope or not. Just find a reason to see him, to talk to him. Maybe he'll confirm your story without knowing it. Ask him if there will be any more sales or if he's through with you. If he talks about it, you have your confirmation."

"And just what good would that do if I'm alone with him? It's still just my word against all this evidence." Digger gestured at the contents of the envelope.

"Not if you record the conversation."

"Record? A wire?" Kate interjected. "Digger Moss wearing a wire? Oh, my Jesus Christ alive! What are we getting ourselves into?"

"Got a better idea?" Mike Reynolds drained his Diet Coke, hook shot it over his shoulder into Kate's wastebasket, and sat waiting.

15

Kate and Digger each seemed deep in their own respective thoughts. Finally after what seemed like several minutes, Kate spoke first.

"How do we do it then?"

Mike Reynolds opened his briefcase and extracted a yellow legal pad. Reaching inside his suit coat for a pen, he began making notes. "The Public Defender's Office uses a private investigator who has some sound recording equipment. I'm sure I can borrow it, no questions asked."

"Do you know how to use it?" asked Kate, beginning to wonder about Mike Reynolds.

"Who me?" Mike feigned surprise. "Wouldn't have a clue, but how hard can it be?"

"Easy for you to say," chided Digger. He was feeling better. The mood in the room had just changed from despondency to anger and then to determination. It was exactly what he had hoped when he decided to confide in these two. They were smart. They were loyal. They were not afraid to take action, if necessary.

Kate noticed. "I detect a change, here. When Digger came in here, Mike, he was so low, the spots on a snake's belly would have looked like the stars in the sky to him. I don't remember if he opened the door or just slid under it. Now listen to him. And you. Does this mean we're going to get the sons of bitches?"

"We're gonna try," agreed Mike. "We've got things to do. Digger needs to get in touch with Greg Larson pretty soon."

Together they made their plans and recorded them on Mike's legal pad. Mike was to get the recording equipment from the Public Defender's investigator. Digger would leave a message for Greg Larson that he wanted to see him. They would meet the next day in Digger's chambers. They agreed that their meetings should not appear as something unusual to the clerks or other courthouse staff. They should not alter their schedules. Even with the crowded court schedules they each had, they should be able to meet during the normal lunch break or at the end of the day. They agreed that everything should appear normal.

Digger sat at his desk, thinking about the envelope. He no longer had it. They had decided that since Larson's note had been taken, his chambers were no longer safe. Mike Reynolds had placed the envelope and its contents in his briefcase. He promised to put it in a safe place in his law office. But he could not get the envelope and its contents out of his mind. He had barely slept the night before and doubted he would get much sleep tonight. It would be difficult to act as if everything were normal. It would be hard to concentrate on the cases before him, but he would try. He felt better than he had since first opening the envelope.   The help and determination of his friends gave him the support he needed to attack this problem and fix it or go down trying.

On his way to his car in the parking ramp, Digger waved to Chief Judge Parker as she drove toward the ramp exit. Everything like normal, he thought. On the way home, he drove with the one-way traffic east along Second Street trying to decide what to tell Judy. She would be home from work by now. The flexibility of her job as an editor in a local publishing house gave her comfortable hours that almost always put her home before he left the courthouse.

The Moss homestead was a three story white colonial with black shutters located on a residential street in the Congdon area of East Duluth. Judy and Digger had worked their way up to the house through a series of homes they tried to buy cheap, fix up, and sell for the top price. By the time the oldest of their children was starting high school, they had accomplished their goal. With three stories, there were lots of bedrooms, bathrooms, closets, studies and playrooms. Plenty of room for three kids and their friends while still leaving some relatively private room for the adults. Each of their children had graduated from Duluth East High School nearby and attended the University of Minnesota Duluth while living at the house. Even UMD was only a few blocks away.

They were all grown and gone now. He and Judy bounced around the house like two marbles in a 55-gallon drum. Digger had realized there were parts of the house he didn't see for weeks or even months. But, they were simply too accustomed to its friendly rooms and walls, its comfortable feeling, and the memories it held to get rid of it just yet. Besides, kids came home often enough that the many bedrooms still came in handy. There even were grandchildren now, who came to visit.

As he turned into the driveway, he made up his mind. He would simply tell her the whole story, take some degree of reprimand for getting into this pickle in the first place, and tell her about the help he was getting from Kate and Mike.

Judy Moss peered into the deep well cooker on the stove to check the progress of the pot roast that had been cooking slowly for several hours, beginning by an automatic timer long before either of them left work. Satisfied, she replaced the cover and turned toward her husband.

"What could you possibly have been thinking, Digger?"

Digger Moss sipped his martini, bracing himself for the reprimand he knew he had coming. His actions worried her. It was because she loved him very much, as he loved her. She sat beside him at the kitchen table, sipped her glass of blush wine and continued.

"What really pisses me off is I didn't know. You're off dealing in hard drugs in some parking lot or dark alley and I'm going blissfully along thinking how wonderful and safe our life is."

"Judy, ..." he tried to interrupt.

"I know, Digger, I know," she cut him off. "Being a judge, there will always be things you cannot talk about, but Jesus, Digger! Participating in a criminal sting operation involving drug dealers is right out of the movies."

"Sorry."

"I should *think* so!" she gave him one of her patented stern looks. "Well that's done anyhow. Tell me how Mike and Katy are going to help."

Digger told her about his conversation with his friends. Judy was not happy about the idea of Digger wearing a wire to a meeting with Greg Larson, but she too was getting mad and she was getting protective of her man. She was all for some direct action to clear Digger of this frame-up. If this all gets straightened out and we find those responsible, Digger thought, they would not want their fates left in the hands of Judy Moss.

The next morning, a full special term calendar of civil and family court motions lay before Digger. He managed to pay attention to the arguments of the lawyers, but it was hard to concentrate on the complex issues they were raising. He found that by consciously taking very detailed notes, it was easier to avoid distraction by the envelope and the problems it had brought his life.

"Your Honor, may I respond?"

"You may," Digger responded automatically. The lawyer proceeded to argue that the statute of limitations had expired before suit was commenced and therefore it should be dismissed. Counsel's argument that the running of the statute should be tolled by the claimed promises of the defendant to correct the problem for plaintiff was simply not supported by the applicable case law, he argued.

Digger took the case under advisement, promised a written order shortly, and called the next case.

"Good morning, your Honor," said Mike Reynolds as he guided his client to the counsel table.

"Good morning," said Digger. Everything like normal, he thought.

To take his mind off the envelope and Greg Larson while he ate lunch alone in his chambers, Digger reviewed his assigned case list and listed the cases he had under advisement. Mike had phoned to say he couldn't get the recording equipment until the afternoon. They would meet at about 4:30 or as soon as court was finished. Digger found himself becoming impatient. He didn't like the waiting. He wished it was 4:30 and they could get on with it.

His telephone rang.

"Hello?"

"Judge Moss, please," was the formal response.

"This is he."

"Judge Moss, this is Greg," the voice continued, "Greg Larson. You left a message that you wanted to talk to me."

"Oh, Greg! Uh, yes, I did leave a message." Digger felt his heart leap and his pulse quicken. Adrenaline, he supposed. Brought on by sudden fear? He wondered. "I wanted to talk to you about that business we discussed when we last met, you know."

"I'm not sure there's much to talk about, Judge," said Larson, "You approved probable cause and signed the complaint. I filed it with the Court Administrator's office. It was for a warrant for the arrest of the defendant. I assume they're looking for him now. I haven't heard that they picked him up, yet. Have you?"

What the hell was he doing? What complaint? Law enforcement officers were always bringing criminal complaints to judges for signature. After being signed by the charging prosecuting attorney and being sworn to by the complaining officer, a criminal complaint is presented to a judge for determination whether the alleged facts constitute probable cause to issue the complaint. Digger had certainly signed a few complaints for Greg Larson over the years, but he didn't remember any in the last few weeks. Larson was being so specific about it. Maybe he's worried about discussing anything over the phone, thought Digger. Maybe he's not alone on his end.

"No, I haven't heard anything," Digger answered. "But I do think we should talk. Is there a time that's good for you?" Digger held his breath.

Silence. Digger was sweating, though the temperature in his chambers was quite cool.

After what Digger thought to be an interminable time, but was probably only a few seconds, Larson responded.

"Well, Judge, I'm pretty tied up all this week. I'm working under cover, you know. I don't want to be seen walking into the courthouse or meeting with a judge. The apartment I'm using under cover is not far from the courthouse, but you might be recognized, if I'm being watched. That would raise some serious questions in the minds of the people I'm currently hanging with."

"Well, I think it's important that we meet." Digger hoped he wasn't being too eager.

"I'll tell you what," said Larson. "We can meet at my home. I can swing by there when I'm out driving around. No one would have any reason to follow me everywhere I go. Besides, I could spot a tail. I can make sure I'm not being followed before I go there. I'll leave the back door unlocked so you can get in and wait for me. I'm divorced, so there won't be anyone there."

"I don't know."

"I think it's the only way, Judge. It'll be easier to do after dark. Wear casual clothes, so you don't look like a cop, or, God forbid, a judge." He laughed.

"How soon can we do it?" asked Digger.

"How about tomorrow night, about eight o'clock?"

Digger paused. He didn't know if he liked a clandestine meeting in some strange place after dark. He *knew* Judy wouldn't like it. Of course, it wasn't any worse than the drug deals in parking lots and dark alleys, he mused. And that's exactly why he knew Judy would not approve.

"I guess that's okay," he said. "Where is it?" Digger picked up a pencil.

"North Sixteenth Avenue East. It's a large red brick duplex on the east side of the street. The address is 620 - 622 North Sixteenth Avenue East. It's a side by side duplex. I live on the uphill side and rent the lower side to UMD students. My unit is 622. If you go around to the back, you'll find an entrance into the kitchen. I'll leave it unlocked. Just go in and wait for me."

Digger replaced the phone on its cradle. His hands were clammy. They never got that way.

He knew the neighborhood where Larson's duplex was located in Duluth's east hillside. The City of Duluth is built on a steep hillside overlooking the western end of Lake Superior. The City is twenty-three miles long and only about four or five miles wide at its widest point, excluding the Park Point peninsula which separates Lake Superior from St. Louis Bay and the Duluth harbor. Most of the long narrow, lakeside city is considerably narrower than at its widest point. Nearly anywhere in the city provides a spectacular view of the blue waters of the big lake. Even the extreme western reaches of Duluth, along the curving path of the St. Louis River, have a beautiful scenic view of the harbor and the lake from anywhere up the hillside. The hill is so steep it once accommodated a cog railway to transport passengers to the top. In the western part of the city, the hill supports Spirit Mountain, a ski area developed within the city limits in the mid-seventies that has a vertical drop of 600 feet and ski runs over a mile long.

Because of the combination of the steep hill, the harbor and adjacent waters of the world's largest fresh water lake, some have called Duluth, "a little San Francisco." Even its weather, although much colder than the Golden Gate, is similarly erratic and subject to sudden changes. Native conversation about the weather is much the same in both communities.

In the downtown area, the streets and avenues are just about 45 degrees off of north-south or east-west directions. As a result, Duluth has its own peculiar language to describe directions within the city. Out the shore of Lake Superior, toward the lake's "North Shore" and toward the Canadian border, which to most out-of-towners would be north, is called "east." The opposite direction, up the St. Louis River, is called "west." The other directions are called "uphill" and "downhill" or "the upper side" and "the lake side."

Larson's duplex was on the east side of Sixteenth Avenue East, six blocks above Superior Street, eight blocks above London Road and eight blocks, an interstate highway, a railroad track and a pedestrian "Lakewalk" above the shore of Lake Superior. Being situated on an avenue, one side of the duplex was significantly downhill from the other, thus Larson's reference to the "uphill" and "lower" sides of a side by side duplex.

Kate Riley repeated herself. "Word for word, Digger. We want the conversation word for word. Leave nothing out."

Digger's last hearing had gone beyond the court's usual closing time of 4:30. When he arrived back at his chambers at ten to five, Mike Reynolds and Kate were there, waiting. Mike had a cardboard box of ominous looking equipment with him.

He repeated the telephone conversation with Greg Larson to the best of his ability.

"We're in!" cried Kate, grinning. "I don't know if I like the time and location, but there's nothing we can do about that."

Digger looked uncertainly at the box of equipment.

"I got some stuff, here, Digger," said Mike reaching for the box, "but I'm not sure how much of it we can use."

"What do you mean?"

"Well some of it is designed so someone can monitor your conversation from a listening station close by, like a car or van. I didn't know if we could use that very well. I mean, can you see Judge Riley or me on a stakeout?"

Kate tried to look offended. "Speak for yourself, Mike."

"Now that you've identified the meeting location, I'm sure it won't work," Mike went on. "We'd be spotted in a minute. Especially, if Larson, a trained peace officer, is going to be arriving after you get there and will be looking for any kind of a tail or surveillance."

"Besides," offered Kate, "Sixteenth Avenue East is so steep in that area, we'd either be falling forward on our faces or lying on our backs trying to stay awake."

"This isn't funny, Kate."

"Digger, I already told you. You're fucked. No two ways about it. You're so fucked it's funny. If it weren't so funny, it would be too depressing to think about it." She pointed a finger at him, her high-gloss, red nail polish gleaming. "If we can't see the humor in it, then we won't be calm enough and cool-headed enough to pull this off. That particularly includes you!"

"She's right, Digger," said Mike. "I, of course, wouldn't know, because I am so vastly much younger than you, but I bet when you were playing All American football, you did best when it was fun and worst when you took it too seriously."

"You're both right," said Digger. "But I do take issue with a couple of things. First, Reynolds, you are not *that* much younger than I am. Second, your wisdom about the thinking of an All-American, Big Ten running back just shows that you hockey players never thought about the game or took anything seriously. You just skated and sometimes scored in between fights."

"Men! You could each go way out on the desert or in the woods up in the Boundary Waters with not a soul within a hundred miles and you'd still be full of shit."

"That's not quite how the joke goes, Kate."

Kate waved her hand at Digger. "Shut up, Digger. I like my version better."

"Okay, already!" Digger slapped his open palm down on Kate's desktop. "We are agreed that I'm really and truly fucked, and that it's funnier than hell. Now what are we going to do about this meeting with Sergeant Larson of the Duluth P. D.?"

Mike reached into the cardboard box. What he brought out looked like an ordinary hand-held dictating machine that each of them used nearly every day in their work. It was black. Made of a tough, durable plastic material, it was a little larger than a package of cigarettes.

"I already have one of those," said Digger.

"Not like this." Mike pulled a coated wire about two and one-half feet long from the box and attached the end with the jack into the small recording machine. The other end was presumably a microphone, thought Digger. So this is the "wire."

"This uses the same micro-cassettes you use in your dictator, but the recording machine is much more sensitive. With this auxiliary mike, you should be able to record everything that's said in the room."

"How do I hide it?"

"We can put it in a jacket pocket or a pants pocket," said Mike. "Hell, we can even put it in your crotch, if you want." Kate tried unsuccessfully to stifle a giggle.

"Let's try it out," said Digger.

"In the crotch, I hope." Tears came to Kate's eyes as she broke out into unbridled laughter. Digger glared at her.

Digger put the small recorder in his shirt pocket and clipped the microphone to the front of his shirt. Mike and Kate, who was still giggling, talked to each other at various volume levels. They walked around the room while Digger stayed by the desk. Then Digger walked around while they stood still and talked. Kate rattled some pens and pencils in a metal holder while Digger and Mike talked.

They regrouped at the desk while Mike played the tape. Everything could be heard clearly. Even when Kate was rattling the pens and pencils, the conversation between Mike and Digger was clear and unmistakable. They were all impressed.

CHAPTER THREE

To say that Judy Moss was less than thrilled with the plan was more than the understatement of the year. It was, thought Digger, closer to the understatement of the fast closing millennium. Maybe not, but in these waning months of that particular one thousand years, he felt confidant in believing that few understatements would be yet made that could truly compete for the honor.

"James Digby Moss, you are truly a phenomenal, uncaring, unthinking asshole!" It was only that she loved him so much, he comforted himself, that she cared enough to berate him in this fashion. After all, he reasoned, if she didn't care, she wouldn't say anything.

"You can't be thinking of going and seeing this person alone and at night!"

"Judy, we talked it over and it's the only way," said Digger. "The evidence in that envelope is so strong it will ruin my career. If that gets out, God forbid, before I've had a chance to clear this business up, I shudder to think what will happen! I will be removed from office, undoubtedly charged with a felony, and probably convicted. Christ, dear, can you see me in prison?"

"Oh."

"Oh, yeah, and there just may be a few of my former customers who would like to see me in prison, preferably the same one they're in."

"Oh, shit."

Digger nodded agreement. "Right. Now you're getting it. I have to do something really effective, really fast, or I'm in a world of hurt, as they say."

"Okay, but you better be very careful, Digger." Her arms went around his broad shoulders. She buried her head in his chest and sobbed. "I put up with Digger Moss all these years and just when you're really starting to get fun, I don't want to lose you, damn you!"

Digger stepped back and held her face in his hands and looked into her deep blue eyes, brimming with tears. "I love you more than anything. I promise I will be very careful. I won't take any more chances than are truly necessary. Okay?"

"Okay, but you better keep that promise." She wiped the tears from her eyes, smiled and kissed him on the mouth for a long moment, squeezing him like she never wanted to let go.

When they broke apart, Digger held her arms with his big hands. "And what is this nonsense about me just *starting* to get fun?"

"You heard me." She jabbed him in the ribs and pulled away quickly.

Digger grabbed for her and missed. She backed away from his grasp, pointing at him.

"Just you remember your promise, Digger ... or I'll *never* let you hear the end of it."

"I'm sure of that," said Digger.

Sleep came very slowly to Digger that night. He was nervous about the meeting. He did not know what to expect from Greg Larson. Was he responsible for the envelope? He would almost have to be, thought Digger, staring into the darkness of the bedroom. After all, he was presumably the only one who knew about the sting in which Digger was used. But on the phone, he seemed normal except for his ruse about a sentencing. It was as if he was willing to talk to Digger, but was afraid of anyone else listening to what they might say. Whose side was Larson on? Who was on the other side anyway? Why were there even sides at all?

Too many questions and no answers at all, he thought. He closed his eyes and tried to sleep.

His bailiff opened court the next morning as usual. "All rise! District Court is now in session, The Honorable James Digby Moss presiding."

Horton vs. Horton was a bitter divorce case involving disputed custody of two little girls, ages five and seven. After several pre-trial motions, the case had finally come before Digger for trial. Both lawyers were experienced family law specialists. Digger knew that they would have tried everything possible to try to get a reasonable settlement for their respective clients. Knowing it would do neither him nor the Hortons and their daughters any good to be preoccupied with the meeting with Larson that evening, he glued his attention to the evidence as the two experienced trial lawyers went to work. Over forty documents were marked as exhibits and received in evidence by the morning break at quarter after ten.

As Digger and his court reporter, Ruth Bailey, stood sipping coffee from styrofoam cups in the hallway behind the courtroom, Mike Reynolds appeared.

"May I see you a moment, Judge?" he asked. "Morning, Ruth."

"Hi, Mike," she answered, moving down the hall to give them some privacy.

"What's up?" asked Digger.

Mike shook his head. "Judge Riley's worried about you. She *ordered* me to come over here to check on you, *and* report back to her. I believe her exact words were: 'Report to me damn quickly, or you'll lose your next case!'"

"Oh good," laughed Digger, "nothing like a little abuse of judicial power to add to our troubles."

"She also said if you refer to '*our* troubles' again, I was to say to you from her, in the best Lone Ranger and Tonto tradition: 'Whaddaya mean 'our,' Kimo Sabe?' "

"Just the kind of support I need," said Digger. "Tell her I'm managing to concentrate on my work, I'm damned nervous about tonight, and she should be worried."

"Will we have a chance to meet before you go to see Larson?"

"Let's get together again at the end of the day."

"Your chambers?"

"Yes."

"Okay, Digger," Mike said, "I'll go report right away so I can preserve my sterling court record in front of the Honorable Kathrine Riley." He turned and disappeared down the hall. Digger returned to the courtroom.

In the late afternoon, after both judges' calendars were completed, the three met in Digger's chambers.

"Still nervous?" asked Kate.

"Underneath this calm exterior," said Digger, "I'm shaking like a leaf."

"You'll be fine, Digger," said Mike. "Besides, if you get hurt or killed, the case someone has built against you either won't seem so important, or won't matter at all!"

"Thanks for that." I look nervous, Digger thought. He could just feel that he looked nervous. Would that matter when he met with Larson? Maybe not, he thought. Under the circumstances, it would be natural for anyone to be nervous, so Larson would not be surprised or suspicious. He hoped.

"What are you going to wear?" asked Kate.

"Larson said come casual," Digger replied.

"I mean have you figured out where you'll have the tape recorder and the microphone?"

"Mike says he's going to set up the mike here and I'll just plug it in to the machine in a jacket pocket."

"What, not in your crotch?" Kate grinned. "I was so hoping you'd do that."

"I told Judy you said that."

"You didn't!"

"I did."

"Digger, Jesus Christ, now I'll have to apologize. You prick."

Mike Reynolds stepped away from the conversation. "I'm not hearing this," he said. "Shall we set up the microphone?"

"Right," Digger and Kate said in unison.

Digger removed his shirt so Kate and Mike could tape the microphone wire to his skin under his arm and down to his waist so it would come out from under his shirt near his belt and disappear into the inside of the jacket he would be wearing.

"All right now what are you going to say to him, Digger? Do you remember?" asked Kate.

Digger went through his side of a conversation they had carefully planned. It would be good only until Larson said something that changed things. Then, he guessed, he would be on his own. Until something happened to change the plan, he was to ask Larson about whether his investigation of the police department had uncovered anything. Did he have more information about who was involved? Did Digger have to do anything more?

If Larson didn't come forward with anything that would confirm the operation in which Digger had been involved, he would go further, indicating that he was nervous about his involvement and wanted something more to explain what he had done and to show that he was working with Larson when the pictures were taken. He wouldn't mention the pictures of course. By this latter approach, they had reasoned, Digger would be describing the operation in more detail. Larson's response would then have more meaning.

Once Digger had what he thought was confirmation that he had been working for Larson, he was to terminate the conversation as politely as possible and get the hell out of there. If none of the plans worked, he was just to get the hell out of there.

At home with Judy, Digger was unable to eat. She insisted that he call her on his cellular phone as soon as he left the meeting. Digger wondered about the use of the cell phone. Were those things secure? Were there records? Could someone tell where he was when he called? He tried not to show it to Judy, but Digger was nervous.

He drove west on Fourth Street. The night was cool and overcast. A slight mist softened the glow of the streetlights. He was reminded of movie scenes of London in the fog. Perfect, he thought, sarcastically. Just like a London spy movie. Dark, cold, foggy, and downright eerie. Just what he needed to maintain the current state of his nerves.

At Seventeenth Avenue East, he turned up the steep hill. Digger had decided not to park near Larson's duplex or drive by it. He had driven by earlier and knew the layout. Turning left on East Seventh Street, he looked for a place to park.

About a third of the way down the block, he found a spot big enough to pull his car in without having to back in. Ordinarily, he considered himself relatively skilled at parallel parking. It was, however, a skill at which he didn't feel at all confident at the moment. He shut the engine off and sat still trying to calm himself and remember the plan.

The car was parked on the upper side of the street. He stayed on the upper side as he walked slowly past the closely spaced residential homes. The lots, here, were typically no more than fifty feet wide and often less. The houses were mostly two-story frame dwellings, often less than ten or twelve feet apart. There were no driveways. Those who did have garages or off-street parking accessed it through the alleys behind the houses.

He approached Sixteenth Avenue East. Stopping to check the tape recorder and microphone, he started down the hill. As soon as he crossed Seventh Street, Digger could see the duplex. The red brick façade stood out among the frame buildings lining the avenue. Digger found some antacid tablets in his jacket pocket and chewed two quickly.

He reached the narrow concrete walk that went along the side of the house to the back door. He turned to take it. As he reached the back door he noticed that, as Larson had predicted, he was fairly out of sight of the street. He pulled open the outer storm door and tried the knob on the main door. He had butterflies so bad he thought they would be getting out if it weren't for the knot in his stomach.

The door swung open into a dark foyer and a dimly lit room beyond. Feeling his way around the foyer, Digger found that it was indeed a small vestibule with large hooks on the wall on which were hung several jackets and a series of hats. He bumped something with his left knee. Peering into the darkness and feeling with both hands, he discovered a plastic kitchen-style garbage container with a plastic garbage bag fitted around its edge. The room beyond, he saw, was the kitchen. Larson had left a dim fluorescent light on that was part of the control panel on the range top and which provided what little light there was. He stepped carefully into the room and began a survey of the surroundings.

A few dirty dishes were still on the stovetop. Since Greg Larson was working undercover and had a separate apartment for that purpose, they might be still there from some meal prepared and eaten several days or maybe weeks earlier. The kitchen was roomy and functional. Two walls contained deep counters and large white-painted cupboards. The stove and refrigerator were not new, but they were not as old-fashioned looking as commonly seen in such apartments. The sink was stainless steel, set into one of the Formica

30

counters with modern looking fixtures. A dishwasher was built in to the cabinets under the counter next to the sink.

Larson was not a man who left much sign of occupancy, thought Digger. He observed that apart from the dirty dishes on the stove, there was practically nothing in the kitchen that was not in the cupboards out of sight. There was nothing on the counters, no canisters, no small appliances, nothing. There was a table in the corner under a window. There was nothing on the table, no salt and pepper shakers, no napkins, nothing. Strange, thought Digger. There were no pots and pans or utensils visible, nothing. Digger opened a drawer. Empty. What the Hell? thought Digger.

He found the living room beyond the kitchen. The only illumination came from the kitchen. He could make out a couch, an end table and an upholstered chair. Digger checked his watch. 8:25. Not knowing whether he should turn on any more lights, he made his way to the chair, sat and waited.

Digger was plain scared. Sitting in the dark, waiting to secretly tape record a conversation with a man who may be behind an attempt to frame him for a serious felony was nuts. Anyone with half a brain would be leaving. He stayed.

After what seemed like at least an hour, Digger rose from the chair and moved to the kitchen door to check his wristwatch in the pale light. Almost 9:00 o'clock. Time was crawling and his skin was crawling.

After awhile, he felt the need to urinate. He adjusted himself in the chair, but comfort eluded him. Damn! he thought. I've got to go. If I don't, he thought, I'll be so nervous, as soon as I see Larson, I'll piss in my pants. That'll be an effective approach. He did not know where the bathroom was located. Somewhere off the living room in which he was seated, he presumed. But, where? He had been leery of turning on any lights as he waited, but he could not find the bathroom in the dark. He imagined that when Larson arrived he would turn on some lights, so perhaps turning on a light now would make no difference. He wasn't sure why he had decided to sit in the dark anyway. He just had.

A lamp on the end table provided ample light for the living room. He observed a hallway leading toward what he guessed were bedrooms ... and a bathroom, he hoped. Along the dark hallway he found an open door on the right. Feeling the wall just inside the door, he found a light switch. As the bathroom light came on, Digger saw the body.

He was lying face down on the hardwood floor at the end of the hallway. Head and shoulders extended into what Digger assumed was a bedroom, which was carpeted. The man wore blue jeans. He wore no shoes or socks. He had no shirt. Digger did not know what to do. At least he had to see if the man was alive. He knew that. As he approached the body, he saw the pool of blood coming from under his chest. From the blonde crew cut, Digger guessed it was Greg Larson. In the doorway, he braced himself with one hand against the door frame and tried to take a deep breath. Larson's shoulders blocked most of the doorway. Digger had to step over the shoulders, avoiding stepping on the head. As he lifted his left foot over the body, his right foot slipped in the blood on the hardwood floor, he lost his balance, careened into the door frame, and fell over the remains of Sergeant Greg Larson.

Digger struggled to get off the body. In the bedroom, he could barely see in the low light from the bathroom door. He searched for a light switch and found one. The ceiling light was bright. He looked at the body. Rolling it over on its back, he confirmed that it was Larson. A huge hole in his chest was the source of the still fresh blood. The gunshot wound was surely fatal and probably instantly so, thought Digger. It seemed almost useless to check for a pulse, but he felt the neck and found nothing. Automatically, his eyes searched the room and spotted the telephone on the bedside table. Moving quickly, he picked up the receiver and began to punch in "9-1- ... stop! How would he explain his presence here? Even if Kate Riley and Mike Reynolds supported him, the contents of the envelope would become public. Any way you looked at it, he thought, I am flat out fucked. I'm ruined. Quickly, he put the telephone receiver back on its cradle, glanced around the room, turned off the light, and stepped back through the doorway, being careful not to slip this time. He passed the bathroom, turning off that light as he went. He had forgotten all about his need for that facility.

In the living room, he turned out the table lamp on his way to the kitchen. In a moment he was in the small back vestibule. Pulling the main door open, he opened the outer door slightly and peered out.

Seeing no one, Digger slipped through the door and restrained himself from running down the walk and up the hill. Trying to appear like any casual pedestrian, he eventually reached his car. Only after he had pulled away from the curb and driven past Sixteenth Avenue East, did he pick up his cell phone.

"Hello, ... Digger?"

"Judy! I haven't much time! I'm out of the house and in the car driving away. I'm coming home, but there's trouble! Call Kate Riley and Mike Reynolds right away!"

"Digger, what happened?"

"I can't talk now, Honey. Call Kate and Mike and ask them to come right over. I'll be right there."

Digger drove west to Chester Park drive, then west on Eighth Street to Sixth Avenue East and up Central Entrance and out the Miller Trunk Highway past the Miller Hill Mall at the top of the hill. He did not want to be seen driving from Larson's house toward his own. Eventually, he took the Haines Road from the Miller Trunk across to the Arrowhead Road and back toward Duluth's East End.

Turning in his driveway at last, Digger saw Kate's Jeep and Mike's Explorer parked on the street.

"Where in Christ's name have you been, Digger," Kate shouted at him, as he opened the front door. "And what the hell happened? You've got us all worried and your wife scared to death!"

"Oh Digger!" Judy ran to him and embraced him. "I was really scared. I ... Digger! That's blood!"

"What?" Digger looked at his clothes. His khaki pants had bloodstains around the knees. His sneaker had blood spattered on the toes. There was even blood on his jacket sleeve. He remembered when he fell on Larson's body. "Oh God! It's not mine. Let's go in the kitchen so I can explain."

At the kitchen table, Digger talked while the rest listened. He told them each detail including his need to go to the bathroom which brought about the discovery of Larson's body. Somehow, he had gone all that time without even thinking about it. When he was done with the first time through the story, he excused himself and was surprised that he barely could go. Where the hell did it go? He shook his head, overwhelmed by the evening's experience and not, in his estimation, thinking too awfully clearly.

Back at the kitchen table the questions began. Did you call the police? Why not? Shouldn't you call them now? Why not? Did you touch anything? You did? What? Did you wipe off the phone? The door frame? The light switches? Why not?

"Digger, what are you going to do?" asked Judy, her hand touching his arm. "You have to call the police," she turned to their friends, "doesn't he?"

"She's right, Digger," said Kate, gravely.

"But Kate!" Digger clutched Judy's hand. "If I get involved in an investigation, all that crap in that envelope will come out. I can see the headline:

LOCAL JUDGE CHARGED WITH POSSESSION OF HEROIN AND COCAINE WITH INTENT TO SELL!!!

"That'll sell papers. Sell papers and ruin me. Sell more papers and send me to prison!"

"Oh, Digger!" Judy gasped.

"That's right, dear, prison." Digger looked at Kate and Mike. "We already decided that I would have to clear myself, hopefully with your help. The evidence is so strong, I lose, unless we can prove it wrong before it is made public."

"Well, it just got a lot harder," said Mike.

"What?" Judy asked.

"That's right," Digger agreed. "My only alibi was murdered tonight."

"Oh, God." Judy Moss buried her head in her hands sobbing. Digger and Kate tried to comfort her.

Judy thanked Kate and rose from the table. Wiping away the tears as she crossed the kitchen floor, she opened a cupboard and extracted four coffee mugs.

"I've got coffee," she said. "It must be pretty strong by now. I put it on just after Digger left. Have you had anything to eat?"

Digger knew that Judy, like the rest of them, had to do something. In times of real stress in the past, he had seen her find relief in comforting others, busying herself providing food or drink, or otherwise waiting on people.

"Eat? How the hell can you think of eating at a time like this?" Kate looked incredulous. "We got trouble, girl."

"Shut up, Katy." Judy placed a large white mug on the table in front of Kate. "I may not be able to come up with the solution by myself, but I can help, and I can sure see to it you guys aren't weak minded from hunger or thirst. Digger didn't eat anything before he went to see Larson. So don't get in the way, 'cuz I'm serving." She brought the coffee pot and stood over Kate. "Besides, Katy, it makes me feel better. So how do you want your coffee?"

"Black and strong. Thanks."

"Digger?"

"Thanks."

"We have another semi-major problem," said Mike, as he held his cup out to Judy.

"Now what?" Judy asked, pouring.

"Before, we had to deal with the obligation Kate and I might have to disclose Digger's illegal activities as violations of the Code of Judicial Conduct or to report to the police that crimes had been committed." Mike sipped the hot coffee. "Now, we have knowledge that a murder has been committed. Even if it did not involve Digger, I'm sure we're obliged to report it, *and* be completely truthful in responding to questions from investigating law enforcement officers."

Kate nodded her reluctant agreement.

"I told you both before," said Digger, picking at the plate of macaroni and cheese Judy had set before him, "this problem is mine. I need your help, but I can only expect so much. You two have done nothing. I can't have you breaching your professional ethics, or even possibly committing a crime because of me."

"Oh, bullshit, Digger," said Kate. "We've probably already done that, anyway. In for a penny in for a pound, I say."

"Don't get me wrong," said Mike. "I'm not suggesting Kate or I give up on you, Digger. But I do think we should be prepared to justify our actions or inaction."

"Any suggestions?" asked Kate.

"Well, I have copies of evidence in my office that indicates Digger may have been involved in illegal drugs. That's scary. So, ..."

"So, ... you better be his lawyer!" Kate finished for him.

"Right! And somehow I think that because you are judges -and that's certainly at least the equivalent of an officer of the court. Hell, you are the Court!- you are somehow entitled to investigate possible criminal activity."

"I think that's stretching it," said Kate. "We're not cops."

"But in this instance, I think we are justified in not going to the authorities. First, we have ample evidence that some one or more persons in the police department, Sheriff's office or City or County government may be directly involved; and second, those persons pose a direct threat to my client and your colleague."

"Well said, counselor," said Kate, nodding her agreement. "It not only says why we've got to help Digger, but justifies why we should. I like it."

"Lawyers." Judy shook her head as she poured fresh coffee. "You guys can make old horseshit smell like fresh roses, I swear." She was feeling better by doing something, and she noticed, so were they. "But I like it."

"You're wasting your time," Digger said sadly, staring at the macaroni. They all looked at him.

"I realize the situation looks tough, Digger," said Kate, "but now is not the time to let depression take over. Don't give up."

"No," Digger said, "you're right, Kate, but that's not the problem."

"Pray, what is?"

"You guys are worried about justifying your failure to report what's happened, but the cops will know soon enough. And, when they do, everything comes out in the open and I'm through, ...ruined."

"I said, 'Don't give up', yet."

"Kate, I touched a lot of stuff when I was there! My fingerprints are lots of places. The cops are going to know I was there!"

"Oh, shit." Kate stared at the ceiling.

Judy asked, "Have you ever been fingerprinted, Digger?"

"Not since the army, that I remember, but don't they have all those prints on some giant computer?"

"Even if they don't have your prints," said Mike, "we have to expect that something will bring them around to you and they'll get your prints as a part of this investigation. Then you're screwed, because by that time they'll know you're hiding something and the prints will close the door on you."

"You're right," said Digger.

"What do we do?" asked Judy.

"I've got to go back," Digger said, looking at his wife.

"*We've* got to go back," said Mike.

"No!" screamed Judy. "Mike, don't you let him. Digger, don't you even think it!"

"They're right, Judy." Kate stood and put her hand gently on Judy's shoulder. "If they don't there's no chance we can help Digger."

CHAPTER FOUR

Mike and Digger parked Mike's Explorer on Sixteenth Avenue East facing downhill just past the duplex. Mike cranked the steering wheel, turning the front wheels in to the curb.

"Ready?" he asked Digger.

"Hell, no, " he replied.

"Gut it up, Marine!" Mike started to open his door, but held the handle so the interior light would not come on. "Let's go."

Digger looked back at the duplex. Everything looked the same, except now there were lights on the downhill side. "Looks like the students are home," he told Mike. "I didn't see any activity over there before."

"Students?" Mike held the door closed, keeping the light off.

"Yeah, students. Larson told me he lives in the uphill side, No. 622, and 620 on the downhill side is rented to UMD students."

"Are they likely to see us going in?"

"I don't think so. The door is in the back. You take that narrow walk along the side. It's on the far side from the students' apartment."

"Then maybe we should stay on this side of the street until we get even with that sidewalk we're going to take. They probably aren't looking outside anyway, but that lessens the chance of being seen."

"Right." Digger resolved himself to the task. "Let's go." He opened his door.

Inside the back vestibule, Mike said, "You know where the lights are?"

"Do we dare turn any on?"

"Don't have a choice, Digger. We came here to clean up. Can't see to clean if we can't see." He felt along the kitchen wall next to the door from the vestibule. Both men were wearing disposable plastic gloves Judy had given them from her house cleaning supplies back at the Moss home. When he found the switch, the room was filled with bright light. It hurt Digger's eyes.

Remembering the sparseness of the kitchen as he had viewed it in the dim light from the stove, he saw that in this bright light it seemed even starker. The cupboards, counters, walls, and ceiling were plain white.   The floor was linoleum tile with a faded pattern and was nearly white.

"Jesus!" breathed Mike. "Like being on the inside of an egg! I thought you said the guy lived here."

"He does, I guess."

"With what?" Mike inquired, gazing around the stark, empty room.

"I don't know, but may I point out that he doesn't live here anymore. In fact he doesn't live anywhere anymore. He's down here."

They went through the kitchen into the living room and beyond into the narrow hallway, Mike turning lights on as they went. At the end of the hall, they found the body, still there, as Digger had left it. Mike even found an overhead ceiling light in the hall which made the corpse on the floor seem larger and more real than it had in the dim light.

"God!" Digger whispered, looking at the death scene under the bright light.

"Jeez, this is bad!" Mike said as he forced himself to look closer at the body. "All right, Digger, let's get to work. We don't know how much time we have. What did you touch?"

They retraced every step Digger had taken earlier, trying to wipe clean everything he touched, restore everything he had disturbed, and erase all evidence of his previous presence. Using clean soft cloths provided by Judy, they wiped clean anything that might have Digger's fingerprints. Mike wiped up blood tracked on the bedroom carpet. The coagulating pool of blood next to the corpse contained a large smear where Digger had stepped and slipped and one perfect print of the sole of Digger's running shoe. Using one of the rags, Mike obliterated the print, smearing the blood around on the wood surface of the hallway floor.

"I hope we didn't forget anything," said Digger, back in the Explorer.

Mike guided the vehicle slowly down the steep hill, turned right on Fourth Street and headed west, much as Digger had done before. Heading the opposite direction of where you wanted to go seemed the thing to do, thought both men without knowing why, really.

"I hope so, too, Digger. Think hard. What could we have forgotten?"

Digger concentrated, thinking about the time he spent sitting in the dark, realizing now that Larson's dead body lay just a few feet away the whole time. Shaking himself to get rid of that thought, he mentally walked through every action he had taken.

"No, I can't think of anything."

"Good! 'Cuz I don't want to go back there." Mike had driven right through downtown, past the courthouse and turned back east on I35 toward Digger's house.

"Well, you certainly took long enough!" Kate said as she opened the front door.

"Good to see you, too, Judge," said Mike as he entered.

"Well, did you get everything taken care of?" Kate asked.

"We think so," Mike replied. "It will still be obvious that someone was there after Larson died, but we hope, at least, that nothing will point to Digger."

"I hope you're right." Kate placed a hand on Judy's shoulder.

Judy Moss stood by her husband. She felt a little out of place with these two judges and a criminal defense lawyer analyzing the issues and figuring the possible consequences of each action. But something bothered her.

"Digger?" she touched his elbow.

"Yes, dear?"

"If this is some kind of blackmail, as you all seem to think," she paused, looking at Kate and Mike, "then why haven't you heard something? Don't blackmailers make a demand for money or something?"

"Right," Mike agreed. "We've been waiting for something to happen, but so far, nothing."

"I don't get it," Digger said. "Nothing since that damned envelope arrived. And now Greg Larson has been murdered. What the hell is going on?"

"They must want something," said Kate. She looked hard at Judy. "You got a bunch of extra wealth hidden somewhere, girl? Somethin' I don't know about?"

Judy Moss smiled. "On a judge's pay? Are you kidding?" Then more seriously: "No, some may think we have a lot of money to pay blackmail, but if they do, they're wrong."

Mike stood to leave. "There's no point in speculating," he said. "All we can do is wait until they contact Digger and make their demand."

"Mike's right." Kate also stood. "It's getting late. We'd all better get home and get some rest. Tomorrow's another day. I have a suspicion Digger will be hearing something soon."

"**P**olice have not identified the victim at this time," said the newscaster's voice as the clock radio on the dresser in the Moss bedroom came on at 6:00 a.m.

Digger Moss bolted from the bed, turning up the volume and reaching for the remote control for the bedroom TV.

"What's that?" Judy wiped the sleep from her eyes as she tried to wake up.

"Listen!" said Digger. "It's on the news!"

As the television screen came to life, Digger saw that the story was on the local news. He turned the radio off. The TV screen showed the front of the duplex on Sixteenth Avenue East. Several police officers were in the picture. The reflection of the flashing lights of squad cars could be seen in the windows of the building.

"... didn't hear anything! We didn't know anything was wrong until the police arrived!" An excited young student was being interviewed by the television reporter.

"And to recap," said the Channel 6 news anchor, seated behind the news desk back in the studio, "early this morning, shortly after midnight, police discovered the body of a man in an apartment at 622 North Sixteenth Avenue East. While police are saying little about their investigation at this time, it appears the man died of wounds from a shotgun. The gun has not yet been found." She brushed a strand of yellow blonde hair from her forehead and continued, looking directly at the camera. "Channel 6 news has reliable information that the dead man was a member of the Duluth Police Department, although that has not been officially verified by Police Chief John Morgan."

Digger listened as he began to get ready for work. While brushing his teeth in the master bathroom, he heard the television announcer say that there would be a press conference held by Chief Morgan later that morning.

Judy stood in the bathroom door, watching Digger. "It sounds like the whole story will be out by noon," she said.

"Not the whole story," Digger mumbled through his toothbrush. He rinsed his mouth and said, "I've got to get to work. Everything must look like normal, remember."

"I know," she sighed, "but it's going to be difficult. Very difficult."

Digger drove to the courthouse along Third Street, the one-way street heading west. As he entered the building, he saw that the wide, marble-floored hallways were crowded with early morning arrivers talking about the news. He headed directly to his office, then stopped and turned to join a group discussing the murder. Everything normal, he thought. After a news event like this, he would be standing in the crowd talking just like every one else.

"Digger!" a voice called. "Did you hear? It's supposed to be a cop!"

Eventually, Digger got back into his chambers and tried to pick up his usual routine. His calendar was scheduled to begin at 9:00. He checked the files that had been set out for him by his clerk, took them into the courtroom, and placed them on the bench with a copy of the written calendar on top. Following his habitual pattern, he then checked his mail basket by the clerks' office. As he approached the counter, he stopped suddenly, a chill went up his spine. There was another envelope!

As nonchalantly as possible, though his heart was pounding and his breath was short, he removed the envelope from the basket and turned to walk back towards his chambers, trying to appear casual as he looked over the envelope. It was the same envelope! The same address label, the same confidentiality warning, and Digger's penciled receipt date he had written in the upper right corner when he got it the first time!

"**K**ate?" Digger said into the telephone receiver.
"Digger?" she answered. "Where are you? Everybody in the whole courthouse is talking about the morning news."
"I know. I was in one of those discussions out in the hallway. I just finally got back to my office and found more trouble!"
"What?"
"Another envelope!"
"What? Where?" Kate sounded truly alarmed.
"It was in my mail basket this morning. I just got it. Now it's on my desk in front of me."
"Digger," she said slowly, as if she was not sure she wanted to hear the answer, "what's in it?"
"I don't know."
"What?"
"Kate, it's the *same* envelope! The *very same* envelope!"
"Digger, that's impossible. Mike has that envelope, remember?"
"It's got my mark on it. I dated my receipt of it like I always do."
"Shit!"
"Is Mike in the courthouse?" he asked.
"If he isn't, I know he will be, Digger," she said. "He's got a sentencing in front of me in about forty-five minutes."
"Mike's usually early for those things," Digger said. "See if you can find him and bring him here."
"What for?"
"Let's open the envelope together this time."
"I'll go find him."

They each stared at the plain brown envelope lying on Digger's desk.
"That was in my office in the back of a file cabinet!" Mike exclaimed, shaking his head, pointing at the envelope. "How could anyone have known where it was? Even if they knew, how could they have gotten to it?"

The three stared at each other across the desk, each wide-eyed and open-mouthed. Then Mike began to look around the room, his eyes moving from wall to ceiling, from radiator to air conditioning vent, from light fixture to wall hanging.

"What?" asked Kate, watching Mike scan the room.

"Shhhh," Mike whispered, holding his right index finger to his lips and motioning to them with his left.

They followed him out of Digger's chambers. He led them down the hall and into an empty law clerk's office. He shut the door to the small room behind them.

"Jesus, Mike!" said Kate, herself whispering conspiratorially. "What the hell are we doing?"

Mike glanced at the open books and files on the desk, the computer monitor showing a WestLaw icon in the center of the screen. To Digger, he asked, "Whose law clerk uses this office? Yours?"

"No," Digger replied, "Jack is next door. This is Judge Anderson's law clerk."

"Good! Maybe we're okay here." He looked at Kate and Digger very seriously. "The only place we ever discussed the fact that that envelope would be in my office for safe keeping was either in one of your offices or Digger's home. The only people present in any of those conversations were the three of us ... and Judy, when we were at their house. Now assuming that none of us told anyone, and further assuming Judy isn't leaking information to anybody, both of which are reasonable assumptions in my view, then the walls have ears ... and maybe eyes!" He rolled his eyes around as if to scan the small office in which they stood.

"Holeee (she drew the end of the word out) shit!" Kate put a hand on Digger's broad, but stooped shoulder. "You mean our chambers are bugged?"

"How else would they know?" was Mike's response.

"My chambers?" asked Kate, the look of apprehension on her face growing.

"If Digger's places are bugged, then they've heard us and maybe seen us. We must assume that our offices are bugged too."

Digger looked overwhelmed. He had the look of defeat, as if he was about to give up. "What the hell are they trying to do to me?" he said. "And who the hell are they, and what the hell do they want?"

They regrouped in the fourth floor jury lounge. Sitting around a round gray Formica table, they carefully opened the envelope and studied its second set of contents.

"Holy Balls! It couldn't be worse, but it is!" Kate threw down a page of the papers from the envelope and looked at her friends in anguish. She wiped a long strand of red hair away from her face. "This is going to be Murder One for Christ's sake! We're talking Grand Jury here!"

The reactions of Mike Reynolds and Digger Moss were no different. The contents of the envelope were devastating.

There were more photographs and another draft Complaint. The photos showed Digger going into and coming out of Greg Larson's Sixteenth Avenue East duplex. One was a picture of a bloody shoe print inside the apartment.

The Complaint was like the first one, proclaiming in its caption that it was the case of the State of Minnesota against James Digby Moss. The charge was Second Degree Murder. First Degree Murder charges can only be initiated in Minnesota by an Indictment by the Grand Jury. The envelope also contained a Notice of Intent to Present to Grand Jury.

"Oh, God!" said Kate as she opened the small white envelope, removed and read the message it contained. She held it up for the others.

YOU DIDN'T THINK YOU WOULD GET AWAY WITH <u>THIS</u>, DID YOU?
[Unless you work with us, you won't!]

Digger's mental state had been bad since he received the repeat appearance of the envelope. It had gotten worse when Mike pointed out the possibility of surveillance of his chambers. It got even worse as they learned the contents of the envelope this time. His friends were worried about him.

Ｉn another part of town Frank Griswold closed his cellular telephone. Milo Bracken had told him what he wanted to hear. The Honorable Digger Moss was scared. He was almost ready, thought Griswold. Bracken was sending the tapes of the latest recordings from his listening station in the van parked near the courthouse. Everything that Judge Moss and his two confidants had said and done so far had gone according to Griswold's plan. The people who hired him for this job should be happy. And, he thought, would pay handsomely for his efforts, he would see to that. He opened the cell phone again and punched in a seven digit number.

"Good afternoon, Whitaker Industries, Power-Plus Battery Division," a soft, melodic voice answered. "How may I direct your call?"

"Randall McCoy, please," said Griswold.

"One moment."

"Hello?"

"Mr. McCoy, this is Frank Griswold. I've got more news." He explained the current situation with the judge.

"Good," said McCoy. "We're anxious to make our demands. Do you think he's ready?"

"Pretty close, I think. Give me a few more days."

"All right, but remember my people are getting restless," said McCoy. "Will we be ready in a day or two?"

"Count on it," said Griswold. The conversation ended. Griswold closed the cell phone and placed it on the night stand.

He stared out over the harbor from his hotel room high above the Holiday Mall on Superior Street. An ore carrier was passing under the Aerial Lift Bridge. He could see the cars lined up on Lake Avenue waiting for the bridge to come down so they could get out onto Park Point, the sand barrier between the Harbor and the Lake. Things were going along very nicely, he thought. He didn't want his employers to think it was too easy. For what they were going to get out of this, they could and should pay him considerably more than the original arrangement. So a little more delay was useful. He would wait just a few more days for effect. Besides, the harder he could make it on that arrogant prick, Digger Moss, the better he liked it. The thought made him smile to himself, but the thought of Judge Digger Moss brought up feelings of anger that were hard for him to control. He concentrated on the view. The ore boat was almost under the bridge now. People who had been standing outside their cars chatting were scurrying to get back in ready to move when the bridge was down.

They met that evening at Kate Riley's home on the beach on Park Point. Judy and Digger brought pizza which Judy was busy serving.

"If you think Katy's and Mike's offices may also be bugged, what makes you think this is safe?" she asked handing Kate a small plate with a large wedge of pepperoni and mushroom.

Digger answered. "We don't know, but at some point they run more risk than it's worth. If they could bug my office, the same person could do Kate's, the law clerks' or anywhere else in the courthouse. Mike's law office in the Alworth Building is much the same, a large building, largely unoccupied at night. This house, our house, private residences would be different. They would require additional risk. We don't know that they even planted anything in our house. We don't know if our house is being watched or not."

Judy shivered, her shoulders shaking as though a chill went up her spine. "It gives me the creeps," she said, "to think of somebody listening to everything we say."

Kate comforted her. "We *are* going to get the sons of bitches, Judy. *Aren't* we boys?"

"One way or the other," said Digger.

Mike nodded agreement.

Digger had once again become despondent, ultimately responding with anger and resolve. His friends and his wife were glad to see this response, but knowing Digger Moss as well as they all did, each was slightly apprehensive about what Digger might do.

Digger said, "If we go to the cops, they lose their leverage."

"But we decided we couldn't go to the police ....," Kate started to say.

"And," Digger interrupted, "if they *think* we're going to the cops, they'll *think* they are losing their leverage." He was up walking now, the others sitting on the couch and upholstered chairs in the Riley living room. Digger crossed to the fireplace, touching a large piece of gray driftwood Kate had collected from the wide sand beach in front of her house. Digger felt the smoothness of the weather and water polished wood. He continued, thinking aloud as he went. "*And*, if they think we are *planning* to go to the cops, they'll think they *are in danger of* losing their leverage and they will have to do something. They'll have to try to make a deal that's better for me than going to the cops."

"*And*," Mike joined in, "they will finally come to you with what they want! Good thinking!"

"Shit, Digger! I knew you were smart!" cried Kate, slapping Judy on the back and reaching for her pizza. Through an enormous bite of pepperoni and mushroom she sputtered, "But how do we make them think you, or we, are going to the cops?"

"Mike, can you tell for sure if my chambers have listening devices?"

"I can't," said Mike. "I'm sure Duluth P.D. has equipment that can locate bugs, but I guess we can't use them."

"No, we can't," said Digger. "What about your private investigator?"

"Right," acknowledged Mike. "I've never had occasion to ask, but I'll bet he can check out your chambers and locate any bugs."

"When can you talk to him?"

"Right now, probably," Mike answered. "Kate, may I use your phone?"

Mike looked up the detective's residence in Kate's Duluth phone book and punched in the numbers. He stood and walked into the adjoining dining room and talked softly into the phone. Moments later, he returned. "He says he can do it. He'll do it first thing in the morning, if it's convenient for you," Mike said, handing the telephone receiver back to Kate.

"That's it, then," said Digger. "We'll find out about their surveillance. If it's what we think, then we'll take control by what we feed them over their own listening devices."

"I like it," said Kate.

"Tomorrow, then," said Digger, rising from his chair and taking Judy's hand.

"Tomorrow," acknowledged Kate and Mike in unison.

CHAPTER FIVE

Milo Bracken listened through a headphone set he wore over his balding head. It pushed the long thin top hairs out of position over his baldness so they stuck out from under the headset's plastic band and curled up in the air. Griswold won't like this, he thought. He reached for the can of Coke he'd removed from the van's fridge some time ago and had forgotten when the headphone's ear pieces had begun to speak to him. He was listening to a conversation in Judge Moss's chambers. That lawyer, Reynolds, and Moss were giving up. The pressure Griswold put on Moss was too much. Bracken thought Griswold was pushing, but it was not for him to comment. He was just paid to listen; listen and report. He guzzled the warm Coke and listened.

"It's gone too far," he heard the voice of Judge Moss say. "We tried to avoid going to the authorities before, but now we have no choice. There's no other way out."

Milo Bracken felt the acid rising in his throat in response to the warm Coke. He unscrewed the top off a glass pint bottle of cheap bourbon and added an ounce to the Coke, spilling some on the rim of the can. He took a long swallow and lit a Pall Mall, all the while listening.

At first, Reynolds, the lawyer, was objecting, thought Milo, but gradually he, too, was for going to the cops. Jesus! If they go to the cops, the deal is over! Milo sucked on the cigarette, drawing the smoke deeply into his lungs, getting tobacco and bits of the cigarette paper stuck to his lips. He washed that down with warm bourbon and Coke. Reynolds was speaking.

"Digger, you know the consequences," he said. "But I've always wondered if we were right in thinking we could ever keep this situation from the police. You have a strong reputation as a good and honest judge. That's worth something."

Milo didn't hear any response from Judge Moss. The lawyer continued.

"One thing is, if we are going to the authorities, the sooner the better. Any further delay just raises questions. When and how should we do it?"

This time, the judge answered. "Today or tomorrow," he said. "As soon as we can put together the whole story, including the documents I have received in the envelope, let's meet with Chief Morgan."

"I'd ask him to have Lieutenant Jackson there too."

"Good idea," said the voice of Judge Moss. The voices were getting fainter as though the two men were leaving the room. Milo didn't hear any more.

Shit! he thought. Griswold *has* done it! Milo sucked on the Pall Mall and washed the smoke down with more tepid Coke and bourbon. His head was pounding from the hangover he still had from the previous night's drinking. The aspirin hadn't helped, but the bourbon seemed to be working a little.

He had to do something. This was going to be a sweet deal for him. It was very good money. He certainly needed that. His life had always been a roller coaster, from riding high to being right at the bottom. It was certainly in the pits at the moment, his third wife had left him and was threatening to divorce him, his Twin Cities detective agency was in financial trouble, his license was being investigated, and he had large gambling debts to dangerous people you just didn't forget to pay. The money coming out of this deal from Griswold was critical to him. And Griswold was fucking it up! He removed the head set and smoothed the thin greasy hair back over his bald spot. I have got to do something, he thought, and now!

"Jesus Christ, Milo!" A young man entered the van from the sliding side door, waving his hand in front of him to clear away the acrid, blue cigarette smoke. "If you don't quit those things they will kill you. If you don't quit smoking them in this van, you're going to kill us both before this job is done!"

"Take it easy, kid. We've got troubles." Milo took a deep drink from the Coke can.

"What? The judge not taking the bait? What?" Vincent Turcotte slid the door shut behind him.

Milo explained the situation. Vince worked for him occasionally in the Cities. He was young, about twenty-six, Milo thought. He did not have regular gainful employment. He was involved, peripherally, in the Minneapolis drug scene, even occasionally coming to Duluth on some transactions. Mostly, however, he just hung around and was available for odd jobs that were usually outside the law and paid well because of that fact. Milo didn't really want to know more. Knowing he couldn't do this job alone, Milo had included Vince for a sizable sum, although nothing like a full share of what Milo expected to get.

"If it goes sour, you think your man will try to stiff us?" Vince removed his aviator's sunglasses and ran his long slender fingers through his greased back black hair. He did not know Griswold's name, anything about him, or how to reach him. Milo had kept it that way.

"I don't know," Milo shook his head and drank.

"The operative word there is 'try,' you know," said Vince. "If he does try, you lead me to him and I'll take care of the problem." He moved his hand to the small of his back, where Milo knew he kept a small pistol stuffed in the waistband of his blue jeans.

This was one of the things Milo liked about the kid. He was working for Milo, so he would back Milo's play whatever it may be, within reason. Even though the kid was involved in illegal activities much of the time, he had a sense of fairness and loyalty that Milo found both unusual and welcome. He could trust him, more than he can trust me, Milo realized.

"Keep it holstered for now, kid," Milo said, grinding out his Pall Mall in the overflowing ashtray. "I'm letting you take over the watch and I'm going to go see the man, now. There must be something he can do to put this thing back on track." He got up from his chair at the equipment desk, grabbed his small canvas bag and moved, hunched over through the van toward the door.

"Milo?"

"Yeah?" Milo turned back toward the kid.

Vince made a motion with his hand toward his own face and hair.

"What?"

"Better stop at the room and clean up a little, if you want this guy to take you serious at all. You look like shit."

Milo Bracken paused in the doorway, rubbing his hand over his unshaven face, feeling his throbbing head and the soreness of his eyes that he knew were bloodshot without looking in any mirror.

"Right, good idea," he said, and left the van, shutting the sliding door behind him. The kid was right. He walked to the aging Ford

Escort the kid had driven from their motel room in West Duluth. He would go back and clean up. Then he would see Griswold.

Mike, Digger and Kate met for lunch in a back booth in Porter's restaurant in the Holiday Mall, just three blocks from the courthouse. Digger sat across from Kate and Mike. They waited for their Caesar salads, a house specialty, to be served before they started talking about the case against Digger.

"How do you think it went this morning," Kate was asking. She poked at the strips of grilled chicken lying across the bed of Romaine lettuce.

"We can only wait to find out," said Digger, "but it better work fast, or it won't make any difference no matter how convincing we may have been."

"Right," said Mike, turning toward Kate. "Basically, we set a deadline for them to contact us with their demands, whatever they are."

"Well," said Kate, "let's hope it works."

Milo Bracken looked like a different man. A hot shower had gotten rid of most of his exhaustion, headache and hangover. A shave and clean clothes had transformed him and given him the spirit and resolve to meet his task. He smoothed out the creases in his suit pants, straightened his necktie and put on the dark gray suit coat, appraising his image in the mirror. Look like a fucking lawyer, he thought and smiled. Now he was ready to see Griswold.

Leaving the dingy motel, he steered the Escort to I35 and headed east into downtown Duluth.

Griswold answered the door of his Holiday Inn Hotel suite. At first surprised, he looked Milo up and down, noting the clean business suit and tie, polished leather shoes, and Milo's neatly combed hair. This was not the Milo he was used to.

"What in the Lord Jesus Christ's name are you doing here?" he demanded.

"We got troubles," Milo answered.

"You mean *you* got troubles!" Griswold jabbed a thick finger into Milo's chest. "For coming here!"

"Can I at least come in to explain?" Milo was already regretting his decision to confront Griswold.

"All right, God damn it, get inside at least, where you won't be seen." Griswold checked up and down the hall for anyone. No one was there, but a maid's cart was parked in the hall about five rooms away. He grimaced as he ushered Milo in. The suite had a living room with a couch and upholstered chairs, a kitchenette area at one end, and a short hallway beyond to the bedroom and bath.

"Five minutes! That's all!" he growled at Milo as he picked a newspaper off the couch and sat down pointing to one of the upholstered chairs for Milo.

Milo sat, as ordered. He described the conversation Digger Moss and Mike Reynolds had had in the judge's chambers that morning. Milo explained his concern that the ability to control the judge was being jeopardized and would be lost if they went to the police.

Frank Griswold listened to Milo, watching him intently, twirling a ball point pen with his fingers. He tried to control the growing anger within him.

As he spoke, Milo noticed Griswold's expression. His lips were closed tightly together, as if he were afraid something might escape from his mouth. His neck had turned red and his face was following. Milo was regretting his decision even more.

" ... and so," Milo continued, "I think we've got to act right away so we don't lose him." Milo finished.

"Think?!" Griswold stood. He was shouting now. "You're not supposed to think! You were hired to listen and report! Only!" Griswold went to the kitchenette counter and poured himself a measure of Scotch whisky into a glass, neat, without ice. He added some soda from a plastic bottle of mineral water, swirled it around in the half-filled tumbler and took a deep swallow. He did not offer Milo a drink. He lurched toward Milo's chair, glass in one hand and pointing a finger at Milo. Milo was afraid Griswold was going to fall on him.

"I hire a cheap, down and out P.I. to come up here to Duluth and do two simple things for me. Listen and report. That's all. Listen and report." Griswold took another drink and smacked his lips. "And for those two simple things, I offered you more money than you could ever have imagined such a job could possibly be worth. Why? Because the job is important and I need you to stick to your two simple things!"

"I know, Frank, but ..."

"And you think we should act right away so we don't lose the good judge? 'We'? This is my operation. '*We*' don't do anything! *I'll* decide what to do and when."

"Frank, I ..."

"Don't 'Frank' me," said Griswold, only barely under control now. "But you're partly right, it is time to contact his Honor, only you won't be involved anymore."

"What?"

"You're fired." Griswold started to open the door to the main hallway. "And your five minutes are up." He glanced in the hall, saw the maid's cart was gone and opened the door all the way, standing, holding it open for Milo to leave.

"Frank, you can't ..."

"I can and I just did." Griswold waved a hand toward the door in a mock gesture almost like a gentleman bowing to a lady and motioning for her to pass. "I don't need your services anymore anyway. The 'listen and report' part of this job is done. I don't need to monitor the conversations of Judge Digger Moss anymore. From now on I'll be in them. Besides the advance I paid you was as much as you'd expect to be paid for a job like this. You said so yourself. So consider yourself well paid and leave."

"Frank!"

"Get the fuck out of here, Milo!"

Milo Bracken turned down the hall toward the elevators. Oh shit, he thought, now what have I done. Once in the elevator he tried to think of what to do. He had not paid the kid anything, yet. The advance went as a temporary payment towards gambling debts with a little held back for a few bottles and cigarettes. At least he was relieved to know that his most aggressive creditors were appeased for a while. At least his legs were still in tact. Milo truly believed that some of his gambling debts were held by people who might follow the old-fashioned underworld debt collection methods. His chance to rescue himself had just gone south.

After Milo left, Griswold got out his notes on Digger Moss's pending cases. Satisfied, he decided to fix another Scotch before calling.

Milo was so predictable, he thought. A loser for sure, Griswold had felt certain he would be able to do the simple job, and Griswold had felt certain he would do something like just now that would give Griswold the excuse to fire him and cut him out of the big money. That had been Griswold's plan from the beginning. Just like he had done with Greg Larson. He had definitely cut Larson out. Sure, it was like a double cross, but not when it was part of the plan from the beginning. Yes, he thought, everything was going according to plan.

"Hello?" Digger Moss answered the phone in his chambers after two rings.

"Judge Moss?" Griswold made no attempt to disguise his voice.

"Yes? Speaking."

"Judge, I know you've had some disturbing communications lately and I want you to know they were from me."

"What?! Who is this?"

"All in good time, Judge," said Griswold. "All in good time."

"He told me he didn't care if we went to the police!" Digger told them. He said he still had a hold on me that would make me come around!"

"What the hell was he talking about, Digger?" asked Kate, resting her hand on the steering wheel. They were seated in Kate's Lincoln Town car parked in her reserved spot on the ground floor of the parking ramp adjacent to the courthouse. Kate was in the driver's seat, Digger in the front passenger seat, and Mike in the rear. Immediately after the telephone call, Digger had found them both and they had gone to this spot where they believed no one could hear them.

"What name did he give you, Digger?" asked Mike.

"No name. He said that would come later, but he did give me a request."

"What?" Kate and Mike both asked.

"He wants me to fix a sentencing."

"What? How?" Kate looked dumbfounded.

"It's a felony sentencing I have scheduled for day after tomorrow. I took the plea about a month ago. He wants me to make a downward durational *and* dispositional departure from the Sentencing Guidelines," said Digger.

"Both durational and dispositional? That seems unusual." Kate drummed her fingers on the steering wheel, thinking.

"How does he know when the sentencing is anyhow?" asked Mike. "Does he know the guy?"

"I don't know," said Digger.

Kate turned to Mike. "He can find out the schedule if he has access to TCIS." She pronounced it "Teesis."

"Tee-what?" asked Mike.

"TCIS. T-C-I-S, the Trial Court Information System on the courthouse computers." she answered.

"Oh, you mean the stuff the courtroom clerks look at on the courtroom computers to find files, dates, and so on?"

"Right."

"I know what you mean, now," said Mike. "I didn't know it had a name. But how would this guy have access?"

"If someone could plant listening devices in my chambers, then that someone could surely use the computers after hours and if he knew how to operate TCIS, he could get any information he wanted about my cases."

Kate said, "I wonder, isn't TCIS shut down after hours?"

"I don't know," said Digger, "but it doesn't shut down right at 4:30, when most people leave. I know that. And it's on pretty early in the morning before most people get here."

"So what about the sentencing, Digger?" asked Mike. "What are you going to do. Is there a plea agreement?"

"Nope. A straight up plea," Digger said. "That's what's so strange."

"What?"

"Well, the Pre-Sentence Investigation report from the Probation Department doesn't recommend a dispositional departure, but leaves the door wide open, even suggests it as a possibility. The guidelines call for 48 months in prison, a commit to the Commissioner of

Corrections.   The range on the guidelines grid is 44-52 months. Probation is recommending a guidelines sentence of 44 months.

"Probation is recommending the bottom of the range?" asked Mike.

"Right," Digger said. "That's novel, isn't it? And a dispositional departure of a stayed sentence with some local time, instead of prison, together with probation is certainly within the realm of reason in this case.   Under the circumstances of the case, even though a plea agreement couldn't be reached with the prosecution, I think the defense lawyer thought a straight up plea was best.   Putting the defendant on the mercy of the court."

"Who is the defense lawyer?" asked Mike.

"Marcy Sullivan."

"No doubt in my mind that you're right," said Mike. "Marcy is a sharp and experienced trial lawyer. She didn't back away from trial without reason. She's decided the best for her client is the plea, agreement or not, and then appeal to your sense of fairness. And I bet she's right. Hell, even if the prosecutor did not agree, there may not be any strong opposition."

Kate nodded agreement. "But why," she asked, "would your guy also ask for a durational departure? I never heard of that. If you are going to stay the prison sentence for local time and conditions of probation, who cares how long the prison sentence is if it isn't much different than the guidelines anyway?"

"Exactly," said Digger, shaking his head.

"Well, let's work this out," said Mike. "If defendant executed the sentence of 44 months that probation is recommending, deducting one-third for good time, he would do 29 and 1/3 months. What did your caller want?"

"43 months."

"That's certainly an unusual number." said Kate.

"Yeah," agreed Digger, "it's one month less than the range on the guidelines grid."

"Just enough to make it a departure," Kate thought aloud.

"So," continued Mike, "if the stayed commit is 43 months, and he ever executes it, with good time, it's ...," he paused, " 28 and 2/3 months, I think, instead of 29 and 1/3 months."

"I don't get it," said Kate.

"Neither do I," said Mike. "No one I know would really ever ask for a durational departure like that. Not when you expect your client not to have to execute it, because it's stayed for reduced local time and probation. And you tell us in this case, the lawyers aren't asking for it and the PSI says the bottom of the range of the regular guidelines sentence with a possible dispositional departure and probation because this guy is somebody nice, or at least nicer than some other people."

"I think I get it," said Digger, slowly.

"Let us in on it," said Kate.

"Maybe it's a test."

"Shit!" said Kate, "That's it! Of course! The lawyers will think you've gone completely 'round the bend, but it doesn't make a hell of lot of difference to anyone in the long run. From what you tell us, this guy won't violate his probation seriously enough to have to go to prison, anyway."

"I think you're right," said Digger nodding.

"A test. Hmmmh." Mike was thinking. "Well what do we do?"

"Digger has to go along with it, to find out what they really want," said Kate.

"I don't like it," said Digger.

"Well, Digger, Sweetheart, I don't think you have much choice."

"You want me to make a decision because someone is blackmailing me?" He looked directly into Kate's emerald eyes.

Kate stared right back at him, her eyes flashing. "God damn it, Digger, I want you to do what is best for Digger Moss, right now. If we are going to beat this son of a bitch, and we are, then we've got to take this fight to him. We can't do that until we find out who he is and what he really wants!"

"The request on the sentence doesn't really hurt anybody. The lawyers might think you've gone wacko on this one, but I suppose that won't be the first time." said Mike, grinning. Both judges turned and regarded him with put on stern looks, and the tension eased.

A Duluth Police Sergeant was using a pointer to explain the evidence contained in an enlarged photograph beside him.

"These are the marks left behind on the carpet. Even though they were faint and hard to see, and even though some attempt had been made to clean them up or at least obscure them, it was a deep pile carpet from which we were able to obtain a foot print. The marks were made by the victim's blood left in the carpet. Our lab people have come up with this footprint." He shifted his pointer to another easel with a black and white drawing. The television camera shifted its angle to follow him.

"Is that the killer's footprint?" a reporter asked.

"What kind of shoe is it?" asked another.

The sergeant waited until the crowd of reporters at the press conference settled down.

"We believe we have concrete evidence that the killer wore a running shoe with this pattern on the sole. Although the pattern is not complete in the carpet stains, it appears clear that it can't be any other shoe than a Nike-Air Verve II."

"Have you got any leads on whose shoe it might be?" asked a voice from the crowd.

Chief of Police John W. Morgan stepped in front of the sergeant to address the media crowd. The noise level reduced substantially, as soon as he appeared. The Chief was an imposing figure. A large black man, he stood over six feet four inches and weighed close to two hundred and fifty pounds. And none of it was fat, some said. During his relatively short tenure as chief, Duluth had had its share of crime. Morgan had showed he could handle situations thoroughly and efficiently.

"Now, people," his deep voice captured the attention of the crowd, "that will have to be enough questions for now. I know you need more, but we will give as much as we can, when we can, without jeopardizing our investigation. And rest assured!" he boomed. "This man killed a police officer, a member of our department and we will not rest until he is identified, arrested, and punished!" Morgan turned and left the room.

"Well, there you have it, Ladies and Gentleman in the viewing audience," said the TV news anchor, pulling a strand of yellow blonde hair away from her face, Chief John Morgan has given us the update on the Larson murder investigation. Just three days ago, at this East End duplex," the screen showed a photograph of Larson's duplex taken the morning of the discovery of the body, "Sergeant Gregory Allen Larson of the Duluth Police Department was brutally murdered in his own home. Police have not yet identified any suspects in the slaying, but as you have seen, clues are being developed which Chief Morgan believes will lead to an early arrest."

Digger switched off the television and put the remote control on the night table beside the bed.

"What are you going to do?" asked Judy, sitting up in bed beside him.

Digger got up from the bed. Stepping into the walk-in closet on his side of the bed, he emerged with his Nike-Air Verve II's.

"I spent a good deal of time cleaning those," said Judy. "Now what are you going to do with them?"

He looked at the pattern of the sole and heel, trying to remember what he had just seen on television. "I don't know," he said. "I suppose I should get rid of them, or hide them."

"Does it bother you that we are doing things that make you look guiltier than if you didn't do them?"

"Absolutely," he agreed, sitting back on the bed, staring at the shoes, "but it's because we dare not go to the police. They wouldn't have any choice but to proceed against me based on plenty of probable cause to believe I had committed several crimes. I don't think we have any choice."

"If you're innocent, isn't that supposed to be all you need? When you are dictating orders here at night, or arguing your cases to me, I hear you talking about defendants being presumed innocent until they are proved guilty beyond a reasonable doubt. Plenty of times, even to my knowledge, you have decided pre-trial issues in criminal cases because at that point the defendant remained not guilty of the charges against him. What about that?"

"True," he answered, tossing the shoes on the floor beside the bed, "but there's a big difference between proof beyond a reasonable doubt and probable cause to go to trial. Kate and Mike agree with me that the evidence sent to me in the envelope is not only enough for probable cause, but probably enough to convict. If I am a criminal defendant, I would have the right to remain silent and would not have to put up a defense of any kind. The burden on the State remains the same, proof beyond a reasonable doubt, but if I don't do anything, I

61

would almost assuredly be convicted even though I am really innocent."

"In other words, we are in deep trouble." She leaned her head on his shoulder, putting an arm around his chest and squeezing him.

"Deep." He lifted her off his chest and took her in his arms. "But, damn it, we will get through this."

The next morning, Digger carefully wrapped the running shoes in several grocery store plastic bags and finally in a large black garbage bag rolled up around itself and tied with heavy brown twine. This package he took to the attic and placed in the bottom of a box of Christmas decorations being stored there until next Christmas. When the box threatened to overflow as he replaced the decorations, he redistributed some of them to the several other boxes of decorations stored in that far corner of the attic. He left a smiling Santa sitting prominently on the box with the shoes, pushing it to the rear of the group of boxes, nearly touching the sloping roof line as it neared the top of the outside wall of the house.

"Where'd you put them?" Digger stood before the mirror, adjusting the knot in his tie. Judy sat on the bed, watching him. "Huh?" she followed up her question when he didn't answer right away.

"Better you don't know."

"Oh, come on, Digger." She came to stand beside him before the mirror. She grinned and gently jabbed him in the ribs. "You *know* when this is all over, *I'll* have to find them for you anyway."

Digger smiled at the thought. She was right, although in this particular case he really thought he would remember. He was pleased she was seeing some humor in the situation. Now that they were doing something again, he felt better too. "Under the red Santa in a box of Christmas stuff in the corner of the attic."

"You," she pointed a long slender finger at him. "You involved my little, soft, red Santa Christmas tree ornament in this mess? Digger! I've had that Santa since I was a little girl!"

"Yes, dear."

"What's next?"

"Well, next, I'm going to work. Remember, we have to keep everything as usual. Tonight, let's go shopping up at the Miller Hill Mall."

"Oh?" Her eyes brightened as she looked at him in the mirror as he put on his suit coat, and adjusted the cuffs of his shirt in his coat sleeves.

"Relax." Digger gave her a reproaching look in the mirror. "Daddy needs new shoes."

"Oh."

"Want to have dinner up there?"

"Dinner! Right." She paused in thought. "Grandma's up by the Mall? Maybe not. Maybe I'd like to come back down the hill to the Pickwick."

"Your choice."

Her eyes brightened again. Something Digger believed she could do whenever she pleased and did so for his benefit when she thought it useful. "I'll decide while you are away earning the price of this meal."

"And the shoes," he responded.

"Don't you think I'm going to skimp on a good Pickwick meal just because you're going to spend some God awful amount on shoes to run in." She straightened her hair, still looking at him in the mirror. "You runners have been completely snookered by a whole industry that feeds on your desire for self importance as athletes. All you do is run, and not very fast at that. Yet you pay more for these fragile shoes that fall apart after a while than the best Florsheim dress wingtips. Come to think of it, why do you need to replace the shoes so fast? Haven't you got more important things to do than go running?"

"Chet will probably call to go out at noon tomorrow, he usually does on Thursdays. Everything as normal, remember."

That night the Mosses drove up Central Entrance to the Miller Hill Mall up on U.S. Highway 53, known locally in the area of the Mall as the Miller Trunk Highway. They shopped at a store in the enclosed Mall dedicated exclusively to footwear and other clothing for amateur runners, walkers, tennis players, cyclists, etc. One entire wall of the long narrow space occupied by Runners' Outlet was devoted to shoes, not boxes of pairs of shoes, but a single sample of each style of shoe, on wall hung brackets from floor to ceiling and back wall to front wall.

"How much do you weigh?" asked a clerk.

"One seventy-five," said Digger.

"How often and far do you run?"

"Three or four times a week," said Digger, "when I can," he added. "Usually, I go three or four miles."

Using a long wooden handled device, the clerk removed a brightly colored shoe with a thick wedge-shaped heel from a high rack. "This Nike series is top of the line. It's one of our most popular shoes."

"I don't think so," said Digger.

"Our customers really like it," the clerk said, raising the tone of his voice slightly at the end of the sentence as if to say, are you sure you aren't interested in this one?

"No," said Digger, pausing to look at the huge display of shoes. "Let me see the New Balance, that one up there." He pointed.

"You sure steered clear of the Nikes," said Judy, as they drove down the hill.

"All they have just now is a pattern of the bottom of a shoe. It's like a composite at that. I don't want anything similar or the same brand."

At the Pickwick, they sat next to the window watching the Wednesday night race of the sailboats of the Duluth Keel Club out on the lake. The start was in front of the Aerial Bridge. Digger could imagine hearing the pre-start whistle of the committee boat as the confused wanderings of the white sails began to turn in a common direction and the sound of the start as the first boats passed the committee boat to start the race.

Back at home, Digger unwrapped the new shoes. He put in the laces. Then, he gently rubbed them around in Judy's flower garden. Back in the house, he cleaned them up a little and examined them. Not bad, he thought. They weren't as bright as brand new shoes always looked.

The sentencing was set for 11:00, at the end of a Special Term calendar of motions that began at 9:00. As Digger suspected, Chester Brand called before 8:00 to see about a noon run. A busy civil insurance defense lawyer, Chet needed to have every thing planned. Even when they were partners at Jensen, Brand, Chet would come to Digger's office first thing in the morning to see if Digger was available to run or sometimes just to tell Digger how he, Chet, planned to spend his day. Chet was a talker. Even running, he was a talker. Digger liked him a lot. He had been a close friend since their law school days at Minnesota. But Chet usually did all the talking. Digger liked to run. Digger liked to talk with Chet. But sometimes he had trouble doing both at the same time. He got out of breath. So, he usually let Chet talk and he ran. He'd told Chet he would meet him at the YMCA at noon if his hearing was over in time. If not, he told Chet not to wait for him.

He finished the Special Term civil motions by 10:40 and recessed until 11:00. At eleven, he entered the courtroom for the sentencing.

"All rise!" The bailiff opened court.

"Please be seated," said Digger, as he seated himself at the bench.

He called the case. "State of Minnesota vs. Page Richard Gilchrist," he announced. "The record should reflect that the defendant is present in court and with his counsel Ms. Marcy Sullivan, and Ms. Marilee Jackson, of the St. Louis County Attorney's Office, is here for the State. Good Morning, counsel and Mr. Gilchrist.

"Good morning, your Honor."

Digger began the routine. "This matter is set for a sentence hearing this morning. The Court has received a pre-sentence investigation report from Mr. Sam Fortner," he glanced up, over the top of his reading glasses, "who is also present in court this morning. I'll ask counsel in turn if they have had an opportunity to review the PSI and if there are any comments or corrections of a factual nature regarding the report. We will begin with Ms. Jackson."

The prosecutor stood. "Your Honor, I have had a chance to review the PSI report. The State has nothing of a factual nature."

"Thank you," said Digger. "Ms. Sullivan?"

The defender rose from her chair beside her client at counsel table. "Thank you, your Honor. I have had a chance to review the report with my client. He has read it through, discussed it with me, and indicates he understands it and the recommended sentence. The

65

defense has no corrections of a factual nature regarding the report." She sat back down.

"All right," said Digger, "the Probation Department has recommended a sentence of commitment to the Commissioner of Corrections for a period of 44 months. Ms. Jackson, what is the position of the State regarding this recommendation?"

Marilee Jackson stood at counsel table. "Your Honor, the State agrees with the recommendation and asks the Court to adopt it." She sat down.

"Ms. Sullivan?"

"Thank you, your Honor," said Marcy Sullivan, rising from her chair. "Under the unusual circumstances relating to this case, the defense requests a dispositional departure from the presumed sentence under the guidelines giving my client a stayed sentence with some time at the Northeast Regional Correction Center and conditions of probation." She went on to argue for a departure as Digger had expected she would. Her client, Gilchrist, had no prior record. He had been of assistance to the police in their investigation that had led to other arrests. He was amenable to probation.

"Your Honor," she finished, "I have talked with Mr. Fortner and Ms. Jackson. And I don't think there is any real opposition to my request."

Digger looked at Merilee Jackson and Sam Fortner, eyebrows raised in question.

"Your Honor, the State has no strong opposition to a probationary sentence in this case." Jackson confirmed the defense counsel's statement.

"Probation has no objection, your Honor. We leave it to your sound judgment," said Fortner. "I have a probationary sentence outlined here for your consideration, if you wish." He approached the bench, handing Digger a single piece of paper and handing copies to each lawyer before he sat back down.

Digger reviewed the paper and spoke. "What Mr. Fortner has handed me calls for a commitment to the Department of Corrections for 44 months stayed for five years of supervised probation including as conditions of probation, one year at NERCC, abstinence from alcohol or drugs, random drug and alcohol testing, and other standard conditions of probation." He looked over the bench at counsel. "I take it from what I have heard, that neither party objects to this sentence?"

The lawyers nodded.

"All right, then, would the defendant please rise?"

Page Gilchrist and Marcy Sullivan stood as Digger read the sentence. When he finished, he followed with a routine question.

"Any comments, additions or corrections? Mr. Fortner?"

"Judge, maybe I heard wrong, but did you say 43 months?"

"I did."

"You saw that the recommendation was for 44 months?"

"I did."

Fortner sat down, a confused look on his face.

"Your Honor?" Marilee Jackson was standing.

"Yes, Ms. Jackson?"

"43 months would be a durational departure from the guidelines presumed sentence," she said hesitantly, and then added, "I'm not sure you intended that."

"I know," said Digger, "and I did." He turned to Marcy Sullivan. "Anything else, Ms. Sullivan?"

"I have nothing more, your Honor." She exchanged a strange look with the prosecutor as she rose to gather her papers.

"All right, then, court is adjourned." Digger tapped the gavel on its clapper and rose to leave the courtroom. Mike was right, he thought. They really think I'm wacko now.

Digger glanced at his watch as he removed his robe on the way to his chambers. 11:40. Good. He could get to the "Y" a little early.

"Hi, Judge Moss!" said the athletic looking blonde young woman standing behind the front counter at the "Y." "Running today?" She was dressed in running shorts and a tee-shirt with the YMCA logo on the front. She held out her hand for his membership card.

"Running scared, Jennie," Digger answered with his usual pun, which, he realized he probably meant literally this time. He gave her his card and fifty cents for which he received in return a locker room key and a towel. She buzzed the door for him as he left the lobby area.

Digger had walked the two blocks from the courthouse to the "Y", arriving five minutes before noon. He had time to get ready before Chet and countless other noontime exercisers arrived. He selected his usual locker, sat on one of the long wooden benches between the rows of lockers and opened his gym bag. The new shoes were on top. He was pleased with his "dirtying" job. They look okay, he thought. He began to change out of his business suit.

Standing with one foot on the bench, he was tying his shoe lace when Pete Myers came around the row of lockers carrying a dark green gym bag over his shoulder. A young internist in a group at the Medical Arts Building, a block and a half from the "Y", Myers ran every weekday but Wednesday, his "day off" he called it. He usually ran six miles, passing Digger on the way out, and then again on the way back. The only reason Digger was not completely humiliated, was their difference in age and the fact that Dr. Myers too would one day be running slower and shorter distances.

"Hey! New shoes, Judge?"

Digger's blood ran cold.

"New Balance, eh?" Myers tossed his bag on the bench and turned to open a locker. "Pretty fancy, Judge."

At least Chet Brand hadn't noticed his new shoes. If he had, it certainly would not have gone without comment, thought Digger. He listened to Chet talk on as they ran east on the Lakewalk up the hill into Leif Erickson Park.

" ... in the Cities for the last two weeks. Asbestos depositions." He knew Jensen, Brand represented a major defendant in the asbestos litigation on a regional basis and it was Chet's baby. "Yeah, Digger, the asbestos cases are a lawyer's job security and retirement program. The only ones making more than the lawyers are the court reporters. Jesus! I swear the one we're using here in Minnesota is getting richer every day. He's easily the best dressed person in the deposition room. Drives the fanciest car, too. He gets orders for about twenty copies of every deposition."

Digger looked out over the lake and to the South Shore in Wisconsin. East of Leif Erickson Park, they were running along the Lakewalk near the water's edge with an uninterrupted view of the blue waters of the big lake. Fishing boats were trolling over on the Wisconsin side.

"You gonna get that cop murder?" Chet asked.

Digger nearly stumbled on the asphalt path. "What?"

"The cop that was killed over on the east hillside the other day. Are you going to get that case?"

"Oh," said Digger, recovering his rhythm, "I doubt it, but I really don't know. There is an order in which murder cases are assigned, separate from the random assignment method for most cases. I don't know where we are at the moment on that assignment order." God, he thought. What if he was assigned the case? Well it won't be assigned until after there is a complaint, maybe a Grand Jury Indictment, and an omnibus hearing. That requires a suspect first, and ultimately a defendant, who, if he isn't careful, might just be Digger, himself.

Chet Brand went on running and talking. Digger listened and tried to keep up, his mind definitely on other things.

"They got to get him, Digger." Chet was beginning to get winded too, as they turned and started back.

"What?"

"They've got to get the son of a bitch and get him quick! This simply is not good for the community, this kind of news, news of a cop killer in Duluth, for Christ's sake! I tell you, Digger, I don't know much about the criminal law you're now doing, but it better put the guy away fast and certainly not let him off!"

Chester Brand, thought Digger, a good civil lawyer, probably more understanding of the criminal law than he gave himself credit for, but opinionated as hell about the case. God help Digger Moss, if the false information he was afraid of got loose in this town.

A blonde man with long wavy hair, dressed in blue jeans and a tan windbreaker was standing near the stairway up to the bridge to Fitgers. Digger remembered seeing him there before as they were on their way out. He's probably smarter than we are, thought Digger, he looks relaxed, in no hurry, and he's not all sweaty and out of breath.

Digger took a quick shower and made it back to his chambers by twenty after one. He had not noticed the man in blue jeans and tan windbreaker a half block behind him as he walked back to the courthouse. In his chambers, he was gulping a sandwich and Diet Coke from the cafeteria, when the phone rang.

"Judge Moss?"

"Yes?" Digger recognized the caller's voice.

"You seemed to have passed our little test. We won't be giving our information to the police just yet, so you can relax, but not too much now, do you understand?"

"I understand."

"We're going to have to meet, Judge," said the caller, "and soon."

"Where?" asked Digger. He was not at all sure he wanted such a meeting, but no doubt it would be necessary if they were to catch this guy and clear his name. But he did not want a meeting before he talked with Kate and Mike.

"I'll tell you where, later. First I want you to give me a list of all your cases currently under advisement and the ones you have coming for trial in the next three months."

Digger was silent.

The caller said, "You can do that, certainly, can't you?"

"Yes," said Digger, slowly. "Yes, of course I can."

"Good. Make one up and leave it on your desk before you leave work tonight, all right?"

"Well, yes, but ..." What was this man telling him, that he could just come in here anytime and pick it up?

"That's the next step," the caller said. "Simple isn't it? And, of course, you know how important this is to you. Do I need to remind you?"

"No, you do not," said Digger, wishing he could get his hands on the owner of that voice.

"Hold on, Judge. I don't want to hear anything but your willingness to cooperate, you understand? Anything else, anything, and this deal's over and you are in deep shit. Got that?"

Digger did not answer.

"Leave the list," the caller said abruptly, and hung up.

A stocky man with long wavy blonde hair, dressed in blue jeans and tan windbreaker was talking on a cellular phone in the skyway over Second Street, between the third floor of the courthouse and the adjacent parking ramp. Frank Griswold closed the cell phone and stood for a moment studying the traffic on Second Street below him. Then he walked towards the parking ramp, down the stairs and out onto Second Street, walking east, towards his hotel.

Digger phoned his law clerk and scheduling clerk to arrange for the list of cases the caller requested. Then he left messages for Mike Reynolds and Kate Riley to meet him later. A meeting was coming. They had to be ready.

CHAPTER SIX

It was gone! Digger stared at his desk. It was Friday morning. He arrived at the courthouse before 7:30. As soon as he opened his door he looked for the envelope in which he had left the caller's requested lists the night before. Gone!

Mike, Kate and Digger had thought about surveillance of his chambers to see if anyone came for the lists and if so, who it was. But, they had decided, it was more important to get the lists to them, whoever "they" were, and move on to the meeting the caller had mentioned. Then, maybe, they would know what demands would be made of Digger.

Digger had checked the lists of cases under advisement and cases coming up for trial in the next few months. There was nothing that particularly stood out. Several civil motions, two civil trials, a couple of divorce cases and several criminal omnibus motions were pending under advisement. Fourteen, in all, that were under advisement awaiting a decision by him.

His coming trial calendar had some interesting cases including a murder case, a personal injury products liability claim in which the plaintiff had been rendered a paraplegic by the failure of an automobile front axle, a crim sex case and a wrongful death civil action. But none seemed to lend itself to any kind of blackmail regarding the result or any of Digger's potential rulings.

Whatever, he thought. They have the lists now. Whoever in the hell "They" are.

"Hello?" said Randall McCoy. "This is Randall McCoy."
"Mr. McCoy, this is Frank Griswold."

"Just one moment, please." Silence. After a brief pause, Griswold heard, "May I call you right back? I have some people in my office right now. You are at the same number I have, aren't you?"

"Right, I'll be waiting for your call."

Five minutes later, Griswold's telephone rang.

"Hello?"

"Griswold?"

"Yeah."

"I couldn't take your call before," said McCoy. "We have to be careful, you know."

Griswold ignored the comment. "Moss came through on the sentencing."

"What? What sentencing?"

"I told you," Griswold said impatiently, "that I was going to test Judge Moss before we submitted any real demand. I also told you," his tone was quite demeaning, "that I would submit your request along with some others, so it wouldn't be obvious which case, if any, was the most important."

"Yes, I guess I remember that," said McCoy.

"Well, now it's time to meet to discuss our next move," said Griswold.

"I wish we didn't have to meet." McCoy's voice sounded concerned. "For obvious reasons, I prefer not being seen with you."

"I know," said Griswold, with understanding, but he thought, you sniveling little prick. You're quick enough to ask me to do your dirty work and then you won't even acknowledge my accomplishments for your benefit. We'll see about that, he thought to himself.

"We can meet somewhere discreet. Here in the Holiday Inn perhaps, maybe out on Park Point or up on the Skyline Drive, but we do need to meet."

"All right, how soon?"

"The next day or so."

"Just a minute." Griswold could hear McCoy shuffling some papers on his desk.

"I'm free tomorrow, about 1:00."

"Fine," said Griswold, "meet me at 1:15 at the parking lot off Lake Avenue on Park Point. It's right where Lake Avenue curves to the right and joins Minnesota Avenue. After that, there's only one street going out the Point. Keep going straight instead of curving and you're in the lot. Know where I mean?"

"Yes, I think so."

"Fine. I'll see you then. I'll either be in the lot or out on the beach right there."

Griswold folded the cell phone to its closed position. He had a surprise for McCoy on Saturday, not expected, but certainly deserved.

73

"**I**'m scared, Digger, I don't have to tell you," said Kate Riley. They met after 4:30 in Kate's chambers. "You know what happened the last time you had a meeting. The other guy came dead."

"Kate, it's the only way to find out what they want. It's the only way to find out with whom we are dealing. It's the only hope of coming up with a plan to get them and save me from disaster, probably prison."

"He's right," agreed Mike. "And all we can do now is wait until this guy calls."

"What's the latest on the investigation?" Kate changed the subject. "I've been on the bench all day. The domestic abuse calendar ran right through the lunch hour. My staff and I had fifteen minutes for lunch and we were back at it all afternoon."

"Nothing new on the news," said Mike. "No new gossip here in the courthouse or on the street either that I have heard."

"Well, right now, that's good for us, I guess," she commented.

"That is exactly correct," said Digger, feeling like he was in a race for time, but had not been told which direction to run or where the finish line was. "We have got to have time to find out who and what we are dealing with and to formulate a plan."

Digger opened his front door to get the Saturday morning paper. He stood in his pajama bottoms, in the doorway, quickly scanning the headlines for the inevitable story about the Larson murder. He went into the kitchen, where he poured fresh coffee that had brewed automatically by timer. Sitting at the kitchen table, he found the story on the case and began to read. Seeing nothing he had not read before, he thought, at least there were no new developments and that was good.

"Well?" Judy entered the kitchen, still in her nightgown. She got a mug from the cupboard and stood at the counter, pouring coffee and glancing at Digger.

She looked tired, he thought. God it would be good for her when this was all over. The stress was definitely showing on her face and in the way she spoke and even moved.

Griswold stared at the big rollers coming in on the beach. An east wind blew cold on the shore of Lake Superior. Because of the direction of the wind, the temperature was probably fifteen to twenty degrees cooler than if it had been calm or the wind had been from the southwest. Duluth sat perched on the edge of a giant cooler, when the wind was right .. or wrong, depending on your point of view. Because of the temperature, the wide sandy beach of Park Point was fairly deserted, except for a few diehard beachcombers and walkers, wearing warm jackets or sweat suits.

Good, he thought. A little cold won't hurt the situation. He waited patiently for McCoy, watching an ore carrier leave the Duluth Ship Canal and move out on the lake. As it pushed through the waves, hauling thousands of tons of taconite pellets from the ore docks, waves crashed against its bow, water shooting up and over its decks, sending a cold spray down the foredeck.

"There you are, Griswold!" Randall McCoy struggled across the sand, leaning against the wind, his expensively styled silver-gray hair blowing wildly. "I looked for you in the parking lot. Whew!" He shivered, crossing arms in front of him, holding his raincoat against him. "It's cold and windy down here! Well, it's Duluth weather. 'Cooler by the lake,' as the weatherman always says."

"Right," said Griswold, looking down at McCoy's gleaming, hand-made Italian shoes partially buried in the sand. He smiled. "Let's walk."

"No. Let's go back to my car where we can be comfortable," said McCoy.

Griswold looked McCoy straight in the eye. He said, his face right in McCoy's face, "Let's walk." He turned and starting walking in the direction of the Ship Canal along the long, wide sand beach, the strong wind blowing off the lake against his right side.

McCoy hesitated, then followed.

"What is it you wanted to talk about?" He shouted, to be heard over the sound of the waves and wind.

"Money." Replied Griswold, walking close to the water's edge where the waves rolled up on the sand.

"What?"

"Money." Griswold repeated.

"I heard you, but what about money?" McCoy's shoes were getting caked with wet sand. The cuffs of his slacks were getting wet.

"I need more."

McCoy stopped. An incoming wave rolled up the beach over his shoes, soaking the cuffs of his slacks, which were stylishly tailored to break just as they touched the shoe.

"No!"

Griswold stopped and turned looking at the comic figure of Randall McCoy, blowing in the wind. Tan slacks, navy blazer, striped tie, Gucci shoes and London Fog raincoat. On a Saturday, for Christ's sake! He stepped back along the beach and towered over the smaller man.

"You listen to me, you little prick!" He almost grabbed the front of McCoy's coat and then thought better of it. Shouldn't go that far, he thought. "I know what kind of a deal you've got going here and how much money is possibly involved. You need me to get it, and I need more money!"

"But we have a deal!"

"Tough shit! You're nowhere without me. Moss came through on his first test with the sentencing on Thursday. Now, I've demonstrated that I can produce. My fee is going up and I'll have half now as a sign of good faith and for my success so far."

"My people will never go for it."

"They have no choice, McCoy."

"All I can do is deliver the message," said McCoy. He sounded dejected, even shouting over the wind and waves.

"Good enough," conceded Griswold. "Let's go back to your car and I'll lay it out for you."

In the quiet and comfort of Randall McCoy's Cadillac, Griswold made his demand. McCoy nearly choked when he heard it, but decided to say nothing at this point. In truth, he was afraid of Griswold. On the beach, Griswold had frightened him terribly. Maybe it was the combination of the cold, the wind, the black and brown waters of the wind-churned Lake Superior and the forcefulness of the man's brutal physical advance. It certainly was not the arena in which he was used to negotiating. Had Griswold planned it that way? He wondered.

And Griswold's demand was outrageous! Six million dollars for the successfully completed job! What's more, he wanted half now, in cash, before he would proceed further! Three million dollars just because Judge Moss had made a slight modification in a sentence at Griswold's request!

Before Griswold got out of McCoy's car, he told McCoy that he wanted no stalling, no delay, and no attempts to negotiate.

"If I don't hear from you, real quick," he had said, "and if I don't see the cash just as quick, we're through, and," he paused, staring directly into McCoy's eyes, "you and your friends are through. Get my meaning?" When McCoy had nodded that he understood, Griswold got out and slammed the car door, disappearing beyond the tall grass back out on the windblown beach.

McCoy was stopped for the Aerial Bridge, lifting for an incoming saltwater ship. He heard the horn of the Vista King excursion boat sound from its dock just inside the harbor at the entrance to the ship canal and Aerial Bridge. He watched it leave the dock, apparently taking some tourists for a ride in the harbor. Normally, it would go out under the Aerial Bridge, but, he presumed because of the wind and waves out on the lake, it was not going on its usual route. Good, he thought. He did not want to wait for another boat. He wanted the bridge down so he could get across and into downtown.

The reaction he anticipated from the rest of the contract holders that were involved in the hiring of Griswold, was something he did not look forward to. But he had no choice. He had to arrange a meeting. And fast.

Frank Griswold stood staring out onto the rough waters of Lake Superior. He had control now. That little slime McCoy, with his superior air was nothing at all. Griswold had handled him like a little kid. His partners wouldn't be any more difficult. Griswold had them and they would soon realize it.

They had no choice but to concede to his demands. He could control them for the same reasons as he could now control the great Digger Moss, because he had something on them. If they did not

77

cooperate, they knew he could expose them for what they really were. He could expose their efforts to blackmail a sitting judge to get a favorable ruling on a case before him. And he could do it without involving himself. He had already prepared envelopes to go anonymously to the Duluth Police Department, St. Louis County Sheriff, and St. Louis County Attorney's office. Each contained photographs and audio tapes identifying McCoy and others and showing where other evidence could be found proving their involvement in attempting to blackmail Moss for their own personal benefit. Similar envelopes were already prepared showing Moss's involvement in drug transactions and the murder of Sergeant Greg Larson.

Griswold was particularly satisfied with himself. He fully intended to go through with the complete job, get the decision out of Digger Moss, get his six million dollars and then send all of the envelopes. They could all face the consequences, he thought, including the Honorable James Digby Moss.

CHAPTER SEVEN

"**T**his is bullshit! He can't do this!" Harry Slater rubbed the back of his neck. "It's a double cross!"

Slater sat at a long, highly polished conference table in the basement boardroom at the Kitchi Gammi Club. Seated around the table were seven other men. Randall McCoy sat at the head of the table. Each of the men was in his late fifties or older. Some were nearer seventy and at least one was over seventy. Most had a look of opulence in their dress and appearance. Some had an air of opulence that simply could not be artificial. A few, however, looked quite ordinary. They all looked nervous, or upset, one or the other or both.

"But he is doing it, Harry," said Orrin Rasmussen, whose sun tanned complexion and pure white hair gave him a look of distinction and wealth.

"I agree with Harry. Can't we do something to make him live up to his side of the bargain?" said the man seated next to Rasmussen.

"And what do you suggest, Bert?" asked Rasmussen.

Bertram Johnson had been with Whitaker Industries a long time. He was there before Charles Whitaker instituted the distribution plan under which most of the men at this table had become quite wealthy. Under that plan, the first group of sales people numbered only nine, besides the old man himself. They were permitted to recruit their own sales men and women, who could recruit their own subcontractors and so on. He was one of the original "founders", as they called themselves, the original first tier of the distribution plan. About half of the original nine were still around. Of the group in the room, McCoy, Slater, McCloskey, and he were the only original founders. Rasmussen and Hood were part of the original distribution system, but were in the second tier, having been among the first recruited by first tier men. Fowler and Vagelli, he did not like. They were what founders referred to as "newbys," men who had purchased the rights of founders, or other original people from lower tiers, by paying a price for an assignment of their contract rights. Vagelli owned a second tier contract. Hollis Fowler had purchased the rights of a founder.

"I suggest we insist on our original agreement with the man," he said. "We made him a very good offer, which he accepted. It's a lot of money. He already got a substantial advance."

"That's one of the problems, Bert," said Randall McCoy, from the head of the table. McCoy, a vice-president of sales and distribution at Whitaker Industries, was one who had both the appearance and air of opulence. "We already paid Griswold more than the job is worth. He can't lose, even if we fire him. But, now that he knows more about what's really involved ..."

"He wants part of the action," finished Charles Hood. "It figures."

"That's right," confirmed McCoy. "And he's got us over a barrel. If we don't deal with him, he'll expose our involvement. We'll all go to jail!"

"Oh, Christ!" exclaimed Slater, wishing he'd never gotten involved with this group.

"Randall, are you sure we are safe, here?" asked Hood, looking around at the paneled walls and windows grated with wrought iron bars.

"Hollis is watching the door for the waiter, or anyone who might come by. We're at the farthest reaches of the building from anything else that might be going on just now. We are fine, here."

"So, what can we do?" asked Johnson. "If he has us over a barrel, than we have to deal with him, don't we? Shouldn't we just give him what he wants? Do we have any other choice?"

"Kill him."

They all looked toward the source of the last incredible suggestion. It came from the man seated by the door.

"Kill him? Jesus Christ, Fowler, do you realize what you're saying?" Bert Johnson mopped his sweating brow with the handkerchief with which he had been nervously cleaning his glasses.

"Bullshit!" A meaty hand slapped down on the dark polished cherry surface of the big table. Frank Vagelli stood and looked around the room. He looked like a fighter, stocky, barrel-chested, arms and shoulders that strained the fabric of his sport coat. He had neither the appearance nor the air of opulence. He ran a hand through his unruly, thick black hair. "You don't like it, but you've been going along with it, so far. So get off your high fucking horses and come down to where the work is being done. We've got a problem, here, and we will fix it. Now quit bitching and help us figure out what the fix will be."

The eighth man, seated by the door, rose from his chair and approached the table. Hollis Fowler had kept watch by the door and had not entered into the conversation, except for his single startling comment. Now he spoke. "We've gotten ourselves into a bit of a pickle, here, it's true. But, we all sat right here several months ago and decided it was worth the risk."

"Not murder!" cried Johnson, his face pale beyond the normal fairness of his skin. He removed his glasses and began cleaning them again with his handkerchief.

"Not murder?" repeated Hollis Fowler, calmly. "Bert, just what did you think, or any of the rest of you for that matter," he looked around the room, "What did you think would happen to Judge Moss when this was all over?"

"What are you talking about?" demanded Fred McCloskey, standing to face Fowler at eye level.

"What do you think I'm talking about?" Fowler stared McCloskey in the eye until the bigger man looked away.

The people at the meeting gradually separated into three factions: Slater and McCloskey, who wanted to pay Griswold what he asked to avoid the consequences he threatened, and to get the desired result from Judge Moss; Vagelli and Fowler, who wanted to permanently eliminate Griswold, but felt that he should be temporarily paid his demand of half his requested fee at this time and killed after the Moss job was accomplished; and Rasmussen, Johnson, Hood and McCoy, who wanted to refuse Griswold's outlandish demands, but agreed with Fowler and Vagelli's plan as an alternative for different reasons. McCoy now hated Griswold for the humiliating and demeaning way in which Griswold had treated him on the beach. Rasmussen, Hood, and Johnson were simply afraid of Fowler and Vagelli.

"Who the hell is going to deliver the three million?" asked Johnson.

"Don't worry, Bert. Jesus Christ!" The contempt in Vagelli's voice was missed by no one, especially Bert Johnson. "We'll take care of that for you."

"Did Griswold say how and where he wants it?" Rasmussen asked, leaning forward, elbows on the table.

"Cash," replied McCoy. "Hundred dollar bills, delivered directly to him."

"Are you going to deliver it?"

"I ... I don't know," McCoy answered slowly. "I suppose I have to."

"No!" Fowler interjected. "No, Randy, you don't. Frank and I will deliver the money. This Griswold needs a slightly different message from us than he's got so far." He turned toward Vagelli. "You agree?"

Frank Vagelli nodded.

Randall McCoy breathed a quiet sigh of relief.

"All right, then, let's put together the three mil," said Fowler.

The meeting was arranged for the next afternoon. McCoy made the call to Griswold and told him to be at the same place on Park Point where they had met previously.

Griswold arrived early, by design. He left his car and walked out onto the beach. In contrast to their earlier meeting, the day was warm and sunny. Families were gathered on blankets, little kids running into the frigid water. Like beaches everywhere, there were people jogging and walking along the beach. A few high, fluffy white clouds floated across the hillside out over the lake. He waited and watched people and the few fishing boats trolling by the Superior entry at the south end of the Point. He was enjoying himself.

He waited. A half hour went by. He glanced toward the parking lot, but could not see the cars for the grassy dune which separated it from the beach.

He waited. Forty-five minutes.

Finally, he walked back toward the sand dune peering over it, looking for McCoy's Cadillac. He did not see it or McCoy. Two men watched him from the lot. One was a stocky, barrel-chested man wearing a green windbreaker. His mop of black hair was windblown and unruly. The smaller man wore a business suit, his white shirt unwrinkled, his tie neatly knotted at his throat. They seemed content to watch him. In fact, they were staring at him.

Griswold turned toward the lake, looking across at Duluth's east hillside. When he turned back, there was still no sign of McCoy and the two men were still staring at him, neither having moved.

What the hell? We'll see what the hell is going on, here, thought Griswold. He walked toward the two men.

"You two have been watching me," he said, as he approached the men in the parking lot. "Can I do something for you?"

"Mister, you're the one who can do something for us." Frank Vagelli started toward Griswold. His manner was clearly aggressive. Surprised and alarmed at the open hostility of the stocky man in the windbreaker, Griswold began to step back, but the other man put a hand out to stop his companion.

"We are here to keep Randall McCoy's meeting with you," said Hollis Fowler, his voice slow and measured. "This is Frank Vagelli and I am Hollis Fowler." He extended a hand in greeting.

Griswold did not take the offered hand. "Where is McCoy?" he asked, still uncertain how to react to these two.

"Mister," growled Vagelli, "where McCoy is doesn't concern you anymore. We are doing the deal and that's that."

"Frank's right, Frank," Hollis Fowler continued in his even voice, obviously amused at the sound of their identical names together. "You don't need to worry about Randall anymore. We come in his stead as the emissaries from the group he has been representing in dealing with you so far."

"I don't know if I like it," said Griswold hesitantly, shuffling his feet on the sand, looking around at the cars in the small lot.

"I don't give a shit what you like or don't like, asshole!" Vagelli looked like he might spring at Griswold any minute. "You deal with us now, like it or not!"

Again Hollis Fowler interceded. "Once again, Frank's right, Frank." He smiled benignly. "We, that is, the group, decided you needed a different message from us than you may have been getting from Randall McCoy, especially in response to your threats."

"Threats? Now, wait a minute."

"No. You wait a minute." The voice of Hollis Fowler remained even and steady, but his tone had turned to pure malevolence. His carefully chosen and spaced words sent a crystal clear message. This was a man who did not threaten. What he said would come true. A promise, not a threat.

"From now on, you report directly to Frank Vagelli or me, Hollis Fowler. You take no orders from Randall McCoy or anyone else. You do not try to contact Randall McCoy or anyone else about this matter. Do you understand?"

Griswold was shaken. He hoped it didn't show. Control was important to him. But these two were nothing like McCoy had been on the beach where Griswold had dominated and even frightened the weaker man. At least he had to stand up to these men and not be like McCoy had been.

"All right." He tried to sound nonchalant. "My meeting was to be on the beach." He nodded toward the lake shore on the other side of the tall grass. "Let's walk where we're less conspicuous."

"No," said Fowler.

"Yes," responded Griswold starting toward the beach.

Suddenly, Vagelli was on him. Griswold felt his shoulders being pulled back, terrible pain from the grip of each of Vagelli's big hands. He was spun around and slammed backwards against a parked car. Vagelli drove a meaty fist into Griswold's stomach. He buckled over and collapsed to the sandy surface of the lot, lying next to the car, holding his gut and retching. Vagelli stood over him fists clenched.

"Fuck you, Griswold!" he yelled down at the writhing figure. "If you want to see our money we'll do it here. Otherwise, no deal, and you are dead meat. Do *you* get *my* meaning?"

Griswold did not answer, although he seemed to be recovering somewhat from the assault.

Hollis Fowler spoke, looking down on Griswold. "You see, Frank, what Frank, here, is saying is that *you* are no longer in control, we are. We have decided to meet your recent exorbitant demands, but because it suits our purpose, not because we are in any way intimidated by your threats. Do you understand?"

Griswold nodded.

"Good." Fowler continued. "It is important that you do understand, because if you do not, or if you do not act precisely in accordance with our instructions, you will end up a lot farther over in that direction than you wish." He nodded toward the beach. "You know the old saying, don't you?"

Griswold struggled to sit up, leaning against the car, still clutching his midsection with both hands. "What saying?"

"Lake Superior never gives up its dead." Hollis Fowler let the old quote hang in the air for effect on Griswold. They had broken him sufficiently for their purposes. He nodded to Vagelli, who turned toward their car a short distance away.

Vagelli returned in a moment with two large nylon carryall duffel bags. He dropped them beside Griswold. "Here's your fucking money!" he snarled.

"That is the first installment as you requested," said Fowler. "Our instructions are that you now communicate our demands to Judge Moss. We understand that you had to do the preliminaries in order to prepare him for our request. We even think you did a fair job of doing that. We also understand that the request has to be carefully done and that doing that properly may take a few days, but we think you should start now." Then Fowler repeated a phrase to which he and Vagelli had, they believed, conditioned Griswold to respond. "Do you understand?"

"Yes," said Griswold without hesitation.

"Good." Fowler and Vagelli walked to their car and drove from the lot onto Lake Avenue, leaving Griswold sitting leaning against the car with the two nylon bags beside him.

Badly shaken by his experience and still in a considerable amount of pain, Frank Griswold struggled to get up and load the duffel bags full of money into the trunk of his car. Even though he had been intimidated, frightened and hurt, Griswold began to seethe with anger as he hunched over the steering wheel driving north on Lake Avenue. He resolved to get even with these two, but how he had not yet figured out. He was in too much discomfort to plan it out now. It was enough that he knew he would get even somehow. For now, he would go along with their orders and bide his time.

Back at the Holiday Inn, Griswold placed the two nylon duffel bags on the bed and opened them. He was feeling better fast, sustained and fortified by the thought of retribution sometime in the future. After all, payback *was* sweet, and this payback would be real sweet. He would make sure of that.

He could not resist the opportunity to look at the money. He spread some out on the bed. For some time he played with the money, studying it, getting the feel of all those packets of one hundred dollar bills. Finally, he carefully packed the duffels and slid them into the safe. They just fit. He knew they would. He had measured. It was part of the determination of how much to demand. He smiled to himself and turned to the television to see what news there was about the Larson murder.

On a small remote television screen in a van parked on the top level of the Holiday Inn Parking Ramp, Milo Bracken and Vincent Turcotte watched the bags of money going into the safe.

"How much do you think it was?" asked Vince.

Milo watched Griswold scanning the channels on the television in his suite. They had placed tiny video cameras in Griswold's suite so they could monitor his activities throughout.

"Don't know," he responded, lighting a Pall Mall, "but I bet it's enough for you and me. He grinned a toothy grin at Vince.

Vince smiled back. "This guy deserves to get robbed ... and worse."

"Easy now, boy," cautioned Milo, raising a hand, palm facing Vince.

"I know, I know." Vince reached for a Coke. "I won't do anything without your okay."

"Good." Milo drew heavily on the strong cigarette, deep in thought.

The local news broadcast Griswold found had nothing new on the police investigation into the Larson murder. Good, he thought. Except for his disastrous meeting with Fowler and Vagelli, things were going very much according to plan.

CHAPTER NINE

Digger Moss stared across his desk at Mike Reynolds and Kate Riley.

"I just don't like it," said Kate, shaking her head. "Nothing's going on! Digger, I can hardly stand it. I don't know how the hell you're still functioning."

"It's difficult," agreed Digger. "But I think it's hardest on Judy. She's scared."

"Christ! She ought to be!" Kate stood up and looked down at the two men. "We can't just sit here! We've got to do something!"

With another scan for bugs, they had determined that the tiny transmitters had been removed. Why? They did not know. It was simply a change in the pattern and presumably meant something was about to happen. What, they did not know. All three were frustrated.

"It's tough all right," said Mike, "but we've got to keep our heads. We have got to remain as calm as possible and follow our regular routines as much as humanly possible ..maybe more than humanly possible." He drank deeply from his coffee mug. "Because if we don't," he continued, "we may either slip up and give away our secrets, *or*," he emphasized the "*or*," "we may not act rationally when something does happen that requires our best reaction."

"He's right, Kate," said Digger. "We've got to stay on our toes. All of this has had a purpose. I'm sure we are about to find out what that purpose is."

"Well, God damn it, I hope so, and soon," Kate answered. "I need to see what it is I'm fighting. When we know what this is all about, then we can nail these bastards' asses, whoever they are."

"There. That's better." Digger grinned. "Tough old Kate. We need you just that way."

"Whaddaya mean 'old'? Digger, you be careful now."

"**J**udge?"

Digger turned from his computer on which he was fine tuning a divorce temporary order that he needed to get out. It was only an hour since his conversation with Kate and Mike. Everything as normal, they had all agreed. Actually he found the effort took his mind off his problem a little. It was a welcome relief. "Yes, Jack?"

Digger's law clerk entered his chambers. John Robert Terwilliger, III., alternately known by friends and family as "Jack" or "J.R.," was a new graduate from the William Mitchell College of Law. He was serving a one-year clerkship for the District Court before beginning his career in private practice. Each judge had one law clerk assigned. Jack was Digger's.

"I got an e-mail from the law clerk for Judge Bradford in St. Cloud, in the Seventh District. He wants to know if you've decided the Power-Plus Battery case. Apparently his judge has a similar case that would be affected by your decision."

"Interesting, Jack," said Digger, leaning back in his chair. Like the order on his computer screen, working with his law clerk helped ease the incredible tension of waiting and worrying. "Which came first, the chicken or the egg?"

"Excuse me, Judge?"

"A poor analogy, Jack. Please forgive me."

"I don't understand." Jack sat across from Digger, listening.

"Well of course we should let Judge Bradford know, through her law clerk, the status of the case in our court and how soon we expect a decision. On the other hand, if she decided her case first, her decision could help us in ours, don't you think?"

"I see what you mean." Jack was already thinking about the benefit of having another judge's memorandum of law when doing the legal research he would have to do for Digger Moss.

"And Ellen Bradford can decide the issue every bit as well as we can." Digger's eyebrows raised slightly as he said to the young lawyer, "You know, she's one of the most brilliant students of the law we have on the bench today, state or federal." With Digger's current preoccupation with his own personal troubles, it wouldn't hurt for her to make the decision and for him to follow, he thought.

"Let's call her."

"Who?" asked Jack.

"Judge Bradford," said Digger reaching for his desk phone. Without removing the receiver, he pressed a button for a dial tone and began punching in the telephone number shown in the directory of State offices.

"Judge's Chambers," said a pleasant voice on the phone's speaker.

"Judge Bradford, please," said Digger.

"May I tell her who is calling, please?"

"Yes, this is Judge Moss in Duluth," Digger answered. "Do you know if she is available?"

"Good morning, Judge Moss," said the voice. "Judge Bradford was in court earlier, but I think she has returned. If you will hold one moment, your Honor, I will check for you."

"Thank you."

Soft music came from the desk phone while they waited on hold.

Digger smiled in appreciation. "I told judges in this courthouse for years that they were the only lawyers in town who answered their own phones and who didn't have a live person to answer them when they were on the bench or out of the office. They needed receptionists then, and they still do now. Listen to what they've got in St. Cloud." He nodded toward the telephone. "I'd sure trust my calls to this person."

The elevator music was interrupted by the receptionist's voice. "Judge Moss?"

"Yes?"

"Thank you for waiting, your Honor, I will connect you now."

"Hello, ... Digger?"

"Ellie, don't say anything bad about law clerks, 'cuz mine is sitting across the desk from me and you're on the box."

"Can I say anything bad about judges with funny nicknames?"

"Shut up, Ellie and meet J. R. Terwilliger, the 3rd."

"Jesus who?"

"Terwilliger, Ellie," said Digger, shaking his head at Jack.

"I'm pleased to meet you, J. R., although since I can't see you I'm left to my imagination regarding your appearance. What would a young lawyer with a handle like 'J. R. Terwilliger, the Third,' who is foolish enough to clerk for the infamous 'Digger' Moss, look like?"

Digger grinned at Jack, still shaking his head.

"Ah! But wait!" Ellen Bradford exclaimed. "Never make an assumption, young man, if indeed that's what you are. Did you graduate from law school after this past school year?"

"Yes, Judge. I did," said Jack.

"And did you go to law school right after college?"

90

"Yes."

"A four year baccalaureate program?"

"That's right, your Honor," answered Jack. "I got a Bachelor's Degree in political science."

"How nice for you, I'm sure," said the voice of Ellen Bradford. "But don't change the subject of interrogation."

Jack looked at Digger who just shook his head. "Don't worry," he whispered.

"Digger! Are you coaching the lad?"

"No, Judge."

"All right, then," she continued. "Did you go to college right after high school?"

"I did."

"And did you graduate from high school at a normal age, or did you drop out for a while, or something like that?"

"No, judge, I did the normal thing. I was eighteen."

"Ah! Good! Then you *are* a young man. About twenty-five, I suppose, depending on when your birthday is," she said. "So the question is in fact what a twenty-five year old baby lawyer working for Digger Moss would look like. I'd guess tall and skinny as a rail. About six-three, dark, short hair ..."

"Long, blonde ...," corrected Digger.

"What?"

"Long, blonde hair," he repeated. "Otherwise, your pretty close."

"Oh good!" she said. "So what do you and your hippie law clerk want of me, today, Digger? Or, shall we let J. R. do the talking? Digger?"

"I'm writing a note to Jack telling him that your simply moderately deranged and that you are in fact harmless." Digger was actually enjoying himself. He liked Ellie Bradford.

"Jack?"

"That's what some of us call him."

"Well Jack, if you believe that note he says he's writing, you might be in trouble if you have to appear in front of me some day."

"I'll remember, your Honor," said Jack."But, what's a 'Hippie?"

"I'll tell you when you're older," replied Digger. "Ellie," Digger began, "I've got this case involving Power-Plus Batteries under advisement. Finished a trial to the court about a month ago. Jack

91

says your law clerk is inquiring because of a similar case you have. Trying to get me to do your work for you?"

"The thought crossed my mind, Digger, but not so, in this case. You've got the deciding case."

"What's the difference?" Digger asked.

"The contract in my case is based on the contract in your case," she said.

"So what?" asked Digger. "Don't you still have to decide your own case on its own facts?"

"Nope," she answered. "Let me get my file."

Jack and Digger could hear Ellen Bradford moving around her chambers. They heard what they presumed to be a file drawer being slammed shut. Then, the sound of rustling paper near her speaker phone.

"Here it is. You got your contract there?" she asked.

Digger nodded to Jack, who reached in Digger's "Under-Advisement" file drawer, extracted a file, opened it and pointed to the contract.

"I do, Ellie," said Digger.

"Turn to page twelve, near the end. Look toward the bottom of the page at Article XXXII." She read aloud as Digger listened and followed in his own contract:

"Article XXXII. Contract Interpretation.
This contract is governed by the laws of the State of Minnesota. The parties specifically agree that any disputes between them which may arise regarding the terms hereof, or any rights of the parties hereunder, shall be controlled by any rulings of the District Court of the State of Minnesota, or any appellate court of that state interpreting, construing or otherwise ruling on that certain contract containing these terms and identified as Contract No. 001."

"Why would mine have that language if it is the 'Contract No. 001' referred to?"

"It's a standard form, Digger. All the contracts have it, including *numero uno*, I guess. Look at the top of page one. The identifying number of the contract is in the upper left corner. What does yours say?"

"001."

"Right," said Ellen. "Mine says, '001-003-114-022."

"What do all the numbers mean?"

"Beats me," she said. "All I know is that the lawyers in my case agree that, because of Article XXXII, decisions of Minnesota courts on Contract Number One control. Since you have a case going on Number One, and it involves the issue in my case, they have asked me to wait, because your decision will control."

Something bothered Digger. His stomach suddenly felt hollow. "What's the issue in your case?" he asked.

"I don't even know the case that well, Digger," she replied. "I don't have it under advisement for decision or anything like that. I'm just trying to move my caseload along, and this case is waiting for you. The issue, as I understand it, has something to do with the per cent of gross sales receipts to be paid by one party to the other. It's real boring stuff."

"It's a bit more complicated than that, but that's about it," said Digger. The hollow feeling was still nagging at him. But he said, "I actually thought it was pretty interesting, but I think Jack agrees with you."

"Smart lad."

"Well, thanks, anyway, Ellie, I guess Jack and I will have to do our own work with no help from you." Digger needed to close this conversation and think about this.

"I'll be waiting for your decision, boys." she replied.

"Thanks a lot, Ellie," said Digger. "I'll see you at the judges' conference."

"Good-bye, Digger."

Digger pressed a button on his phone. The line went dead.

"So much for that idea," said Jack.

"What?"

"I said …"

"Never mind," said Digger, apparently deep in thought, "I heard you. I was just thinking about something else." Something else indeed, thought Digger. I'd better get hold of Kate and Mike right

away. It seemed he might be onto what was coming. What they were
waiting for.

"**B**ut a judge can't really sway a decision," said Kate.
"Certainly a little, in some situations, I suppose, but
nothing obvious, and certainly not contrary to law. Even if a judge
wanted to, or was being forced to, it would be too obvious. It wouldn't
work."

"I agree," said Digger, "but maybe not in this case."

"What's different about this case?" asked Kate. "It isn't a case
where you could favor one party just a little. You are going to make a
determination completely one way or the other. They either pay the
increase or not. The losing party appeals and that's it. If you're right,
it stands. If you're wrong, it comes back. It's out of your hands."

"Not quite." Digger removed his reading glasses. "This contract,"
he tapped the photocopy in front of him, "contains some ambiguity as
to the fifteen year increase. It doesn't defeat the entire contract. The
parties have been operating under its terms for over eighteen years.
It does, however, allow the introduction of evidence outside the
document itself, including facts and circumstances surrounding its
formation, even oral statements by the parties prior to and at the time
of the contract."

"You're saying the Parol Evidence Rule doesn't apply?"

"Right. While ordinarily it would prevent attempts to use verbal
statements made prior to or contemporaneously with the signing of
the written agreement to modify the terms of the writing, there is
enough ambiguity here that the rule permits such evidence. The
parties don't dispute that. That's what the trial was all about."

"So you're not just interpreting the language of the contract, you
are going to have to decide what they intended."

"Exactly," Digger declared. "It's all a question of fact and I am
the finder of fact. As you know, different juries can reach different
results and so can different arbitrators or different judges when they
are making findings of fact. The fact that I decide one way, when
someone else might have decided another, does not make my decision
wrong, if it is supported by the evidence."

"And, assuming no error in the trial, the only issue on appeal would be whether the decision is contrary to the evidence, just like a jury case. Well?" Kate looked at Digger, inquiringly.

"Well, what?"

"Were there any errors?" she asked.

"None," Digger answered. "There weren't even any disputes. No motions, no evidentiary objections. They even agreed that parol evidence was admissible. The trial went as smooth as silk."

"And what's the correct decision?"

"That's just it. It could go either way. I could find for either party based on the evidence and still be in the range of findings of fact reasonably supported on the evidence. It just depends on whom I believe and what weight I give to the testimony of the various witnesses."

"So you are in control and the possibility of reversal is virtually non-existent."

"That's it."

"What about the other contracts? You say that Article XXXII makes them dependent on your case, but isn't the parol evidence different in each case? Doesn't each case have to stand on its own facts?"

"No. Those contracts are not ambiguous."

"I thought they were the same."

"They are all exactly the same."

"Digger, don't play with me," Kate glared at him, "or you could get in trouble."

"The other contracts are not ambiguous, ... "

"Deep trouble."

"... even though the language is verbatim." He grinned.

"Digger!"

"Okay, Kate. I couldn't resist that," he said. "Article XXXII is the reason the other contracts aren't ambiguous. It's clear as a bell on its face. The parties to those contracts agreed, as they had the ability to do, that any issues, including any ambiguities of the contract would be controlled by the decisions on the first contract. They might have wanted to do that in order to avoid costs of litigation or arbitration. The desire for uniformity of the contracts within the pyramid may have been the motive. In any event, there won't be separate trials on this issue because the Parol Evidence Rule *does apply to those cases,* to eliminate modification by parol, because Article XXXII is unambiguous on its face."

"Let me get this straight, then," Kate said. "You are being threatened with the destruction of your career, the ruin of your life, and probable incarceration, if you don't decide in favor of the plaintiff, in a case in which your decision cannot be overruled, or really even questioned. True?"

"True."

"Well, then it's a no brainer. Plaintiff wins." She threw up her hands, palms up.

"Kate!"

"I know, I know," she said. "The great Digger Moss would never consider it and besides, they can't afford to let you off the hook when it's over anyway. Right?"

"Right."

"So where do we go from here?"

CHAPTER TEN

"**H**ello?"

"Judge Moss, please."

"Speaking, who is this?" Digger thought he recognized the voice from before. He fought against the feeling of foreboding beginning to overtake him.

"We've spoken before," the voice said.

"Yes."

"And, I must say, you passed our little test just fine, but you're not ready for the real thing, yet."

"What does that mean," asked Digger, uneasily.

"We have another test for you," the voice continued.

Having recovered now from the beating Frank Vagelli gave him, Frank Griswold sat comfortably on the couch in his Holiday Inn suite, Scotch and soda in hand, a small thin cigar smoldering in a glass ashtray, as he toyed with Judge Moss. While he was enjoying himself immensely, he did want to be careful not to show it. He did want Moss to believe that they needed another test and not suspect that this was the real thing.

"A little civil case, I think," he said into the telephone, gazing out the window at the big lake. "You did well on the criminal matter. Now let's see how you do on a civil case."

"A civil case might be more difficult," said Digger. "In the criminal case, because the sentence was stayed, a few months on the criminal sentence didn't really make much difference. In a civil case, I won't have much opportunity to make a decision that doesn't have more effect on someone's rights."

"Exactly the point, Judge!" said Griswold. "That is why we need another test, you see."

"Oh."

"Here's the deal, Judge," Griswold continued. "You have a civil case under advisement, I see from the list you gave me - thanks, by the way - called "PowerPlus Batteries against Nickerson, *et al.*"

Digger's hand trembled when he heard the name. He nearly dropped the telephone. This was it! This was no test! Control, he thought. Don't let this guy know you know!

"Yes," he said as calmly as he could.

"Right, well we want you to find for the plaintiff on that contract issue," said Griswold. "You are about to decide that case, aren't you?"

"Soon, I guess."

"Soon is right," said Griswold, adding, "You get my meaning?"

In the van, Milo Bracken spat cigarette tobacco onto the floor. He took a swig from a can of Coke.

"God damn this guy, Vince," he said, lighting a fresh cigarette. The air in the van was blue from his smoke. "He is a first class prick!"

"What? We already knew that," Vince answered.

"I know, but Jesus Christ! I never had anything against this Judge Moss, but I sure do against Griswold. And the way he's treating the judge I don't like either. What an ass!"

"Milo, relax, like you tell me. Like you keep saying, let's just wait here and keep our eyes and ears open and our chance will come. Right?"

"Right."

"It's a pyramid scheme!" Mike Reynolds told Digger and Kate at lunch the next day. Mike had arranged a small dining room on the second floor of the Kitchi Gammi Club so they could speak in private and discuss the demand which had finally come. But Mike had new information he'd uncovered after their first conversation about the PowerPlus Battery case.

"What do you mean, like a pyramid letter?" asked Kate.

"No, but sort of similar, I suppose," Mike answered. "When old man Whitaker was looking for a way to expand the market for his small battery line, he and his lieutenants devised a pyramid distribution scheme like those used by some companies for cosmetics or cleaning products."

"You mean like Amway or Avon ?" asked Kate.

"More than you know, Judge," Mike answered. He handed them each a three page document.

"What's this?" asked Digger, taking the pages from Mike's outstretched hand.

"This is a photocopy of a Duluth News Tribune article about Charles Whitaker, the head of Whitaker Industries back in 1986. It's from an interview when Whitaker donated the monies for the new Whitaker School of Business at UMD. Whitaker was always shy of the news media. He stayed out of the limelight even though he sponsored several scholarships in the company name, provided the funds for the Whitaker Hockey Arena, and managed to be very involved in local civic matters, albeit from behind the scenes. It refers to the story of the pyramid I'm talking about. You'll see it also refers to an authorized biography done a year or so before. It doesn't say much and it was fairly well hidden in the article. It would not have been like Whitaker, apparently, to make much fuss about it, brag about it, or even advertise it much. He simply directed the reporter to the biography for information."

Mike reached into his briefcase and extracted a hard bound book from the Duluth Public Library. The dust jacket proclaimed its title as "WHITAKER," by Ansel Brunner. "I copied the part I'm talking about for you." He handed them each another set of photocopied pages.

Kate and Digger read in silence. The part of the book Mike had copied read as follows:

> One day in the summer of 1980, Whitaker stood staring out the office window. The sight of the shimmering waters of Lake Superior in the midday sun did little to distract his thoughts.
>
> From his office on the third story of the Lake Superior Commercial Storage Battery Company, Charles Whitaker enjoyed the view he had known most of his life. From the time he was a small boy, his father had brought him to this office on Saturday mornings. Charlie had played while his father worked at the big desk. He had often stared out this window at the ore boats passing by to enter the Duluth Ship Canal and go under the Aerial Bridge. In the midsummer, he would see

fisherman trolling and sailboats racing or heading up the lake toward the Apostle Islands on Wisconsin's South Shore. The original factory and all the offices had all been in this one building, located on the lake shore a few blocks beyond Leif Erickson Park to the east, by Duluth directions. He had grown up with this view, later working for his father at each part of the commercial storage battery business. Now he was nearly sixty years of age and the business was changing.

In 1980, the need for the large commercial storage batteries that had once been the mainstay of the company's rather specialized business no longer existed. Years before, with his father's encouragement, a young Charles Whitaker had worked on development of a small battery design for longer life than those available on the market. Through hard work, innovation, and a fair amount of luck, he thought, he had succeeded. A battery design was patented which was applicable to all the various small batteries from the "large" six volt flashlight batteries, to "D" cells, "AA", "AAA," etc. Even the rectangular nine volt and smaller camera, hearing aid and watch batteries could be produced with the patented design giving them longer power life than what could be purchased in the stores.

With little fanfare, the company had added a line of small batteries to its products. Charles' father had been in business supplying his batteries to a very specialized market. Distribution was made by direct sales contacts. There was no advertising. The policy did not change with the addition of the line of smaller batteries. Whatever the size, except the tiny watch batteries, they were plain red with a white stripe about two-thirds of the way toward the top. Below the stripe and parallel to the length of the battery was the name and added slogan: "Power-Plus - - -50% longer life!" The only other message to the consuming public was on packaging. Batteries sold in pairs, threes, or sets of four or more were encased in plastic against a backing card which proclaimed, "Lasts 50% longer than other batteries at less cost. Try it! You'll see!"

Even Charles' father had known the importance of getting the message to the market. He was not against that. He simply did not like to make a big noise about it. He had often told Charles how he had moved into the market ultimately dominated by Lake Superior Battery Company. "Stealth," he called it. "I sneaked up on the other guys," he used to laugh. "Seriously, Charlie," he would always say, "Go to your market with a damned good product, a reasonable price, and good service. If you don't make to much fuss about it, you'll have the other guy's customers before he even knows you're around. And by the way," he would point out, "there's nothing wrong, illegal, or even sneaky about providing a good product at a fair price instead of blowing a lot of steam about a lesser product at a higher price."

Charles Whitaker had taken his dad's teachings to heart. Using direct sales through independent brokers and sales men and women, a reasonably small sales staff at Lake Superior Batteries had placed its line of small batteries, along with a line of cordless, rechargeable, power hand tools in hardware stores, building materials supply stores and discount stores throughout the country. Now after nearly fifteen years of that type of marketing, and still with no advertising, Lake Superior had a whopping ten per cent of the market for small batteries. The big boys, Everready® and Duracell®, generally split the rest except for about five percent spread among several other specialized smaller manufacturers, whose batteries were usually specific to some particular use.

The market, of course, was also growing dramatically as the number of small appliances and devices were produced and sold that required batteries. Children's toys and games alone represented a market increase of gigantic proportions. The public, especially those who had young children, were looking for an economical long-lasting battery, even if they did not realize it. Manufacturers who were willing to avoid the phrase "Batteries not included," could get a good price on Lake Superior's Power-Plus batteries to include in their packages and Lake Superior got its long lasting plain red batteries in front of the consuming public.

Charles Whitaker had much more in mind, however. For ten per cent of the national market to be owned by a small still privately owned company was phenomenal indeed, but Charles wanted more for his company, for his employees, and for his family. Over the years, as the small battery market and sales developed, he had continuously put the profit back into production. Manufacturing plants were now operating in Tennessee, northern Kentucky and Ohio, from which delivery around the country was more economical then from northern Minnesota. Now Charles wanted his loyal employees and his own family to profit from the success for which they had worked so hard.

His goal was a greater share of the market. His present manufacturing facilities could handle it. They had been built with increases in production in mind. It could be done, but quietly as his father would have done, while the titans of the industry were sleeping, or fighting among themselves, with their noisy advertising, their pink bunnies and their "copper tops."

He had begun by renaming the company and reorganizing it into separate divisions. It was now Whitaker Industries. The line of small batteries which had become the company's main business was the Power-Plus Batteries Division of Whitaker Industries. What he needed now, Charles knew, was a change in the distribution system. He needed more loyalty and a more aggressive approach than they got from the independent brokers. That was the problem he pondered now.

At his large East End home, Charles Whitaker sat sipping a dry martini as he watched the evening news about the presidential election campaign. His wife was working in the kitchen.

The door bell rang.

Charles set his martini on a wood and felt coaster on the end table and rose to get the door. "I've got it!" he called to his wife.

"Thanks, dear!"

He opened the door. "Yes?"

"Avon® calling!" a pleasant looking middle aged lady sang out in a melodious voice.

Charles watched as his wife gladly interrupted her dinner preparations to meet this lady, go through her catalogs, and order cosmetic and skin care products. When she was leaving, Charles spoke to her.

"Are you an employee of the Avon® company?" he asked.

"Not directly." She smiled as she answered.

"Do you mind my asking how it works?"

"Charlie!" his wife exclaimed. "I'm sure Mrs. Pruitt has a busy schedule."

"Oh no!" she responded. "I don't mind at all." To Charles, she said, "I'm happy to explain it to you. It's interesting, the way it works."

Charles listened with interest as Mrs. Pruitt explained the business of being an "Avon® Lady."

On the very next day, back in 1980, Charles Whitaker and the top executives of Whitaker Industries met in the conference room overlooking the blue waters of Lake Superior.

When they finished their reading, Kate and Digger looked up.

"Interesting," said Digger.

"And, it was pretty effective," said Mike. "It got those plain little red batteries with the white stripe into every hardware, building supply, drug, convenience and grocery store in the country. Since this distribution system was adopted in about 1980, PowerPlus has gone from a very respectable ten per cent of the market to an enormous thirty-five per cent!"

"What?" Digger looked incredulous.

"That's right. It's one of the best kept secrets around."

"Batteries are big business. We must be talking about a lot of dollars, here," said Digger.

"You can't imagine," Mike answered, reaching for his water glass. "Whitaker Industries is privately owned, so I could not get as detailed or current information, but I can tell you what the major manufacturers in the market did last year, based on their public

Dave Sullivan

corporation filings. The big boys, who pretty much split the rest of the market are Everready and Duracell. Everready had gross sales last year of $2.3 billion. Duracell did $2.29 billion."

"Holy shit!" Kate cried. "You are talking serious money. But I still don't know what difference it makes, or what it's got to do with Digger," she added.

"I think I'm beginning to see," said Digger.

"See what?" Kate picked at her chef's salad.

"Judge, did you ever dream about being rich, when you were young?" asked Mike, immediately regretting his last words.

She gave him a strange look. "Of course I did, when I was young!"

Mike recoiled from her look and her tone, but recovered and continued. "Some people just dream of having a million dollars. Others imagine having a penny for every star in the sky or every drop of water. Still others fantasize about getting a royalty, of say a nickel, for every can of Coke that's sold, or every pack of cigarettes, and so on."

"Actually, I have done that." Kate smiled. "But what's that got to do with Digger?"

"Digger tells us his case deals with an increase of two per cent of gross sales after the first fifteen years," said Mike. "In his particular case, the amount claimed to be due already is about $75,000. Into the future, it continues at the rate of about $22,500 per year on that particular contract, depending on sales."

"So?"

"So, there are hundreds of contracts!" said Mike. "It's like a five cent royalty on every can of Coke. The people at the top of the pyramid get the $75,000 past due and the $22,500, or so, per year from a hundred or more contracts! If a top man had a hundred contracts below him like that in Digger's case, he'd get seven and a half million now and 2.25 million per year if Digger finds for the plaintiff. There are a dozen or so top men like that at PowerPlus."

"Oh, my God!" Kate put her fork on her plate.

104

CHAPTER ELEVEN

"**H**e has made the demand," Hollis Fowler reported to the assembled group in the basement boardroom at the Kitchi Gammi Club.

"When do you expect we'll hear something?" asked Orrin Rasmussen.

"He has had the case under advisement for about a month or more." said Fowler. "In a case like this, I'm told that four to six weeks is about average for Judge Moss. I suspect we're talking any day, maybe a week or so."

"How will we find out, Hollis?" asked Bertram Johnson, anxiously.

"Relax, Bert," Fowler answered him. "We will find out in the ordinary course of the court system. Judge Moss will file his decision and Order for Judgment, the clerk will enter it on the computer, mail it out, and our lawyer will get a copy in the mail. Our lawyer will call us, or send us a copy." He paused to let them consider his response, and then added, "We don't want anything different than the usual method of receiving a court decision. Nothing that even seems unusual. In fact," he stood and leaned over the end of the table, "we don't want any unusual reaction from any of us. Agreed?"

Around the long polished table, each man nodded his agreement.

Digger drove home without noticing any of the traffic control signals along the way. He was barely conscious of turning onto his street and into his driveway. He turned the engine off and sat. With the information about the PowerPlus pyramid sales system and the huge amounts of money involved, he knew they were all in trouble, not just Digger Moss, but Kate Riley and Mike Reynolds ... and, God help them all, his wife Judy, too. They had all been together, monitored electronically, so their conversations and knowledge were known to people who had the ability and motive to put them out of the way, permanently.

"Oh shit!" he said aloud, slamming a fist against the steering wheel. Somehow he had to straighten this whole mess out. But, how?

He opened the car door and walked slowly up the front steps to his home.

"Hi, dear!" Judy Moss met him at the front door. As soon as she saw the expression on his face, she knew he was not faring well under the pressure. "Something new happen?" she asked.

"Sort of," he answered. "Mike gave us some information he dug up ... at the public library, for Chrissakes. It makes things look bad."

Judy ushered him to the living room couch, sat him down and sat down beside him. She kissed him on the cheek and said, "Tell me."

She listened intently as Digger related the story of the PowerPlus pyramid and the amounts of money involved in the civil case in which he was being blackmailed into making a particular decision. Instead of reacting with horror at the realization that she was in danger along with Kate and Mike, instead of just Digger, she seemed to take it in stride. Her expression even seemed to relax, as if what Digger was telling her was not that bad after all.

Digger saw it. "Don't you realize what I'm telling you?"

"It's okay, Digger," she smiled. "All this time I have been so worried about you and felt so helpless, like I really wasn't involved, except of course when I had to clean your bloody shoes." Her mouth quivered almost breaking into a grin. "Now at least I'm part of the danger as well. Hopefully, I can be more of a part of the solution, too."

What a fantastic woman, thought Digger. She can be tough when she wants to.

"Whoever the hell is doing this to us will be stopped," she said, standing up from the couch, placing her hands on her hips.

Apparently she wants to be tough now, he thought.

"What do Katy and Mike say?"

"They are coming over tonight, after dinner."

"Well, thanks for telling me, dear." She pushed him over on the couch and landed on top of him. She wrapped her arms around him and said, "We'll get through this, my love." She hugged him. Then, as quickly, she was up. "What time are they coming?"

"About eight."

"Then we better get dinner out of the way." She turned and headed for the kitchen.

Later, Judy and Digger sat with Kate Riley and Mike Reynolds in the Moss living room.

"So what are we going to do?" Kate asked for the third or fourth time.

Mike answered. "I don't know, but two things have happened that we must consider. First, we know who they are, and second, the stakes just got a lot higher."

"What do you mean?" Kate wasn't sure she wanted to hear an answer.

"Think about what we know," said Digger. "This isn't just about extortion to get a billion dollar plus legal decision. This isn't just about Digger Moss anymore." He told them the same thing he had told Judy earlier. "This involves so much, they have got to kill me when it's over. They have been monitoring our conversations. They know all of you know. They have got to kill us all to get away with it clean."

For once Kate Riley was silent. She had nothing to say. She ran a hand through her thick auburn hair. Everyone looked at the floor, at the ceiling or anywhere except to make eye contact with one another.

"We need a plan," said Mike, "worse than ever. The problem is that we're in the middle, between the cops investigating the Larson murder and the PowerPlus people who have the evidence against Digger, and the rest of us." He looked around at each of them in turn.

"Well, you can't decide the case right away, Digger, or we'll lose every bit of leverage we have, which sure isn't much." Kate Riley had stood and was pacing the room.

"Katy's right, Digger," said Judy. "If you're right, and you decide the case now, they'll come after all of us as soon as they can."

"We have to delay, then," agreed Digger, "but how?"

"Do what judges usually do, Judge," said Mike.

"What's that?" asked Digger.

"Nothing."

"Mike!" Kate stopped her pacing and glared at Reynolds. "A little more respect for the bench, if you please."

"Actually, I'm serious. Judges take various lengths of time to make a decision in a matter taken under advisement. It depends on the judge, or the complexity of the matter, or whatever reason, but all we lawyers and our clients know is the judge has not made the decision, yet. We never get progress reports. Even if we ask, we just get the response that the judge is working on it."

"What's that got to do with Digger?" asked Kate.

"He can do the same thing ... nothing. Simply delay. If he's contacted, he can just say he is working on findings and a memorandum supporting his decision."

"Mike's right." Judy Moss entered the conversation. "Digger, delay is actually easy. You just don't make a decision. What are they going to do? If they release their 'evidence' against you, they'll never get their decision."

Digger agreed. "You're both right. It will work for a few days or a week or so. In that time we have to do whatever it is that will exonerate me and save all of you."

"I wish we could go to the police." Judy poured more coffee. "Isn't there anyone you can trust?"

"I thought I could trust all of them," said Digger, holding his cup up to his wife as she poured. "But, since Greg Larson's sting operation was to uncover drug dealing at the highest levels in the Police department and city government, we don't know whom he was after."

"And so," Kate Riley finished the thought for Digger, "we have no idea which police we can trust, if any!"

"It wouldn't matter if we did know who was clean," said Mike.

"What?" asked Judy.

"Yeah, Mike," added Kate. "What the hell are you talking about? We could use a couple of honest police officers about now."

"No question about that, but ..."

"Mike's right," interrupted Digger. "Even if we found honest police, or if Larson's sting was off base and the police department is fine, they're not going to help."

"Whaddaya mean, Digger?" Kate exchanged an exasperated look with Judy. "All this time you have been against going to the police because of the sting and the fear that you wouldn't know which officers you could trust!"

Mike explained. "Think about it. We have agreed that the evidence against Digger is so overwhelming that he will be convicted, even though we know him to be innocent, unless we prove his innocence. If we go to the cops, even if they are all clean and trustworthy, or if they get the evidence some other way, they have to run with it. They have to arrest him. The County Attorney has to charge him. Even if they are willing to listen to Digger's explanation, they have no choice but to proceed."

"That's right," said Digger. "And remember, we aren't just dealing with the evidence of possession and sale of drugs, they will have evidence of the murder of a police sergeant."

"Oh God," Kate sighed. "They can't be nice to a cop killer, even if they wanted to help you out, which they won't."

They sat in silence for a while, each concentrating on the problem, trying to think of a helpful solution. Judy went to the kitchen and returned with the coffee pot, busying herself freshening their cups.

Kate Riley stood, holding her coffee cup in one hand and the saucer underneath it in the other. She sipped from the cup. She said, "Well, for the umpteenth time, I ask you, what do we do now?"

Digger was doodling on a yellow legal pad on the coffee table in front of him. "We can't delay the decision too long, but maybe as long as it takes to trap these bastards." He wrote a number 1 on the pad and next to the number he wrote, "Delay decision." Below that, he wrote a number 2 and poised his pen to write the next step.

"A trap," thought Mike aloud. "Maybe that's not so hard," he said. "They know Digger knows who they are, or at least that they are at Whitaker Industries and that they're involved with the battery contracts. If Digger wanted to talk, he could send some kind of message, ask for a meeting."

"Oh, sure, Mike," said Kate, "and go wearing a wire, I suppose. Last time we tried that, it worked lousy."

"Look," said Digger, "these pricks need me. At least, they need me until I've made the decision. They won't hurt me before then. It's too important for them. It's just too God damned much money."

"There has to be a purpose of the meeting," said Mike.

"I'll ask for a cut," Digger replied.

Kate Riley and Judy Moss looked at Digger in shock.

"I thought you'd say that," said Mike, shaking his head, as if to suggest they were going to get in deeper trouble.

"A cut!?" stammered Kate. "A cut? Are you nuts? They'll kill you!"

"Not when I haven't made their decision yet, they won't," said Digger. "They can't afford to."

"Well, then," Kate continued her opposition, "how about credibility? Who would believe that the great 'Digger Moss' would take a money bribe to make a decision in a certain case? 'Digger Moss,' who never did anything wrong in his life, except smoke a little grass in college!"

Judy Moss looked at Kate Riley curiously.

"Thank you for the accolades, Kate," said Digger, "but I think they'll believe me."

"Maybe he's right," Mike interjected. "They've got so much on Digger that he has no choice but to work with them and they know it. There's so much money involved, that, if he's figured it out, it would not be at all unreasonable for Digger to try to get enough payment for what they've asked him to do so he can slip away and live comfortably somewhere far away. I think Digger is on the right track, here."

"How do you get to the right people, Digger?" asked Judy. "I'm sure not everyone at PowerPlus Batteries is involved. I don't think Charles Whitaker or his family is involved."

"We'll go through my contact. When he calls, I just tell him I have to meet with his principals before I do anything. What choice does he have? What choice do they have?" Digger made a note on his legal pad. He was down to number 4 now.

"When?" asked Kate. "When will you do it?"

"The sooner, the better," said Digger. "If the cops get onto me, it will be too late."

They continued planning Digger's next move. Digger made notes on his pad, while they figured just what he should ask for and how he should do it. They couldn't control how soon Digger would be contacted. They could only hope it would be soon. They were not disappointed.

Chief of Police, John Morgan stood in front of City Hall before a bank of microphones addressing a large group of news reporters and photographers.

"We are continuing to develop the evidence," he said, "but at this time, we are not prepared to identify any suspects in the investigation."

"*Are* there any suspects in the investigation, Chief?" yelled a reporter from the rear of the crowd.

Morgan paused and was saved by another question.

"Chief Morgan, was Sergeant Larson working on anything special at the time he was killed?"

"We are considering that," Morgan's deep voice answered. "However, as you might expect, we have to be careful not to disrupt those ongoing investigations in which Sergeant Larson was involved. We will let you in on that information when it is no longer confidential."

"Any more information about motive, Chief?" asked another voice from the center of the group.

J udy Moss pressed a key on the remote control which muted the television. She turned to Digger.

"Well, it's good that there aren't any more clues," she said. "The police aren't any further than when they found the shoe print."

"A few days ago, I would have agreed with you," said Digger. "But, it's been too long, Jude. Morgan's been putting the media off too long. He's getting desperate for a suspect. If they get any of the information about me, they'll jump on it, just to have something to report. Also, they don't have any clues about the real killer. That'll make it harder to steer them away from me if I become a suspect."

"Crepe hanger!" she accused, pointing at him. "I try to be optimistic, and you ruin it."

"Relax, sweetheart." He put an arm around her shoulder. "It just means it's important that our plan succeeds soon, before something happens that makes me a suspect."

"When will you hear from that terrible man who contacts you?"

"Soon I hope."

"W ell, I'll be God damned!" Frank Griswold put down the phone. "James Digby Moss is getting some guts!" he said aloud to himself.

Griswold rose and went to the kitchenette counter in his Holiday Inn suite. He poured a large Scotch whiskey, took a long drink, and smiled. Let him have his fucking meeting, he thought. Let them all have their fucking meeting. I've got my three million out of those greedy battery salesmen. Now just to get even with the Honorable James Digby Moss! Then I am outa here! He took another long swallow of Scotch.

In the van, now parked on Fourth Street above the Holiday Inn, Vince said, "The judge is going to get himself in more trouble than he can handle, I think."

Milo agreed. He had begun to develop a liking for Judge Moss, stemming, no doubt, from his increasing dislike for Frank Griswold. He did not like the idea of Judge Moss meeting with Griswold, or the desperate men he represented.

Milo and Vince had found parking spots on the street and in some small parking lots up the hill from the Holiday Inn. Because of the steep hill in Duluth's downtown area, these places provided excellent locations from which to monitor the electronic devices they had set to watch and listen to Griswold and monitor his phone conversations. Instead of being further away, the height they gained by moving up the hill gave them a better position than they would have had in a flat city. That fact also allowed them a variety of parking spots so they would not be at one place every day and attract unwanted attention to themselves and their van.

"We'd better be there to monitor any meeting," said Milo.

"Right," agreed Vince.

"I don't know," said Digger. "He didn't say. He just seemed to get mad. Then he said he'd talk to his people, but he expected them to be real disappointed. He said, 'You know what that means.'"

Kate Riley and Mike Reynolds listened. Kate rose from the chair behind her desk in her chambers. "What you guys said the other night still holds," she said. "They can bluff and bluster, but they can't afford not to deal with Digger, at least for now."

"Have you got the recorder?" asked Mike.

"I do."

"Nothing fancy, now," Mike cautioned. "Just in your inside suit coat pocket where you might ordinarily carry a dictaphone. Don't turn it on until you think you're in. Go to the bathroom or turn toward the wall or something to hide the movement it takes to turn it on."

"Right." Digger didn't like this "spy" business.

"Have you tried turning it on while it's in your inside coat pocket, Digger?" asked Kate. "Do you think you can do it?"

"I think so," he answered.

CHAPTER TWELVE

"**W**ell, you've got your meeting," the voice said. "Frankly, I think it's a mistake for you, but then you don't want my advice, right?"

"I want the meeting," said Digger. He looked across his desk at Kate Riley, who was with him in his chambers when the call came in.

"Okay," the voice said. "the Kitchi Gammi Club at noon tomorrow."

"That soon?" asked Digger, surprised.

"I told you before, Judge, these guys aren't fooling around. They want their decision ... and they want it pretty soon ... if you get my drift."

"I understand," said Digger. The line went dead.

"Tomorrow noon at the Kitch," he said to Kate.

She sighed. "Well, you wanted it soon. Looks like you got it."

"That's for sure."

"Are you ready?"

"I hope so."

Milo Bracken and Vincent Turcotte ate avocado and bacon sandwiches and drank dark imported beer in their van behind Sir Benedict's on the Lake, a restaurant next door to the Kitchi Gammi Club. Remodeled from an old gas station, the restaurant served specialty sandwiches and a variety of wines and imported beers. Patrons dined inside or on its outside deck.

They enjoyed their sandwiches and beer in the sunshine coming through the windshield. The listening equipment in the rear of the van was set on speaker so they could hear. Milo could see the small television monitors displaying the video signals from the tiny cameras they had installed at the Kitchi Gammi Club earlier, posing as electricians from a local electrical contractor. Since learning the day before of the scheduled meeting, they had been very busy, arriving at the Club early in the morning. Fortunately, the boardroom had no meetings before noon. Milo and Vince were able to make their hasty, but nearly undetectable installations before the staff came to set up for the lunch meeting. Resting and enjoying the bright sunny day and the blue waters of Lake Superior, which they could just see alongside the east wall of Sir Benedict's, they waited for the meeting to begin.

"What time is it?" asked Milo.

"Just past noon," Vince answered, looking at his cheap wristwatch. "Where's the judge? He's late."

"Don't worry," said Milo, "I think we can count on the judge being here. He may have been in court until noon. Also, I bet he doesn't mind making them wait a little." Milo smiled.

"What?" Vince took a swig of amber beer from his bottle. "He's gettin' himself into enough trouble as it is. Don't you think it would be a mistake to piss these guys off?"

"The judge is a cool character, by my read of him. I think he doesn't mind at all if they wait. It will set the mood that he isn't coming crawling to them, he isn't begging, but that he is also dealing from strength."

"What strength?"

"If he doesn't give them their decision; if he goes to the cops and tells his story; no matter what happens to him, they don't get their decision and their money; *and*," he emphasized the "*and*," "the police and everyone else will know about their blackmail efforts against the judge. It may even come out that they were involved in the murder of that cop." Milo bit off a large mouthful of the thick sandwich.

"Jesus!" Vince sighed, thinking over Milo's explanation.

Milo wiped his mouth with a crumpled paper napkin. "It's like a standoff," he said. "Like two guys in the movies standing at point blank range pointing guns at each other. One says, 'You put your gun down.' The other man says, 'No, you first.' See? These hot shot, big time executives have the judge's reputation, his career, and even his life in their hands, but the judge has got them too. He can expose them, sure, but they can deny it, and he probably doesn't have any concrete or written evidence against them."

"So what's his weapon in the standoff?" Vince interrupted.

"He can decide the case against them. There goes all their millions."

"Jesus. He *is* a cool character."

"There he is!" Milo straightened in his chair, put his sandwich down on the dash and moved to the rear to examine the pictures on the monitors. Vince moved back to join him.

Two of the screens showed the boardroom itself viewed from small video cameras hidden in the air conditioning vents in the ceiling. Their overhead views overlapped, showing the entire room and each of the men sitting at the large polished table.

The third camera was positioned over the door to the boardroom facing the basement sitting area through which anyone arriving or leaving for a boardroom meeting could be seen. It was this third camera that had drawn Milo's attention. They had already watched the others arrive. They had seen them waiting in the boardroom with increasing impatience. They had even heard some of their remarks about the time over the speakers in the van that played the audio from the microphones they had planted. There were no microphones outside the boardroom where the third video monitor now showed Judge Moss arriving and being greeted by two men.

They watched.

Digger walked through the east entrance to the Kitchi Gammi Club, what for many years had been known as the Ladies' Entrance, women not being allowed to enter the main door in front or the back door from the alley. Reluctant to change, the Kitch had finally replaced the common name of the east entrance with something more appropriate and even allowed women to become members of the club.

Walking past the desk, he acknowledged the attendant behind the desk.

"Hi Matt," he said.

"Good afternoon, Judge," the attendant responded. "How are you?"

"Fine, Matt. How's everything going today?"

"Just great, Judge. Are you here for the Whitaker meeting?"

"I am."

"Downstairs in the boardroom, Judge. They'll be serving lunch soon."

"Thanks Matt." Digger continued past the front desk to the stairway and started down to the basement.

As he walked toward the boardroom at the west end of the building, he was greeted by two men, one in a conservative business suit and the other in khaki pants and a green windbreaker. The first man wore a dark gray, double breasted suit, an expensive light gray shirt, and wide gray and black paisley tie. The cuffs of his shirtsleeves extended a tasteful half inch beyond the sleeves of his coat, displaying large gold cuff links. His silvery hair was neatly groomed and carefully combed, not one hair out of place. The other man was larger, his appearance a marked contrast to that of his companion. He was big, stocky, and barrel-chested. His thick black hair was uncombed. The first man looked calm and polite, even friendly, as they approached him. The second man exuded anger and hostility.

"Judge Moss?" said the first man.

"Yes."

"Good afternoon, Judge. This is Frank Vagelli," he gestured toward the larger man, "and I am Hollis Fowler." He stepped toward Digger, extending his right hand.

Digger shook hands with them both. The limp handshake of the man called Fowler was overcompensated by the vice-like grip of Vagelli, whose eyes conveyed his acrimony notwithstanding the peaceful origins of the handshake greeting.

"Judge," said Fowler, "under the circumstances of this meeting that you have requested, you'll understand that we have to search you first."

"What?"

"We gotta search ya, is what he said." Vagelli moved toward Digger with such aggression that Digger wondered if he was about to be assaulted.

Vagelli squatted on his powerful haunches and began a pat down search. As he moved up Digger's body, he was not gentle. His big, meaty hands pushed, shoved, squeezed, and pulled at Digger's clothes. It was extremely intimidating to Digger. God, what happens when they find the recorder? he thought. The way the big man was searching him, Digger had no doubt the recorder would be found.

"What the hell is this?" demanded Vagelli, as a big hand bumped the hard case of the recorder in Digger's inside breast pocket.

117

For a moment, Digger considered running, but he noticed that Hollis Fowler had moved behind him, in a position to block Digger's flight, if he tried.

Frank Vagelli did not wait for an answer to his question. He roughly opened Digger's coat and yanked the small recording device out of the pocket. He held it up for Fowler to see.

"Judge?" said Fowler, inquiring.

"It's just a dictating machine," answered Digger. "I often carry one, for dictation in my car, or at home." He added, "There's not much time to do that sort of thing during the day because nearly all my time is scheduled on the bench in the courtroom."

"Bullshit!" muttered Vagelli.

"Shit! They're searching him!" Vince Turcotte turned toward Milo. "I told you he was getting into trouble!"

Milo studied the small TV monitor, straining his eyes to see what was going on in the basement of the Kitchi Gammi Club.

"I wish that big prick would pick on somebody his own size. Maybe he'd like to try that on me!"

"Vince!" Milo said. "You're smaller than the judge."

"You know what I mean. Look how he's treating him!"

"Wait!" Milo leaned toward the small screen. "They've found something."

"What is it?" Vince leaned in close, too.

"Oh, Christ! It's some kind of recording device!" Milo slammed a hand on the counter. The small monitor bounced, the picture fluttering in response. "What the hell was he thinking?"

"What difference does it make, Milo?"

"Huh?"

"Well, the way you explained it, they've got a standoff. It's still the same standoff, whether they took his recorder or not."

Milo thought about Vince's remark. "You're right," he said. "I just hope Judge Moss realizes it."

"I don't believe it!" growled Frank Vagelli. "You brought this in to record what we say in there!" He held the small machine up in Digger's face, his big hand threatening to crush it like an empty cigarette pack. "Be God damned careful, Mister," Vagelli leaned in toward Digger, his face inches away from Digger's face, "or you won't be able to hear or see what goes on in that boardroom!"

"Frank,... Frank," Hollis Fowler spoke calmly and evenly, as he put a hand on the shoulders of each of the men. "We don't want to prevent the judge from having his little meeting, now, do we? Let's keep that thing and take Judge Moss in to meet with our friends."

Digger observed that it took a moment for Vagelli to regain control, the anger in him was so great. It was obvious to Digger that Fowler was clearly the senior man, that he used Vagelli's rage as a tool, and that without Fowler's presence, Vagelli would be out of control and extremely dangerous.

In the van, there was a collective sigh of relief and two bottles of the imported dark beer were simultaneously raised as Milo and Vince watched the scene on the third monitor close with Digger Moss being led into the boardroom, as yet unhurt.

"Shit! That was close!" said Milo.

"You got that right," said Vince. "I couldn't hear what that big prick was saying, but I could tell his meaning. The judge got off lucky."

They both turned to watch the remaining two monitors showing the boardroom. Their view was like watching an overhead shot of a hockey game, giving the scene a surreal quality. They did not have a good view of the expressions on the men's faces, but they could clearly hear what each was saying.

They watched as Digger Moss was escorted into the room by Vagelli and Fowler, men whom Vince and Milo had watched, but whose names they did not yet know.

John Morgan sat in his office in the headquarters of the Duluth Police Department in City Hall. Across the desk sat two of his senior officers. On the desk between them lay the contents of the file on the investigation of the murder of Sergeant Greg Larson. Chief

Morgan was clearly unhappy. He lifted a styrofoam cup of black coffee that looked more like tar and gulped some down.

"I know you guys are trying, but damn!" he grumbled, his deep voice seeming to descend to new depths. "The mayor's on my ass, and I've heard from two City Councilors already this morning! We have got to come up with something!"

"We know, Chief," said Lieutenant Joe Walters, a long-time veteran of the detective bureau. "We've got practically everybody on it. There just isn't much to work on."

"That's right," added James Pelton, who was one of the department's two Assistant Chiefs. "We'll get 'em. That's for sure. But it's going to take time, unless we get a break."

"Well, something has got to happen ... and happen pretty God damned soon!" Morgan boomed. An officer outside the glass walls of Morgan's office turned to look at them.

"What about the shoe print?" he asked, lowering his voice.

"We've got men working on it, but nothing so far, Chief," said Walters. "There were a hell of a lot of those Nikes sold nationwide, and a hell of a lot of them right here in the Twin Ports."

Assistant Chief Pelton added, "Normally, you'd say if a local gets killed, it's done by someone local, unless it's mixed up with drugs, gangs, or some other crime pattern. But because Greg was investigating undercover, we have to assume his killer could be from anywhere; just visiting Duluth for criminal purposes, like taking advantage of the higher drug market, or something like that."

"I know," muttered Morgan. "The killer could be from Chicago or Detroit or anywhere. The likelihood that he's from the Twin Cities is just as great as his being from Duluth."

"And that's a lot of shoes ... and a lot of shoe stores," added Walters.

"Any clues from what Greg was working on, Jim?" asked Morgan.

"Not really," answered Pelton. "He was undercover in the local drug scene. Had a small apartment in the Central Hillside he used for his cover." Pelton leaned forward, putting a hand on Morgan's desk. "There were a couple of strange things, though."

"Yeah?"

"Well, they are probably nothing, but Greg had some contacts with a drug dealer, new to town, named 'Zorro' that didn't seem to fit the usual pattern, and he had some strange contacts with a judge, Judge Moss."

"Digger Moss?" Chief John Morgan straightened in his chair.

"That's right, John, but I'm sure it's nothing. We just couldn't figure out what they were, that's all."

"Well, find out, and keep me advised," said Morgan, standing to indicate the meeting was over.

A t the Kitchi Gammi Club, the meeting was not over. Still parked behind Sir Benedict's, Vince and Milo listened and watched intently.

I n the boardroom, Orrin Rasmussen was speaking. He removed his glasses and ran a hand over his white hair. Placing his glasses on the table before him, he turned his blue eyes toward Digger, who was seated at the end of the table nearest the door. Hollis Fowler sat next to Digger. Frank Vagelli stood behind them near the door.

"Judge," asked Rasmussen, "even if we negotiate a monetary deal with you, as you seem to suggest, how can we all be assured that you will come through with the decision and remain quiet afterward?"

"I have no choice," was the answer. "With the false evidence you have against me, I have no choice but to cooperate. I've just decided to take a course of action that protects me and gives me and my wife some security in the future."

"But the evidence you talk about presumably gives you no choice anyway," said Rasmussen.

"Right," added Harry Slater. "What's changed?"

"I have," said Digger, with a controlled calmness that surprised even him and drew considerable respect from Milo and Vince in the van.

"What makes you think you have any option to change?" demanded Slater, shifting in his chair, obviously unnerved by the judge's actions.

"As I see it," responded Digger, "I don't have many other options. You have put me in a position where my only option is to try to insure survival ... and that's what I'm doing. That's why I'm here. That's why I asked for this meeting."

"Bullshit!" Frank Vagelli moved closer to the table from his position by the door. "You came here to get these guys to talk about the deal so you could record the discussion and have some evidence against us. That fell through when I found this fucking recorder you brought along!" He slammed the small machine on the polished table top. Several of the men around the table looked at the small black recording device in alarm.

"Now you're fucked and you know it!" Vagelli stared down at Digger Moss, his accusation hanging in the air.

Several of the men nodded their understanding and agreement.

Digger Moss showed no reaction.

"Well?" asked Slater, waiting for a response from Digger.

"He's wrong," said Digger, calmly, "but it doesn't make any difference."

"Yeah, right. The hell it doesn't," muttered Vagelli from his position by the door to which he had returned.

"I'm afraid Mr. Vagelli is right, Judge," said Orrin Rasmussen. "You really don't have much of a leg to stand on, here."

"He's wrong."

"What?"

"Vagelli is wrong." Digger's calmness, his lack of reaction, disturbed the men around the table.

"No, Judge, Frank Vagelli *is* right." Hollis Fowler stood and looked at the men seated around the table, then down at Digger Moss. "Without this recorder," he tapped the small black machine on the table in front of Digger, "you have lost the leverage you came to try to obtain. Don't you agree?"

"No."

It was not the style of Hollis Fowler to lose control of negotiations, but for a moment, a very slight reaction of frustration showed on his face. He regained his normal cool control and asked, "Well, Judge Moss," his smile clearly intended to be demeaning, "we are all waiting. Just what is it you think you can do?"

Every face turned toward Digger Moss, waiting.

"I'll decide the case against you."

The room was silent.

"Damn!" exclaimed Vince. "The judge has balls, I'll give him that. He ain't takin' any shit from these guys."

Milo was studying the view of the top of the head and shoulders of a man in a far corner of the boardroom whom he had not noticed before. He was a stocky man, dressed in navy slacks and a green windbreaker. Milo could not see his face, only his long wavy blonde hair.

"Griswold!"

"What? Who?" asked Vince.

Milo pointed at the small screen. "That's Griswold! The slimy son of a bitch is at the meeting! See him? Over in the corner."

Vince studied the monitor with interest. While he had never met Griswold, he had watched him on their surveillance monitors before.

"There is the bastard," he whispered. Then, in a louder voice, he said, "I can't see his face. I'd really like to see his face to see what he's thinking."

"Right," Milo agreed. "He's the one we're interested in."

In the boardroom, no one spoke for a long time. Each man thinking over the implications of what Digger Moss had said. Finally, Hollis Fowler broke the silence.

"Judge," he said, "I think we have come to a point where we have to discuss some issues outside your presence. The easiest way to do that is for you to leave for a few minutes. Frank will accompany you to the sitting area by the fireplace just outside this room. We will let you know when we are ready to talk to you again." He nodded to Frank Vagelli, who came forward and took Digger's arm starting to help him to his feet.

"No," said Digger, removing Vagelli's hand from his arm.

"What's that?"

"Listen you ..." growled Vagelli, reaching for Digger's arm again.

"No," repeated Digger firmly, getting to his feet under his own power. "No. I *am* going out that door, but I'm not sitting by the fireplace with this jerk or anyone else. I'm leaving the Club. Now. I'm not coming back. I have a hearing at 1:30." He glanced at his watch. "I plan to be on the bench at that time."

Digger started for the door. He put a hand on Fowler's shoulder. "Excuse me," he said.

Frank Vagelli started for Digger, but Fowler put out a hand to stop him, shaking his head. Digger reached the door, stepped outside, shutting the door softly behind him. He was gone.

In the van, Milo and Vince clicked their beer bottles together in a toast to Digger as they watched him walk through the Kitchi Gammi basement and disappear from sight.

"He's good and he's tough!" said Vince, taking a pull on the long-necked bottle.

"But maybe a little foolish," added Milo.

"Whaddaya mean?"

"What do you think they're gonna do with the judge, Vince?"

"I dunno, what?"

"Can't let him live, can they?"

Vince stared at Milo, letting his remark settle in. "God, you think they're gonna kill him?"

"Do they have a choice?"

Vince thought about it. Finally, he said, "You're right, the sons of bitches. You think the judge knows?"

"Unless I'm very much mistaken, he does," answered Milo.

"Then he really *is* a cool customer," said Vince.

The two sat in silence, each in his own thoughts about Digger Moss as they continued monitoring the meeting in the boardroom.

CHAPTER THIRTEEN

Digger Moss was shaking as he steered his car out of the Kitchi Gammi Club parking lot and up the hill to First Street where he turned left to return to the courthouse. It was ten minutes after one. The walk through the basement of the Kitchi Gammi Club had been one of the most difficult walks of his life. Even though Hollis Fowler had stopped Vagelli, Digger expected them to change their minds or Vagelli to act on his own and come after him. He could not keep himself from looking back over his shoulder several times as he walked through the Club to the East entrance and across the avenue to his car.

Driving west on First Street, he called Kate Riley on his cellular phone.

"Judge Riley's chambers," said a young male voice, which Digger recognized as Kate's law clerk.

"Mickey?"

"Yes?"

"Mickey, this is Judge Moss. Is Judge Riley there?"

"Good afternoon, Judge Moss. Just a moment. Judge Riley is right here."

"Digger?" Kate Riley's voice sounded apprehensive. "Where are you?"

"I'm okay, Kate. A little unnerved is all. I'm on my way back to the courthouse now. Can you find Mike and meet me when I get there?"

"Okay, I'll try, but where?"

"Your chambers, I think, Kate."

"I'll be here, and Mike, if I can find him."

"Thanks."

Digger drove on toward the courthouse, trying to think what they would, or could, do next. That Hollis Fowler, Frank Vagelli, and their friends were an ongoing threat to the safety of Digger and anyone else helping him or who had knowledge was clear.

"**W**e have to get all of them!" Digger told Mike and Kate in her chambers.

"What do you mean, 'get them,' Digger?" asked Kate.

"I mean take them out of commission, eliminate them, prevent them from being able to do anything, whatever," he answered. "I mean we need to do whatever it takes to keep any of them from being able to eliminate us so the truth will never come out."

"Oh."

"Actually the first and most important step in that direction is clear," said Mike.

"What's that?" Kate asked.

"Yeah, what's so clear?" asked Digger.

"You can't ever give them the decision they want." Mike answered.

Digger and Kate contemplated Mike's remark in silence for a moment. Kate rose from her seat, walked to her small refrigerator and returned with three Diet Cokes.

"Mike's right, Digger," she said. "Even if you give them a favorable decision as a ruse, intending to change it later, they'll be coming for you as soon as the ink is dry on your signature."

Digger agreed. "They can't afford not to. Once they have the decision, they need to clean up the loose ends and eliminate any possibility of anyone talking."

"But, Christ, Digger, you can't find against them, or they'll turn you into the police somehow, as they have threatened to do," said Kate, "and you can't go very long without making a decision. So what *are* we going to do, now?"

"Whatever it is, it's got to be fast," Digger replied, gulping his Diet Coke, thankful for the cold, soothing liquid on his parched throat.

"That's for sure," said Mike Reynolds. "From what you tell us, they're sitting over at the Kitch, deciding what to do with you, right now."

Assistant Chief Pelton spoke as he rose to leave Chief Morgan's office.

"I'll take Kathy Winslow with me. We'll go see the judge, now."

"Good," the Chief answered. "Maybe he can shed some light on this mess."

"We can only hope, Chief." The tall, thin assistant chief smiled as he opened the office door.

Morgan nodded. He certainly did hope. He hoped something would happen on this case, anything. The lack of evidence and the lack of progress was driving him crazy. It had the same effect on his whole department. They did not like the reaction they were getting from the public and the public officials. Judge Moss was a pretty good man, thought the chief. Maybe he has something that will help.

"A fternoon, Judge! Have you got a minute?" Pelton leaned in the doorway of Digger's chambers.

"Come on in, Jim," said Digger, from the chair behind his big desk. "What can I do for you, today. Need a signature?"

"No thanks, your Honor," he replied. "Just need some information. You know Sergeant Winslow."

"I do." Digger rose and extended a hand across to Kathy Winslow who smiled and accepted the handshake. "Please, sit down."

The two police officers sat across from Digger. Assistant Chief Pelton began the discussion. "Judge Moss, what can you tell us about Sergeant Greg Larson?"

Digger felt his stomach roll over and his bowel tighten. "What about?" he asked, hoping he didn't give away the dread he felt.

"Greg Larson," said Sergeant Kathy Winslow. "Judge, as you know we're investigating Sergeant Larson's murder, and," she paused, "without a lot of success."

"So I read in the paper," said Digger, recovering from his initial shock and regaining his composure, he hoped. "You have my sympathy. What can I do to help?"

"We saw your name and phone number in some personal notes we found in Greg's desk. It looked like maybe he was working on something that had something to do with you. Do you know what it could be?"

Digger tried his best to look like he was trying to remember something, while his mind raced as he considered what to do. What did they know? What did they think? He began to form his decision as he said, "I've talked with Sergeant Larson, of course. Like many of you, he comes in once in a while with a Complaint to be reviewed or an application for a search warrant, something like that. But I don't recall anything else." There. He was committed.

"Did you have any telephone conversations with him? Did he call you, or you call him?"

"Not that I recall," said Digger. "Oh, I'm sure I've talked to him at some time by phone. He has probably called to see if I was a available to review a search warrant or something, but nothing recently."

"Well, all we've got are his notes which don't really say anything," said Pelton. "We thought maybe he had called you."

"Nope."

"Then I don't suppose you had any idea what he was working on before he was killed?" said Winslow, making a question out of her statement by lifting her voice slightly at the end.

"Not a clue," said Digger. "I see in the paper that he was working undercover on drug cases. I always saw him in plain clothes, but I had no idea what his assignment was."

"Well, Judge, we thank you for your time," said Assistant Chief Pelton, rising from his chair. "If it's any consolation, you have been as much help as our other leads. We just aren't getting anywhere on this case."

"I wish I could be of more help." Digger stood as they prepared to leave.

"Thanks again, you have a good afternoon."

"Thanks, Judge." Sergeant Winslow smiled as she turned toward the door and followed Pelton out the door and down the hall.

When they were gone, Digger sank into his high-backed desk chair, putting his head back against the leather. He exhaled slowly, realizing that he had held his breath at the last as the two police officers left his chambers. That was close, he thought. Thank God he had guessed right, that they had no idea whether he and Larson had actually talked. He had been very lucky.

"He's lying! Why?" asked Kathy Winslow, as she and Jim Pelton crossed the distance between the County

Courthouse and City Hall.

"I wish I knew. The Chief will want to know about this!" declared Pelton.

"**W**hat the hell?" Chief John Morgan was astonished. He had assumed that since there was some contact between Greg Larson and Judge Digger Moss, the judge might have some information that might be helpful. God, anything would be helpful. But they had clear records that Greg had called the Judge and the Judge had called him! The judge was lying!

"We know, Chief," said Pelton. "We can't figure it either."

"Are you sure he didn't misunderstand you?"

"Not a chance, Chief," said Sergeant Winslow. She pulled a small notepad from the pocket of her uniform and referred to it. "I asked him specifically if he had any phone calls with Greg. He answered, 'Nothing recently.' "

"I don't know what the hell is going on, but we're going to do something about it."

"What?"

"Get somebody in here to do a search warrant application."

"On Judge Moss?" asked an incredulous Assistant Chief Pelton.

"On Judge Moss!"

Chief Judge Carrie Anne Parker studied the search warrant application which Sergeant Kathy Winslow and Assistant Chief Jim Pelton had presented to her. My God, she thought, a search warrant to search the office and home of a sitting District Court Judge! She looked up at the two police officers standing on the other side of her desk.

"Judge," said Pelton, "we came to you because you are the Chief Judge of the District. We figured it was better to come to you under the circumstances."

"I suspect you were right to do that," Judge Parker acknowledged, "but this is a little thin isn't it?" She gestured at the typewritten application.

"He knows something he is hiding from us, Judge," said Winslow. "This is a homicide investigation, a cop was killed."

"I know, I know," sighed the judge. "All right, let's get on with it. You swear this is all true?"

"I do and it is," answered Pelton, watching carefully as Chief Judge Carrie Parker signed the application and the search warrant.

"Thank you, Judge," said Pelton, as he gathered up the papers and hurried from the judge's chambers.

Frank Vagelli crawled out from under a red Cadillac Seville in the Whitaker Industries parking garage. Executives of the company parked on the first level of the ramp. Their cars were cared for by company employees who washed them regularly, kept them filled with gas and windshield washer fluids, checked the oil, tires, and belts and even did oil changes at the recommended mileage intervals.

The Cadillac belonged to Harry Slater. Slater was a coward, thought Vagelli. At the meeting at the Kitchi Gammi Club, after Judge Moss had left, Slater was one of two of the men who had refused to accept the inevitable. Hollis Fowler had explained it to them.

"We have got to go along with Moss," Fowler had said. "We have got to agree to his monetary demands, but when he makes the decision we have got to kill him. We have no choice!"

Most of the men reluctantly agreed with Fowler's logic. He had intimated as much before. But Harry Slater and Bertram Johnson could not accept it. Hollis had told him later that they were weak. He said that a chain was no stronger than its weakest link. He said that to strengthen a chain you got rid of the weak links. He said Bert Johnson and Harry Slater were two weak links.

He got into the Cadillac and gently returned it to Slater's reserved parking space.

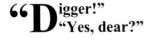 **D**igger!"
"Yes, dear?"

"Come look at this!" She was in the kitchen preparing dinner. The six o'clock news was on the small television on the counter. Digger came into the kitchen.

"What?"

"Look!"

The local news anchor was speaking as the screen showed a wrecked automobile, surrounded by onlookers and uniformed police, their squad cars parked with overhead lights flashing.

"The car belonged to Harold J. Slater, a Duluth resident and an executive at Whitaker Industries. Police are still uncertain what happened, but witnesses said the car came speeding down 2nd Avenue West and crashed into the concrete wall of the Downtown Park parking ramp on Michigan Street at the bottom of the hill. Live at the scene, our Lisa Maki has more. Lisa?"

"Thank you, Don and Beth, we're here at the corner of 2nd Avenue West and Superior Street. Behind me, just a short block down the hill, you can see the car. Witnesses say it was speeding up all the way into the wall. It never slowed down."

Digger looked at Judy. "You know I don't believe in coincidences."

"I know."

"There's a connection. He must not have gone along with the program, whatever that is, and they killed him, or he committed suicide."

"Oh, God," sighed Judy Moss. She put a hand on his shoulder. "What have we gotten ourselves into, Digger?"

"We'll be all right, Jude." He held her hand in his. "We just can't give up and we just can't let down our guard."

God! Digger thought to himself. They're taking out their own people! His thought that when this was over, they would clean things up by killing people who knew anything was clearly confirmed.

The phone rang.

"Hello, Moss residence," said Judy into the receiver. "Yes, Mike, he's right here. Just a minute."

"Digger?"

"Here, Mike."

"Did you see the news?"

"I did."

"Jesus Christ, Digger! What are they doing?" Mike's voice was tense with excitement.

"I know, Mike," said Digger. "They're not fooling around, and they won't fool around with us!"

"No shit, Sherlock!" Mike said, starting to calm down. "We know for sure now what they'll do to you, eventually. Don't you think you better go to the police and tell the whole story?"

"No!" Digger was adamant. "Nothing has changed. I suspected these people would be as rough as they have just shown they will be. We still can't straighten this out if I am in jail."

The doorbell rang. Judy looked at Digger questioningly and left the kitchen to go through the dining room to the front foyer.

"Good evening, Mrs. Moss, is the judge at home?"

From the kitchen doorway, Digger could see two uniformed police officers and two plain clothed officers talking to his wife. One of the plain clothed men held up a gold detective's shield.

"Mike!" Digger whispered into the phone. "The cops are here! At my front door! We got trouble!"

"Hold on, Digger," said Reynolds. "Can you tell what they want?"

"Unless I miss my bet, they've got a warrant!"

"For your arrest?"

"Either that or to search the place!"

"I'll be right there!" The phone went dead.

Digger stood for a moment in the doorway of the kitchen holding the dead receiver in his hand. Finally Judy turned and looked at him, her expression clearly asking for help. He put the phone down and moved through the dining room to the foyer.

"Can I help you officers?" he said, putting an arm around Judy's waist.

"Good evening, Judge," said one of the plain clothed detectives. "Sorry to bother you at this time, Judge, but we have a search warrant here which we are supposed to execute this evening." He held out an 8 ½" x 11" page of white paper for Digger to see.

"What? A search warrant?" Digger grabbed the paper and examined it. It was a warrant to search Digger and Judy's home. It was signed by Chief Judge Parker.

"Digger?" Judy put a hand on his shoulder, looking at the paper which Digger held.

"It's all right, Jude. It's all in order." He looked at her, gave a reassuring nod, and said to the police, "Okay, gentlemen, I guess the place is all yours."

"Sorry about this Mrs. Moss," said one of the men as they entered the foyer. "We'll try not to disturb too much."

As the policemen began to spread out through the rooms of the Moss home, a screech of tires signaled Mike Reynolds' arrival in front.

"What the hell is going on?" he demanded of one of the men as he came through the front door.

One of the men in plain clothes put a hand out in front of Reynolds to stop him. "Hold on counselor, we have a search warrant from Chief Judge Parker here." He held out the piece of paper Digger had previously examined.

"I don't give a shit what you've got!" said Mike leaning into the detective's face. "You don't need to come in here unannounced at this time of the evening to the home of a District Judge!"

"Come on, counselor, you know the rules," said the detective. "We never give the subject of a search warrant advanced notice of when we are going to do the search. In fact, we are conducting a search of Judge Moss' chambers at this time."

Digger was startled by the detective's last comment.

"Right now?" he asked.

"Yes, Judge," said the detective, and added, "It's standard procedure."

Digger thought, What might they find at my office? He couldn't think of anything except the envelope, and Mike had that. Maybe they'll find Greg Larson's note explaining the sting operation and my involvement with it. That would be nice, he thought, but he knew it was not there. He had searched every possible place in his chambers for it. It had been stolen and would not turn up again.

"Do you have the application?" Mike demanded as he finished studying the search warrant.

"Yes," the detective answered.

"Well?" Mike held out his hand. The detective looked to his partner, who gave a slight affirmative nod. He handed a two-page document to Reynolds. Mike read it carefully and handed it back.

"Digger, let's go into the kitchen," he said. Judy led them back through the dining room to the kitchen table. She poured three cups of coffee and set two of them on the table for the men. She remained standing, leaning a hip against the kitchen counter near the coffee pot, sipped her coffee and listened.

"Digger, did you read the application?" asked Mike.

"No. What does it say?"

"It's an affidavit, sworn to in front of Judge Parker, that says you lied to the police!"

"What?"

"Someone from the police talked to you, right?"

"That's right," Digger answered. "Jim Pelton and Kathy Winslow stopped to ask me some questions."

"Well, the search warrant application says you lied to them!"

Digger looked sober. Judy came toward the table resting a hand on Digger's shoulder.

"I guess that's right," Digger said.

"What?" Mike and Judy said in unison. Judy said, "It must be some kind of mistake. Isn't that so, Digger?"

"No, I guess not," he answered, taking his wife's hand in his. "They asked me if I had had any telephone conversations with Sergeant Larson and I said no. They must have had records that say otherwise."

"How could that happen, Digger?" Mike pressed him.

"I think they set me up," said Digger. "I got the impression that they didn't know of any phone conversations with Larson, so I went with it. Obviously, I was wrong." He shook his head. Judy squeezed his hand.

"Well, I think the warrant is pretty God damned skinny," said Mike. "If the fact that you lied to the police is probable cause to search your home and chambers, I'd like to have a judge tell me that after a contested omnibus hearing to challenge the constitutional validity of the search warrant. And if a judge does that, I'd like to hear it from some appellate judges, too.

"You're assuming I'll be charged, aren't you?" said Digger. Judy gasped at the realization of what Mike and Digger were saying.

Mike stared into his coffee, shaking his head.

"I can see why Carrie Parker signed it," said Digger.

Mike nodded agreement. "Yep. A high publicity case. The police and the public screaming for answers. Not a good time for one judge to appear to be protecting another."

"Right," agreed Digger. "Better to sign it and leave the police to deal with whether they did a good enough job in the application."

"Will they find anything in your chambers?" asked Mike.

"Nothing I can think of," answered Digger.

"How about here?"

Digger and Judy looked at each other.

"What?" Mike asked.

Just then one of the uniformed officers came into the kitchen. "Sorry, folks," he said. "I drew the duty on this room." He looked apologetically at Judy Moss, as though he felt guilty for invading her domain.

"That's all right, officer," she said. "You go ahead. We'll get out of your way." She motioned for Mike and Digger to move. They did.

They stood outside on the front porch as the police searched through the house, through the Mosses' private belongings. Judy felt violated in a way she had not previously experienced.

"Okay, guys," whispered Mike, "what was that look for just before the cop came in?"

"What look?" asked Judy.

"Come on, Jude. This is friend Mikey, here. Are they going to find something, here?"

Judy looked at Digger.

"The shoes?" he said. "You think they'll find the shoes?"

"The shoes?!" Mike nearly shouted, but caught himself in time for his voice to sound like a horse whisper of a person suffering from laryngitis. He continued to rasp, "Jesus Christ! Are the shoes here?"

"In the attic," Digger whispered.

Judy put a hand on Digger's shoulder. "Digger," she whispered.

"Judge?" It was the plain clothed detective who stood at the open door to the foyer.

"Yes?" said Digger, taking Judy's hand in his and moving toward the door.

"Judge, we've finished with the downstairs. I just wanted you to know that we are going upstairs now, if you care to observe.

"Thanks," said Digger.

CHAPTER FOURTEEN

Frank Griswold sat watching the same television news program in his Holiday Inn suite. Those fuckers! he thought. "Those God damned sons of bitches," he said aloud, taking the remainder of his Scotch in one swallow. He stepped to the bar to freshen his drink, keeping one eye on the television.

The picture showed the red Cadillac compressed like an accordion against the gray cement wall of the parking ramp at the bottom of Second Avenue West, just a block from where Griswold was staying. A crowd of onlookers watched as the Gold Cross Ambulance crew worked, the flashing lights of the ambulance and several police squad cars gave the scene an hallucinatory character.

The too pretty announcer smoothed her yellow blonde hair and said, "Mr. Slater was well known in Duluth and active in civic affairs. He was a long time executive at Whitaker Industries in the PowerPlus Battery Division. Slater leaves surviving him, his wife, two grown sons and their families."

Jesus! He realized that the picture he was seeing wasn't live, but he didn't think he'd ever heard the victim of a fatal car crash identified so quickly. He supposed because Slater was so well known in Duluth, the news would be out anyway.

Griswold took a long drink from his glass, the Scotch whiskey burning his throat, raw from too many cigarettes.

It's time to get out, he thought. The bastards are starting to play real rough. Rougher than he had imagined they ever would. It's those two tough guys he met at the beach, he knew, Fowler and Vagelli. Griswold thought about his current position with the battery people and with Judge Digger Moss. He had Moss where he wanted him. He had the evidence to send the good judge to where he had himself sent so many. And soon the police would have it too. With the boys from PowerPlus Batteries, he knew he would meet a fate similar to Harry Slater's as soon as he became expendable. But, he wasn't expendable yet. They still needed him to deal with Moss. The meeting at the Kitchi Gammi Club was necessary, but they far preferred their communications with the judge to be through a third person. Griswold was that third person.

But as soon as he turned the evidence against Moss over to the police, would that make him expendable? If the cops have Digger Moss for murder, he's not going to be deciding any civil case he has under advisement. The Whitaker boys will be running for cover, hoping Moss doesn't say anything about their blackmailing him to get the PowerPlus decision made in the company's favor.

Griswold moved to the window overlooking Superior Street, drink in hand. He looked to his left, seeing the corner of Second Avenue West and Superior Street. Just a block below that, Harry Slater's Cadillac had squashed itself against an unforgiving concrete wall after a high speed run down Duluth's very steep downtown hillside. No, Griswold wasn't going to stick around for that to happen to him, he decided.

He finished his Scotch and got out his materials on Judge Moss. He had previously figured how he would get the information to the police. It was time. When he was done, he would pack his bags and get the hell out of Dodge, Duluth, actually.

Griswold knew that some of the materials would not be admissible evidence, but it would convince the cops, and the public, of Moss's guilt of both drug dealing and murder. After they had that, they would concentrate on Moss alone. They would have enough circumstantial evidence to convict him.

Photographs and documents were placed in two large, thick, manila file folder envelopes. They were closed with a large flap over the side and an elastic cord that wrapped around to keep them closed. Each of these he placed in even larger manila envelopes and sealed their gummed flaps. On the outside he affixed a computer processed printed label addressed to, "Duluth Police Department, Attention: Chief Morgan."

Frank Griswold poured himself another Scotch and surveyed his work. He smiled, sipped his drink, and lit a cigarette. He had waited a long time for what he was now about to do.

Back at the Moss home, the search continued. Judy, Digger, and Mike watched as the officers carefully searched the bedrooms and bathrooms on the upstairs levels of the home. Because of its size and the many bedrooms, closets, playrooms and other storage rooms, the search was a lengthy process. On the third floor, where the last of the Mosses' children had lived during college, in what amounted to an apartment, Judy watched in distress as the officers disturbed their daughter's personal belongings left there when she graduated and moved away. Judy had chosen not to change these rooms when Margaret had moved, keeping some memory of when she and the other kids inhabited the house, giving it a vitality and energy it had not had since they all left. Only at holidays, with adult children and spouses, and little grandchildren all over the house did their home take on that quality it had for so many years. Judy enjoyed those times as she had enjoyed the original. While she missed those times, she also liked the peace and quiet of their home with just her and Digger. But, she did not like seeing these men opening drawers and pawing their contents where her daughter had lived not so long ago.

One of the plain clothed detectives opened a dark stained oak door in the hall. He stared up yet another stairway, this one enclosed on both sides, the steps uncarpeted and unfinished wood.

"What's this, Judge?" he asked. "Another story?"

"That's the attic," answered Digger. "Nothing up there that we need very often, just old stuff we stored, holiday decorations and things like that."

The detective looked at his partner. The uniformed officers waited.

The partner said, "We better look." He motioned to the two uniformed officers and nodded toward the stairway beyond the open door. "We're almost done, boys. This will only take a minute." The uniforms disappeared up the stairs, the plain clothed detectives following behind.

Digger could feel himself sweating, although the temperature on the third floor was quite cool.

Delivery of the envelopes to the police had to be carefully done. Griswold had given it a lot of thought while he had been in Duluth. Rejecting several possibilities, he had decided that the best and simplest way to accomplish the delivery was to leave the envelopes in a commercial establishment where they would be found and then brought to the attention of the police department. He had chosen a downtown restaurant away from his hotel and the restaurants he had frequented during his stay.

For his evening meal, he enjoyed an order of shrimp scampi and a bottle of Chardonnay at the Top of the Harbor restaurant on the revolving top floor of the Radisson, a few blocks west of the Holiday Inn and just down the hill from the courthouse. The restaurant was on the top floor of the cylindrical shaped hotel. The curving outer walls were of tinted glass, giving diners a panoramic view in all directions. As the dining floor revolved around the stationary center core which included the elevators, bathrooms and hostess station, patrons enjoyed a magnificent view of Lake Superior, the Duluth Harbor, the upper reaches of the St. Louis River, the Duluth hillside and the Duluth Civic Center. The full revolution of the restaurant took a little over an hour.

Griswold smiled as his view turned away from the harbor to look at the civic center just up the hill. Lit by street lights and small white decorative lights on the trees on Fifth Avenue West, he could clearly see the centerpiece, the St. Louis County Courthouse where Judge James Digby Moss worked. Up 'til now, that is, he thought. He smiled at the thought and forked another garlic-laden shrimp into his mouth.

When he had entered the restaurant, stepping off the elevators, he had the envelopes concealed beneath his jacket. He went into the open cloakroom next to the elevators, leaving his jacket on a hanger as far from the entrance as he could, and the envelopes on the shelf, close to the entrance and in easy view. When he was seated for dinner, his part of the delivery had already been accomplished. Now he had just to wait.

The courthouse was impressive from the view he had from the top of the Radisson. Trees, grass and brick walkways formed a park in front of it, framed by the Federal Building on the left and City Hall on the right and the County Courthouse in the center. Impressive, indeed, thought Griswold. I wonder what commotion my little envelopes will cause in that building before long?

After assuring herself that he was finished, his waitress cleared his dishes and soon returned to thank him and leave the check.

Eventually the turning restaurant brought him back near the Maitre d'hotel station, where, as luck would have it, he saw the hostess and a waiter looking at the envelopes and engaging in a lively discussion. They disappeared around the corner, apparently in search of someone with more authority than they wished to exercise. Griswold rose and approached the station to pay his bill.

"**O**kay, we're done," said the plain clothed detective in charge. "Come on boys, it's getting late." He turned to Digger and Judy, still standing in the third floor hallway at the entrance to the attic. "Sorry to cause you so much trouble, folks. You know how it is."

"Well," Mike grumbled, "what did you find?"

The detective looked at Mike. "You know that we have to report to headquarters and file an inventory of the results of the search, counselor, so I can't really tell you anything ....," he paused, "but you don't see us carrying much, do you?" he added, and started down the stairs.

Digger had watched them leave, hardly able to breathe. Finally, as the squad cars pulled away, he sighed with relief.

"Well, I don't think they found anything," said Mike. "I thought you were worried about the shoes."

Digger replied, still trying to catch his breath. "I was. I can't believe they missed them, up in the attic, in with the Christmas decorations!"

"Digger?" Judy nudged her husband.

"Yes, dear?"

"I moved them."

"What? Where?" asked an incredulous Digger Moss.

"I told you they made me nervous, sitting up there in our attic while the TV newscasters kept talking about 'the bloody shoe print.' So, I moved them. I put them in the trunk of my car, down under the spare tire."

"Oh, God!" sighed Mike. "I know I shouldn't be hearing this. And I am sure they are going to be searching your cars."

"Why didn't they?" Digger asked.

"Beats me, Digger. Remember, the search warrant did not say anything about searching vehicles. Maybe it was an oversight. Maybe the cops thought if they did it would be bad because they are not mentioned in the warrant."

"You think?"

"I'd sure be challenging it later, if I were the lawyer for the defense."

"You are," said Digger. Judy was startled by his remark.

"Hold on, Digger," said Mike. "There's no defense needed, yet."

Griswold laid out his suitcases on the bed in the bedroom, opened the clothes closet, and began to pack. Soon the police would have his deliveries. Not long after that the police would either arrest Judge Moss or at least the public would know of his involvement in the crimes. It was time for Frank Griswold to leave Duluth.

Our boy is gettin' ready to leave, Milo," said Vince Turcotte, his eyes glued to the small screen. Milo sat up in the captain's chair in the front of the van and looked.

"Shit! He's outa here!" he shouted. "Let's get ready to roll!"

"What about the equipment?"

"Leave it! Someday, if we get a chance, we'll come back for the cameras and transmitters. Maybe it won't be worth it."

Milo Bracken shifted into the driver's seat, started the van and headed for their motel. They would have just enough time to throw their stuff in the truck and get back to catch Griswold as he left the Holiday Inn. They knew where his car was in the hotel parking ramp. Griswold had never seen their van, so he thought they could follow him without too much trouble.

"Better stand on it, Milo," said Vince, who settled into the front passenger seat after securing their equipment in the van while it was already moving. "We don't get back before he pulls out of the ramp, we're fucked."

"I know, I know," agreed Milo, his hands clenched on the steering wheel.

"How's our gas?"

"Up to the top as always," Milo answered. "I knew we'd be hit with a move on short notice."

A short twenty minutes later, the van was back, parked in the Holiday Ramp on the fourth level, in sight of Griswold's white sedan.

"Here he comes!" exclaimed Vince, staring out the passenger window of the van.

Milo watched Frank Griswold struggling with his travel bag hanging from a shoulder strap on one shoulder, a smaller duffel strapped over the other shoulder, and the two money bags. He held one large nylon duffel bag in each hand.

"And there's the money," Milo whispered. Vince nodded silently, eyeing the two bags Griswold carried.

Griswold reached his car and fumbled with the key in the trunk lock. Finally, the trunk opened and he dropped his bags into the large trunk. Milo and Vince watched as he carefully placed the two duffel bags on the floor of the trunk and laid the other two bags over the top of them.

"What's he doin' that for?" asked Vince shaking his head. "Does he think if somebody is looking they won't find the money under his suitcase?"

"Beats me," Milo responded. "If I had three mil in my trunk, I might cover it up, too."

"Where's he going?" said Vince with some alarm, straightening in his seat, where he had been slouching, thinking it made him less obvious.

Griswold had closed the trunk and was walking away from the car, back toward the elevators.

"I dunno," said Milo. "Maybe he hasn't checked out yet. But don't worry, Vince."

"What?"

"Don't worry, he'll be back," said Milo, lighting a Pall Mall, blowing a cloud of smoke across the van, "and he won't be gone long."

"Yeah?"

"Yeah. Remember the money. It's right over there." Milo nodded toward Griswold's white sedan.

"Unless he put those big duffels in there as a decoy," said Vince, staring at the sedan.

"Jesus!" Milo threw his cigarette out the window. "Thank you for sharing that possibility with me."

"Never mind, here he comes." Vince pointed toward the figure of Griswold, hurrying along the row of parked cars towards the white sedan.

In a moment, Griswold was steering his car around through the driving lanes of the parking ramp, descending to the exit level, with Milo and Vince slowly following. They knew that at the ramp exit, Griswold had to turn left onto First Street, which is a westbound one-way street. Once they also paid and exited the ramp, Milo figured it would be easy to catch sight of Griswold before he turned off First Street.

In fact, Milo assumed Griswold was heading for Minneapolis and he would take First to Fifth Avenue West, right in front of the courthouse, turn left and proceed down the hill to I-35 and head west out of town. That's exactly what Griswold did. A few minutes found Milo and Vince a comfortable distance behind Griswold's car as both vehicles climbed up Thompson Hill and began the two-hour trip to the northern suburbs of the Twin Cities.

Chief John Morgan stared across his massive desk at the two senior detectives seated in his office. Two large manila envelopes and their contents were spread out in front of him. Assistant Chief Jim Pelton stood in the corner listening to the conversation.

Chief Morgan's secretary, Lizabeth Wilson sat beside the desk taking notes in old-fashioned shorthand. Like her boss, she was African-American. Like her boss, she, too, was an imposing figure. There, any similarities ended. Liz Wilson was tall, but slender. A beautiful woman with long flowing black hair, she stood five feet eleven inches without shoes. She had the thin athletic build of a long distance runner, which she was. She was the only local woman to finish in the top fifteen women finalists in **Grandma's Marathon**, run from **Two Harbors** down the North shore to **Duluth** each June. She had done that the last three years.

Sitting on a hard chair next to Chief Morgan's desk, her long muscular but slender legs crossed, steno pad on her lap, pen poised, she listened for the next comment from her boss. Inevitably, it came.

"Just exactly what the fuck is going on here?" he boomed. "Pardon my French, Liz," he muttered toward the lady without whom he was convinced he could not begin to do his job right. Her large dark eyes turned toward him and a nearly imperceptible smile crossed her full lips.

His apology accepted, he turned to the detectives. "You say somebody just left this stuff at the Radisson?"

"That's right, Chief," said a detective, "on a shelf in the coatroom at the Top of the Harbor, addressed to us."

Morgan shook his head in wonder. "Somebody's sure got a hard-on for Digger." He looked at Pelton in the corner, raised his eyebrows, and asked, "I wonder why?"

Pelton shook his head and had no answer for the Chief. Instead Pelton turned to the detectives. "Has forensics gone over the envelopes?"

"Thoroughly," said one of the detectives. "Of course there were a lot of prints from handling by the people at the restaurant and even our own people before anyone realized a need for a forensics exam. Initially, there was more concern about whether the envelopes presented any danger."

"Like a bomb?" asked Pelton.

"Or something," answered the detective. Liz Wilson made a notation on her pad.

"So what did forensics turn up?" asked Morgan, clearly becoming impatient, not with the detectives, they knew, but with the strange circumstances. People did not send incriminating evidence to the police department like this.

"Not much, Chief. The envelopes and the paper are standard stuff you can buy anywhere. They didn't find any finger prints that weren't identified as friendlies. They're all from hotel or department employees."

"Whoever sent us this stuff was careful," said Pelton.

"Careful," repeated Morgan. "That's for sure, but why?" He propped his elbows on the desk in front of him and folded his big hands together. "That's what bothers me. Why? And what does that say about the quality or truth of the evidence, what we're looking at here?" He gestured at the papers and photographs in front of him.

"I know how you feel, Chief," said Detective Joe Walters. "Nate and I felt the same way." He nodded toward his partner, Lieutenant Nathaniel Jackson. "But look at the stuff. I don't care how we got it, how can the judge explain this?" He picked up a blowup photo of Digger Moss engaged in what appeared clearly to be an exchange of money for drugs. He held it up along with a photo of Moss and Sergeant Larson talking in a downtown parking ramp, and two time-stamped photos of Digger entering and leaving the Larson duplex. The time stamps showed the date of Larson's murder and times consistent with the coroner's determination of the time of death.

"The more you look at this stuff, Chief," added Nate Jackson, "the more you become convinced that that son of a bitch," he pointed to one of the pictures of Digger, "killed Greg Larson! Why, I don't know, but I sure intend to find out."

"Sure don't seem to be in any hurry, does he?" Vince pulled a cold beer from a cooler behind the front seats of the van, popped the tab, and took a long pull of the cool liquid as he watched Griswold's white car traveling several cars ahead of them at exactly the speed limit.

"If you had three million in the trunk, would you want to be picked up for any traffic charge?" asked Milo.

"No, I guess I sure wouldn't," Vince agreed.

"On your toes!" said Milo, suddenly. "He's taken the off ramp to Hinckley. Must be time for a pit stop."

"I got him," said Vince, leaning forward staring out the windshield.

They watched Griswold heading up the ramp toward the state highway crossing over the freeway. By the time they turned the van off the road and began the climb up the ramp, they saw Griswold turning left to cross over the freeway. Following him, they watched him pull into the Holiday Gas Station and park next to the building.

145

"I guess he doesn't need gas," said Milo, as they drove past the station and stopped the van in the Hardee's parking lot. Milo turned off the ignition and left the key. "You keep watch for him. I'm going to take a leak and get some food. Want something?"

"Yeah, a roast beef and some fries," answered Vince, watching out the passenger window, his eyes fixed on the white sedan parked next to the Holiday. "Hurry up," he added.

A few minutes later, Vince saw Griswold come out of the Holiday station carrying a paper bag. Instead of walking to his car, he started walking toward the van!

"Holy shit!" Vince said to himself, slumping down in his seat. Nervous, he watched as Griswold headed directly toward the van. As he approached, he clutched the paper bag tightly. Vince brought out his revolver, prepared for whatever might happen. Griswold walked right on past the van without looking at Vince and stepped into the Hardee's Restaurant.

Vince Turcotte took the first breath he had taken since Griswold left the Holiday Station. That was close! He thought. Then it occurred to him. Griswold knew Milo. Milo was in Hardee's. Griswold had just gone in there! Vince jumped out of the van and opened the door to Hardee's. He stood between the two glass doors that formed a foyered entrance to the restaurant. He could see Griswold standing in line to order. Where was Milo? Griswold looked at him, curiously, then turned to study the menus on the board above the cash registers on the ordering counter.

From his right, Vince saw Milo coming from the restroom, about to turn the corner to go order food. He would run right into Griswold!

Vince pulled open the inner door and stepped directly in front of Milo, almost colliding with him.

"What the hell?"

"Shut up, Milo!" Vince hissed at him, pushing backward. He pointed toward the ordering counter, hidden by the wall against which he had pushed Milo. "Griswold!" he whispered.

"What?" gasped Milo.

"You gotta get outa here!" whispered Vince.

Keeping his back to the counter, Milo quickly left the building and got to the van, where he hid in the back behind the front seats. Vince stayed in Hardee's, taking a seat in the front until Griswold left with his order. Then Vince ordered some sandwiches for himself and Milo and hurried back to the van.

"Shit! That was too close!" said Milo, climbing into the driver's seat.

"Did he see you?" asked Vince.

"Nope. I was in the back when he walked by. I can't say he didn't see me in Hardee's, except he didn't look like I expect he would if he had recognized me. I think we're okay."

Milo eased the van out of the parking lot as he saw Griswold's sedan leave the Holiday lot and head over the overpass to the ramp back onto the freeway.

J udy Moss answered the ring of the front door chimes. She looked through the small glass window in the thick oak door which allowed a view of the front porch. Her heart sank. She saw a marked Duluth P.D. squad car parked on the street at the end of their front walk. Two plain clothed and two uniformed police officers stood outside the door.

"Mrs. Moss?" asked one of the plain clothed detectives as she opened the main door.

"Yes?"

"Is the judge at home?"

CHAPTER FIFTEEN

The jailer escorted Digger toward the small consultation room. Behind a glass window, a uniformed deputy nodded to the jailer as she depressed a switch to unlock the secure door. Digger wore the orange jail uniform that was worn by new prisoners or those who were classified as high security risks. Other prisoners wore dark blue uniforms. As the door lock emitted an audible buzz, the jailer reached for the handle. Seated at the table in the center of the small room were Digger's wife and his lawyer. The jailer left them alone in the room and closed the door behind them. The room had another door which opened into the reception area of the St. Louis County Jail. It was also locked and controlled electronically by the deputy at the control panel within the glass enclosure.

"Digger!" Judy had been obviously startled to see her husband in the orange jail jumpsuit. Now she ran to embrace him. "Oh, Digger!"

The emotion Digger Moss felt at that moment almost overcame him. "I'm sorry." His whisper was nearly a sob. "I never should have hoped we could get out of this!"

"Digger! You stop that!" Judy Moss was recovering quickly. She would not accept defeat in her husband. She would support his standing tall, even if he didn't want to. "This is not your fault ... and we will work this out!"

"Digger, we do have to talk," said Mike Reynolds, still seated at the table. "You'll be having your first appearance in court tomorrow or the next day. They will set bail and give you a date for an omnibus hearing. Every time you go to court will be a media circus, you know that." He pulled a yellow legal pad from his briefcase. "We have to discuss how we are going to handle these things."

Digger sighed and nodded, taking a chair across from Reynolds and staring down at the Formica surface. Judy sat down next to him.

"We also," Mike lowered his voice, although he knew and believed that the consulting room was private and they could not be heard, "have to figure out what we're going to do next to deal with these assholes and get the information to clear you."

Digger raised his head and looked directly into Reynolds' deep blue eyes. "You'll do nothing," he said. "It's over. We lost."

"Wrong!" Judy announced. "We aren't giving up yet, Digger, and don't you try to tell us to."

"She's right Digger," agreed Mike. "We can't give up. Remember, Judge Riley and I agreed that the evidence against you was overwhelming. If you want to get out of this mess, you can't rely on your innocence and the criminal justice system to do it. You have to come up with affirmative evidence to clear you of the charges."

"I don't like it," said Digger. "It's dangerous and you will get hurt. And," he stared into Mike's eyes again, "if you put my wife in danger, or get her hurt, I'll personally see that you regret it for the rest of your life!" His tone left no doubt that he was very serious.

"Digger!" Judy nearly screamed in his ear. "You take that back! Mike is your friend and he is only trying to help you! Goddamit, Digger, if you don't straighten around, *I'll* make *you* regret it, you can be sure of that!"

Slowly, Digger began to smile. "Okay, Jude," he said. "I'll try to avoid being despondent by realizing the reality of the situation, but I don't want you, or Mike, or Kate Riley taking chances on my account."

"Don't worry about us, my lover," she said, putting an arm around his shoulders. "You just work on keeping a good attitude. We need you to stay strong. Be the Digger Moss we're used to."

As they got down to discussing the criminal charge, Mike Reynolds made notes on his legal pad. The charge was Murder in the Second Degree. They knew the State would convene a Grand Jury to request an Indictment for Murder in the First Degree. Mike was right. It would be a media circus.

As Mike Reynolds drove his car out of the parking lot of the St. Louis County Jail and turned south on Haines Road, Judy Moss watched him from the passenger seat.

"What are we going to do, Mike? We have to meet with Katy, don't we?"

Mike Reynolds stared at the road ahead. He brought the car to a stop for a red light at Arrowhead Road. Instead of turning left to take

Judy back to her east end home, he drove straight ahead, saying, "Let's go see the judge right now. You're right Judy. We have to take some action and keep Digger thinking positive. Otherwise, everything may be lost."

"I know," she sighed.

"**H**e says what?" asked Kate Riley, when they met in her chambers. "Jesus Christ! Digger can't give up or he's just plain fucked!"

"It gets worse, Judge," said Mike. "They found Digger's shoes."

"What?"

"Digger's tennis shoes. The ones he was wearing the night he went to Greg Larson's duplex. They got another search warrant."

"Oh, God, the bloody ones?" She looked at Judy, who nodded, concern and even fear apparent on Judy's face.

"That's them," Mike answered, "but apparently they can't find any blood on them."

Kate turned from Judy to look directly at Reynolds. "Not even for DNA testing?"

"They say not."

"Well that's something," she said. "DNA would have shown Larson's blood and that would have pretty much ended it. Digger would have been truly fucked for sure."

"We have to do something, Katy." Judy's statement was more of a plea than a comment.

"I know, Judy," answered Kate, "and we damn well will." They both looked at Mike.

Mike responded to their inquiring looks. "The problem remains the same," he said. "We still have to get some proof that Digger was set up and that he was being blackmailed into throwing a civil decision. Nothing short of that will clear him."

"Well we have tried twice with Digger and both times the result was disaster or near disaster," said Kate.

"That's right," agreed Mike. "Now we have to take an entirely different approach."

"Like what?" asked Judy.

"Like we hire some outside help," said Mike.

They both looked at him in surprise.

After the near disaster at Hardee's in Hinckley, following Frank Griswold into the Twin Cities had gone relatively smoothly. Once in the heavier traffic of the metro area, they had nearly lost him, but between Milo and Vince, they had managed to keep him in sight most of the time and had ultimately followed him to his destination at an apartment building just off Rice Street in St. Paul. Just north of Highway 36, the apartment complex was actually in Roseville, one of St. Paul's northern suburbs.

From a distance, they watched Griswold unload his bags and enter the building. The faint beep of the sedan's horn indicated Griswold had used a key chain remote to lock the car as he walked away toward the building.

"Hear that, Milo?" asked Vince. "He ain't comin' back."

Milo agreed. After waiting only a few seconds after Griswold disappeared into the building, he pulled the van into the lot and up to the door. Vince got out and checked the entryway. The outside door opened without a key. Inside, there was a small foyer between the outer door and an inner locked door. On one wall of the foyer, was a register with the names and apartment numbers of the tenants. An intercom phone hung alongside, so visitors could contact residents of the secure building. Residents could release the inner door lock from their apartments after identifying the visitor over the intercom phone. Vince studied the names and returned to the van.

"Well?" asked Milo as Vince climbed into the van and Milo steered it out of the lot.

"He's not hidin' anything," Vince answered. "Right there on the wall it says, 'Apartment 417: Mr. Frank Griswold,' in big letters, plain as day."

They were silent, both men thinking about the situation and about the money, as Milo drove a short block to Rice Street and turned north. Two blocks later he pulled into the parking lot of the Hoggsbreath Saloon.

Inside the Hoggsbreath Saloon, they ordered draft beers and ate salty popcorn, compliments of the house. Patrons threw darts at electronic dart boards in the dimly lit lower level of the saloon.

Vince filled his mouth with popcorn, chewed slightly, washed it down with a long swallow of beer, and spoke. "He's got the money with him."

"We know that," replied Milo.

"How long will he keep it in the apartment?"

"We don't know that." Milo lit a cigarette and blew smoke across the booth. Lifting the heavy glass to his lips, he said, "That's what we have to find out," and he drank.

"How we gonna do that?"

Milo looked at Vince. "Surveillance, Vince, surveillance."

"Again?"

"Again."

"But what if he takes the money to the bank, or something?" Vince asked. "If we're watching him do it, won't it be too late for us?"

"Maybe," said Milo, "but it's a risk we have to take. We want the money, but we don't want to get caught, by Griswold or anyone else. Besides, I don't think he's just going to show up at a local bank and deposit three million dollars."

"I suppose not," agreed Vince. "Okay, when do we set up the equipment?"

"We'll have to wait until he leaves," Milo answered. "Any problem getting inside?"

Vince had seen the foyer and the security. "I don't think so. I think I could have us in there almost as fast as if we had Griswold's own key." He smiled and raised his beer.

"That's my boy, Vince." Milo raised his beer and their glasses clicked. "Now, what we have to do, is get set up for round the clock. Let's run you home to get a car. You can get what you need and then spell me so I can do the same. I think he will sleep in his own bed tonight. Why don't we go back and watch until after midnight and take care of things after that."

They finished their beers and within a few minutes, they were parked near the apartment complex watching the door and Griswold's white sedan.

Shortly after eight o'clock that evening. Frank Griswold went out. He did not carry the duffel bags with him. Vince and Milo thought about breaking into his apartment to steal the money right then, but decided there were too many unknowns and too many risks. So, they followed Griswold at a discreet distance. They were right not to take the risk of breaking in. With two quick stops in a nearby strip mall at a grocery store and a liquor store, Griswold was back entering his building within thirty minutes.

After midnight, his surveillance team set about making their own arrangements. Milo drove the van over to Minneapolis where he dropped Vince off at his own place. He returned directly to continue their stakeout of the apartment building in Roseville. Later Vince spelled Milo in the van while Milo went home to get a change of clothes and some supplies so they could keep steady watch on the apartment in relative comfort.

It was 2:30 a.m. when Milo returned. He loaded his things into the back of the van and then climbed in beside Vince with a large thermos of hot coffee. He handed Vince a copy of the Minneapolis Star Tribune and, as he poured them both some of the steaming coffee, said, "Take a look at that!"

Vince unfolded the newspaper against the steering wheel and looked at the big headline.

Duluth Judge Arrested!
For Murder!

"Oh, Holy shit!" exclaimed Vince.

"Yeah," said Milo handing him a mug of the coffee. "It gets worse."

"Worse? How could it get worse?"

"Read on, boy." Milo pointed to the news story. "Read about the evidence they got on him."

They sat in silence as they sipped the strong, hot coffee and Vince read the story. Milo stared out the window at Griswold's white car and the apartment entryway. He was deeply troubled by the story, although it really didn't affect him. Especially now that he wasn't even in Duluth.

"Jesus Christ! They've got pictures of the judge coming and going from the dead cop's house before and after he was killed!"

"See what I mean?"

"See what you mean? See what you mean?" Vince repeated. "Look, Milo, I kind of felt sorry for the judge, felt he was bein' framed, but," he nodded at the news story, "he fucking killed the cop!"

"I don't think so."

"What about all this?" Vince held up the Tribune.

"My bet is that's compliments of our friend in there." He motioned toward the apartment building.

"No shit? But how'd he do it?"

Milo started his explanation, thinking out loud as he went. "We know Griswold has been watching Judge Moss and every move he's made for quite awhile. Hell, at the courthouse, we were Griswold's eyes and ears."

Vince nodded.

"So, I think Griswold was there when the judge went to the cop's house. You notice the cops are pretty mysterious about how they came by those photographs. You got to figure an anonymous informant. Otherwise, they would have had them a long time ago."

"Yeah?"

Milo had been trying to pull something from the back of his mind and now he had it. "Remember those big envelopes Griswold was fussing with the night before he left? Right before he went out to dinner?"

"Yeah, he took them to the car when he left for dinner."

"I'll bet anything they were full of pictures and stuff and left somewhere for the police to find. Hell, that's probably why he left when he did. That's probably why he demanded the big money with half down in advance."

"Did you read this whole story, Milo? They found the judge's shoes hidden in the trunk of his wife's car. The shoes matched a fucking bloody footprint near the dead cop's body for Christ's sake!"

"I know, I read that," said Milo, grinding out a cigarette but into the overflowing ashtray and lighting another, "but I still think the judge is innocent and has been completely framed by our friend Griswold. I don't have a doubt that Judge Moss went to the cop's house. The pictures prove that. He probably had some kind of a meeting or appointment with him. Hell, he probably even found the body. That would explain the shoes. If he did, he sure as hell had to hide it. Remember, the cop was killed *after* Griswold sent his first envelope to the judge with the stuff on the drug dealings that Moss thought he was doing undercover for the cop."

"That's right," said Vince, remembering their early surveillance of the judge's chambers. That seems a long time ago, he thought. Then he remembered something else. "Even after the cop was killed, Griswold sent another threatening envelope to the judge, and it had to do with the cop killing, remember?"

"Exactly right," Milo nodded. "If I had to bet, I'd say our buddy Frank, here, offed the cop before the judge got there and took his picture coming and going. Then he threatened the judge with turning him in, but I don't think he told the judge about these pictures."

"That prick." Vince stared toward the apartment building trying to stare through the brick walls into Frank Griswold's residence. "What a fuckin' double-crosser. He threatened Judge Moss. He blackmailed him. But it looks like he was going to get him all along."

"Yeah," agreed Milo. "I wonder why."

"That double crossing son of a bitch!" Frank Vagelli nearly shouted at the rest of the men in the Whitaker Industries boardroom. They were all there. Reduced in number by the tragic death of Harry Slater in his Cadillac at the bottom of Second Avenue West, eight men sat around the big conference table. Orrin Rasmussen's flowing hair was still as white as fresh fallen snow, but his usual tan complexion looked gray and pallid. Bertram Johnson simply looked frightened. Fowler and Vagelli believed that, although nothing had been said about the real cause of his "accident," the message which could be drawn from the death of Slater was not lost on Johnson.

Each of them looked visibly upset. Fred McCloskey and Charles Hood sat slumped in their chairs at the foot of the table. Randall McCoy had surrendered his usual place at the head of the table to Hollis Fowler, who sat there, conducting the meeting, with Frank

Vagelli at his side, hovering like some kind of attack dog, waiting to be unleashed.

"We should have taken him out when I said," continued Vagelli, straining at his invisible leash.

"Frank's at least partly right," said Hollis Fowler to the others, who seemed too shocked to participate in the conversation. "We do have to do something about Griswold. Maybe we should have taken care of him earlier as Frank suggests, but there were reasons to do what we did before. Now we need to remove him, and right away."

Vagelli sat back in his seat, comfortable with Fowler's backing.

Finally, the other men began to speak.

"Why now?" asked McCloskey. "Even if we may have had to do something before, that's changed, hasn't it? Getting rid of those who knew of our actions was one thing, but now, since the judge is arrested, the whole thing is over. What's the point in doing anything more, now?"

Hood and Rasmussen nodded their agreement. McCoy sat in silence. Bert Johnson cowered in his seat, saying nothing, and giving no sign of joining the other men in questioning Fowler and Vagelli.

Hollis Fowler stood slowly, resting his hands on the edge of the table. He spoke in a low measured voice, directly at Fred McCloskey.

"It is not over, Fred," he said. "Even with Judge Moss under arrest, our case has to be decided by someone. It will be reassigned. We will have another judge to influence."

"Do it all again?" asked Orrin Rasmussen, the color draining even further from his face. "We can't go through this again ...," he looked around the table, "... can we?"

No one answered, at first. Then Fred McCloskey spoke again. "Orrin's right," he agreed. "We can't do it again."

"I don't think you two remember how much is involved, here," said Fowler, in the same carefully measured voice. "Remember, if the amounts to be realized by each of us from the simple signature of a judge on a relatively insignificant appearing order was enough to undertake to influence the judge before whom the case was pending, it's still a good enough reason. Nothing's changed."

"Besides," said Randall McCoy, entering the discussion for the first time, "Griswold can't be trusted. He knows too much about us."

He leaned forward, pressing against the table edge, looking back and forth at the other men. "He's got to be eliminated."

Vagelli nodded vigorously.

"But Judge Moss will talk!" exclaimed McCloskey. "What about that? We can't go through this again because he will tell what we did and everyone will know what we are doing."

"Fred," said Fowler, in a conciliatory tone, "the judge won't say anything. He hasn't until now. He's still trying to deal with the charges against him. If he tries to tell a story about us, it will hurt his case. No one will believe him. If he is convicted, no one will believe him and it will not do him any good."

"That's right," said McCoy. "And the dangers of his talking are the same whether we go after a new judge or not."

"We were talking about the bastard, Griswold," said Vagelli.

"Do we even know where to find him?" asked Charles Hood. "You said he's gone from the Holiday Inn."

"We'll find him, all right," growled Vagelli. "He's got more balls than brains. He's somewhere in the Cities, I bet you your founder's interest." His twisted smile showed the contempt he felt for the other men.

Fowler, still standing at the head of the table interrupted, defusing a possible situation he did not want. "Frank's right," he said. "Griswold has not shown the height of wisdom in his actions, so far. We will find him without difficulty, I am sure."

"Good!" said Randall McCoy. "Get him ... and get our money back."

"*You* gonna do it?" muttered Vagelli.

McCoy retreated into his chair, away from the table's edge.

"Easy, gentlemen," said Fowler, maintaining the role of peacemaker and mediator and rapidly gaining the position as clear and sole leader. He was using Vagelli's volatile temper to his own advantage. "Frank and I will take care of Griswold. We will find him and we will take care of him. He will not be a problem or a risk any further. You will be protected. And for that, you will pay us a fee."

"What?" asked McCloskey. "What do you mean, a fee?"

"Well actually, it is a kind of contingent fee," said Hollis Fowler.

"What do you mean?" This time it was Orrin Rasmussen who spoke.

Dave Sullivan

"I mean," replied Fowler, "that when we find Griswold, and take care of him, if he still has the money, Mr. Vagelli and I will split it, as compensation for services rendered."

No one said anything. Vagelli smiled his twisted smile.

CHAPTER SIXTEEN

"All rise!" commanded the booming voice of the bailiff. "District court is now in session, the Honorable Andrew L. Forsythe presiding."

Judge Forsythe ascended the steps to the bench as the bailiff opened court. As the announcement concluded with the judge's name, Forsythe tapped the gavel on its clapper and said, "Please be seated."

It was Digger's first appearance, referred to by some as his arraignment, or, because he was charged with a felony, his Rule 5 hearing. At a first appearance on a felony or gross misdemeanor, the court would do three things. First, the judge would establish that the defendant understood his rights and that he had read the complaint. Next, it would be determined if a public defender would be appointed, if one was requested. And third, the Court would set the date of the next hearing, which was the omnibus hearing.

Ordinarily a Rule 5 hearing would be with the morning "grist," or morning arraignments, that occurred every weekday morning from 9:00 to Noon. Digger's hearing had been scheduled for a special time. Even though it was short and followed this specific routine, no local judge would preside at that hearing. It had to be given a special time for a judge from outside the district to hear it.

Chief Judge Parker even declined to make the assignment, requesting that the Supreme Court assign a judge to hear the case against Digger Moss. Judge Andrew Forsythe, from the Hennepin County District Bench was selected. Digger knew him to be a well-respected judge noted for his fairness, but also noted for his law and order attitude towards criminal defendants, once their guilt was established.

The courtroom was crowded with media and other observers.

Given the privilege of wearing civilian clothes instead of the usual jail uniform, and given the advantage of entering the courtroom from the hallway behind before the courtroom was opened to the public, Digger Moss sat next to Mike Reynolds at one of the two counsel tables.

"State of Minnesota vs. James Digby Moss," announced Judge Forsythe as he called the case. He looked out over the courtroom, focused on Digger and Reynolds and said, "The record should reflect that the defendant is present in court and with his counsel Mr. Michael Reynolds." The judge opened a file folder in front of him on the bench and studied it a moment.

"Mr. Reynolds, the Court's file has a 'Felony-Gross Misdemeanor Acknowledgment of Rights' form signed by the defendant. While some may think it goes without saying in this particular case, I do want to establish for the record that Judge Moss understands his rights. You have talked to him about this case?"

Mike Reynolds rose and addressed the Court. "I have, your Honor."

"And do you believe you have had ample opportunity to talk with him in preparation for this hearing and are you ready to proceed?"

"We are ready to proceed, your Honor."

"Are you satisfied that the defendant understands his rights?"

"I am."

"Has he read the Complaint?"

"He has, Judge, and we will waive a formal reading at this time," said Reynolds.

"Thank you." Judge Forsythe paused for a moment. "And that brings us to conditions of release."

"Your Honor!" The voice came from the other counsel table. The speaker, at that moment rising to address the Court regarding bail, was a tall, very thin, hawk-nosed gentleman with narrow dark eyes beneath nearly non-existent eyebrows and thinning dark hair combed straight back from his forehead.

"Mr. Wilkins?"

When the case was charged out, the St. Louis County Attorney had declined to prosecute a local judge and had requested prosecution by the State Attorney General's office.

The A.G. sent H. Gordon Wilkins, an experienced, ambitious criminal lawyer whom everyone thought wanted to be the Attorney General someday, or U. S. Attorney, or even Governor.

Seated on the bench behind the prosecution table sat Marilee Jackson of the St. Louis County Attorney's office. While the County Attorney had declined to prosecute, he had, however, assigned

Marilee to monitor the case. So, she was present at hearings, but not assisting the prosecution.

"Your Honor," Wilkins continued, "the State requests that defendant be held without bail or if bail will be set that it be in the amount of Three Million Dollars."

A murmur was heard from the onlookers. The bailiff stood. The judge lifted the gavel and stared out over the audience.

Digger sat without reaction to the request for bail. Mike Reynolds remained silent. They had discussed that bail would be high enough that Digger would not get a pre-trial release without giving up nearly everything he and Judy owned. Resigned to the possibility that he might be convicted, Digger had decided he would sit in jail rather than jeopardize Judy's future.

"Well, Mr. Wilkins," responded Judge Forsythe after some thought, "as to your request that the defendant be held without bail, the Court believes the federal and state constitutions require that reasonable bail be set. Mr. Reynolds, do you wish to address conditions of release?"

Mike Reynolds stood. "Your Honor, we are satisfied that your Honor knows all there is to know about my client and the allegations against him. Except to say that the charges are totally untrue and Judge Moss is completely innocent, we will rely on your good judgment regarding the matter of bail."

"Very well," said the judge. "The Court will set bail at Two Million Dollars. Anything else on this matter, then counsel? Mr. Reynolds?"

"Nothing, your Honor."

"Mr. Wilkins?"

"Nothing further your Honor."

"Then court is adjourned." With that, Judge Andrew Forsythe rapped the gavel on its clapper, rose, and left the courtroom.

Newspaper, radio and television reporters moved in on the counsel table area. Microphones were pushed at Digger and Mike Reynolds. With the help of the sheriff's deputies, they left the courtroom as they had entered. Prosecutor Wilkins, however, was not so anxious to get away. Digger looked back as he went through the door, seeing Wilkins beaming as he prepared to address the media.

"Reynolds Law Office." Her voice carried that perfect, melodious tone that callers found pleasant, but which still conveyed a sense of formality and attention to business. Martha Baxter was a small woman in her late thirties. Her auburn hair was pulled back and held in place by a wide, black headband, which accentuated her thin attractive face, red lips and large brown eyes. Martha had been with Reynolds for nearly twenty years. She started just two years after finishing high school at Duluth Central. A nervous young business school graduate when she began, she had learned how to handle Mike Reynolds' business, his clients, and even Mike himself with skill, pleasantry and confidence. She was indispensable. She knew it, but did not act like it. Martha was happy in her job. During her employment with Reynolds, she had married and had three children, one of whom was in high school. Reynolds had always made sure she had time off when needed for family.

"Mike Reynolds, please."

She smoothed a stray chestnut-colored strand into place and said, "One moment, sir, I'll see if he is available."

"Mike," she said, opening the door to his private office, "I think it's that private detective from the Cities you called about Digger. Harry Beecher. He's on line two."

"Hello? This is Mike Reynolds."

"Harry Beecher, Mike. I think I've got what you're looking for."

"Go ahead, Harry."

"The guy's name is Frank Griswold. A small time entrepreneur, that's what they call them nowadays, some times legal, sometimes not."

"Just a minute, Harry," interrupted Mike. "Let me put you on the speaker phone so Martha can hear you, too. She'll probably be making some notes." He nodded to Martha, who brought a legal pad and sat across from Reynolds.

"Okay, we're ready, Harry. Go ahead."

"Hello, Ms. Baxter."

"Hi, Harry Beecher."

"What about it, Harry?" asked Reynolds, grinning at his secretary.

"Like I said, the dude's name is Frank Griswold. He was at the Holiday Inn in Duluth. He used a different name, but he listed his car properly and that was easy enough to trace. He wasn't too careful, or maybe he wasn't too smart." He paused. Mike and Martha could hear the rustle of paper as Beecher consulted his notes.

"Here it is. He lives in Roseville. It's an apartment complex just off Rice Street. He's there, now."

"You mean he is there right now?" asked Reynolds. "As we speak?"

"Well, he was there this morning," Beecher answered the question. "We don't have a stakeout on him, but that's where he lives, and he left Duluth four days ago. We know that from the hotel. Anyway, he's home now."

"Well, thanks, Harry," Mike said. "This is what we were looking for. But we still need to know more about him. Can you stay on the job a little longer?"

"It's your nickel Mike. Right, Ms. Baxter?"

"Right, Mr. Beecher."

"Well, Mike? Whadda ya want?"

Mike Reynolds gave brief instructions. Martha Baxter made notes. Harry Beecher said, "Yes," "I understand," and "You bet" a number of times.

"Harry, give me the address of this Griswold's apartment."

Martha noted the address on her pad.

Hanging up the phone, Mike said, "I hope this is worth it."

Martha Baxter pushed her pencil behind her ear. "Worth it? Mike, Digger Moss is one of your oldest and best friends. How can you ask that question?"

"Your right, as usual, of course," he said. "I suppose the question is whether this will work. Will it do any good?"

"Work? Help Judge Moss?" Martha looked at him, eyebrows raised. "Mike, you better hope it helps the judge."

"Griswold? Frank Griswold?" Digger Moss shook his head. "The name doesn't mean anything to me."

"I don't know why it would, Digger," said Mike Reynolds. "There's no reason why you would know the goon that the Whitaker executives would find to hire to blackmail you for them."

"Who cares who he is?" asked Judge Kathrine Riley, running a hand over her dark red hair, her green eyes reflecting the intensity of the situation.

They sat around the small table in the consultation room at the jail. Although the conversations between an inmate and his lawyer were privileged and protected, they spoke in low tones, as though afraid they were being recorded, or at least overheard.

"The question," continued Kate Riley, "is what are we going to do, now that we know who and where he is?"

"I'm not sure there's anything we can do," said Digger, staring at the table top. "This Griswold has already spilled his guts to the police. It's too late for me."

"Jesus Christ, Digger!" Kate raised her voice. "I know this situation is depressing. It's depressing to us too, but snap out of it, boy." She reached across the table and took his hand. "We have got to do something!"

Digger held her hand a moment, looking into those incredibly intense eyes. "Kate, I'm not wallowing in depression. I'm not languishing, here. I'm thinking. And, I think, clearly enough. But, I can't do anything, here." He motioned with his hands to the cramped surroundings and to his orange clothing, the uniform of the St. Louis County Jail for new prisoners and for prisoners requiring high security, or protection. Digger, a District Judge who had sentenced many of the other inmates at one time or another, fell into the last category.

"The point is," he continued, "neither of you can do anything. You'll get in as much trouble as I'm in."

They sat in silence for a moment, both Kate and Mike thinking about Digger's declaration, while Digger also thought, quietly. But Digger was thinking about something else. The beginnings of a plan were forming in his mind.

"Well, we have got to try to do something," Kate said emphatically.

"I agree, Digger," said Mike. "We can't just sit by and do nothing. This Griswold character knows your innocent! We need to get him to come clean."

"No!" Digger slammed the heels of his manacled hands on the table's Formica surface. "Promise me, you two, that you will not do anything about Griswold. It won't do me any good, and it will do you both a great deal of harm."

"Well, Digger, I'll promise you this," said Kate. "I'll promise you I won't do anything without talking to you first, but I'm not going to sit back and see you convicted of crimes you didn't commit!"

"I'll accept that promise, for now," he responded. "Mike?"

"I'll give you the same promise, Digger."

"Good. Thanks. Now, what's the address where Griswold lives in St. Paul?"

In the van near Frank Griswold's apartment Milo Bracken drank deeply from a can of Classic Coke and lit another Pall Mall. He stared at the apartment entryway and at Griswold's white sedan parked nearby.

"Don't he ever come out?" asked Vince Turcotte, reaching into a large bag and coming out with a handful of potato chips which he crammed into his mouth.

"Not very much," agreed Milo. "I don't get it. He's just pulled off a big deal. Three million! And he just sits there. Goes out only for a few groceries and liquor ... and just sits there. I don't get it!"

"Well, we don't know what he's doing there. We can't see him. He hasn't been gone long enough for us to bug the place. If he does go, how will we know if it's safe to go in?" He reached in the bag for more chips. "If we do get to go in, why put in our video and audio stuff at all? Why not just grab the money and run?"

"It is frustrating sitting here," agreed Milo. "I wish we could see him and hear him, too. But we just have to wait until the right time. I want to get the money, but I want to know more about what he's doing."

"Uh huh, I thought so, Milo," said Vince. "You're after somethin' more than the money ... ain't you?" Turcotte finished a mouthful of potato chips, drank from a can of Mountain Dew and lit a filtered cigarette.

Milo turned toward Vince, tapping the ash off his cigarette. "I am, Vince," he said. "I really don't like this asshole. I don't like what he did to me ... us. And I really don't like what he's doing to Judge Moss."

"Hey, I'm not arguin' with ya. I like the judge. He's got guts. He's a good man and he's getting' screwed. But what are you goin' to do about it? What can you do about it?"

"I don't know."

"Well, Milo, when you figure it out, lemme know, will ya? Cuz I'm with you all the way ... within reason." He held his revolver in the air and grinned at Milo.

"Thanks." Milo turned to stare at the apartment building again.

Inside the apartment, Frank Griswold was not "just sitting." On a personal computer, he was researching on the Internet, making his plans to leave St. Paul, for good. This included a plan for safe and secure deposits and investments for the money, so he would have wide and varied sources of funds, available at just as varied locations around the country and outside the country. He had identified airline tickets to be used for his initial departure and a series of flights thereafter for which he would use different names, so his ultimate destination could not be traced back to St. Paul, or to him. He had arranged by telephone for several passports and changes of appearance which would be provided, for a substantial price, by a woman who operated from a duplex down below west Seventh Street in downtown St. Paul. She had been referred to him as a skilled and discreet businesswoman.

Griswold rose from the computer and went to the kitchen counter, where he poured himself a large Scotch whisky and took a long drink. In a few days, he thought, I'll be out of here and far enough away, no one will ever find me, if even anyone bothers to look. He smiled and sipped from the cheap, chipped glass. I'll be financially fixed. I won't have to say, "Yessir" or "No sir" to nobody. A new life. That's the ticket, and I've got it.

Frank Griswold did not believe that Digger Moss could find him or do anything to him, especially from prison. He smiled at that thought. Similarly, he did not believe that that sniveling little prick, Randall McCoy, would try to do anything to him, or could do anything to him. If he did try, he had plenty on them. They didn't have the guts anyway.

No, he thought, I'm leaving for two reasons. First, is the opportunity for better climates and the enjoyment of the money. The second reason, he was being honest with himself, was the possibility of trouble from Hollis Fowler and Frank Vagelli. Those two had really frightened him. Those fuckers might come after him. If they did ..., Griswold didn't want to think about it.

So, he stayed in his apartment, eating TV dinners, drinking Scotch whisky, and making the plans for his future.

CHAPTER SEVENTEEN

Digger Moss sat by himself in the holding cell. He had been transported from the St. Louis County Jail with other prisoners being brought to various types of hearings in their cases. Unlike the others, who were grouped together in a holding cell to wait, he was alone. Unlike the others, who were dressed in jail uniforms of blue or orange, depending upon their status at the jail, he was dressed in civilian clothes, a business suit, white shirt and tie. The others were restrained by handcuffs and leg shackles. He was not.

Digger had been brought to the courthouse for an omnibus hearing. Mike Reynolds would advise the judge what pre-trial issues he intended to raise, what constitutional challenges would be made, and what issues reserved. It had been two weeks since his first appearance. The time in the jail seemed interminable. Even with regular visits from Mike as his attorney, and from Judy, he thought he would not survive it much longer. What must prison be like? He tried not to think of the hundreds of men and women he had sentenced to time in the jail, the local corrections center or to prison in one of the State's correctional facilities.

At the jail, Digger was kept in the most secure section for his own protection. Furniture was all built in as fixtures or bolted down. Nothing moved. There was nothing that could be moved. It was impossible for a prisoner to do any damage or find anything with which to do damage, even to himself.

Since his first appearance before the law and order judge from Hennepin County, Digger definitely did not look forward to another appearance before Judge Forsythe and the crowd of onlookers.

"Okay, Judge," the deputy said, opening the cell door and motioning to Digger. "They're ready for you."

Digger followed the deputy out into the holding area and towards the door to the first floor hallway. They passed the courthouse's rear public elevator and turned into the main hallway toward a short hallway to a private freight elevator used to carry prisoners. They passed first floor Courtroom No. 3, which was originally constructed in the early seventies for Conciliation Court. Now, because judges hearing Conciliation Court calendars did so in their own courtrooms, it was used by the Minnesota Court of Appeals on its occasional visits to Duluth, and for other proceedings for which there was not a regular courtroom available.

Digger looked at the crack between the double doors to the courtroom. It was dark and he could not see the silver dead bolt that showed when the doors were locked. He concluded, therefore, that the courtroom was empty, dark and unlocked. Making one of the most difficult and fastest decisions of his life, he turned and ducked through the doors into the courtroom, pulling them quickly and quietly shut behind him. He turned the handle of the dead bolt lock. He knew it was only a split second before the deputy turned and saw he was missing. He moved down the center aisle toward the counsel tables and the bench, moving from his memory of the courtroom in which he himself had held court many times. When the front of his left leg touched one of the counsel tables, he felt for the chairs and moved quickly to his right, feeling for the side wall of the courtroom and the door to the adjacent robing room.

As he found the door handle, turned it and slipped inside, he heard someone rattling the locked doors to the courtroom. In the robing room, the lights were on. He noted the positions of the other two doors and hit the wall switch, sending the room into blackness. Crossing to the door on his left, he turned the handle and eased the door open a crack. As he had hoped on this afternoon, the arraignments courtroom was empty. It was normally used only in the mornings for the daily arraignments calendar. Someone had left the small recessed lights over the audience seats turned on. Without the main lights over the bench and pit area, the courtroom was dimly lit, the smaller lights giving the bright blue audience seats a soft glow.

Digger mentally thanked the bailiff, clerk or maintenance engineer who had thought to leave the small lights on. Taking advantage of the dim light, he moved quickly to the courtroom doors, cracking them and looking across the hallway to Courtroom No. 2. One of the doors was standing open. Like the arraignments courtroom, only the small lights over the rows of green audience seats were on. Nothing was going on in the courtroom. He had to move fast. He crossed behind the bench in the arraignments courtroom and eased the door to the criminal clerks' office open slightly. He saw no one.

He had to keep moving. It had only been seconds since he left the deputy. He figured the deputy would search by himself for a moment before he sounded the alarm. He was counting on that to give him the few extra seconds he would need. His choices were two. He could go through the main doors of the arraignments courtroom, dash across the hallway to Courtroom No. 2 and go through that courtroom and out into the narrow private hallway behind the courtroom, or go through the clerks' office to the same hallway and hopefully, to the east outside door to the courthouse. His right hand rested on the handle of the door to the clerks' office.

He pushed the door open and stepped into the clerks' office. At that moment, the only one in the room was the receptionist. Her back was to him as she spoke on the phone, making reference to her computer and answering the caller's questions about the scheduling of some hearing, no doubt. The office was in the shape of an L, wrapping around the courtroom. He had entered the room from the courtroom in one of the two sections, while the receptionist was in the other which faced the open counter and the main public hallway beyond.

Quickly tiptoeing past the receptionist, he entered the private hallway that ran behind Courtroom No. 2 and Courtroom No. 1 beyond. No one was in the hallway. No one had seen him, he was sure, from the main hallway outside the clerks' office. He turned left immediately into the foyer of the east door. No longer used as a public entrance, the clerks and others who smoked used the wide walkway and patio area outside the door as a smoking area. With no clerks but the receptionist in the first floor clerks' office, Digger was afraid some of them would be standing just outside the door taking a smoke break. At a glance, he was sure no one was out there. Because the door remained locked, the smokers had a small piece of wood they placed in the door as it shut to insure they could get back in. The piece of wood was not there. The door was closed tight. He checked anyway, looking through the glass panels of the door. No one. He glanced around the foyer. His luck held. There on the coat rack used by the bailiffs and some of the attorneys was a tan raincoat and a felt cap with a brim. He grabbed them, threw on the coat and was adjusting the cap down over his forehead as he went through the door to the outside.

Meanwhile, the deputy sheriff had decided to sound the alarm. He did so by running into the Sheriff's office across the main hall from Courtroom No. 3. The Sheriff, himself, came running from his office in the back when he heard the commotion. The deputy explained that Judge Moss was right behind him following him out of the holding area walking toward the secure elevator. When he turned to go down the hall to that elevator, he noticed the judge was not there. He tried the courtroom doors they had just passed, but they were locked. He checked the hallway toward the criminal clerks' office, saw nothing and came to report.

"It's some kind of mistake," said a tall deputy in civilian slacks and sport shirt, automatic pistol in a small leather holster on his hip. "Judge Moss isn't about to try to escape!"

The younger, uniformed deputy looked relieved. "That's what I thought," he said.

"Maybe he took the public elevator up to the hearing," said the Sheriff. "Where were you going?"

"To Judge Parker's courtroom on the fourth floor," replied the young deputy. "Judge Forsythe is using it for Digger's hearing this afternoon."

"Check up there," the Sheriff commanded the tall deputy. "Let's get this cleared up quick."

The hesitation of the Sheriff's office to believe that he, of all people, would try to escape, gave Digger valuable time. He had counted on that. By the time they had anybody on the fourth floor, and before they realized that he really was trying to escape, he was past City Hall and into the skyway system through the State Office Building. From the skyway, he ducked into a parking garage and out onto Second Street two blocks east of the courthouse.

While in the State Office Building, he had taken a great chance and used valuable time. He had no money. He could not use a pay phone. He had removed the raincoat, holding it over his arm, and stopped in an office off the first floor hallway and asked to

171

use the telephone. As he had hoped, the business suit gave him some appearance of authority. At least the receptionist in the office where he stopped must have thought so. She had smiled and handed him the desk phone, reminding him to dial "nine" for an outside line.

"Good afternoon, this is Judy Moss." He had heard his wife's voice answer her office telephone. "How may I help you?"

"Yes," he had said without greeting her or acknowledging her by name. "This is James Digby, can you have someone meet me with a car?"

"Digger! What the hell ..."

"That's right, along Fourth Street, going east, between Second Avenue West and Lake Avenue. Can you send someone right away? Good!" He smiled at the receptionist. Into the phone he said, "Thank you very much." He had returned the phone, then.

"Everything arranged then?" said the receptionist.

"Yes, indeed," replied Digger, "and thank you very much. You have a nice afternoon."

"Thank you. You, too." She had waived as he left the office.

Now, he stepped out of the parking garage onto the sidewalk on Second Street, hurrying to the corner and up the hill toward Fourth Street, where, if his luck held, Judy would pick him up in a few minutes. He was beginning to have hope and a positive attitude about his decision. It was, he knew after all, his only hope of saving himself.

In Judge Parker's chambers on the fourth floor of the St. Louis County Courthouse, however, the attitude of those present was not positive at all.

Judge Forsythe had the lawyers brought back into chambers from the courtroom as soon as he heard. He was wearing a dark business suit and had not yet put on his robe.

"Mr. Reynolds," said Judge Forsythe, "what do you know about this?"

"Nothing, your Honor," answered Mike Reynolds. "I was waiting for them to bring Digger up from holding, just like the rest of us." He nodded toward the prosecutor, Assistant Attorney General H. Gordon Wilkins, his assistant, also from the State Attorney General's office, and Marilee Jackson from the county attorney's office.

"Well," said the judge, "it appears that Judge Moss has decided to leave the custody of the Sheriff and has eluded discovery in the initial search for him. Perhaps we all should not have been so eager to allow him the privilege of wearing civilian clothes and being without the leg and wrist shackles that I see your prisoners regularly wear here in Duluth."

"Judge, I'm sure there is some mistake," Mike said. "Digger Moss would be the last defendant to try to escape. He's part of the system, himself."

"Normally I would agree," said the prosecutor Wilkins, "but, Mike, maybe he has flown because he is guilty. That's a reasonable inference." Wilkins' young assistant stood stiffly next to his boss, displaying his best effort at a look of righteous indignation.

Mike stepped toward the prosecutors, looking down directly into the raised eyes of Wilkins. "You be very careful, Gordy ..." Mike knew Wilkins did not like the nickname, "Gordy." He did not like the man or his litigation tactics. He did not particularly like being on a first name basis with him and did not invite it.

"Whoa! Easy boys!" Judge Forsythe rose from the chair behind the desk. "Let's not get into personalities, here. Judge Moss has gone missing. Maybe there is an explanation. Maybe not. Regardless, we must treat him as an escaped prisoner until we learn otherwise. It is a little early for inferences and he does stand innocent of the charges against him until the State proves otherwise. But let's see what can be done to find him."

The judge turned to the Sheriff and one of his deputies. While they talked, Merilee Jackson stepped behind Mike and put a hand on his arm. "Mike, I'm sorry," she said softly. "This doesn't look good for Digger."

He turned to face her. "Tell me about it," he whispered, shaking his head as they left the judge's chambers and returned to the crowded courtroom.

"Mr. Reynolds!" called H. Gordon Wilkins, waving to him through the crowd. As he reached Mike, he put a hand on Mike's shoulder and pushed a piece of paper toward him. "I had planned on serving this at the Omnibus Hearing, but I guess this will have to do. He turned on his heels and left through the crowd, stopping to talk to a local television news reporter.

Mike looked at the paper. It bore the caption of Digger's case, "State of Minnesota vs. James Digby Moss." It was entitled, "NOTICE BY PROSECUTING ATTORNEY THAT MATTER WILL BE PRESENTED TO GRAND JURY."

Under Minnesota law, the prosecuting authority could only charge a homicide as high as second degree murder. A charge of Murder in the First Degree, which carried a mandatory life prison sentence, could only be brought by Indictment by a Grand Jury. The notice said the Grand Jury would convene to consider evidence against Digger in less than a week.

Judy Moss drove her green sedan slowly east on Fourth Street, looking for Digger. What was he doing? She knew nothing except what he had said on the phone. None of that made any sense, but she knew he was in trouble, that he needed her, and it was urgent. That was enough for her ... for now.

Suddenly she saw him. He darted out from the right side of the street, just behind the car ahead of her. She had to slam on the brakes to stop in time. He grabbed the rear door and leaped into the back seat.

"Drive!" he shouted.

Judy looked in the rear view mirror, but could not see him. Glancing back she saw that he was lying down on the seat to avoid being seen from outside the car. She stepped the accelerator down and brought the car up to normal traffic speed.

"Drop down to Second Street and drive east," he told her. "When you get to 21st Avenue East, take it down the hill to London Road and head east out to the Lester River and on up the lake shore."

She followed his instructions without comment. They rode in silence. Judy could hear sirens in the distance behind her. Oh God, she thought. We're both going to jail!

"How close are you to the Lester?" Digger was still lying on the back seat.

"Coming up on 60th Avenue East, now, Digger. We'll be over the Lester in a few seconds. What do you want me to do then?"

"Take the Old North Shore Highway along the lake shore out to O'Malleys."

"What!?"

"Go to the O'Malleys' house," he repeated.

"Digger," Judy hesitated, but turned off the highway onto Old U. S. Highway 61, the popular twenty mile scenic drive up the shore to Two Harbors, "can we talk about this? I don't even know all the details of what has happened or why you called and ended up in my car, but are you sure it isn't a mistake to get the O'Malleys involved?"

Robert and Margaret O'Malley lived in a log home on the shore of Lake Superior a few miles south of Knife River on the way up to Two Harbors. They were Lake Superior sailors. Their thirty-eight foot sloop was docked at the Knife River Marina. Bob was an architect. Peggy was an artist. Both were actively involved in the Duluth Playhouse, organizing, working on sets, and acting in some of the several plays performed by the group annually. The Mosses and the O'Malleys were very close friends. Some years ago, Digger had been in a few of the plays and Judy had worked hard on the productions, becoming intimate friends with Peggy O'Malley.

"Let's let them decide," said Digger, finally sitting up in the seat. He leaned forward and kissed Judy on the back of the neck. "Thanks," he whispered in her ear.

"It'll take more than that, Digger," she said.

The screams of the wailing sirens accentuated the feeling of pandemonium surrounding the courthouse. The overhead lights of several Sheriff's and Duluth P. D. squad cars flashed against the building and gave the surrounding grounds and the interior offices an unreal atmosphere. Several news media trucks were broadcasting from vehicles parked in the loop drive in the front of the building. Many had already been on hand for Digger's scheduled omnibus hearing and were all set up to begin broadcasting when they heard he had escaped.

"Jesus Christ, Mike! What the hell is Digger thinking?" Kate Riley had found Mike Reynolds as soon as she had heard the news.

"I know what you're thinking, Kate," he said. "There's no way, that I can see, that Digger can work his way out of this mess."

"Poor Digger," said Kate, "I wish we could find him and talk to him."

"Poor Digger' is right," said Mike, handing her the notice of the Grand Jury.

"Oh my God!" she gasped, studying the document. "First Degree Murder! Oh my God!"

Peggy O'Malley came to the door in tan shorts, a white tee shirt and a light blue smock covered with dabs of various colors of oil paint. She was barefoot and carried a long handled artist's brush in one hand. There was paint on her hands and even some on the tip of her nose, as if she had scratched it with a painted finger. Peggy's thin face was framed by her steel gray hair, which hung down well past her shoulders. She was an artist and an actor, lived in an artists' community, and looked very much the part.

"Judy!" she cried, opening the screen door. Behind her was a large living room with expansive windows looking out onto the blue waters of Lake Superior a few feet away.

"Digger?" she gasped, seeing him come up behind Judy.

"Peggy, we've got some trouble," said Judy. "May we come in?"

They followed Peggy O'Malley through the enormous log home to her studio where she had been painting. She began cleaning up her paints. On an easel near sliding glass doors to a deck overlooking the lake was a canvas of a seascape with a long sand beach and an abandoned commercial fishing boat of the style used in Lake Superior. Long thin beach grass grew around the wooden hull. A single sea gull sat perched on the bow rail, waiting.

Peggy O'Malley had comforted Judy after Digger was arrested, while other friends had ignored her and even avoided her. Now here they *both* were, in her home! She finished with the brushes and turned to them.

"Okay," she said, "tell me."

Halfway through their explanation, Peggy called her husband at his office. "Come home, now," was all she said to him, hanging up the phone and returning to the Mosses.

CHAPTER EIGHTEEN

Judy's green sedan pulled away from the stop sign ahead of him. She went straight across Old 61 and on north to the freeway to return to Duluth. Digger turned left and headed toward Duluth on Old 61, returning the way they had come. He felt strange in the dark wig, mustache, and glasses Peggy and Bob had put on him. Expert at costumes and make-up, they had selected a look that made him look natural, not unusual and not like Digger Moss. He wore a pair of Bob's blue jeans, leather deck shoes, a pullover shirt and light tan jacket. He drove a rusty, old, charcoal gray Ford Mustang registered to Rick O'Malley, a son who was traveling in Europe, trying to find himself, according to his parents.

At the Lakeview Castle, he tested his disguise. He walked into the bar, ordered a Coke and used the pay phone.

"Reynolds Law Office," a voice answered politely.

"Mike Reynolds, please," Digger said, unable to keep himself from looking around to see if anyone was watching him.

"Hello?"

"Mike?" There was a silent pause.

"Digger?" Mike whispered into the phone. "Are you nuts?"

"Meet me on Four Pipe," Digger said quickly and hung up.

Mike hung up the phone and rose to leave. It was 5:00 o'clock. Martha was leaving.

"You're leaving early aren't you?" she said when he went out the door with her.

"Oh, this Moss thing has got me going," he said. "I've got to see what the cops have and maybe go out and see Judy."

Mike pulled his Explorer out of the Medical Arts Annex parking garage behind the Alworth Building and headed east on Michigan Street. Turning up the avenue toward Superior Street, he turned left on Superior Street and aimed the Explorer toward I35 and then west out toward Spirit Mountain.

177

Presumably afraid of bugs on Mike's office phones, Digger had kept his conversation very short. Four Pipe was an intermediate ski run on the western side of Spirit Mountain's wide slope. Although obvious to Mike and Digger who regularly skied at Spirit, perhaps it would not be so obvious to others. Mike thought Digger was taking a big chance. He thought the odds were good that if the call were intercepted, the name of the ski run would be recognized and someone would be waiting. But, they didn't know if the phone was bugged, and, if so, by whom. Probably not by the police, at least not yet.

He drove past the road into the chalet and up to the top of the mountain. There, he parked in a small lot adjacent to the very top of the ski hill where the triple chair lift and the quad lift terminated. He walked alongside the quad lift, down the hill and a little further west to the top of a smaller double chair lift. That was the top of Four Pipe. He looked down the slope, along the edges of the trees. It was different seeing the ski run with green grass and foliated trees instead of white snow. He saw no movement. He saw no one.

Then a stranger stepped out of the trees a couple of hundred yards below him. He did not recognize the man. Someone found out! he thought.

The stranger wore blue jeans and a light tan jacket. Mike studied the man, looking for something he would recognize. He had thick, dark hair and a mustache. Mike thought of the deputies and officers he knew in the St. Louis County Sheriff's office and the Duluth P. D. No one came to mind.

The man was waving now and starting up the hill toward him. No, thought Mike, as the man got closer, I do not know this man.

"Mike!"

No it couldn't be! "Digger?"

"Right! Over here!" Digger Moss motioned toward the trees on the side of the ski run.

The two men stepped into the thick woods at the edge of the grassy slope. Digger explained how he had escaped and about the disguise.

"Digger," Mike could not contained his excitement, "if you think you were ever in trouble before, you are really in deep shit, now! They served me with notice of a Grand Jury, Digger. They'll indict you for Murder One, for sure, now that you've escaped."

"I guess we knew that was coming," said Digger. They had expected it, certainly, but hearing it was still a shock. Murder One!

Digger put a hand against the trunk of an aspen and supported himself. He was exhausted, both physically and mentally. Mike stepped closer to him and put a hand on his shoulder.

"What are we doing, now, my friend?" Mike asked.

"Nothing's changed, Mike," Digger answered. "I still have to get the evidence to clear me or I'm off to prison, forever. I'm even beginning to get prepared for that outcome, except I'm damned if I'll let that happen to Judy!"

"You're not working alone, remember."

"I know, and I'm grateful," acknowledged Digger. "I know you and Kate will help, but we still need me outside of jail to get the job done."

"A lot of people are pretty excited, you know," Mike said. "I'm not sure we can meet very often without my getting caught. I assume they'll be keeping an eye on me."

"I figured," said Digger. "We need a foolproof communication system and I think I've got one. You know Peggy O'Malley?"

"**Y**ou really think he'll try to contact Reynolds?" asked a deputy. "Won't he just head as far away from Duluth as he can get?"

"Where could he go?" asked another deputy. "As word of this gets out, and it already has, it'll be one of the biggest manhunts you ever heard, nationwide. The hunt will be for a district judge/ cop killer. It doesn't get any bigger than that!"

"Where is Reynolds, now?" asked the Sheriff.

"We don't have him yet," said the first deputy. "His office in the Alworth Building was closed when we checked and he hasn't been to his home yet."

"Keep on it," the Sheriff ordered. "When you get him, keep on him."

"Electronic surveillance?"

"Not yet, and not without the approval of the County Attorney or the A.G.," the Sheriff replied. "All we need to do is screw this up by violating Judge Moss's constitutional rights, you know what I mean?"

Dave Sullivan

The deputies nodded.

Mike Reynolds pulled the Explorer into the driveway of his East End home. He knew Digger was taking a great risk. He knew that he should probably report his meeting with Digger to the police, but it was clearly an attorney/client communication. He also knew that Digger was right. With him in jail, they had almost no chance of clearing him. The evidence was overwhelming. H. Gordon Wilkins, the prosecutor, was taking an ever increasingly righteous position with the press. People who had believed there must have been some mistake, were beginning to believe that Judge James Digby Moss was a drug dealer and a cold-blooded cop killer. They were beginning to cry out for justice. Digger did not have much of a chance if he depended on the criminal justice system and his own innocence, Mike thought.

CHAPTER NINETEEN

D igger Moss' thoughts were exactly the same as Mike Reynolds'. He was traveling south on Highway 23, the "Evergreen Memorial Highway", through the pine forests that gave it its name. As Mike was pulling his Explorer into the driveway of his home, Digger was already past Wrenshall and Holyoke, on his way to St. Paul. He gripped the wheel of the old Mustang. He could not depend on the criminal justice system, the very system of which he was a part. If he did, he would almost certainly be convicted of murder. So much for the presumption of innocence, he thought. How often he had instructed juries about that presumption and how it abided with the defendant until the defendant was proved guilty beyond a reasonable doubt. Well he wasn't willing to rely on that presumption in this case. In a few days, a Grand Jury would meet to consider indicting him for First Degree Murder. With what they had to work with at the present time, Digger and Mike would not be able to obtain an acquittal. He would be given the mandatory sentence of life in prison.

He drove on with determination, unconsciously gripping the steering wheel of the Mustang, like a race driver, as he sped around the sharp curves of the old two-lane highway. He had chosen this scenic back route as a precaution against the possibility of police surveillance or even roadblocks along I-35. Highway 23 would eventually take him back to the freeway just past the town of Askov. By then he hoped he would be far enough south to avoid the most intense police dragnet. His disguise and the old Mustang should do the trick from there, he hoped. He slowed to just three miles above the fifty-five mile an hour speed limit. He could not afford to get stopped. The disguise might fool someone, but he had no identification. All he had was the cash Peggy and Bob O'Malley had given him.

He had been back on I-35 for about fifteen minutes when a highway sign told him he was two miles north of Hinckley.

"Heads up! Here he comes!" Vince Turcotte turned to the back of the van where Milo was napping. "Wake up, Milo!"

In a moment, Milo Bracken was in the front of the van watching Frank Griswold walking toward his car. From a distance Griswold held his hand out, obviously using the remote key to unlock the car. He climbed in and sped out of the parking lot.

"He's in a hurry!" said Vince. "Do we go after him, or go inside and do our thing?"

Milo paused in thought for a moment. Then he made up his mind. "Let's go!" he said, nodding toward the apartment building.

They were outside the van in less than a minute, each carrying a small duffel with equipment and tools. True to his word, Vince had the security door open in no time. They took the elevator to the fourth floor.

Inside the apartment, Vince asked, "Are we looking for the money, this trip?"

"We haven't got the time, Vince," Milo answered. "Besides, if we found the money before he got back, and we took it now, that would change Griswold's plans completely. I want to know what he's up to and where he thinks he's going."

"I figured," said Vince, inserting a small transmitter into the receiver of the living room telephone. "You're still worried about the judge."

"Damn right I am, Vince," Milo agreed.

Griswold returned about two hours later. He carried an old fashioned, hard-sided suitcase, a plastic bag full of TV dinners and a narrow paper bag from the liquor store.

"Well, at least it looks like he'll be here a while," said Vince. Together, they settled into their captain's chairs in the back of the van to monitor the video and sound equipment they had installed in the apartment.

"This is better," said Milo, lighting a Pall Mall. "Eyes and ears again. I felt deaf and blind before." He watched the three small television monitors showing different rooms in Griswold's apartment, waiting for him to arrive.

Vince laughed. "You do have a way with words, my friend. You *were* deaf and blind before!"

"Shut up, Vince. Here he comes." They both concentrated on the small screen as Griswold appeared, entering his fourth floor apartment. He set the suitcase on the floor inside the door and carried the bags to the kitchen. He returned from the kitchen, picked up the suitcase and set it on the large coffee table in front of the couch. He opened it and examined its contents, laying the items out on the table.

"Jesus Christ!" exclaimed Vince. "That looks like spook equipment!"

"What?"

"Look!" he said, pointing to the small screen of the living room monitor. "The fucking guy's got wigs, glasses, a mustache, looks like a fake nose, there, and unless I can't see straight, those are passports and false ID's."

Milo studied the screen. "You're right. Our boy is planning a major trip and doesn't want anyone to know where he's going, or that it's even him going there."

Griswold disappeared from the screen and reappeared on the bedroom video. He went into the walk in closet next to the head of the bed. Momentarily, he reappeared with the two large nylon duffel bags.

"Aha! The money!" said Vince.

Milo smiled.

"But why is he bringing it out now, Milo. Think he's getting ready to leave right now?"

"Maybe, but I don't think so. It's late enough, he's going to settle in for dinner and probably drink a half a bottle of Scotch. I don't think he's packed. I don't think he'll leave at night."

"Then why bring out the money, now?"

Milo smiled again. "If I had three mil in my closet, I'd want to see it every day. I'd want to hold it and look at it."

"You and Griswold must think alike," said Vince, now looking at the living room monitor, where Griswold had reappeared, placed the two bags on the couch, opened them and had taken out some bundles of bills which he placed on the table among the items Vince called "spook equipment."

After getting gas at the Holiday Gas Station in Forest Lake, Moss pulled the old Mustang around into the McDonald's next door. With a Big Mac, fries and a Diet Coke on the seat beside him, he drove back onto the freeway, about twenty-five miles north of St. Paul. Just south of Forest Lake, I-35 split into 35E and 35W. 35W veered west to Minneapolis and its northern suburbs. 35E went straight south through White Bear Lake to St. Paul. Digger took 35E.

He was going to the address Mike Reynolds had given him for the apartment where Frank Griswold lived. He was the man who had created all of Digger's trouble. Digger was concerned that he had no particular plan, although he had recording equipment on his person, he had a sock filled with coins to use as a blackjack, and he had a thin bladed knife in a sheath in his jacket pocket. He had thought about getting a gun and then dismissed the idea. He didn't want to kill the man. He didn't even want to hurt him, at least no more than it would take to get him to come clean while the recorder was running.

He traveled south on I-35E to the off ramp for Highway 36. From 35E, he drove west a short distance to Rice Street and turned north into the City of Roseville. Watching the street signs carefully in the dark of late evening, he turned left a few blocks north of Highway 36 on the street of Griswold's apartment building. He found it about a block and a half off Rice Street.

Once he located the apartment building, Digger drove back to Rice Street where he found a gas and convenience store. He filled his gas tank to be sure he was ready to travel quickly and without the need of stopping. He bought some snack food and soft drinks. After pulling away from the gas pumps, Digger parked the car alongside the building and went back inside.

"Do you have a restroom?" he asked the young attendant.

"In the back," she replied, pointing to the far corner of the store.

Digger took off the glasses and studied himself in the mirror. He began to carefully remove the false mustache and dark wig. Placing them in a paper bag he'd brought with him, he combed back his short gray hair. Welcome back, Digger, he thought. Here goes nothing. Hell, here goes everything!

Back at the apartment building, he parked the Mustang a few rows back from the driving lane in front of the entryway. He opened a Diet Coke and waited, watching the entryway.

W e got company, Milo," said Vince, who was looking out the windshield at the parking lot, while Milo watched the monitors.

"What? He's right there, Vince. Sitting watching TV, eating pretzels and cheese, and building up a pretty good snootful, I'd bet."

"I know, he's been hittin' the booze pretty good," agreed Vince. "I'm talking about here."

"What?" Milo moved to be able to see the lot. "Where?" He squinted at the parking lot which was lit by two mercury vapor lights on tall poles on each side of the lot.

"Over there," said Vince, pointing. "See that rust bucket of a Mustang over there?"

"Yeah?"

"It drove in a few minutes ago. It's not a car I recognize, and I know what cars regularly come and go, here."

"Don't you be getting paranoid on me, Vince."

"What?"

"A little suspicious, aren't you?"

"He's still sitting there."

"What?" Milo leaned toward the windshield staring across the lot at the old car.

"He's been sittin' there for at least five minutes, drinking pop or beer from a can and eating something, all the time watching the front door. You figure it has something to do with our guy in there?"

"I don't know, Vince," said Milo. "I don't know."

A t that moment a dark blue Buick sedan pulled into the lot. Digger got out of his car and walked toward the entryway as the Buick pulled into a parking place. He carried a small, portable radio and tape player/recorder in his left hand. He entered the foyer and picked up the intercom phone. He was looking at the tenant register, with his back to the entrance as the couple from the Buick

185

entered and the man used his key to open the inner door. As they went through, Digger caught the door before it closed and slipped inside. He waited a moment and then walked around the corner to the elevator.

"Holy shit, that was the judge!"
Vince and Milo scrambled into the back of the van to look at the monitors, wishing they had installed one in the hallway outside Griswold's door. They watched the living room monitor which showed the door of the apartment, waiting to see Griswold answering the door.

"What the hell does he think he's doing?" asked Milo.

"I said it before and I say it now, Milo, the judge has guts, although I'm beginning to wonder about his brains."

"There goes Griswold! He's got a gun!"

They watched from the tiny, overhead video camera as Griswold walked across the living room toward his apartment door. In his right hand he carried a menacing looking automatic pistol. Over the audio speakers in the van, they could hear the sound of the living room television set, playing an old movie Griswold had been watching.

"You hear somethin', Milo?"

"You mean the TV?"

"No. Music. Different music than the TV. Hear it?"

Milo strained his ears to listen to the speakers. "Yeah," Milo listened, "sounds like old time rock and roll, to me."

"Right," said Vince. "I think it's coming from outside the apartment. I think Griswold hears it."

"The judge?"

"Maybe."

They watched as Griswold looked through the peephole in the apartment door, then carefully set the pistol aside on a shelf near the door. He unlocked the two chain locks on the door before opening it slightly to peer out into the hallway.

Digger was waiting, the portable radio on the floor blaring out the music of a Twin Cities "Oldies" station near the end of the FM dial. When Griswold's door began to open, he went into action. He did his best to duplicate his old football stance, dropped a shoulder and charged. In the best "Digger" tradition, he charged, wedging the door open and hitting Griswold with his shoulder, sending him reeling backwards across the living room. Digger grabbed the radio from the hallway and kicked the door shut behind him.

"Holy shit!" Milo and Vince were astonished, staring at the small screen of the living room monitor.

"What the hell?" gasped Frank Griswold, struggling to get up from the floor where he had fallen over a foot stool of the chair where he had been watching television.

Digger stood over him, one hand in his pocket clutching his homemade blackjack full of pennies. "Get up, you piece of shit!"

Griswold hesitated. He wasn't sure what was going on. The surprise at the door and too much Scotch so far that evening didn't help. And what was that God damned music?

The music stopped. Digger put the silenced radio down on the coffee table.

"What are you doing? Why are you here? How did you get here?" Griswold asked nervously as he slowly got to his feet. His eyes darting around the room.

"Watch out for the gun, Judge!"

"Shhh, Vince!" cautioned Milo. "If you're any louder, they'll hear you up there. Or somebody may hear you down here, he nodded toward the parking lot beyond the curtains that closed off the front of the van so the illumination from the monitors would not attract attention.

When Digger walked across the parking lot carrying the portable radio, he was seen by others besides Milo Bracken and Vincent Turcotte observing from their van.

"The Honorable James Digby Moss, as I live and breathe," said Hollis Fowler.

CHAPTER TWENTY

"What the hell is he doing here?" snarled Frank Vagelli, leaning forward to see out the window from the back seat of the big Lincoln Town Car.

"Easy, Frank," said Hollis Fowler, seated beside him. "An excellent opportunity seems to be at hand."

"What?" Vagelli was still staring at the back of the judge as he walked toward the apartment entrance. Then his expression changed as Fowler's words began to sink in. "Oh," he said, the beginnings of a twisted smile forming on his lips, "kinda like two birds with one bullet, eh?"

Hollis Fowler smiled. "Something like that."

"Change in plans?" said the man in the right front seat. He was a big man, who wore a tan trench coat-styled raincoat and a cloth hat. He was big enough that the Town Car seemed almost too small for him.

The driver was also big, and dressed similarly, except for the hat. Together, they looked capable of causing considerable discomfort to anyone who created trouble for their employer, whoever that might be at any particular time. At the moment, it was Hollis Fowler.

"No Lew, not really," said Fowler. "We might just have a little more work for you this evening, that's all."

"Okay by us," the man said. "Right, Max?" he said to the driver, who nodded.

"Right," said the driver. "As long as the price fits the job."

"And it will, gentlemen," said Fowler. "It will."

In Duluth, Chief John Morgan was pacing behind his big desk. H. Gordon Wilkins was seated across from him. Detectives Nate Jackson and Joe Walters were also seated there. His secretary, Lizabeth Wilson sat beside the desk, steno pad and pencil poised. Assistant Chief Pelton stood in his usual place in the corner. Sergeant Kathy Winslow stood in the opposite corner. Outside in the night, the lights of the city illuminated the downtown streets.

"I tell you, Wilkins, we haven't got anything yet. He can't hide forever. In fact he can't hide anywhere for very long. You can be sure that we will have him in a matter of a short time."

"Chief, it has been twelve hours now." said H. Gordon Wilkins. He consulted a gold watch, which he withdrew from a vest pocket by means of a gold chain.

"I know, Wilkins," said the Chief. He did not like the skinny prosecutor. And he did not like him sitting in his office making demands. He had enough trouble with Digger Moss having escaped custody without this jerk interfering. Thank God, he thought, it was the Sheriff's department who lost him and not Duluth P. D. Although he knew that the same thing might have happened to him or his men in the same situation. Digger goddammit Moss! What the hell had gotten into him? And where the hell was he?

"Mr. Wilkins, if you'll excuse us, we'll get back to work on finding your missing defendant."

Beth Wilson looked at her boss. His tone and demeanor were unmistakable. Just beneath the surface, the big man's temper was near its limit. Mr. H. Gordon Wilkins would be well advised to exit quickly while there's still time, she thought. She straightened her long legs and stood in one fluid, graceful movement.

"Here, Mr. Wilkins," she said, pleasantly, "I'll see you out."

"But ....," flustered Wilkins, "I'm ..."

"That's right, Mr. Wilkins," said Beth, taking his arm. "We'd better let the Chief get back to the work of apprehending Judge Moss."

As they left the room, the four police officers who remained, exchanged looks with each other and Chief Morgan. Lizabeth Wilson had commanded the respect of all of them for some time now. She had just earned it again.

"Hello!" said Milo. "Now, what do we have here?"

"What's up, *now*?" asked Vince.

"Two tough guys just got out of that big Lincoln in the back row. If they're not muscle for somebody, I'll eat my hat."

"Look at 'em!" Vince remarked in amazement. "No-neck city! Bet they're packing some heavy artillery under them coats."

"Whoops! Two more guys with them," said Milo. "Oh Christ! It's those guys from the meeting with Judge Moss, the ones who searched him."

"You're right. There's that big prick who started to rough up the judge. I'd like a piece of him."

"You may get your chance, Vince. I'd say the judge is in a heap of trouble, right now."

Oblivious to what might be coming toward him, Digger was trying to force Griswold to give him something, anything which would clear him.

Although Moss had the upper hand for the moment, Griswold was beginning to utilize the futility of the judge's position, hoping to talk enough and to move around enough to get to his gun on the shelf.

"Why would I give you anything that would help you?" he hissed. "You can't do anything to me. How could you possibly hurt me?"

"I can physically hurt you," said Digger, moving toward Griswold, his grip tightening on the blackjack in his jacket pocket.

"Oh, come now, Judge," said Griswold, his confidence gaining. He backed away from Moss, but moved a few feet to his right, as he began to circle the perimeter of the room toward the shelf by the door. "Sure, you can rough me up a bit, but what will that do? I might even get a few licks in on you before we're through."

Digger was not sure what to do next. The man was a contemptible coward who could not be trusted for a second. But even if he beat him physically, what good would that do indeed, if he didn't give Digger anything to work with? Then it came to him.

"Get your coat," he commanded.

"What for? I ain't goin' anywhere."

"You are."

"Where?"

"Duluth."

"Duluth?" said Griswold. "Bullshit. I just came from there. I don't think I'm goin' back anytime soon."

Digger stood firm. "We're going now. Get your coat. We're going to Duluth right now, so you can have a little talk with the police, up there."

As they talked, Griswold had kept moving, just a little at a time, so they were kind of circling each other. All the while he was getting closer to his gun.

They circled the room like animals, each wary of the other, each watching for the opportunity to strike. Digger was nervous. He could match Griswold for weight and he still had some of his athletic ability, but he'd never been in a street fight, never a fight where the stakes were the highest. He didn't know what he would do to subdue Griswold, if he could, but he was pretty sure Griswold planned to do more than just temporarily subdue him. The hate in Griswold's eyes told Digger that.

Griswold edged further to his right, his leg bumping a low coffee table. He didn't even glance at it. He adjusted his stance and began slowly moving around the obstacle as he continued slowly circling to his right. Almost there, he thought.

Digger tried a new tack. "Why did you send evidence to the police?" he asked Griswold.

Griswold straightened slightly in surprise, the sound of Digger's voice interrupting his concentration and the silence of the two men, each crouched, poised for attack or defense against one another. "What?" he snarled.

"Why did you send the stuff on me to the cops?" Digger asked again. "What was there to gain? You lose your blackmail leverage and your employers at PowerPlus Batteries get nothing."

"I have my reasons." Griswold resumed his crouch, sidestepping slightly further to his right, concentrating on avoiding looking at the target of his maneuvers, the pistol on the shelf by the door.

"That's what I mean," said Digger. "What are your reasons?"

Griswold stopped and stood straight, arms still held out to his sides, tense and ready to spring. "Look, you sanctimonious prick, I hate your guts, if you must know, and for God damned good reason ... that's my reasons."

"Why?" Digger didn't know if it was good or not, but his questions were getting to Griswold and distracting him, perhaps. Making him angry might make him less effective, less controlled, less dangerous.. Yeah, he thought, like pissing off a wounded and hungry grizzly bear. "Why do you hate me?" he persisted.

"You don't know, do you?" Griswold hissed. "Since you found me, here, I know you know my name, now. But, you haven't recognized it yet, have you?"

Digger thought. Griswold. Familiar, now that he thought about it, but he couldn't place it. Griswold edged further to his right. Digger jumped at the move. Careful now! He thought. Don't lose concentration, or he'll have you. But Griswold had done to Digger what Digger had been trying to do to Griswold. Griswold had him thinking about something other than the battle at hand. Digger's leg bumped a chair. He glanced down, then quickly back at Griswold who was crouched like a big cat, unblinking, eyes staring at him.

Griswold, thought Digger. Must be some hearing he had conducted. He didn't remember the name. But he would expect to remember the face.

Once while driving to a judge's conference in the Twin Cities, Digger had tried to mentally calculate the number of hearings a trial judge in the Duluth courthouse had each year. By his mental calculations, without pencil and paper, he figured between 5,000 and 7,500 hearings each year. Most were short hearings of course, but of the total, a three week murder trial or a complex products liability case would only count for one hearing. He couldn't remember them all, or even anywhere near half, they went by so fast.

Griswold. It didn't ring a bell, hard as he tried to remember, even at considerable risk, if he lost track of Griswold's moves.

"I don't remember you," he said, finally.

"Not me, you ass!" Griswold actually lurched forward as he spoke, then withdrew back to the circle they were scribing. "Do you remember my brother?"

"Who?"

"My kid brother." Griswold answered slowly, still edging imperceptibly to his right. "His name was Billy, Billy Griswold. You sent him to prison for assault. He could have done local time and been on probation, but you sent him up for ten years!" Griswold's face was purple with rage, now. His colorless eyes staring right through Digger. "He died in prison! He was killed!"

Digger remembered. A First Degree Assault charge. It was a particularly vicious assault. The defendant had a prior criminal history. The Minnesota sentencing guidelines called for a presumptive commitment to the Department of Corrections of 122 months. At sentencing, both sides argued for a departure from the guidelines. The State wanted a double upward durational departure, the maximum usually allowed, to twice the presumed sentence, because of the viciousness of the beating. The defense asked for a dispositional departure to a stayed sentence with some local time and probation. Digger had followed the guidelines.

"I remember," he said.

"Well," snarled Griswold, "that's my reasons."

The two men crouched facing each other in silence once more, continuing their inevitable circling to the right by infinitesimal and almost imperceptible movements.

Digger switched back to his original tack and renewed his demand. "Get your coat!"

"Even if I went back to Duluth with you, you think the police would believe me, if I told them you were clean?" he said, edging further to his right. "The evidence against you is so overwhelming, there's nothin' I could do for you, if I wanted to." Just a few more feet.

"Well, that is what we are going to do, so let's go." Digger moved toward Griswold.

Griswold's right hand flashed toward the shelf on the wall by the door. Digger looked and saw the pistol, but too late. In an effort to stop Griswold he pulled the sock full of pennies from his pocket and hurled it at Griswold. It went high and wide, striking the wall with a loud thud above and behind Griswold's head. Griswold had the gun. It was pointed directly at Digger. The black hole that was the end of the barrel stared at him, menacingly. Frank Griswold stared at him, just as menacingly.

"Let's see, now, Judge," he said, straightening his arm slightly, bringing the gun closer to Digger, "we were talking about a trip, I think."

Digger was beaten. He had known he was taking a big chance, but did not know what else to do. Now things were worse, if that was possible. Griswold was unpredictable and not a little drunk. At least, so Digger had thought, until he saw Griswold's quick move toward the gun. He must have a great tolerance for the Scotch on the table next to the chair where he had been watching television. But even if he could handle the booze, it might make him mean enough to do something crazy. Digger began to believe there was a good chance he would not get out of this alive. He might not see Judy again. He wished with all his soul that he had stayed in custody and had not come to St. Paul this night.

"Well, Judge," Griswold said waving the gun, "I ain't goin on a trip, just now. You might, but not me. Yeah," he paused, "you might."

Splinters of oak flew through the room as the door frame shattered when the door burst open. The impact of the door striking Griswold in the back caused his finger to involuntarily tighten on the trigger. The explosion of the pistol shot in the small room was deafening. Digger fell backwards against the TV chair, knocking over the bottle of Scotch, the amber liquid flowing out onto the carpet.

The big men in trench coats followed the door into the room, one with a large nickel plated revolver, the other with a sawed off shotgun. The man called Lew, who had been the passenger in the Lincoln, shot Griswold. Griswold spun in pain, grabbing his right upper arm, and dropping his own pistol. The driver, Max, held the shotgun on Digger, while Griswold, now on the floor, writhed in pain.

Digger saw that two other men entered the room. He recognized Hollis Fowler and Frank Vagelli from the meeting at the Kitchi Gammi Club. Vagelli had scared him good that day, but it was Fowler that he thought was really dangerous.

In the confusion, Digger had thought he may have been shot by Griswold, but he found that was not the case. The earsplitting noise of the shot and the door bursting open had so shocked him, he had fallen, but the bullet had not found him.

Griswold was not so lucky. He was holding his hand over his wound to try to control the heavy bleeding. Lew bent over to check him. "Went right through, Boss," he said, looking up from Griswold and at the wall across the room. Eventually, he straightened and walked to the far wall, taking a pocket knife from his coat pocket. Digging at the drywall surface, he eventually pulled something from the wall. He held it up between two fingers. "Here's the slug," he said. "No point in leaving it here."

Hollis Fowler came further into the room and surveyed the situation. Frank Vagelli stood behind him, looking over the shorter man's shoulder, grinning that twisted grin at Digger.

"Well, Judge," Fowler said to Digger, "what sort of trouble have you got yourself into here?"

When Griswold had gotten around to get his gun, Milo and Vince got their own guns ready and prepared to assault the apartment building. When the door came crashing in and the first shot was fired, they stopped and watched the monitors. They had no intention of charging into a war, especially if the judge was already dead. When they saw that he was not dead, and in fact that he appeared unhurt, they left the van, running toward the entryway. Milo carried a small hand-held video monitor which was tuned to the frequency of the living room transmitter. As Vince worked the lock, Milo watched the scene above.

"This ain't going to be easy, Vince," he whispered.

"No shit, Milo," Vince answered, swinging the glass door open. He added, "But nothin' good ever is." He pulled his pistol from his pants and started for the elevator.

Milo followed, also with gun drawn.

"What are you going to do?" asked Digger.

"A good question, Judge," answered Fowler. "A very good question. One to which I myself did not have the answer until just now." He turned toward the man called Lew. "I take it what you just dug out of the wall over there came from your gun?'

"It did that," Lew grinned, "after going through this guy's arm first."

Griswold moaned. His arm felt like it was on fire, but it wasn't broken. The bullet had apparently missed the bone, making a clean path through the muscle. By direct pressure with his hand and the sleeve on his shirt, he had managed to control the bleeding somewhat.

"So, there is no evidence of our presence here?"

"None, so far," Lew answered, "except for the hole in the wall over there." He nodded toward the place where he had dug out his bullet.

"And that could have been made by any bullet?" asked Fowler.

"Oh, sure, I guess so," said Lew. "What are you getting at?"

"You don't happen to have a gun that cannot be identified, do you?" asked Fowler.

With his big pistol, Lew motioned toward his partner, Max, the driver, holding the shotgun on Digger.

"Never without one," said Max. "Always a use for a clean gun." He reached down to his left shoe, lifting up his pant leg, revealing an ankle holster from which he removed a lethal looking short barreled revolver.

"Excellent," said Fowler, taking the revolver from Max. "Now, Judge, to answer your question." He stepped to one side, being careful not to touch anything. "You are an escaped murderer. You came down here to get even with Griswold, here, but Griswold had a gun. So did you." He held up the small revolver from Max's ankle. "A shoot out occurred and, sadly, you both died. You shot each other."

Vagelli spoke. "I like it, Hollis," he said. "No one left to tell it different."

"Whatever you're gonna do, it better be quick," said Max, swinging the shotgun around pointing it to the walls separating them from other apartments. "We've got two shots fired, somebody is going to report it."

"Right, Max, but first," he looked at Griswold, "there is the matter of the money. Lew, do you think you can find a spot on Mr. Griswold that would be painful enough that he would be willing to answer a question?"

Lew lightly pressed a big foot on Griswold's upper right arm. Griswold screamed in pain. Holding his arm, still lying on the floor at Lew's feet, he gasped, "It's ... it's in the bedroom closet."

"Good!" said Fowler. He looked at Vagelli, indicating the bedroom. Vagelli stepped over Griswold and disappeared down the hall past the bathroom. A moment later, he appeared with the two large nylon duffel bags. He was smiling.

"Now gentlemen, we need this gun wiped clean and held in Judge Moss's hand to get authentic prints. Then we need Griswold, there, killed with this gun and the judge killed with Griswold's gun. And, as Max suggests, let's be quick about it."

Max held the shotgun on Digger as Lew went to work.

"Oh, and one more thing," added Hollis Fowler. "Fire a round from that little gun out the window, so we can account for the hole in the wall over there. The police may not mind that they can't find the slug, but we don't want them with guns that fired fewer shots than we have bullet holes."

"Smart," said Vagelli. He turned that twisted smile of his on Digger, as if to say, "I'm going to enjoy seeing you die here in just about a minute."

Vagelli's look sent a shiver down Digger's spine.

Lew had donned plastic gloves to handle the guns. He brought the ankle gun over to Digger, pushing it into his palm and forcing his fingers to close on it. With that done, he stepped away from Digger, turned, and without ceremony or compulsion, he shot Griswold in the chest. Griswold's body writhed and twitched violently for a moment and then lay still. Lew found a window in the dinette that opened. He fired a shot through it and closed it. The gun, he laid on the floor not far from Digger's feet. Working methodically, he crossed to Griswold's body and picked up Griswold's gun. He turned toward Digger.

"Hold it right there!"

Hollis Fowler spun around in surprise.

Frank Vagelli dropped the money bags.

Lew turned more slowly, Griswold's gun in one hand, reaching for his own weapon with the other. Max turned bringing the shotgun around to bear on the new arrival.

Several guns fired at once. The shotgun roared as Max fell forward, blood spurting from the awful wound in his neck made by the bullet from Vince Turcotte's revolver. The blast from the shotgun went high disintegrating several ceiling tiles in the far corner of the room.

Lew got one shot off from Griswold's pistol. Milo shot him before he could get to his more powerful pistol. Lew went down in a heap on top of the late Frank Griswold.

Frank Vagelli had drawn a pistol from a belt holster. He raised it, hesitantly, uncertain at whom to shoot, then aimed it at Milo while Milo was fighting Lew. Vince saw him and fired a round that struck Vagelli in the shoulder. Vagelli fired wildly as he went down. His bullet struck Hollis Fowler in the back. Fowler fell forward, striking the television set, which was still playing the old movie Griswold had been watching not long before.

At first, Digger was too shocked to move, then with shots being fired from what seemed all directions, he dropped to the floor and tried to stay out of the cross fire. As the firing ceased, a big hand reached down and dragged him to his feet. He looked into the eyes of a large man with thin strands of hair that looked like they were intended to be combed over his bald spot, but which hung away from the side of his head, giving him a ridiculous almost comic look. But the look in his eyes was anything but comical.

"Get out of here, Judge!" the man commanded.

"But I ...," began Digger.

"Now, Judge!" the man repeated. "Get out of here, right now!" The man pulled Digger near the door and literally hurled him through the door, into the hallway. Digger looked back. The man stood in the doorway, his right arm hanging down at his side, a pistol in his hand. He nodded at Digger, then turned back to the chaos inside.

Who were they? Why had they come? Why had they saved him? What was going on? These questions and more ran through Digger's mind as he ran down the stairway. One thing he decided he would not question further, was the balding man's direction to get the hell out of there.

Twenty minutes later, Digger Moss was traveling north on 35E, gripping the wheel of the old Mustang, his disguise reapplied. He had made an effort that had failed, miserably. He had almost gotten himself killed. He would go back to Duluth and let fate take its course.

He pressed a redial number on the cell phone Mike Reynolds had given him. Earlier he had dialed the number in advance without actually making the call so it could be dialed simply by touching a single button.

"Hello?"

"Peggy?"

"Digger?"

"Yes, Peggy. I need you to get a hold of Mike for me."

"Oh, Digger, are you all right?" she asked. "Everyone's been so worried." She knew better than to ask where he was. Digger didn't think anyone knew about the O'Malleys, but it was better to be safe.

"I'm okay, Peg," he said. "Better than I have a right to be."

"What do you need?"

"Tell Mike to meet me in Big Blue."

"When?" she asked. Since she didn't question the location, he assumed that she recognized the name of a Spirit Mountain parking lot. The O'Malleys were skiers. Also, she may not have recognized it, but simply did not ask, wanting only to help him in whatever way she was able, without question. Peggy O'Malley was like that.

He passed a road sign indicating Rush City a short distance ahead. "In about two hours, Peg."

"Digger, it's after Midnight now."

"I know."

"I'll find him, Digger. You be careful."

"Thanks, Peg." He closed the phone and put it on the seat beside him.

Digger was north of Hinckley when the phone rang. He nearly lost control of the Mustang, he was so startled. Nervously he reached for the ringing telephone, opened it and said a tentative, "Hello?"

"Digger, it's Mike. I got your message. What's going on?"

"Mike? I didn't expect a call."

"I gave you the phone, Digger. I know the number."

"You know where to meet?" Digger asked.

"Yes, I'll be going there shortly."

"Any chance you'll be followed?"

"Maybe," said Reynolds. "I'll leave early and drive around a bit. Maybe come in from the back way."

"Good idea. Mike, I'm coming in. I'll turn myself in, but the way I want to do it. You and me going to Chief Morgan. Maybe you should call him."

"That may cause more problems," Mike said. "Let me think about it. I'll see you at Big Blue."

Digger closed the phone, put it back on the seat, and drove on through the night.

CHAPTER TWENTY-ONE

The Big Blue parking lot is one of several dirt parking lots on the road into the chalet at the top of the eastern runs at Spirit Mountain. Mike Reynolds sat in his Jeep and waited. It was about 2:25 a.m. when he saw the Mustang pull into the lot.

Digger parked the Mustang and hurried over to the Jeep. He still had his disguise. As he climbed in the Jeep, he said, "Let's go."

As he steered the Jeep onto the road, Mike said, "I have a plan, Digger."

"Good, I could use one."

"I think we'd have trouble getting into police headquarters in City Hall. And I think you're right about John Morgan. He'll treat you right."

"So what's your plan?" asked Digger.

"I didn't call Morgan."

"What?"

"We're going to see him."

"I don't understand," said Digger.

"We're going to go wake him up, at his home."

John Morgan was a sound sleeper. His Park Point home was on the bay side of the Point out past the Bayside Market and across from Hearding Island. Traffic went by his house all night long, especially in the summer, often with expensive stereo automobile sound systems that could be felt as much as heard. He had learned to sleep through it all. When they arrived at his door, it took a while for him to become fully awake, even with his wife's help.

He stood in a bathrobe in the doorway to his home. "Reynolds. What do you want, Mike?" he asked. "Christ, it's after three in the morning."

Reynolds stood on the front step to the Morgan home. "I've got a surprise for you Chief."

From the darkness beside the front porch, Digger Moss, disguise removed, stepped into the light of a hurricane lamp style electric porch light.

201

Dave Sullivan

"Jesus Christ!" was all the Chief was able to say.

Digger and Mike had judged the Chief of Police correctly. Without fanfare, he put Digger in his own unmarked car – he did insist on handcuffing Digger – and drove him up to the jail. Mike Reynolds followed. At the jail, Chief Morgan walked his prisoner in, arranged for him to be processed and placed back in the high security section of the jail, and left. On his way back to his home, he called police headquarters and reported to the desk that Judge Moss was back in custody. He asked that all of the officers working on the case be notified and that the County Attorneys office and the court be notified in the morning. He drove home and went back to bed. The sun was rising over Lake Superior as he crawled back into bed. He decided it was worth it to try to get more sleep, even if it was only an hour or so before he had to arise to get ready for work and be at City Hall by his usual 7:30. This day he might be a little late. Thirty minutes or so.

It was just past nine when prosecuting attorney, H. Gordon Wilkins came marching into Morgan's office. He was followed by two young attorneys carrying briefcases.

"Why was I not informed when the defendant was apprehended?" he demanded. He stood across from Morgan, framed by his two assistants, who, like their boss, were dressed nearly identically in dark conservative suits and wingtip shoes.

"I sent word." Chief Morgan did not look up from the document he was signing. "Didn't you get it?"

"Directing your desk sergeant to have the County Attorney's office called in the morning is hardly good enough. I expected to be notified as soon as something happened, anything." His face reddened and his voice rose in volume.

"Why? So you could get in on the bust?" Morgan looked up now. He surveyed Wilkins and his minions. "By the time we knew anything, Judge Moss was already in my car on the way to the jail. It was all over." Raising one bushy eyebrow at Wilkins he added, nonchalantly, "I went home to bed."

202

Wilkins face was crimson. He was nearly bursting. The arrest of Moss was news, big news, and he, the lead prosecuting attorney in charge of the case, had been cut out of it by this small town police chief, who seemed singularly unimpressed with Wilkins' presence on the case.

"Anything else?" Morgan had returned his eyes to the papers on the desk in front of him.

"What?"

"Do you want anything else, Mr. Wilkins?" Chief John Morgan rose from his chair and straightened to his full height, dwarfing the slender prosecutor. "Or are you going to just stick around and interfere with my work for a while longer." His tone was unmistakable. H. Gordon Wilkins turned on his heels and left, his two subordinates following behind.

Assistant Chief Pelton smiled as he passed Wilkins and his entourage. "Getting yourself into more trouble, Chief?" he chided.

"I suppose I should have been more courteous," Morgan acknowledged, "but that little prick annoys the hell out of me."

Pelton stood in his usual corner. "What you don't understand, Chief, and what lawyer Wilkins does," he crossed his arms in front of him, "is that this is not your case. It's his. It is not for you to screw around with that basic premise. Understand?"

"Huh! That'll be the day!"

Wilkins was livid. As he strode across the Civic Center from City Hall to the county courthouse, his aids could hardly keep up with him. People enjoying the big centrally located Joe Priley fountain or reading the names carved into the war memorial, stopped to stare at him, his rage was so apparent. Neither assistant dared say a thing as the elevator rose to the fifth floor, seemingly powered by Wilkins' anger.

"That God damned Morgan!" he shouted at the chief prosecutor in the St. Louis County Attorney's office, pointing a bony finger. "You've got to get me more cooperation from him!"

Marilee Jackson entered the office, as the chief prosecutor, Andrew Preston, began to answer Wilkins. "Listen," he began, "you're here because we chose not to prosecute a sitting judge in our own county. We asked the A.G. for help. If you can't get cooperation out of the local police, may I suggest it might be your attitude?"

"Wha. ..What do you mean?" stuttered Wilkins.

"I mean if you treat them right, they'll treat you right." He looked at Marilee Jackson and added, "But if you shit in your own nest, you'll have to sit in it by yourself."

H. Gordon Wilkins' disposition was not improved by Preston's remarks. He stormed out of Preston's office on his way to the office of the County Attorney, himself. His assistants had been waiting in the hallway. They fell in behind him as he marched down the hall.

Thornton Pederson had been St. Louis County Attorney for seventeen years. Like his predecessor, he was not a trial lawyer. He was a good attorney and a good administrator. He managed the office well. The members of his staff were constantly aware of their luck. He supported them. He gave them wide latitude and broad authority and discretion in how they represented the county, in civil cases and criminal matters.

He was also a politician. He calmed the raging Wilkins, told him he understood the frustrations of the situation, and promised to speak to Chief Morgan, with whom he had a long and friendly working relationship.

Thus comforted, Wilkins and his troops returned to the offices the County Attorney had provided them. Wilkins did not, however, like the thought of his missing a wonderful opportunity to be involved in bringing Moss back before the court. But, he thought, it's not too late.

"Schedule a hearing for this afternoon." he commanded.

"What?" asked a young lawyer. "What kind of hearing?"

"A Hearing hearing," snapped Wilkins. "Get a hold of the clerk who's doing the scheduling on this file and tell her to call the jail and have them bring him up this afternoon. This time in a jail uniform and leg and wrist shackles." He grinned sarcastically at the thought of "the Honorable Digger Moss" appearing in front of Andrew Forsythe in an orange jail suit with handcuffs and leg irons. The only thing that would be better would be if he were dressed in the humiliating wide, black and white horizontal stripes of the Lake County Jail uniform. His brief reverie was interrupted.

"Is Judge Forsythe here in Duluth?" asked an assistant.

"Yes," answered Wilkins, "I think he is here. He'll be instructing the Grand Jury tomorrow. But you better check on it."

"And what kind of hearing did you want me to ask for?"

Wilkins was impatient. "Anything!" he said. "Just tell the clerk we need a hearing right away. He ran from his scheduled omnibus hearing, for Christ's sake! I think most would agree that he needs to be brought before the judge."

As the assistant was leaving Wilkins' temporary office, Wilkins added, "Oh, and by the way, when you get the setting, call the media people and let them know."

They sat across from each other at the Formica table in the visiting room. Neither had spoken for several minutes. Judy held his hands, which were bound by handcuffs chained together. Digger had been allowed to see Judy twice and his attorney twice since he arrived at the jail in the custody of Chief John Morgan early that morning.

Although unimaginable not long ago, they were both relieved that Digger was in the county jail. After he related the story of the Roseville apartment and how two strange men had undoubtedly saved him from certain and immediate death, they both felt whatever happened would be better than they might have had just a few hours before.

"Digger," asked Judy, "what will happen now?"

"The Grand Jury meets tomorrow," he answered. "With what's happened now, I don't think there's any doubt they'll indict for First Degree Murder."

"Oh, God," she sighed.

The door opened and a uniformed jailer entered. "Sorry folks, but we've got to get the judge ready to go to court."

"What?" asked Digger.

"That's right, Judge," he answered. "You got a hearing this afternoon."

"What kind of hearing?"

"Haven't a clue, Judge. All I know is that you're in front of Judge Forsythe in Judge Parker's courtroom at two o'clock. We have to take you in the van with the group going up right after lunch."

Randall McCoy surveyed the men seated around the big table in the boardroom in the basement of the Kitchi Gammi Club. They were nervous. They did not know what to do. They had only the news coverage of a blood bath in a Roseville apartment belonging to one Frank Griswold. The coverage had identified three of the five bodies found in the apartment as the tenant, Frank Griswold, a businessman, Hollis Fowler, of Minneapolis, and one Frank Vagelli. The other two bodies had not been identified.

McCoy was not unhappy with the situation. He would not miss Fowler and Vagelli. Griswold he had positively hated. He was actually pleased with Griswold's demise.

McCoy sat at the head of the table, again.

"What about the money?" asked Orrin Rasmussen, his color still several shades paler than his normal rich tan.

"Yes," said another. "Where is our Three Million Dollars?"

"I do not know the answer to that question," answered McCoy. "I suspect we never will."

"Is that a problem?" asked Charles Hood.

"Except for being out the money, it shouldn't be." This was Fred McCloskey. "It was cash, in small bills. Not traceable to us. Right, Randall?"

"That's right," agreed McCoy. "The money is not traceable. As far as the amount goes, its loss is the least of our worries. We can afford it."

"What *is* the most of our worries?" inquired an obviously nervous Bert Johnson.

"If the money was not found by the police, does that mean someone else was there?" asked another.

"No," said McCoy. "I thought about that. I'm sure the money wasn't there. Griswold would have had it in some more secure place, either a safe deposit vault, or actually deposited in one or more banks."

"What are we going to do?"

Randall McCoy resumed command of the group. It was a position he had missed. The humility suffered at the hands of Griswold that day on the beach and then the not so subtle takeover by Hollis Fowler and his henchman, Vagelli, had not gone well with McCoy, but now, he was back in charge.

"Nothing right now," he said. "Fowler was right, Judge Moss is not going to do anything. In the first place he has no proof. We saw to that. Griswold didn't give him anything he could use against us ...and Griswold is gone."

"And later?" asked one of the men.

"And later," repeated McCoy, "we'll see. Maybe we won't have to do anything. Maybe we'll be dealing with a different judge. Fowler was also right when he said that all the reasons we got into this scheme are still there. We may want to do something with the next judge, too, but it will be different. It depends on who the judge is."

He looked around the room, at the walls of gleaming polished paneling, the leaded glass windows, and finally at the men gathered around the table. They were nervous and uncomfortable, but he would lead them through this, and all to their substantial financial gain, he was now certain.

CHAPTER TWENTY-TWO

T he "Hearing" hearing went just as Wilkins had wanted. Digger was brought to the courthouse amid plenty of fanfare and media attention. He did wear a St. Louis County Jail orange jumpsuit. He was shackled, both wrists and ankles. It was exactly the demeaning experience H. Gordon Wilkins had wanted it to be.

Digger was taken up the private back elevator to the courtroom, but getting there from the first floor holding area was a very public affair indeed. Four armed deputies escorted him through the main hallway of the first floor which was jammed with reporters who had learned he would be brought through the area. They walked him past the door to Courtroom No. 3 through which he had escaped during transport to his last hearing.

Getting off the elevator on the fourth floor, he was taken directly to the holding cell between the courtrooms on the west side of the building. Chief Judge Parker's courtroom was one of those and was where Digger would be appearing before Judge Andrew Forsythe.

Only when everyone was in place, would Digger be moved to the courtroom. Mike Reynolds sat with him in the holding cell, waiting. There was nothing to do or to talk about. No preparation for the hearing to be done. Digger had escaped and returned of his own volition. The prosecutor had been denied a messy apprehension and the opportunity to make Digger look even worse. They would say nothing, make no argument, and let H. Gordon Wilkins, III, rant on for a while, as he seemed so bent on doing. After all, not much was going to happen. Bail was already set at Two Million Dollars. More wouldn't matter.

Outside the westerly facing, iron-barred window of the holding cell, the gray, stone building that formerly housed the St. Louis County Jail was a bleak reminder to Digger of his possible prospects.

Finally, the deputy came to get them. With Mike Reynolds following behind, Digger shuffled along the hallway, unable to walk normally because of the shackles around his ankles which were held together by a very short chain. His wrists were in handcuffs, also chained together and to a chain encircling his waist. Digger also wore a stun belt. The sheriff's deputies were taking no chances.

It was in this manner that Digger entered the courtroom through one of the doors by the judge's bench. He faced a waiting audience, all watching him. Two more armed uniformed deputies stood by the rear door to the main hallway.

H. Gordon Wilkins sat at the prosecutor's counsel table with his two young assistants. Despite Wilkins' gaunt features and his normal sour expression, he actually looked pleased with himself. He had, thought Digger, what could only be described as a "shit-eating grin."

Behind Wilkins' counsel table, the benches were packed with news reporters and spectators. They all watched Digger as he entered. They saw how he was shackled. They held eye contact with him and seemed to silently communicate to him, "Now we've got you! You won't get away from us again!"

Digger shuffled his way across the pit toward the defense table. He crossed that area between the counsel tables and the imposing oak judge's bench, taking tiny steps across the deep blue carpet, the chains on his legs rattling with each small step.

Mike Reynolds held a chair out for him. Judy rose from the first row of benches and came to him, her face full of compassion and concern. Her large oval eyes were rimmed with red from tears not too long before. She reached for his hand, but a deputy, apologetically but forcefully, intervened.

As soon as Digger and Mike Reynolds were seated, Judge Forsythe entered and the courtroom was called to order.

"State vs. James Digby Moss," Forsythe announced, looking at the file in front of him and also a printed hearing calendar the clerk had clipped to the file. After a moment, he looked up and addressed counsel.

"I'm not entirely sure why we are here," he said. "Mr. Prosecutor, perhaps you can help me out here?"

"Certainly, your Honor," said Wilkins, rising from his seat. "H. Gordon Wilkins for the State, your Honor. We scheduled this hearing after the defendant's apprehension following his escape from custody."

"Bail is already set, correct?" asked the judge. "Two Million Dollars, if I recall," he added, leafing through the file.

"That's right, Judge," said Wilkins. "We simply wish to make a record of what has occurred, request an increase in the amount of the bail and reschedule the omnibus hearing."

"All right, go ahead," muttered Forsythe, who thought he had yet to hear any real good reason to have this hearing. Bail was already high, the omnibus hearing could be scheduled by the clerk, and there was no real reason to "make a record" about the prisoner's escape which was certainly well documented. He leaned back in his chair to listen, wishing he were at his desk taking care of some matters that *did* need his attention.

"Thank you, your Honor. May it please the Court, we are here because the defendant, Judge James Digby Moss, here," he pointed to Digger in the orange jumpsuit and shackles, grim satisfaction apparent in Wilkins' expression, "escaped from this very courthouse!" Wilkins stood beside the end of the counsel table, his thin frame leaning against the wood, a long slender index finger touching the polished wooden surface.

"Judge," he tapped the finger on the table top, "at the Rule 5 initial appearance on these charges, we asked that the defendant be held without bail or that bail be set at least Three Million Dollars. We repeat that request at this time."

"Mr. Reynolds?" Judge Forsythe looked over toward the defense table.

"No comment, Judge Forsythe," said Reynolds. "The defense does not oppose such a request."

"Hmmh," muttered Forsythe. "All right, bail is increased to Three Million Dollars. Anything else?"

"The omnibus hearing, your Honor?" said Wilkins.

"Let's wait for the Grand Jury," said Forsythe. "Let's find out what charges we are dealing with before we schedule anything further. Mr. Reynolds, is your client requesting a speedy omnibus hearing on these charges?"

"Not at this time, your Honor," answered Reynolds.

"Very well, then, we'll adjourn at this time." Forsythe rose to leave the courtroom.

The Grand Jury proceeding went smoothly and quickly. Behind closed doors, Grand Jury members heard testimony and reviewed evidence offered by H. Gordon Wilkins, III. The evidence included a number of photographs of the defendant, which the police had received anonymously and which, for that reason (lack of foundation witnesses), Reynolds hoped to keep out of the evidence at trial.

The Grand Jury proceeding is strictly a presentation to the Grand Jury by the prosecutor seeking an indictment. The defendant is not represented in the proceeding. Witnesses are not cross examined or exhibits objected to by any attorney representing the defendant.

After a day and a half, they voted to indict Digger Moss for Murder in the First Degree.

The next weeks flew by for Mike Reynolds as he tried to meet the obligations of his regular practice and work with Digger on his defense strategy. For Digger, they crawled by like the tortoise in the famous race with the hare: slow, but steady, and with the destination inevitable. He was unable to do anything. Before he was arrested, and after he had escaped, he was able to take action to try to clear himself. Now, he just sat. Being naturally from Mars, as opposed to Venus, a distinction made famous in a best selling book about the difference between men and women, which Judy had demanded that he read, Digger wanted to take action. He wanted to fix the problem ... now! Sitting idle while the problem remained was not suited to his character or his personality.

At the omnibus hearing, they waived any pretrial issues, entered a Not Guilty plea and asked that trial be set.

Digger sat in the St. Louis County Jail, waiting. He was held in the high security section, reserved for prisoners who were high security risks or who needed special protection from other prisoners. Arguably, Digger qualified for both. In any event, after his escape, the sheriff's office would take no chances with him. In this section of the jail, everything was stainless steel and built in. Nothing existed that wasn't nailed down. The atmosphere was depressing. Digger was not at all sure he could survive the wait for the trial.

Finally, the trial itself approached. Mike and Digger reviewed the trial preparation, put together a trial notebook in a three-ring binder which Mike would use during trial, and made an extra copy for Digger, although he was not allowed to have it at the jail except when he was visiting with Mike.

Now the trial approached. Digger consciously used his anticipation to battle the misery of the jail surroundings as he waited.

The trial would begin with v*oir dire*, the jury selection process. And it would begin very soon.

CHAPTER TWENTY-THREE

Voir dire, or jury selection, began in Digger's case on a Tuesday morning. On the previous day, 150 jurors had reported in two separate groups of 75 each. The first group reported to the Fourth Floor Jury Lounge at 8:30 a.m. The second group arrived at 1:30 p.m. Clerks from Court Administration met them and got them settled in at the tables and chairs in the jury lounge.

For orientation, each group was addressed by the Deputy Court Administrator who had the duties of Jury Commissioner. She explained the practical matters such as parking, location of the cafeteria and restrooms, and showed them a thirty-minute video tape about the court system and the duties of the judge and jury.

After the video, nine-page questionnaires were handed out to the prospective jurors to be completed by them individually. As each juror completed the questionnaire, that juror was free to leave to report back when summoned. The jurors took from twenty minutes to an hour and a half to complete the questionnaire.

In the first paragraph, the questionnaire contained a simplified description of the case, including Digger's full name and occupation; the name and occupation of the victim, Sergeant Greg Larson; and the names of the lawyers for both sides. A list of possible witnesses who might testify in the case was also included at the beginning of the questionnaire. The jurors were sworn under oath by the clerks before beginning to answer the written questions.

The questions had been proposed by the lawyers and ruled upon by Judge Forsythe. They were designed to assist counsel in the jury selection process which, in a murder case, could be quite lengthy.

On that Tuesday morning when *voir dire* began, after the lawyers had had an opportunity to review the jurors' completed questionnaires, Judge Forsythe called for the first juror for individual *voir dire* examination.

"All right, Mr. Hackett," Judge Forsythe addressed the bailiff, "you may bring in the first juror."

213

H. Gordon Wilkins, III and his entourage were settled in at the counsel table closest to the jury box to the left of Judge Forsythe. Assistant St. Louis County Attorney Marilee Jackson sat on the first row bench immediately behind the prosecutor. Mike Reynolds and Digger Moss sat at the other counsel table. Judy Moss sat on the bench behind them. Peggy O'Malley sat on one side of her. Margaret Elizabeth Moss Winfield, Judy and Digger's daughter, sat next to her mother on the other side. Their two sons sat beside their sister, closest to the wall opposite the jury box.

The clerk stood holding a computer printout. "The first juror is Alice Radloff," she announced as the bailiff started down the aisle for the door. He passed between two distinct groups. On his left, behind the prosecutors' table, were members of the victim's family, fellow police officers and acquaintances. On the right, besides Digger's family, were a scattering of courthouse employees and a large contingent of media representatives. While the media would certainly follow and report the several days of jury selection, it was the lull before the storm. It only signified that the trial would soon begin. The real circus would be when the trial began in earnest, with opening statements and the testimony of witnesses.

However, in this case, even the *voir dire* was of special interest. Even with 150 jurors in the panel of prospective jurors, everyone wondered if a fair and impartial jury could be found. Many believed one could not.

Bailliff Hackett appeared in the rear door of the courtroom with a tall thin woman with thick eyeglasses and dark brown hair pulled tightly back into a bun. Hackett pointed toward the bench and followed her as she walked hesitantly up the aisle. The clerk stood and directed her to the witness box, saying, "Ms. Radloff, you are still under oath for this examination. Please have a seat in the witness stand and state your full name for the record, spelling your last name."

Alice Radloff climbed the steps to the witness box, seated herself, and rolled the witness chair close to the microphone.

"Alice Marie Radloff, R-A-D-L-O-F-F." she spoke nervously into the microphone, so closely that her voice was heard only through the sound system's speakers, the amplified voice carrying throughout the crowded courtroom.

The court and counsel had agreed that because the general questions Forsythe might normally have asked of a jury panel were covered in the first few questions in the written questionnaire, *voir dire* would begin with defense counsel rather than the Court.

"Ms. Radloff, my name is Mike Reynolds. I represent the defendant, Judge Moss, here." Mike gestured toward Digger, seated beside him. "In your questionnaire, you answered that you have heard of Judge Moss, but have not met him, is that correct?"

"Yes, that's true."

"What have you heard about him?"

The prospective juror looked toward the high ceiling, thinking what to say. "Oh, I don't know," she answered. "I do read the paper and I watch the local news. I guess I've heard his name that way. I know he's a judge."

"Can you remember any specifics?" asked Reynolds. "Any decisions or rulings he made?"

"I'm not sure," she responded. "I remember one case where the judge ruled in favor of a Bed and Breakfast going into one of the big old mansions in the East End. It was a big controversy in the city. I think that was him."

Digger smiled and nodded.

"Were you disappointed in that decision?" asked Mike.

"No, I didn't care," she said. "It's not my neighborhood."

"Well, thank you Ms. Radloff," said Mike. "Let's shift gears a little and talk about what you may have heard about this case."

Alice Radloff had definitely heard about the case. Who hadn't? Mike Reynolds' questions disclosed that she had followed the case closely, that she had formed a definite opinion that it was an open and shut case against Digger, and that she wanted to be on the jury.

Under the circumstances, Reynolds challenged the juror for cause. H. Gordon Wilkins opposed the challenge. Judge Forsythe asked the proposed juror if she could follow his instructions including that the defendant was presumed innocent until proven guilty beyond a reasonable doubt. She said she could. Reynolds exercised his first peremptory challenge which excluded Alice Radloff from the Digger Moss jury.

The score: O for one. One juror examined, none selected.

Ordinarily, the entire jury panel would be in the courtroom for *voir dire*. A certain number would be called to the jury box for *voir dire* examination by the judge and the lawyers. That number would be calculated by starting with the size of the jury, twelve in felony cases; adding the number of alternates desired, usually two or three; and adding the number of peremptory challenges, three for the State and five for the defense.

Peremptory challenges are those challenges by which a party may eliminate a prospective juror for any reason ... or for *almost* any reason. In modern jurisprudence, the United States Supreme Court has prohibited the use of a peremptory challenge to exclude a prospective juror based upon race. Except when faced with a *Batson* challenge, so named after that Supreme Court decision, the reasons for the exercise of a peremptory challenge need not be disclosed.

When both sides have passed the jury panel for cause, meaning they don't challenge any of them for specific reasons for which the judge should excuse them, the parties then exercise their peremptory challenges, thereby "selecting" the jury and alternates.

However, in a first degree murder case, such as this, the rules are different. Jurors are examined individually instead of as a panel. The number of peremptory challenges is larger. The State has nine and the defendant has fifteen. Also, instead of deciding the peremptory challenges after the entire panel has been passed for cause by both sides, the challenges must be made or not at the end of the examination of each individual juror.

"The next juror is William Marshall," announced the clerk.

Bill Marshall was an easy going retired railroad engineer who had read about the case, but held no opinion. He had heard of Judge Moss, but didn't know anything that would affect his ability to be fair. Mike Reynolds passed him for cause.

It was H. Gordon Wilkins' turn. It soon became apparent that Wilkins' strategy was argument and indoctrination rather than inquiry about background or possible conflict of interest or bias. He kept stressing the fact that the victim was a police officer and the defendant was a judge.

"Do you think this defendant deserves any special consideration in this case because he is a judge?" he asked.

"I do not," said Marshall with conviction.

"And do you understand, Mr. Marshall, that as the prosecutor, I have the burden of proving to you that the defendant is guilty beyond a reasonable doubt and that his Honor, Judge Forsythe will so instruct you?"

"I think so," said the prospective juror.

"And do you understand, Mr. Marshall, that proof beyond a reasonable doubt is not proof beyond all doubt or beyond all possibility of doubt?" Wilkins looked straight at the juror in the witness box.

"I do," said Marshall. "If there's doubt, it has to be reasonable."

Mike Reynolds winced. It probably didn't matter, and there weren't other jurors listening, but he hoped Marshall didn't think there had to be reasonable doubt to acquit as opposed to there having to be proof beyond a reasonable doubt to convict. It might seem a subtle distinction to a prospective juror, but before Mike was done with them, they should understand the difference clearly. He would stress the presumption of innocence *vis-à-vis* the burden of proof more carefully with the subsequent panel members.

"I pass Mr. Marshall for cause, your Honor," proclaimed H. Gordon Wilkins.

After a brief discussion with Digger, Reynolds exercised his second peremptory challenge.

O for two.

"The next juror is Ms. Naomi Altman," declared the clerk.

They examined seven prospective jurors that first day. By 4:30, the lawyers were exhausted, although H. Gordon Wilkins sat ramrod straight and refused to acknowledge the fatigue he was feeling. Of the seven questioned, they had only agreed on one. Reynolds had exercised two more peremptory challenges, bringing his total to four. The State had exercised two of its nine challenges. The process promised to be slow and lengthy.

The lone juror selected had been carefully instructed by Judge Forsythe not to talk about the case with anyone else, to avoid all news coverage, to immediately advise the Court Administrator's office if she was approached by anyone, and to report back for the trial when she was notified. Her name was Laura Kilbane, a medical transcriptionist employed by St. Mary's-Duluth Clinic, or SMDC

Health Center, the largest health care provider in the area. It had been born of the merger a few years earlier of the Duluth Clinic and St. Mary's Hospital. Ms. Kilbane was twenty-nine, married, and had three children, ages seven, six, and three. Her husband was a lineman for a rural electric company that supplied power up the North Shore, beyond the reaches of Minnesota Power & Light Co., more commonly known as "Minnesota Power," which supplied the City of Duluth and other outlying areas.

Laura Kilbane recognized the name of Judge Moss, but knew nothing about him. She had no connection with law enforcement, knew very little about the case ("When you have three little kids, you don't see the news much."), and she was sure she would be fair.

They had agreed to have three alternates to the twelve-person jury.

One for seven. One down and fourteen more to go.

Kate Riley had decided to keep a low profile during the trial. She did, however, find her way to the holding cell where Digger, Mike Reynolds, and Judy Moss had been allowed to meet before Digger was transported back up to the jail for the night. The door to the holding cell remained locked and guarded by two armed, uniformed Sheriff's deputies. One of them recognized Judge Riley as she approached and unlocked the door for her to enter the cell.

"Well?" asked Kate of the group.

"Not much to tell, Kate," Digger answered. "It's my trial and even I had a few moments where I nearly fell asleep in my chair. Andy Forsythe was stifling yawns for the last hour and a half."

"It is slow," agreed Mike Reynolds, "but individual *voir dire* like this always is ... slow and repetitive."

"When do you think you will have a jury?" asked Kate.

"At this rate, about three weeks," answered Digger, shaking his head and adjusting his weight in his chair to relieve a pinch from the stun belt he wore under his shirt and suit coat. After his escape, the Sheriff's deputies were taking no chances.

"It will start to go quicker, I think," said Mike. "It always does. I'm sure we'll have a jury in five or six days now."

But he was wrong.

He continued. "We've got to make it go fast, if we can do it without jeopardizing our selection of jurors," he said.

"I understand your wanting to get it over with," said Kate, "but what's the rush?"

Mike answered. "The prosecution's most compelling evidence is the stuff that came to them in the anonymous envelopes. They had to disclose it in discovery. It's the pictures of Digger outside the Larson residence, allegedly before and after the murder, and the pictures of the drug exchanges, the drugs and the money. You know the stuff, Judge. It was undoubtedly sent by the man we now know as Griswold, who died in his apartment in Roseville."

"Yes, I remember," she acknowledged.

"Well, at this point, we don't think there's any foundation for it. They don't have the photographer or the camera and therefore they can't lay a foundation for the photographs speaking for themselves or actually being evidence of what they purport to show."

"Most photographs don't come in that way, anyway, Mike," Judge Kate Riley responded. "Almost always, the foundation is simply whether the photo fairly and accurately represents the particular scene or thing in the picture." She went on, lecturing on the Rules of Evidence, partly for Judy's benefit, and partly just to think aloud. "You don't need the photographer. It doesn't matter when the picture was taken, by whom, or under what circumstances. If a picture is of an accident scene, for example, and a witness who saw the scene testifies the picture fairly and accurately represents the scene, it comes in." She looked at Judy Moss, who was listening intently but appeared somewhat confused. "It could be a picture of the moon, at that point, and it wouldn't matter, as long as it looked like the accident scene." Judy Moss looked toward Kate Riley, her look of confusion even more pronounced.

"And who would that be, Judge?" asked Mike.

"Who? What who?" Kate's carefully penciled eyebrows raised in query.

"Who is the witness you are talking about?" Mike persisted.

"Well, I don't know," said Kate. "I haven't thought about it before."

"We have," said Mike. "And we're sure that H. Gordon Wilkins, III and his minions have given the subject considerable thought. We don't think there is anybody."

Kate thought a moment. She went through the pictures in her mind. She remembered the scenes of Digger exchanging drugs for money in a Duluth parking lot with a known drug dealer. Then there were the photos of Greg Larson's body and photos of Digger going to and coming from the house where the body was found. Each photograph was time-stamped by the camera. The times purported to show the time of the photo of the body as between the times of the photos of Digger's arrival and departure.

"Digger can lay the foundation," she finally answered. "He knows about the drug deal photos and he knows he was at Larson's house coming and going as the pictures show. If he is asked on cross-examination, he'll either have to lay the foundation that the pictures fairly and accurately portray what they purport to show, or he'll have to lie on the witness stand."

"But Digger doesn't have to testify," said Mike.

The room was silent for a moment. Gradually Kate Riley realized what they were saying. "Oh, my God," she said slowly, in a voice just above a whisper. "Are you serious?"

"We are," said Mike. "We've talked about it. It's the smart thing to do, at this point."

"Digger?" Kate looked past Mike at her friend and colleague.

"That's right, Kate," he responded. "We've talked about it a lot. Without the photographic evidence, we don't think the State can meet its burden of proof."

"But, Digger," Kate said, "don't you *have* to testify? You are talking about asking a jury to decide the case without hearing whether you even deny what they claimed happened?"

"It looks like the smartest move at this time," said Mike, trying hard to think like Digger's lawyer and not his good friend.

"Katy, do you disagree?" asked Judy. "Digger and Mike have talked to me about whether he will testify, but I don't think I understand all the legal ramifications."

"I don't know that I disagree with their legal judgment, Jude," said Kate. "I'm just concerned with the impact of Digger deciding not to testify in this case. I think in any criminal case, the jury wants to hear from the defendant. But they understand and they are instructed that the defendant has an absolute right to remain silent; that if he or she chooses to do so, it cannot be used against him or her; and the burden of proof on the state remains the same." She ran the fingers of her right hand through her fiery hair and continued. "But, in this case, I think not only the jury, but the community, and even the nation are waiting with bated breath to hear what the Honorable Judge James Digby Moss has to say in response!"

Judy nodded and looked at Digger and Mike. Digger shook his head, acknowledging Kate's point. People expected him to tell his story.

Mike Reynolds interrupted the silence that followed Kate's statement. "Look," he said, "we've got to think legal strategy. We've got to think about the evidence. We've got to think acquittal. If the State hasn't met its burden of proof when Wilkins rests, we should get out, right then and there!"

"I guess you're right," said Kate. "A motion for directed verdict wouldn't do any good. Andy Forsythe would never take this case away from the jury."

"Right," agreed Digger.

"All this assumes," said Kate, "that the pictures haven't come in, in the State's Case-in-Chief."

"Right," Mike agreed. "And that's the point. We need to get this case going before they get more foundational evidence for those damning photographs."

"What about Zorro?" asked Kate.

"Who?" asked Judy.

"Zorro. The drug dealer in the photos with Digger," Kate answered. "Zorro could lay the foundation for the pictures he was in."

"That's exactly right," said Mike, "but he's not on the State's witness list. We don't think they have found him. If we can get a jury picked and get going, we could get through the State's case in a few days. Oh, Wilkins will try to drag it out, but if we keep the pictures out, how much more do they have, and how much of it, if any, proves that Digger is the one who killed Greg Larson?"

"What do you intend to do?" asked Kate.

"Speed up my *voir dire* and not be so quick to use our peremptories," said Mike. "Just get rid of those who say they already have an opinion against Digger that won't change."

"Well, I hope it all works," Kate sighed. They all nodded their solemn agreement.

"We'll get a jury in five or six days and then we'll see what Wilkins has."

But he was wrong.

In Minneapolis, Milo Bracken followed the story in the papers. He was reading the St. Paul Pioneer Press, having already finished the "Strib" and the Duluth News-Tribune. A Pall Mall cigarette butt smoldered in a heavy glass ashtray already full of butts of cigarettes smoked down to almost nothing. He sipped from a can of Coke and continued reading.

Jury selection was going slowly. More than one reporter had raised the question of whether it would even be possible to achieve the selection of a fair and impartial jury in the courthouse where the defendant, a sitting trial court judge presided in the city where the victim, a city police officer had been brutally murdered.

The case was also the subject of national television news coverage. Nationally known legal experts commented on the case, uniformly noting the unusual character of the trial of a judge accused of murdering a police officer. On CourtTV, Johnnie Cochran was himself in awe, a considerable accomplishment in itself, at the difficulty in getting a jury in such a case.

"I don't see how they can do it," he told the camera from a backdrop lined with thick law books. "But neither side wants a venue change." He smiled a knowing smile to show he was drawing upon his considerable expertise. "They both think that the fact that the defendant is a local judge cuts in their favor. But," and he narrowed his eyes at the camera and spoke up close and personal, "somebody is going to end up very wrong!"

On NBC, Harvard professor Arthur Miller, gray, three-piece suit trim and immaculate, handkerchief in coat pocket with matching, perfectly knotted necktie, smiled at the camera as he analyzed the legal issues for the benefit of the national television audience.

Milo smoothed his comb-over with his hand, carefully arranging the long thin hairs over his baldness, and sipped his Coke. Poor Judge Moss, he thought. He's in the thick of it now. It was that God damned Griswold. What a snake. Milo drank more Coke to calm himself. It didn't help. He thought about something stronger to do the job.

Over the next several trial days, four more jurors were selected. They were examining the twenty-first prospective juror when it happened.

"And have you heard anything about this case?" Mike Reynolds had asked.

"Yes, I have," answered prospective juror Emily Wainwright, a heavy set, pleasant-faced, middle-aged woman with a troubled look on her face.

"And, Mrs. Wainwright," Mike began the usual inquiry since nearly everyone had heard something about the case, "can you tell us what you have heard and from whom or where?"

"Well, I've read about the case in the papers and seen it on the news," she answered, then paused for a moment and continued, "before I was called as a juror." She glanced at Judge Forsythe who nodded, smiling.

"Well, Mrs. Wainwright," Reynolds continued, "is there anything about what you've read or heard that makes you think you shouldn't sit as a member of the jury who decides this case?"

"I don't think so," she said hesitantly, glancing down at the counter before her. Mike Reynolds stared at her. She would not make eye contact.

"I'm sorry, ma'am," he began, "but I sense that you are uncomfortable with your answers. Is something bothering you about this case?"

The prospective juror did not answer.

"Mrs. Wainwright?"

Still no answer. She stared at the counter in front of her.

"Ms. Wainwright?" The judge leaned over toward the witness box. "All you all right, Ms. Wainwright?" At a nod from the judge,

Bailiff Hackett came forward with a water pitcher and a box of tissues.

She accepted a tissue from the bailiff and daubed at an eye before answering the judge. "No," she said, "I'm not all right. They told me it would be okay. They told me I would be doing a service for the people and upholding their constitutional right to information." The audience stirred, especially the reporters who had clearly become bored with the repetition of the *voir dire* examination. They leaned forward to hear. Maybe something was happening.

"What!?" exclaimed the judge. "Who?" he demanded.

Mrs. Wainwright turned slowly and faced Judge Forsythe, the look on her face clearly apprehensive, while searching his features for understanding and help.

"The people from Law & Justice," she answered.

"Who?"

"Law & Justice, the network TV show. You know, it's on Sunday night, with Eric Seifert. They said he would interview me after the trial and I would be paid money. A lot of money, they said. My husband's laid off, right now. We could use the money."

The audience was buzzing. Notes were being hurriedly jotted on small pads. None of the reporters left the courtroom, although some looked ready to spring for the door as soon as they heard enough more to get something to their editors and producers.

Judge Forsythe was astounded at what he had just heard. Had a national television program actually contacted a prospective juror? And how did they get her name? "I'll see counsel in chambers for a moment," he said, rising to leave the courtroom. He paused as he was descending the steps from the bench. "Ms. Wainwright," he said softly, "please remain in the witness box. We'll be right back."

Emily Wainwright felt like she had confessed to a major crime, but she felt a sense of relief for it. She also saw in the judge's eyes the understanding she was looking for. But she felt under a spotlight sitting there in the witness box, with everyone in the courtroom looking at her.

In chambers, Forsythe was furious. Wilkins, his entourage, Mike Reynolds, Digger, and Forsythe's law clerk were all there.

"Jesus Christ, what the Hell is going on?" demanded the judge. "You guys have enough trouble with this case without this! I have enough trouble with this case and you guys without this!"

"It's worse, Judge," said the law clerk.

"What?" Forsythe regarded the young man who had served as his law clerk for almost a year. He was an able researcher of legal issues and very helpful in the courtroom. Forsythe insisted that he come to Duluth for this trial. Any help for a trial like this away from his own courthouse in Minneapolis was important. "What have you got George?"

George Coker approached the big desk and handed Forsythe a pink telephone message slip. "It's a call from our first juror. Laura Kilbane called for you during Mrs. Wainwright's *voir dire*. She's been contacted by some reporter also ... from Law & Justice."

Forsythe looked at the small pink slip of paper. He struggled to control his anger with the media people and what they were doing to interfere with the case. He looked at the lawyers seated across from him. Finally he spoke. "I want to hear from each of you," he said, "but I'm thinking we may have to declare a mistrial, here. The jury panel is tainted."

"I'm not sure it's a mistrial when the jury hasn't been selected and sworn, yet," said H. Gordon Wilkins. "The trial has not really started yet."

Forsythe nodded. "You're probably right. Whatever, we'll have to excuse the jurors and start over. Since somebody has obtained the list of the panel members, we will have to call in a new panel and start over with the questionnaires and everything."

The lawyers shook their heads in disappointment and finally nodded their agreement.

Forsythe was not happy. He, too, was getting tired of the repetition of the *voir dire* questions, starting over with each new prospective juror. So, he was sure, were the lawyers. But it was their job, and it was his job. His weariness really grew out of his impatience to get going. He had a job to do. He wanted to get this case tried, efficiently, without unnecessary interruption, without an exorbitant amount of fanfare if that was possible, and, above all, fairly to both sides. He was anxious to get going and accomplish that somewhat formidable task.

Rising from his chair, Forsythe spoke to the lawyers. "Then we had better get started," he said. "We'll go back in the courtroom, excuse Ms. Wainwright, adjourn for the day, and meet back here with the Court Administrator to arrange for a new jury panel to come in to do the questionnaires. I can't tell you now if that would be tomorrow, or the next day. Either way, we won't be starting *voir dire* again until Monday. Sorry about that, gentlemen."

"Judge?" said the law clerk, George Coker.

"Yes, George?"

"How do we know it won't happen again?"

The lawyers looked at Judge Forsythe, awaiting his answer.

"*That's* another matter, gentlemen," he muttered, his voice low and menacing. "After we have arranged for a new replacement panel, we'll take up the question of what to do about Mr. Seifert and his investigative television magazine." Judge Forsythe began moving toward the door of the judges' chambers. The lawyers and George Coker quickly cleared a path for a man they knew was not in his most pleasant mood.

The media reporters were on the edge of their seats when Judge Forsythe ascended the bench again. He came in in such a rush that bailiff Hackett did not have time to command the audience to rise. The judge wasted no time seating himself and getting right to business.

"Ms. Wainwright," he turned to the prospective juror in the witness box, "you are excused from jury service in this case. Please accept our sincere gratitude for your participation in the process and our *sincerest* apology for the way you have been treated. Thank you for reporting these events to us. I can assure you," the judge leaned closer to her and spoke in a low voice, "somebody will be held responsible for what was done to you and to this process."

The reporters were leaning forward, straining to hear Forsythe's last remarks. When Judge Forsythe stood and announced, "Court is adjourned for the day," reporters scurried for the door. One however, remained and called out.

"Judge Forsythe!" he shouted.

Forsythe paused as he was about to take the first step down the three-step stairway to exit the courtroom. He turned and looked out over the courtroom, his expression showing his annoyance at being interrupted from the audience as he was leaving, having adjourned the court.

"Yes?" he said, formidable as he stood somewhat impatiently in his huge black robe, waiting for a response.

Undaunted, the brassy reporter demanded, "Judge, when will court resume? What's going to happen next judge?"

He stood with pad and pencil poised. The other reporters had paused by the door. Stopped by the calling of the judge's name, they waited expectantly.

Judge Forsythe gave a short response. "The parties will be notified when court will resume again," he said and turned on his heel and began to leave the courtroom.

"Judge!" The brazen reporter shouted again. "How will we know what's happening next?"

Judge Andrew Forsythe ignored him and left the courtroom.

H. Gordon Wilkins' young assistants quickly organized the piles of papers on the prosecution counsel table into boxes and briefcases which they piled onto two collapsible, two-wheeled luggage carriers. Each pulled one behind him as they followed H. Gordon down the aisle and out of the courtroom. They took the elevator to the fifth floor and entered the county attorney's office looking like a small safari with the hunter followed by his bearers as they wound around through the reception area, typing pool and down the hallways to their assigned offices.

Once within the confines of the small temporary office he had been given, H. Gordon gathered his troops.

"Get hold of the sheriff's office and our police witnesses," he told them. "We have an opportunity, here. Time is of the essence. Let's use it to find the witness who can lay the foundation for those God damned pictures!"

The two assistants scurried out of the office on their assigned mission. H. Gordon Wilkins leaned back in his chair and tried to sort out the day's turn of events.

A short two days later, Andrew Forsythe again sat on the bench in Chief Judge Parker's courtroom.

"Thank you, Judge," said a tall richly dressed lawyer, as he stood at Forsythe's invitation to note his appearance for the record. "Peter J. Hubbard, of Nelson, Locke & Butler, Minneapolis, for Law & Justice Productions and Eric Seifert. Your Honor, I appear as local counsel. With me, today, from New York is Law & Justice Productions' regular counsel, Mr. Julius Norton, of Penner & Block, New York City. At this time, your Honor, I would like to move the admission of Mr. Norton, *pro hac vice*, to argue our clients' position in this case."

"That motion is granted," said Judge Forsythe. "Mr. Norton, you may address the Court."

"Thank you, your Honor," said Julius Norton, rising to speak. "We are here because of my clients' concern about the Order which you issued imposing a fine against my clients and banning them from this courthouse and from observation of the proceedings in the trial of Judge James Digby Moss. I'm sure you will agree, your Honor, that the Order was a little unusual."

"Indeed," agreed the judge, trying not to become irritated by the demeaning tone of the New York lawyer. He spoke as if he had come way out here to the Midwest and found himself having to teach the hayseeds from Minnesota what the law was all about. Forsythe took a piece of hard candy from a dish on the bench.

"Judge, Mr. Seifert and his staff are only doing their job, protecting the public's right to know and fulfilling their need to know." Norton picked up a document and held it in the air, obviously Forsythe's Order. "A fine of $25,000 is an inappropriate restraint of the right of these citizens to pursue information and their right of free speech in disseminating that information. This sanction and the ban in your Order unduly infringe on those very rights which are protected by the Constitution."

Andrew Forsythe sucked on the hard candy. Lawyers Hubbard and Norton were the only lawyers at counsel table. No other parties were represented. The courtroom was, however, packed with spectators, principally other news media representatives. Law & Justice Productions and its program's emcee, Eric Seifert, had been cut out of one of the biggest court cases in the country by the stroke of a pen by Judge Andrew L. Forsythe. They were not happy about it. Julius Norton was here to try to do something about it.

"Judge, I realize that something went wrong, that you perceived that my clients were interfering with your handling of this criminal case, but I can assure you nothing could be further from the truth. My clients never intended that their actions would in any way interfere with the case or jeopardize the rights of both parties in any way." Norton pleaded with the judge, "I urge you to understand this, your Honor. They were just doing their job."

"The way they did it caused a mistrial, Mr. Norton," said Forsythe, leaning forward on his elbows. "I don't want that to happen again."

"And it will not, I assure you, Judge," said Norton. "If the Order could just be vacated, my clients could return to their job of investigation and reporting the news about what is happening in the courtrooms around this country."

"But not this one," said Forsythe.

"I beg your pardon?" asked Norton.

"I said your clients won't be investigating or reporting on this case," said Judge Forsythe, pausing and then adding, "because of my Order."

"Your Honor," Norton responded, "we will be forced to seek a Writ of Prohibition from the Court of Appeals."

As the judge rose from his high-backed leather chair, his demeanor was unmistakable. He was irritated and quite possibly agitated. "Mr. Norton!" he boomed. "You do whatever it is you think you have to do, but I will not have your clients interfere with this case any further! My Order stands, and, by the way, I expect the fine to be paid promptly or contempt proceedings will be held!" He left the courtroom. So did all the waiting reporters. News of the sanctions against one of their own was news, too.

In the consultation room at the jail, Digger Moss talked with Mike Reynolds. Judy had accompanied Mike to the jail. She sat beside Digger at the conference table, holding his hand in hers, barely listening to their conversation.

"This delay is bad," said Mike. "If they are given long enough, they'll find a way to get those pictures in evidence for their substantive value. If those pictures come in, we've got troubles."

"Do you really think they'll find a way?" asked Digger.

"Given long enough, I do," Mike answered. "Digger, Gordon Wilkins will try anything to get the pictures in. You watch, he'll offer them without any foundation ... and he'll show them plenty to the jury while he's doing it so they know all about them even if we manage to keep them out."

"How long before we begin jury selection again, Mike?" asked Judy, squeezing Digger's hand in hers.

"Not until next week, now," answered Mike. "Judge Forsythe ordered a new panel, but there was some delay in getting the notices out, so they won't have the questionnaires completed for a couple of days. We'll get copies to review and start the questioning next week."

Judy sighed. Next week. Start all over again. She knew this was hard on Digger. She was very apprehensive about the ultimate result. She knew from their conversations that Mike, Katy and Digger were not ignoring the possibility that he might be found guilty. She could not fathom that. As a result, she was not sleeping at all. She was exhausted, but she tried to hold up for Digger's sake. The case had to get over and soon.

But soon was not to be. Not enough jurors responded to the initial notice to 150 panel members. Less than 100 appeared on the day in question. Another 75 were notified to appear. Sixty-two showed up on the next scheduled day, completed their questionnaires and went home to be called later. With a panel of 162, Judge Forsythe ordered the *voir dire* to begin.

Again, the process was slow and repetitious. It took nearly three weeks, but a jury of twelve with three alternates was finally selected. Judge Andrew Forsythe continued to battle with the Law & Justice program and its New York and Minneapolis attorneys. He did not back down from his Order sanctioning and restraining the TV program's staff. The Minnesota Court of appeals denied a Writ of Prohibition against him, thereby leaving his Order in place. Apparently, the judges of that appellate court did not want anything to go wrong in the Digger Moss murder case, either. When the jury was finally selected on a Wednesday afternoon, Judge Forsythe adjourned court to begin the trial on the following Monday morning.

CHAPTER TWENTY-FOUR

The courtroom was packed on the first day of trial. Duluth had had some high profile cases in the past, but nothing like this. The trial of a sitting judge in his own courthouse for the crime of First Degree Murder, of a police officer, was more than anyone could imagine. Reporters from the print, radio and television media jammed the two rows of benches in the rear of the courtroom which had been reserved for them. Other reporters were gathered in the wide hallway outside the courtroom and still other onlookers and media people sat in the Fourth Floor Jury Lounge across the hall, centered between the two courtrooms on the east side of the building.

The jury lounge was filled with tables and chairs normally used for jury panel members while they waited to be called for jury selection to one of the several courtrooms where jury trials were conducted. Pursuant to Judge Forsythe's order, audio speakers had been connected to the courtroom sound system, so people could sit at the tables and listen to the trial.

Local reporters had to fight to get entry into the courtroom itself. There were reporters from the wire services, CNN, CourtTV, and the national networks. National news anchors were present, interviewing anyone who would talk to them. Clerks, bailiffs, and other courthouse staff had been admonished by their supervisors to be careful that they didn't misspeak in some way. Judge Forsythe had placed a gag order on the lawyers involved in the case.

It was a media feeding frenzy. Outside the front of the courthouse, the circle drive was filled with news vans and trucks. Equipped with cameras, elaborate broadcasting systems, satellite antennae, and other tools of their trade, they had enough heavy duty power lines stretched everywhere to transform the normally beautiful grounds of the civic center into something that looked like the area behind the attractions of a carnival. Microphones and cameras were prohibited from the courthouse itself, so the technicians and some of the reporters waited outside, poised to jump at the chance to interview anyone coming out of the building who might be of interest.

Judges, prosecutors, public defenders and other courthouse staff not connected with the case, learned quickly to exit the normally unused first floor east door of the building that allowed them to walk past the uphill side of City Hall and on to the skyway system or the downtown streets from there. The reporters and cameramen learned just as quickly to watch that door as well.

The bailiff called the courtroom to order as Judge Forsythe entered and climbed the steps to his seat at the bench.

"State of Minnesota vs. James Digby Moss," he called, his voice booming through the sound system's speakers. "This matter is set for trial today. Jury selection having been completed," he nodded to the fifteen jurors sitting in the jury box, "I will ask counsel, is the State ready to proceed?"

"We are, your Honor," said H. Gordon Wilkins, popping out of his seat like a jack-in-the-box.

"And is the defendant ready?"

Mike Reynolds rose more slowly than his adversary. "The defendant is ready to proceed, Judge," he said.

"Very well," said the judge, turning to face the jury. "Ladies and gentlemen, at this time I will invite the lawyers to make their opening statements." He turned toward the counsel tables. "Mr. Wilkins, you may address the jury."

H. Gordon Wilkins, gathered some papers and a yellow legal pad and approached the podium. He raised the podium microphone, arranged his papers, and finally stretched his gaunt figure to its full height as he directed his dark eyes at the jury and spoke.

"May it please the Court and counsel. Ladies and gentlemen of the jury," he began, "this is a murder case. The charge against the defendant is First Degree Murder. He has been indicted by the Grand Jury of First Degree Murder. The victim of this horrible crime was Sergeant Gregory Allen Larson of the Duluth Police Department. A police officer, ladies and gentlemen, that's right, a police officer!"

"The defendant," he continued, his abrasive tone rising as he spoke, and pointed a slender, shaking finger in the direction of Digger and his attorney, "is a District Judge, that's right, a District Judge!" He stood pointing at Digger, looking directly at Digger, holding eye contact until, finally, Digger looked away. Then he returned to look at the jury triumphantly. He dropped his voice to a raspy whisper and stooped to speak directly into the microphone. "That's right, ladies and gentleman, a District Judge!"

The jury and the audience were spellbound by the performance of this peculiar man. He stood at the podium, facing the jury, but he was speaking to every person in the room and through the loudspeakers to many persons outside the courtroom. And he knew it. His voice rose and fell, sometimes in volume, sometimes in tone, with each point he made. The opening statement is not supposed to be argument, but H. Gordon Wilkins was clearly arguing the State's case. Finally, Mike Reynolds interrupted.

"Judge," he said, "ordinarily I would not interrupt another lawyer's opening statement, but we have gotten into argument here, and I feel obligated to interpose an objection at this time."

"The objection is sustained," said the judge. "Mr. Wilkins?"

Wilkins continued, apparently not affected in the least by the judge's ruling or the look the judge gave him as the objection was sustained.

"The events with which we are concerned occurred just a few months ago, right here in Duluth. The body of Sergeant Larson was found brutally murdered in his own home. You will hear evidence and see photographs that will prove to you beyond a reasonable doubt that the person who killed Sergeant Larson in such a brutal fashion, was the defendant in this case," he pointed toward Digger again, "District Judge James Digby Moss!"

Wilkins began going through the evidence and witnesses, telling the jury what he expected them to see and hear. He spoke for more than an hour and a half. The jury was engrossed in his presentation. Despite the length of his opening statement, each juror paid perfect attention to him until he said, "Thank you," and resumed his seat.

Reynolds' opening was necessarily noncommittal on the evidence, but he asserted his client's innocence and declared that the State could not meet its burden of proof. "Often," he said, "that is the only defense asserted by a defendant because that *is* the defense, simply that the charges are not true and cannot be proved. That, ladies and gentlemen," he finished, "is certainly the case, here."

The opening statements had taken the entire morning. Judge Forsythe declared the noon recess, the testimony to begin after lunch.

CHAPTER TWENTY-FIVE

The State's Case-in-Chief began that afternoon with the testimony of two of the police officers who had investigated the case. The discovery of Sergeant Larson's body was described in gruesome detail, with photographs of the grisly scene. For the rest of the day and all the next day, Wilkins presented a chain of superbly marshalled evidence, leaving nothing out, carefully tying everything together as he built his case against Digger Moss.

Wilkins even got the tennis shoes in. Over Mike Reynolds' strong objection, Judge Forsythe allowed them, saying however after his ruling in chambers, "Without anything from the victim's apartment on the shoes, the Jury will have to determine the weight to be given the fact that the defendant owns the same type of shoes the police believe were worn by someone in the apartment after the murder."

There was little Reynolds could do with these witnesses on cross-examination, except to point out that all the evidence was circumstantial, very little of it had anything to do with his client, and they knew of no direct evidence showing any involvement of Digger in the death of Sergeant Larson.

As the third day of the trial opened, Judge Forsythe started the proceedings.

"All right, Mr. Wilkins," said the judge, "You may call your next witness."

H. Gordon Wilkins rose from his seat, gathered some documents from the table in front of him, and strode purposefully to the clerk's desk beside the bench. He handed the documents to the clerk and stood silent beside her desk, occasionally glancing at the jury box and smiling as the clerk marked the exhibits. When she was done he took the exhibits, moved to center himself between the bench and jury box, held up the exhibits, and addressed the Court.

"Judge, at this time, the State offers the following photographs which have been marked for identification. The first is a picture of the defendant exchanging money for a package in the parking lot of the ..."

"Just a minute, your Honor!" screamed Mike Reynolds. "We object! Counsel is referring to exhibits that have not yet been received in evidence. I haven't seen them yet!"

Reynolds was seething. He could not believe the slimy little son of a bitch was trying to put the photos in without any witness! And trying to tell the jury what they were before the judge ruled on whether they would be admitted into evidence. He was stepping over the line, but Mike didn't want to move for a mistrial and start all over again. Digger couldn't take it. Besides, Judge Forsythe would do anything to avoid a mistrial and having another trial, especially with the trouble they'd had picking a jury for this one.

"Judge, all of these pictures were provided to Mr. Reynolds in discovery," said Wilkins calmly, as if he were surprised there was any objection. "He has seen them."

"I'll see counsel in chambers," said Forsythe. As he rose from his chair, he looked out at Wilkins. "And bring the exhibits," he added.

In Chief Judge Parker's chambers, Forsythe was waiting for the lawyers as they entered. He had removed his robe and tossed it on one of Judge Parker's burgundy upholstered wing-backed chairs. In his shirt sleeves, seated behind her big desk, Forsythe did not look happy.

"Gordon, God dammit," he growled, "don't you turn this into another mistrial by screwing around with the evidence!" Forsythe was very conscious of the fact that the court reporter was not present and what was said was not on the record. So was Wilkins.

"That was pure bullshit in there, Gordon," Forsythe continued. "You know you can't tell the jury what's in these pictures until they have been received in evidence. I don't know, and I don't want to know, what you thought you were trying to do, but it won't happen again!"

Wilkins stood at attention in front of the desk and said nothing. He appeared entirely unruffled, his three piece suit immaculate as usual, without a single wrinkle. His shirt looked crisp and fresh, with necktie perfectly knotted and centered on his collar. His assistants quivered behind him as they literally hid from the wrath of Judge Andrew Forsythe.

"Now," said Forsythe, "let's see those exhibits."

Wilkins placed the photos on the desk. Forsythe studied each one. Finally, he looked up. "Your objection, Mike?" he asked.

"No foundation, your Honor," Reynolds answered "I..."

"Sustained!" interrupted Forsythe, handing the exhibits back to Wilkins without giving him any chance to argue the point.

As they left the judge's chambers, Mike Reynolds and Digger glanced at each other, sharing the satisfaction of blocking Wilkins attempts at the damning photos and the hope that their plan might work indeed.

Back in the courtroom, in the presence of the jury, Judge Forsythe said for the record, "Defendant's objection to State's Exhibits 23 through 61 on the basis of lack of foundation has been sustained. Mr. Wilkins, you may call your next witness."

"Thank you, your Honor. The State calls Carmen Diego."

"Your Honor, may we approach?" said Reynolds.

"You may." Forsythe rolled his chair to the side of the bench away from the jury as the lawyers approached. He leaned over to hear Mike Reynolds whisper.

"Judge, this name was not on the witness list."

Forsythe looked to Wilkins for explanation.

"Judge, we did not know about this witness until recently. He is a witness called to lay the foundation for the photographs," said Wilkins, "necessitated by Mr. Reynolds' objections," he added.

Reynolds said, "We object. We are totally surprised by this witness."

"In chambers," commanded the judge.

In chambers, Wilkins explained. "Judge, our witness is the other man in the pictures. He is a drug dealer. His street name is Zorro. He can identify the pictures of him and the defendant, and also the pictures of the drugs and cash."

Judge Forsythe studied the photographs again. "All right, I'm going to permit it ..."

"Judge!" interrupted Reynolds. "Even if you allow the witness over our objection on the ground of unfair surprise, we object on relevancy! Pictures of some claimed drug deal don't have anything to do with the murder charges here!"

"One step at a time, counsel," said the judge. "I'm only ruling on your objection to the witness. Until the witness has testified, the exhibits won't be re-offered. When they are, your relevancy objection can be made. The relevancy will depend in part on what the witness says."

They turned to go back to the courtroom.

Forsythe said, "Just a minute. This witness only deals with Exhibits 23 through 50, relating to the drug transactions. The pictures of defendant outside the Larson residence aren't affected. He cannot lay the foundation for them, can he?"

"No, judge," answered Wilkins. "They'll be re-offered on the record on their own foundation."

"But very carefully," warned Forsythe. "You may argue their admissibility on the record if you wish, but it must be out of the hearing of the jury."

"Yes sir," Wilkins acknowledged the admonition.

"Carmen Diego. D-I-E-G-O," said the witness, as he had been instructed to do by the clerk. Diego was a short, slightly built Latino. His long, shiny black hair was combed back. Black eyes stared out from beneath heavy black eyebrows. A thin dark mustache adorned his upper lip. He was thin to the point of being gaunt. His nervous fidgeting suggested he had used more than his share of the merchandise in which he dealt.

All eyes in the courtroom were on him as he approached the witness box, climbed the steps and seated himself.

"Mr. Diego," began H. Gordon Wilkins, "will you tell the jury where you reside?"

"Chicago."

"Illinois?"

"Yeah."

"Did you live in Duluth for a while?"

"You could say that," he said, shifting in his chair, one hand nervously playing with the base of the microphone. His gentle, nervous tapping could be heard over the sound system's ceiling mounted speakers. "I was just here on business," he added.

"And what business was that?" asked Wilkins.

Diego hesitated, looking down at the counter in front of him. The sound of his nervous tapping increased.

"Mr. Diego," said Wilkins, "have you been promised immunity for testifying here today?"

"Yeah," Diego answered. "That's right."

"You understand, then, that you may tell the truth about your 'business' without fear of being prosecuted?"

"That's what I was told."

"Well, then, what was the business you were in Duluth for?"

"Drugs."

"What?"

"Drugs. I was here to sell drugs."

"What kind of drugs?"

"Mostly crack, some speed or meth, and sometimes heroin," said the witness.

"Did you bring these drugs with you to Duluth from Chicago?" asked Wilkins.

"When I first came, I did," he answered. "After that, I had a supplier who brought the drugs in. Sometimes I went back to Chicago for more."

"To whom did you sell the drugs?"

"Who did I sell to?"

"Yes."

"I had contacts. People who wanted to buy and had the cash could find me."

Wilkins paused to consult his notes. He held the courtroom in silence for just the right amount of time. Then he looked up at the witness and asked, "Did you deal with Judge Moss?"

"Objection! Relevance!" inserted Reynolds.

"Overruled."

The witness looked confused, glancing at the judge, then back at Wilkins.

"You may answer," said Wilkins.

239

"Yeah, I did," he said.

"What happened?"

"Whaddaya mean?"

"Did you sell drugs to Judge Moss?"

"Objection! Leading."

Forsythe paused a moment. The lawyers waited. "Overruled," he said, finally.

"Should I answer?" asked Diego.

"Yes," said Wilkins.

"I sold him cocaine, speed, and heroin," he said.

"When?"

"I don't remember when."

"Was it about six or seven months ago?"

"Objection, your Honor," said Reynolds. "The witness has already testified he doesn't remember when. There is no foundation and counsel is leading the witness."

"Sustained," said Forsythe.

"Where did you sell drugs to Judge Moss?" asked Wilkins.

Diego thought for a moment. "Various places in Duluth," he answered.

"Your Honor, may I approach the witness?" asked Wilkins.

"You may," was Forsythe's automatic response.

Wilkins strode purposefully towards the witness box brandishing before him, especially so the jurors could see, the photographs he had offered earlier. He smiled at the witness, smug in the satisfaction that his plan was working perfectly. He had said enough about the pictures before so the jury had an idea of what they were about. He had peaked their curiosity so they wanted to see them. As expected, Reynolds had objected, putting himself in the undesirable position of being the one trying to keep information from the jury. And now it was H. Gordon Wilkins, III, servant of the court and jury, who had gone to the trouble to find this witness and get these important photos to the jury. An excellent strategy that was going according to plan.

"Now, Mr. Diego," began Wilkins, "I am showing you these photographs which have been marked for identification, *and were previously offered into evidence*." He made a production of turning to look at Reynolds, then to the jury, and finally back to the witness. He continued. "Please look through the photos and tell me if you recognize them."

Diego quickly leafed through the pictures and looked up. "I do," he said.

"Did you take them?"

"Pardon?"

"Did you take these pictures with a camera?"

"Nope."

"How is it that you are familiar with them, then?" asked Wilkins.

"You showed them to me."

Reynolds started to rise to object, but Wilkins kept going.

"Do you recognize what they are pictures of?" he asked.

"I do."

"How do you know that?"

"I'm in 'em."

The audience stirred.

"You are in these pictures?" Wilkins repeated for emphasis, turning to look out over the spectators.

"Some of 'em," answered the witness.

Reynolds was helpless. Wilkins was carefully manipulating him into being the one trying to keep the evidence from the jury. But he had been compelled to object, if for no other reason than to protect the record and the right to claim reversible error on appeal. If he didn't object at the time the pictures were offered, he could not raise it for the first time on appeal. But his objections coupled with Wilkins careful manipulations were adding more significance to the pictures than they deserved. The pictures, however prejudicial to Digger, did not, in Reynolds' opinion, have anything to do with the murder of Sergeant Greg Larson.

"These pictures that you are in," continued H. Gordon Wilkins. "Is Judge Moss in them also?"

"Objection!" cried Reynolds, rising to address Judge Forsythe. This time he would make his position clear to the jury, he thought. Two could play at that game. "Your Honor, he is doing it again! Mr. Wilkins knows better than to describe the contents of an exhibit before it is received in evidence. I have no choice but to object on my client's behalf."

Wilkins stood by the witness box, photographs in hand, showing no reaction to Reynolds' protest.

"Sustained," said Forsythe without emotion.

"Mr. Diego," Wilkins continued, undaunted, "do these pictures fairly and accurately reflect a meeting between you and Judge James Digby Moss here in Duluth?"

"Objection, leading."

"Overruled."

There it was, thought Reynolds. The foundation for the pictures. If the witness said yes, the pictures were coming in. The judge would not keep them out on relevancy alone.

"You may answer," said Wilkins.

"Will you ask the question again?" asked the witness.

Wilkins asked that the court reporter read the question back.

"Yes," said Diego, after hearing the question again.

"And, Mr. Diego," asked Wilkins, "were you at the meetings with Judge Moss when these pictures were taken?"

"Yes."

"What were you doing?"

"Selling drugs to him."

"Objection, your Honor," said Reynolds. "Relevancy. Move to strike."

"Overruled."

"Did Judge Moss pay you for the drugs?"

"Yes."

"Did you sell him drugs?"

"Yes."

"Do these pictures show meetings where those transactions were going on?"

"Yes."

"Your Honor," said Wilkins, turning to the bench, "the State offers Exhibits 21 through 50."

"Objection, relevancy," said Reynolds.

"Overruled," said Forsythe. "State's Exhibits 21 through 50 are received in evidence."

"Your Honor," said Wilkins victoriously, glancing at Reynolds, "may I publish these photographs to the jury?"

"You may," answered the judge.

Wilkins did not simply hand the 5" x 7" photos to the jurors for each to examine and pass around the jury box while everyone was waiting, which was the usual method of publication of photographs to a jury. Instead, he motioned to one of his assistants, who popped out of his chair and brought from alongside the end of the jury box a small, rolling metal table on which was a modern overhead opaque projector. Another of Wilkins' minions was setting up a screen on the far side of the courtroom directly across from the jury. The screen was high enough so everyone could see it, including most of the audience. Those seated against the same wall as the screen leaned over or moved to stand where they could see it and waited in anticipation. So much of the time, what was presented to a jury was not seen by the spectators, but H. Gordon Wilkins, III was making sure everyone would see these pictures.

When the equipment was set up, Wilkins handed a photo to his assistant who placed it on the flat glass surface of the projector. Side lamps were clicked on, brightly illuminating the photo on the glass. With a flick of a switch, the large screen burst into life and there, in all his glory, thought Reynolds ... and Wilkins ... was Digger Moss buying drugs from the witness, Zorro, in the parking lot of the Pickwick on Superior Street in Duluth. The clarity was astonishing. The size was larger than life. The effect was profound. The audience stirred. Someone coughed. More than one person, including one juror, gasped at the sight.

Digger felt himself sinking into his chair. From his seat, closest to the screen, the images were huge. He felt the eyes of the spectators and jurors watching him for reaction.

Wilkins continued displaying the photos for the jury and the audience. With each photo, he asked the witness to identify where the meeting had occurred, to identify the parties in the picture, himself and Digger Moss, and to explain exactly what was going on.

After the pictures of Moss and the witness were shown, Wilkins put on one of the pictures of the drugs. He produced a laser pointer from his inside coat pocket and pointed to the enlarged photograph. Placing the small red spot the laser put on the screen directly on the drugs centered in the close-up photo, he asked, "What is this?"

"That's the drugs I sold him," answered Diego.

"How can you tell?"

"Look at the wrapping there, the brown wrapping paper from the package that was in the other picture, see it?"

Wilkins approached the witness box and handed the laser pointer to the witness. He found the small button switch that operated it and the red spot appeared on the screen. Diego moved the spot to the brown wrapping paper that was spread open and on which the smaller cellophane bindles of drugs were sitting.

"See there," he said. "There's some numbers written on the paper. You look at the other pictures and you'll find the same numbers."

"Are you able to say that this is the same package of drugs you sold to the defendant in the parking lot in the other picture?"

"I am."

They went through the pictures again and again, comparing the package in the close-ups to the package in the pictures of the meetings and comparing the close-ups of the cash to what could be seen of the cash Digger was handing to Zorro in the photos of the exchanges. Each time a photo was put up, Digger felt like he was in the front row of the theater watching an old Cinerama wide screen action movie.

Finally, with a close-up photo of cash on the large screen, Wilkins asked, "Mr. Diego, if you got this money from Judge Moss for the drugs you turned over to him, why are there photos of it? I think you have already said you didn't take them, right?"

"Right."

"Can you explain?" Wilkins looked around the room, his eyebrows slightly raised.

"I assume the police took them."

"What?" Wilkins sounded surprised.

"I assume the police, or at least Sergeant Larson took them."

"Why do you say that?" asked Wilkins, feigning ignorance and irritating Reynolds by doing so. Mike Reynolds knew that whatever the witness was going to say, Wilkins knew exactly what it was.

"Because it was a sting," said Diego. The audience reaction to this new information disrupted the courtroom. The jurors had been sitting straight, their attention glued to the witness. Now they turned to observe the audience.

"Order!" shouted Forsythe striking the gavel hard on its clapper. "Order!" he said again, as the crowd began to settle down.

Wilkins waited until the courtroom was silent, then he waited a little longer, so everyone was concentrating on him and the witness, waiting. "What do you mean, Mr. Diego?" he asked slowly and carefully. "What do you mean by a sting?"

And then it happened. He said what no one expected, except perhaps Wilkins and his crew.

"Sergeant Larson came to me and asked for my help. He said he was investigating possible drug involvement by a District Judge. He wanted to catch him in the act of buying drugs and wanted me to sell them to him. He gave me the drugs, confiscated drugs from the police evidence locker, I guess. Judge Moss, there," he pointed to Digger, "contacted me and arranged for a buy. Those are pictures of some of the buys. There were several."

Judge Forsythe could not control the reaction of the audience this time. The courtroom was in an uproar. This news was too startling for the audience and especially the media people to keep quiet about. Rather than make an attempt at control, or clearing the courtroom, Forsythe instructed the bailiff to remove the jury and he recessed the trial for thirty minutes.

Reynolds and Digger were in shock. The pictures were bad enough, but now this unexpected testimony, if believed by the jury, arguably gave Digger a motive to kill Larson. They needed a miracle. Mike found himself wishing he had a court trial instead of a jury trial. Although an argument could be made for a motive, it was still weak legally. There was not a strong enough connection. A judge, he thought, would see it that way, but maybe not a jury. A jury might be more influenced by the collective emotions of its members. And these photos and this last testimony did stir one's emotions.

When Judge Forsythe reconvened the court, H. Gordon Wilkins unnecessarily triumphantly announced, "No further questions, your Honor!"

"Cross-examination, Mr. Reynolds?" asked the judge.

Mike Reynolds faced the dilemma of cross-examining a witness whose testimony had been strong and was not likely to change with his questions. He kept it short and simple. Simply pointing out that the witness was an admitted drug dealer, selling illegal drugs right here in Duluth, and that he had made some kind of a deal with the prosecutor, he ended the examination quickly, hoping he had raised logical and serious questions of credibility in the jurors' minds.

Court adjourned for the day.

CHAPTER TWENTY-SIX

"**A**ll rise!" Digger stood beside his lawyer as Judge Forsythe stepped up to the bench and waved everybody to be seated. The judge got right to business.

"All right, Mr. Wilkins, you may call your next witness."

H. Gordon Wilkins rose from his seat and paused for effect. Then, he solemnly declared, "Your Honor, the State rests!"

A murmur ran through the audience. Digger's heart skipped a beat. He felt a constriction in his bowel. That was it! The State rested! Had they met the burden of proof beyond a reasonable doubt?

The satisfied look on Wilkins' gaunt face as he stood to announce the close of the State's Case-in-Chief signified, and communicated to the Court and jury, his knowledge that the State had amply met its burden of proving the guilt of the defendant Judge James Digby Moss, in the matter of the cold-blooded, senseless murder of Duluth Police Sergeant Gregory Allen Larson.

Digger watched Wilkins. He was acting for the jury. That look was his communication to the jury, and the media, that he had done his job and that the case was all but over. Anything more was just a formality preceding a guilty verdict.

Mike Reynolds also watched Wilkins. Smug little bastard, he thought. But there was a reason for his smugness. With the pictures of Digger in, the prospects looked dim indeed. Mike constantly worried whether he should be representing his friend, Digger. But Digger would hear of nothing else. He trusted Mike. He gladly put his fate in Mike's hands and said no to any other representation. Now, Mike was not so sure it was a good idea. He's still a smug little bastard, Mike thought.

"Mr. Reynolds?" said Judge Forsythe.

"Yes, your Honor?" Mike responded.

"Are you ready to begin defendant's Case-in-Chief?"

"Judge, may we approach?"

"You may."

At the bench, Reynolds, Wilkins and the judge had a brief whispered conversation. Then, the judge said to the jury, "Once again, ladies and gentlemen, we have some matters to attend to outside of your presence. I am going to ask the bailiff to take you back to the jury room for a few minutes. I remind you not to discuss the case and wait there until we call you back. Thank you." He turned to face the courtroom and announced, "The jury is temporarily excused from the courtroom. Counsel will remain."

When the jurors had filed out of the courtroom and the heavy oak door was closed behind them, Judge Forsythe said, "The record should reflect that the jury has now been excused. Mr. Reynolds, you had a motion?"

"Yes, your Honor," said Mike Reynolds, standing to address the Court. "Defendant moves for a directed verdict at this time. The State's evidence is completely circumstantial and simply does not meet the State's burden of proof beyond a reasonable doubt. That high burden of proof is mandated for the protection of innocent defendants like my client." He paused, looked at Digger seated beside him, then at H. Gordon Wilkins, and finally back at the bench. "Judge Moss is entitled to the protection that burden of proof affords."

Reynolds went through the evidence in detail. Except for the pictures and the testimony of the drug dealer known as Zorro, Mike believed that none of the evidence was truly relevant to murder. Nor did he believe that of the pictures and Zorro's testimony, except that it did at least point to a possible connection with Sergeant Larson, a possible motive. When he was done, he told the judge that justice required a directed verdict at this point in the trial and that Digger Moss should be exonerated from these charges and set free.

"Thank you, Mr. Reynolds," said Judge Forsythe. "Mr. Wilkins?"

H. Gordon had been sitting in his usual ramrod straight posture, staring straight ahead while Reynolds argued, patiently waiting his turn. Now he stood, angling himself slightly so he could address the Judge and the courtroom audience at the same time.

"Your Honor, thank you," he began. "I am not sure where my brother lawyer Reynolds has been these past days, but it cannot have been in this courtroom, Judge. The evidence here is certainly circumstantial, but it's overwhelming in its proof of the guilt of the defendant. Of course it's circumstantial. No one saw the defendant kill Sergeant Larson except the defendant! But we have absolutely clear evidence that he lied to the police, that he concealed information from them, and that his drug dealings, of which we have direct evidence, gave him a clear motive for murdering the victim in this case!" The last few words were directed at the audience.

"Judge Forsythe," he continued, "I know that you will instruct the fine ladies and gentlemen of the jury that the State may prove its case by direct evidence or by circumstantial evidence or by both *and*, I believe I am correctly quoting your instruction, ' ... *the law does not prefer one form of evidence over the other*!'" Wilkins, too, proceeded to go through the evidence thoroughly, dwelling on the parts that were so damning to Digger, his reputation and his character. Finally, he sat down.

Judge Forsythe recessed the court for fifteen minutes to consider the motion. He called his law clerk and court reporter to join him in chambers. Digger was taken to the holding cell behind the courtrooms where he could wait with his lawyer. His wife and family were not allowed to join them. The rest of the spectators gathered out in the hallway, used the restrooms and waited.

It was thirty-five minutes before the bailiff called the court back into session. The jury remained in the jury room.

Judge Forsythe entered the courtroom, ascended the steps to the bench, seated himself and arranged some notes on the bench before him.

It had taken longer than the judge had indicated. Both Mike Reynolds and Digger were hopeful, that given the length of time deliberating by the judge, he was struggling with doubt, reasonable doubt. Likewise the audience, especially the court watchers of the media were speculating about the meaning of the time it took for a decision on the motion. Everyone in the courtroom was nervously expectant when Judge Forsythe began to speak.

"I have given considerable attention to this issue throughout the testimony in the State's Case-in-Chief anticipating such a motion as the defendant has made," he said. "After due consideration, also, to the arguments of counsel, the Court finds that the evidence is sufficient to proceed to the jury. The motion is denied." He looked at the counsel tables. "Anything else, counsel?"

"Judge, we'll need some time before starting our Case-in-Chief," said Mike.

"I can appreciate that," said the judge. He looked up at the clock over the courtroom door. Half past ten. He leaned over to whisper to the clerk. Straightening in the high-backed leather chair, he went back on the record. "Tomorrow is Friday. The Court could use some time back in the Hennepin County Government Center to attend to matters that have gone wanting for attention while we have been up here. Court will adjourn to Monday morning at 9:00 a.m. to begin defendant's Case-in-Chief. Now, if you will please wait, I'll have the jury brought back so we can excuse them on the record for a long weekend." Which he did.

Reynolds, Digger, and Judy gathered in the holding cell. After a few minutes, Kate Riley joined them. "With those pictures in evidence," said Kate, "your first plan doesn't sound as good. What are you going to do?"

"It may still be our best move," said Mike. "Only the drug dealing pictures got in. They don't prove anything about murder."

"What about motive, based on that witness Diego's testimony?"

"I think it's a stretch," said Mike, "but it's a possibility, you're right about that."

"Whatever," said Kate, shaking her head, "the pictures sure cast doubt about Digger's character, especially if they go unexplained."

"Yeah," said Digger, "and my explanation sucks!" Digger was despondent. They all could see it. Judge Forsythe's ruling had shocked him, not because he thought it was wrong - he probably would have done the same – but because it unnerved him to hear it, to hear the judge say that the evidence was sufficient to go to the jury. That meant, no matter what, if no further evidence were received, the jury *could* convict him of First Degree Murder, and Judge Forsythe would have no option but to impose the mandatory sentence of life imprisonment.

"So what will you do?" persisted Kate Riley.

"The only thing we can," said Mike. "Think about it for this whole long weekend and come back Monday and do whatever we decide." He shook his head.

No one said anything else. The four sat in thoughtful silence until, finally, the sheriff's deputy interrupted them to take Digger back up to the jail.

In the relative comfort and seclusion of the basement boardroom of the Kitchi Gammi Club, Randall McCoy and his fellow Whitaker executives discussed the case.

"See?" said McCoy. "The State has gone through its whole case and there's been nothing about us! We're in good shape. This whole thing will blow over and we'll be in the clear."

"I wish I could be as certain as you," said an obviously worried Bertram Johnson.

"Yes," agreed Charles Hood. "Why won't Judge Moss blow the whistle on us when he testifies?"

Orrin Rasmussen joined in, running a hand back over his perfectly coiffured gleaming white hair. "That's right, Randall," he said. "Why won't the judge tell his story? It would seem to be his best defense."

"You all need to relax," insisted McCoy. "The judge won't talk, I tell you." He stood and looked next door, out the leaded glass garden level windows towards Sir Benedict's On the Lake, thinking about his next remarks. "He stands charged with murder." McCoy turned back to the men seated around the large polished table. "He and his criminal trial lawyer are plotting strategy. That's all they are doing. That's all they have been doing since this case began. Everything they say or do, including anything Judge Moss may testify to, is designed toward one thing and one thing only, the effect on a jury verdict of guilty or not guilty. Everything they consider or plan is designed to get a verdict of not guilty by raising reasonable doubt as to the State's case."

"Well, I guess that makes sense," said Hood, "but what does that mean, really? I still don't understand why Orrin and Bert aren't right. I still don't understand why Moss won't tell what he knows about us."

Fred McCloskey, who had been silent, simply nodded his agreement.

"What I am trying to get through to all of you," McCoy was not able to disguise the impatience in his voice, "is that Moss and his lawyer don't care about us. They only care about what gives the greatest possibility of an acquittal." He returned to his seat at the head of the table. Placing his hands in front of him on the polished wood surface, his fingers entwined almost as if in prayer, he said, "A story about blackmail by respected executives in this community, and with respect to a civil case, is just too preposterous to be anything but a weak attempt at an explanation by someone who is grasping at the last straws available. It's a story which most will say, if it were true, it would have surfaced a long time ago."

The other five men sat silently thinking. McCoy made sense. He understood the thinking of the criminal lawyer and his client better than they. How, they didn't know, but at least he was making sense. It did seem possible that nothing may ever come of what they had done and what they had tried to do. An indication of understanding, agreement, and some degree of relief could be seen on their faces.

Satisfied from their expressions, McCoy felt that none of them would do anything drastic which would ruin them all. He wished he felt as sure as they now seemed to. He made a mental note to arrange a business trip in the next several days to one of the coasts with arrangements for possible sudden departure for places unknown, if needed.

CHAPTER TWENTY-SEVEN

"**H**is name is Bracken, Milo Bracken," said the jailer Friday morning, consulting his clipboard. He came to get Digger, informing him he had a visitor. But Digger didn't know any Milo Bracken.

Milo Bracken had driven up from the Cities and directly to the St. Louis County Jail on Haines Road near the airport. He had debated using a false name, but he had no criminal record, there was nothing to link him with Griswold or the others killed in the apartment. His name meant nothing. But if he had given a false name, someone might have caught it. False name to a police officer was a crime. In this case it would have been a Gross Misdemeanor. He didn't need that. Didn't need that at all. So he had written his real name, consistent with the identification he was carrying and which he showed the deputy with whom he registered and asked to see Judge Moss.

"Who?" asked Digger.

"Bracken. He's waiting in the visiting room."

Digger was shackled and led from his cell to meet someone he had never heard of. But as he entered the room, he recognized the big man immediately. Digger would never forget this man.

"You!" he whispered as he sat and rested his shackled hands on the table.

"Hi, Judge," said Milo Bracken.

"What are you doing here?" Digger asked. "Who are you?" He could not get over his astonishment at seeing the man who had saved him those few weeks ago in the apartment down in the Cities.

"Take it easy, Judge." Milo looked around the room, at the walls and doorways. He examined the ceiling fixture. He looked at Digger and rolled his eyes toward the surroundings and whispered, "They bug your conversations in here, do they?"

Digger suddenly looked around himself. "I don't know," he said.

"Well," Milo whispered even more softly, "we'll be careful, then."

"Who are you?" Digger insisted.

"I'm Milo Bracken, Judge." He put out his hand. "Pleased to meet you. Oh, sorry," he said when he saw the difficulty in a friendly handshake when one party was cuffed and chained the way Digger was. He went on.

"I'm a private detective from Minneapolis. Can't say the work has been too good the past few years. Neither has my luck ... been too good, that is."

"Well, I owe you my ..."

Milo put a finger to his lips and rolled his eyes again.

"... but I don't know how I can help you," Digger finished without finishing the first part of his sentence where Milo had cut him off. This Bracken did not want them to say much the jailers could make sense of, if they were monitoring the conversation.

"Thanks for the thought, Judge," said Milo, "but I'm not here to get help *from* you. I'm here to give help *to* you."

"What do you mean?"

While trying to avoid saying too much, Milo tried to explain, encouraging Digger to engage in the same mildly disguised discussion.

"As I said, lately the P.I. work hasn't been too good for me the last couple of years. Then I got this great job. Up here. Surveillance. Worked for the fella you were visiting when we first met ... in person, that is."

Digger's eyes widened. He shifted his weight in his chair. Griswold! He thought. But he said nothing, his attention riveted on Bracken, waiting for him to say more.

"Yeah, I worked for him and he worked for some corporate types, if you know what I mean." Milo pulled a pack of Pall Mall's from his shirt pocket, then looked around for an ashtray. Seeing none he put the pack away. He continued.

"Anyway, this dude double crossed us and left us in the cold."

"Us?"

"I had a partner, assistant, whatever you want to call it."

"So what happened?" asked Digger.

"Well, then, we surveilled *him*!" Milo said under his breath, so softly that even Digger could barely hear him.

Digger whispered back. "But I'm not sure how that has anything to do with me."

"Let's just say that surveillance is not only watching, but the gathering and keeping of evidence, if you get my drift." Milo smiled knowingly at him.

254

A shred of hope began to form in Digger's mind. Was this big, unkempt man telling him there was help? That there was reason to have hope? He dared not think about it, for fear he might lose it.

"Anyway, I've put together a little package you and your lawyer might be interested in. Thought I'd leave it with him. Okay with you?"

"Y-yes," said Digger trying to conceal his excitement. "Do you know who he is and how to find him?"

"I do," assured Milo. "Reynolds, right?"

"Why are you doing this?"

"Because." Milo leaned forward, his face inches away from the prisoner, and spoke in a whisper so low that Digger knew except for him, no one could hear. "Because I know you're innocent and because I think you're gettin' fucked royally, from more than one direction!"

"How can I ever repay you?" Digger could not believe that something might actually happen to help him.

"Not necessary, Judge," Milo answered. "You know that fella you were visiting was paid a lot of money by those corporate types. A lot of money."

"But ..."

"Judge," said Milo, standing to leave. "you know they never found any money where you last visited our friend." He winked. "Judge, you take care." He reached out and placed a big hand on Digger's shoulder, then turned and waited at the door to be let out by the jailer. In a moment he was gone and Digger was being escorted back to his cell.

L ater, Digger got to call Mike Reynolds. He was so excited he could hardly stand not to tell Mike about his conversation with Milo Bracken. He just told him it was important and asked him to come to the jail. Mike arrived within a half-hour. Even with the assurance from Mike that the conversation between lawyer and client would not be monitored or recorded, Digger spoke in hushed tones describing the conversation he had with his visitor.

"But where is he, Digger?" demanded Reynolds, his strained voice exhibiting the frustration he felt at possibly being close to some evidence that would help Digger, but without the witness necessary to use it. "Did he tell you how to get a hold of him?"

"I don't think we will be able to find him." Digger smiled. "I think he is about to disappear."

"Goddammit, Digger!" Mike's tones were not so hushed. "I don't know what he's got for us, but you know it probably won't be admissible in evidence, at least not without him, and it does nothing for us if we can't use it!" He did not look happy. "Goddammit!" he said again.

Digger was surprisingly calm. "Relax, Mike," he said. "Wait for the package and we'll see."

Martha Baxter hurried into her boss's office. She carried a large cardboard box wrapped in brown paper. It had been brought to the office by a large sloppy looking, balding man with a substantial paunch and tired looking eyes. But he was very polite and he said that Mr. Reynolds would want to see the package right away. She asked if he would wait until Mr. Reynolds was off the telephone. No, he could not stay and talk to Mr. Reynolds himself. He thanked her and left the office as quickly as he had appeared.

Mike Reynolds took one look at the box, shot an inquiring glance at Martha, and, when she told him the man had apologized for not being able to stay and had left, he bolted through the doorway of his private office, on through the reception area and out into the hall. No one. Nothing. Whoever it was was gone. He returned to Martha and the box.

CHAPTER TWENTY-EIGHT

Monday morning at 9:00 a.m., Bailiff Hackett called the courtroom to order. Judge Forsythe wasted no time.

"The State having rested its Case-in-Chief, we will begin the defendant's Case-in-Chief at this time. Mr. Reynolds, is the defense ready to proceed?"

"We are, your Honor."

"Very well, then, you may call your first witness."

"Your Honor, the defense calls the defendant, Judge Moss, to testify," declared Mike Reynolds.

H. Gordon Wilkins was startled at first on hearing the unexpected announcement. Then he leaned back in his chair fairly salivating at the thought of cross examining Digger Moss. Oh, the questions! he thought. So many wonderful questions! What about the tennis shoes? What about the Zorro pictures? And, most important, what about you coming and going from the murdered police sergeant's residence? Huh? What about that, Judge Moss?

He began making notes. Although his trial preparation had included preparing for cross of the defendant, if he testified, enough had happened that the questions would be asked differently now. They would be asked for maximum effect on the jury almost regardless of the answers.

The clerk looked apologetic as she stood in front of Judge Digger Moss and raised her right hand. As he raised his own hand, her voice was a whisper compared to her usual loud and clear formal delivery of the oath.

"James Digby Moss," said Digger into the microphone after seating himself in the witness box. "M-O-S-S." He waited for the questions to begin.

Mike Reynolds arranged some papers on the counsel table. He took his time. At this moment, the slightest sound could be heard in the crowded courtroom, the quietest cough or clearing of the throat, or the proverbial pin dropping. All eyes were on Digger Moss or Mike Reynolds waiting. And Mike knew it.

The courtroom trial was a drama in which the lawyers and parties performed, and this was an important part of it. Digger Moss was

going to testify! This was the moment the audience had waited for.
They could not be sure if it would ever come, because a defendant
may choose not to testify, and that was almost this case, thought
Reynolds. But next to the delivery of the Jury's verdict, this moment
was the most important to the spectators and media. And now it was
here. It would not do, knew Reynolds, to move too quickly, to
minimize in any way the significance of the testimony about to come.
He took his time, aware of the waiting silence.

Finally, he started his direct examination in the case against
Digger Moss.

"Judge Moss," he began, "Where do you reside?"

"3177 Greysolon Road in Duluth," answered the witness.

"And I know everyone here knows already," Reynolds smiled,
"but just for the record, what is your occupation?"

"I am a District Judge in the Minnesota State District Court. I am
chambered in the Sixth Judicial District, in the St. Louis County
Courthouse here in Duluth."

Keep it simple, thought Reynolds. Keep it brief.

After he and Digger got the box from Milo Bracken, they talked
and planned at great length. The contents of the box changed their
whole strategy. The big change in their plan was that, with the
evidence supplied by Bracken, Digger would testify. But also, they
changed the strategy completely to rely almost exclusively on the
Bracken material. Digger would deny the charges, of course. He
would tell the complete story from his own knowledge and use the
Bracken evidence, nothing more. They would not offer other various
explanations or arguments that might be available. If you had to use
five reasons for something, you didn't have one good one. So the
Bracken evidence was all the corroboration they had for an otherwise
tall, tall tale. The million dollar question, the critical question for
Digger, that which would determine his fate, was whether the Court
would allow Bracken's material in evidence with the slim foundation
they had, slim by the standards of the Minnesota Rules of Evidence.

So, they would steer a straight course to the Bracken material. He
would keep it simple and focused. The formalities over, Reynolds went
right to work.

"Judge Moss, you have been seated here throughout this trial and
you have heard the testimony of the State's witnesses against you?"

"I have," sighed Digger.

"Was it difficult?"

"Very," Digger answered.

Too late, H. Gordon Wilkins clambered to his feet to shout, "Objection, irrelevant!" And then he added, realizing Digger had answered, "Move to strike."

"Sustained," responded Judge Forsythe. "The answer is stricken. The jury is instructed to disregard the witness's answer."

The audience stirred. Mixed feelings could be discerned from their expressions. At once they felt hostility toward this apparent cop killer and sympathy for this possibly innocent man who had been and was still going through an incredible ordeal. Those who had these mixed feelings had them because they did not know what to think. Here he was about to tell his story. If he had one, maybe there was some truth to his lawyer's assertion that he had nothing to do with the death of the victim, Sergeant Larson. Whatever, they certainly understood that sitting through the trial would be very difficult for Digger and they would not be able to disregard his answer to that effect. Nor would the jury, they thought.

Reynolds continued his examination.

"There were some pictures introduced showing you and a drug dealer in the Pickwick parking lot and some other places in Duluth. Do you remember that?"

"Yes."

"Your Honor, may I approach the witness?" asked Reynolds.

"You may," was Forsythe's immediate response.

Mike Reynolds walked toward the witness stand. He stopped in front of the court reporter and sifted through the pile of exhibits. Turning toward Digger, he said, "Showing you what has been received in evidence as Exhibit 23, do you recognize this photograph?"

"I do."

"It is of two men making an exchange in the parking lot of the Pickwick Restaurant here in Duluth, is that so?"

"Yes."

"And, Judge Moss, are you one of the two men?"

"I am," answered Digger.

The audience and the jury were hanging on every word. Straight, direct and simple, thought Mike Reynolds as he continued his questions.

"Now the State's witness testified that he was exchanging drugs with you for money in return. You remember that testimony?"

"Yes."

"Is that testimony true?"

Members of the audience shifted in their seats. Some leaned forward trying to hear better. A juror dropped her notepad on the floor in the jury box.

Digger answered the question. "Yes. It's true," he said.

One of H. Gordon Wilkins assistants smiled knowingly at his boss. Wilkins, himself, remained impassive, revealing no reaction to the testimony.

The audience, however, did react, with facial expressions of shock, or of satisfaction at having their beliefs confirmed, with whispers to other spectators, and with a flurry of note taking by the news people.

Judge Forsythe leaned forward at the bench and glared the audience into silence.

Now it came. The first moment of Digger's explanation, his defense. The moment was critical.

"Judge Moss," Reynolds asked slowly, "what were you doing in the parking lot of the Pickwick exchanging drugs for money with this 'Zorro' character?"

"It was a sting, as the witness testified," explained Digger, "only it was I who was working with Sergeant Larson. Or at least I thought I was."

"Would you please explain?" asked Reynolds.

"Objection, your Honor!" barked Wilkins. "We object to a narrative answer. We request that the examination be in question and answer form, so we can interpose objections where appropriate."

"Sustained. Mr. Reynolds, counsel does have that right."

"Of course, your Honor," said Mike. "I would be happy to oblige Mr. Wilkins. Judge Moss, you said you were working with Sergeant Larson. Did he contact you regarding any sting operation?"

"Objection, leading."

"Oh, I'll permit it," said Judge Forsythe. Wilkins was going to make it as hard as possible for Reynolds.

"Judge Moss? Did Sergeant Larson contact you?"

"He did."

"How?"

"He came to see me."

"Where?"

"In my chambers, here in the courthouse."

"When?"

"About three months before he was murdered."

"At this meeting in your chambers, what did Sergeant Larson say?"

"Objection! Hearsay," said Wilkins.

Forsythe considered the objection for a moment. Finally, he said, "I think the important thing here is that he said what he said and not necessarily the truth of what he said. That being true it is not hearsay under the rule. The objection is overruled."

"Judge Moss?" asked Reynolds.

"Greg Larson asked me to participate in a sting operation," said Digger. "He said he was working undercover on a drug investigation that involved members of the police administration and some other government officials suspected of dealing in illegal drugs. He said it might possibly include drugs seized by law enforcement in other investigations."

"What did you do?"

"I agreed to help."

"Was anyone else present at the meeting?"

"No."

"Do you have any documentation or other evidence that the meeting took place?"

"No."

H. Gordon Wilkins did react this time. A purposeful but nearly imperceptible nod of the head done strictly for the benefit of the jurors, at least two of whom saw it.

"Did you ... have any documentation?"

"I did," Digger answered. "I had a note from Greg that I kept in my desk drawer. It explained the sting operation and what I was doing. It was signed and dated by him."

H. Gordon's head jerked toward the witness as he listened and waited.

261

"Where is it now?" asked Reynolds.

"It was stolen," said Digger. "I don't have it anymore."

Wilkins relaxed perceptibly. He repeated his knowing nod of the head for the benefit of the jurors and the audience as if to say, Oh sure, you expect anyone to believe that?

There were some similar reactions among jurors and spectators. Reynolds and Digger knew there would be. They had decided it was best to address it first rather than have it somehow come out later on cross and make it look like the prosecutor had discovered something they had tried to hold back.

"Judge, when did you first see these pictures?" asked Reynolds, holding a bunch of the drug transaction photos in the air.

"They came to me in an envelope, delivered to me at the courthouse."

"When?"

"About a week before Greg Larson was murdered."

"Was there anything else in the envelope?"

"Yes, there was a draft of a criminal complaint charging me with possession of drugs with intent to sell, but it was not signed by any police officer or prosecuting attorney."

"Anything else?"

"There was a typed note that said something like, 'DID YOU REALLY THINK YOU COULD GET AWAY WITH THIS?' or something like that."

"Do you have that complaint or the note."

"No, it was stolen, also."

Someone in the audience groaned. Could Judge Digger Moss really expect anyone to believe this?

"Did you ever see the envelope again?"

"Yes."

"Please explain the circumstances, if you would."

"Well, the envelope came back, but with different pictures and stuff," said Digger. "This time it contained different pictures and a different complaint draft."

H. Gordon Wilkins, III, was on the edge of his seat, now. They had to be the pictures of Moss coming and going from the murder scene! Moss had chosen to testify and now he had him!

"Do you have the pictures or the envelope?" asked Reynolds.

"Not anymore," said Digger. "When the police began to investigate me, I destroyed them. I felt that they were too incriminating and would hurt me before I had a chance to establish my innocence."

Wilkins had to catch himself from falling right out of his chair. He destroyed the evidence! He admits it! How much better can it get?

The audience was enthralled. Where was this going? How could Judge Moss help himself with what he was saying? But he was saying it right out and still professing his innocence. The suspense was overpowering. When Judge Forsythe declared the morning break, no one was even interested. Coffee could wait. They wanted more testimony. Even the bathroom could wait. Their obvious interest and their reaction to the announcement of a recess notwithstanding, Judge Forsythe called for the break.

"Court will recess until 10:40," he said, tapping his gavel on its clapper and rising to leave the courtroom.

They spent their break in the holding cell. Judy was nervous.

"Mike, I don't think we're doing too well," she said. "People in the audience and even on the jury look pretty skeptical. If I didn't know the truth, I'd be pretty suspicious of Digger about now."

"Honey, we talked about this," said Digger.

"That's right, Judy," said Mike. "We know we've got to go through this so nothing is left open. We have to tell the whole story and count on the stuff from Milo Bracken to be received in the evidence and corroborate Digger's story."

"Will you be able to get it in evidence?" she asked. "I thought you weren't sure."

"Well, we'll have a hell of a fight from Wilkins, that's for sure," Mike replied.

"What will he say?" she asked.

Digger answered. "Audio tapes and video tapes are easily altered or edited, Jude. There are usually objections unless it can be shown that they have not been edited, or that the original unedited version is available for inspection."

"Have these been edited?"

"We don't know," said Mike. "I'm sure they have not, but it takes the video photographer or the person who recorded the audio tape and," he glanced at Digger, "we don't have him available."

The holding cell behind the courtrooms had windows facing west out over Second Street. Standing behind her husband's chair, Judy Moss turned and stared out through the security bars at the old jail across the street and the decorative crabapple trees that lined the sidewalks. She turned back to the two men at the table.

"When will you try to use the tapes?" she asked.

"Soon," Mike answered, "very soon."

"Mr. Reynolds, you may continue your direct examination," said Judge Forsythe as court resumed after the break.

"Thank you, your Honor," said Mike Reynolds.

Reynolds led Digger through the rest of the story. He marked the civil contract file as an exhibit. He had Digger explain the pyramid scheme of Whitaker Industries' PowerPlus Battery marketing distribution. He watched the jury who appeared confused, but he saw their obvious astonishment when they heard the amounts of money involved.

Digger described how he had been approached by Griswold, how he had been tested with a request on a criminal sentence and how he had ultimately been asked to swing the PowerPlus Battery case decision.

H. Gordon Wilkins was fairly animated in his obvious reaction to the story and his opinion of it expressed to the jury by his body language. He shifted in his seat, rolled his eyes, and did all but comment out loud as Digger told his story.

"Judge Moss," asked Reynolds, carefully, "did you ever meet with the people that this man represented?"

"You mean the executives from Whitaker?"

"If that's who he was representing, yes."

A slight commotion in the audience, caught Forsythe's attention. People were whispering. He knew that the mention of Whitaker executives would arouse interest. Whitaker was a major employer in Duluth, and in Minnesota. Its executives were known as generous and philanthropic, public minded citizens in their personal lives as well as their management of the company. An attack on the character of any of them was a dangerous tack, Forsythe thought.

"Yes, I met with eight of them," said Digger.

There it was. Digger Moss was saying he was innocent and that he had been blackmailed by executives of Whitaker Industries of Duluth, Minnesota. And not just executives in general, but eight specific ones, who would presumably soon be identified. The reporters were beginning to drool.

"Judge Moss," Reynolds began. He did not call Digger by his first name or by his famous nickname. Other clients in criminal cases, he often addressed in court by their first names. It was less formal and made them seem more friendly and likable. Technically, that degree of familiarity was prohibited by the Rules of Decorum for the courts which require that parties and witnesses be addressed by their surnames only. They once had been part of the procedural rules called the "Civil Trialbook," but were moved to make sure it was clear that they applied to criminal lawyers as well as to civil lawyers. Since this rearrangement of the rules, Reynolds had seen little change in the practice of using first names to improve the image of criminal defendants for judges and juries. It was flat out easier to convict and to punish "Mr. or Ms. Hardcase," then "Jim" or "Sally." But, this case was different. This was a sitting trial judge. Let his formal title and position be his image, here.

"Judge Moss, are you aware of any documentation or evidence of your meetings?" Reynolds asked.

Once again, Wilkins looked nearly ecstatic. It was Christmas! And there wasn't even the usual foot or two of snow on the ground! It was like he was opening one colorfully wrapped package after another! Reynolds was digging his client's grave. Each part of Moss's story seemed even farther fetched than the one before, and each time, Reynolds confirmed the lack of any corroborating evidence. Wilkins probably wouldn't even have to cross examine. But of course, he would. Would he ever!

"I am," Digger answered.

The courtroom was stunned. What? Was there evidence? What? Who?

Wilkins came out of his reverie and leaned forward aggressively, his eyes bearing in on the witness. Coiled like a tightly wound spring,

265

he was ready to leap to his feet to object. His right hand was palm-down, flat on the table top for added take-off assistance in jumping to his feet when the time was right. How dare they claim any corroborating evidence to a story which was interesting only by its total fabrication?

"And what type of documentation would that be, Judge?" asked Reynolds.

"Video and audio tape recordings," answered the witness.

"Objection!" Wilkins sprang up so fast his feet nearly lifted off the floor. "Your Honor, may we approach?"

"You may," answered Judge Forsythe. He stood and started for his chambers, a signal to the lawyers that their bench conference was not to be at the bench, where the jurors might overhear.

In chambers, H. Gordon Wilkins was furious, his face nearly purple with rage.

"Your Honor, this is highly improper! We've never seen any video tape or audio tape. Until just now, we never knew anyone claimed that any such evidence existed!" Wilkins was shouting. In the confines of the judge's chambers, it was deafening. Wilkins' two assistants cowered behind him, occasionally trying to look defiant and righteous, but mostly intimidated by the sheer volume of their boss's oration. Andrew Forsythe was beginning to get irritated, but he understood Wilkins' frustration. You prepared a trial a certain way, according to a certain principal theme. If you got surprised, bushwhacked, it was not at all easy to take. If it was thought to be improper or unfair, the hackles on the back of a lawyer's neck would stand straight up and not relax for quite a while. Forsythe took charge.

"Just a minute, Gordon," he said, in an understanding tone. "I think you should be able to present your objections on the record."

"Thank you, Judge." Wilkins sat down in a captain's chair opposite the judge's big desk.

"George," Forsythe said to his law clerk, "get the court reporter to bring her machine in here. Thanks."

George Coker scurried toward the courtroom.

A few minutes later, the court reporter was seated in a wooden chair next to the judge's desk, fingers poised over her stenograph machine.

Facing Judge Parker's massive oak desk were three oak and brown leather captains' chairs. Wilkins occupied one. Digger and Mike Reynolds were seated in the other two. Wilkins' assistants sat on the edge of an antique overstuffed couch positioned along one wall. Law clerk George Coker stood in a corner behind the judge.

"The record should reflect," said Judge Forsythe, as the court reporter's expert fingers began to work their magic on the keys of the stenograph, "that the Court and counsel, *and* the defendant are in chambers, out of the hearing of the jury. Mr. Wilkins, you may argue your objections."

"Thank you, your Honor." H. Gordon Wilkins leaned forward, glancing at a yellow legal pad lying on the desk in front of him. Digger noticed that Wilkins' expression was much less ruffled than before Judge Forsythe had sent for the reporter. While his delivery displayed outrage and his tone and volume showed agitation, he had changed. Digger recognized that the emotion Wilkins now showed was intentional. It was perfectly controlled as he made his argument to the judge.

"The tapes that have been mentioned cannot be received in evidence, your Honor. They are a complete surprise to the prosecution. We have no way to assess the foundation for these exhibits. We have no way to know if they have been edited, or whether the originals are available to examine." He paused to let the truth of his remarks sink in. "In other words, we simply don't know enough, *you* don't know enough about this evidence to weigh its probative value in these proceedings or whether it meets the requirements of the Rules of Evidence!"

Mike Reynolds straightened in his chair, about to respond. Forsythe put up a hand to stop him.

"You are exactly right, Mr. Wilkins," he said, addressing him formally, for the record. "We really do not have any foundation for this evidence, whatever it is."

"But, Judge Forsythe ..." Mike Reynolds tried to interrupt, but he was again stopped by Forsythe's raised hand.

"However, we are here somewhat prematurely. The tapes to which you now object have not been offered. They have not been marked for identification. They haven't even, as far as I am aware, been seen in the courtroom. The Court understands Mr. Wilkins' concerns. His arguments are well noted, his position well taken. I specifically wanted to give him the opportunity to voice his concerns on the record so we all would be aware of them and any appellate court later reviewing this matter would know we were." He made a note on a pad on the desk. "While we haven't seen these alleged exhibits, *if we do*, and I expect we will," he looked solemnly at Reynolds, "counsel must be very careful with the way they are handled and with any further reference to them. We know the prosecution intends to object. Being adequately forewarned by Mr. Wilkins, he must be given every opportunity to do so at the appropriate time, and before the jury becomes aware of the content of the proposed evidence. Is that clear, Mr. Reynolds?"

"Yes, sir."

They all filed back into the waiting courtroom except Judge Forsythe who waited for the court reporter to set up her equipment before he entered.

When seated at the bench, he said, "All right, Mr. Reynolds, you may continue."

"Thank you, your Honor. Judge Moss, you testified that you were aware of some video or audio tapes of the meetings you said you had with Whitaker Industries executives?"

"Yes."

Mike Reynolds removed two VHS size videotapes from his briefcase and walked toward the clerk. Handing them to the clerk, he waited patiently as they were being marked, knowing that every eye in the courtroom was on him and on those tapes.

"Your Honor!" Wilkins was standing. "May we approach the bench?"

"Come ahead."

Forsythe leaned toward the front edge of the bench to hear the whispered comments of the lawyers.

"Judge, I object to Mr. Reynolds display of these tapes before the jury!" Wilkins rasped. "We still don't know what they are! They could be anything!"

Forsythe answered, keeping his voice low. "I know, Gordon, but we'll never know what they are until they are marked and until there is some testimony about the marked exhibits. I understand your position, but I have got to let Mike mark them and ask his identifying and foundational questions. But," he turned to Reynolds and pointed a finger that the jury could not see in Reynolds' direction, "you be very careful, here."

Mike Reynolds nodded. Wilkins returned to counsel table and Reynolds to the clerk.

The clerk announced, "Defendant's Exhibits 62 and 63 have been marked."

"Thank you," responded the judge, making a note in his book.

"Your Honor, may I approach the witness?" asked Reynolds.

"You may."

"Judge Moss, I am handing you what have been marked for identification as Defendant's Exhibits 62 and 63. Can you identify them for the Court and jury, please?"

"They are two video tapes of meetings of certain executives of Whitaker Industries which were held at the Kitchi Gammi Club, here in Duluth."

"Were you at these meetings?"

"One of them."

"Objection, your Honor!" Wilkins interjected. "May we approach?

Forsythe sighed, being careful not to show any reaction to the jury. This was going to be difficult, he thought.

At the bench, Wilkins whispered, "Your Honor, if he was not at one of the meetings, then he cannot lay any foundation for that tape!"

Forsythe looked at Reynolds.

"Judge, I'm not through with my questions, yet. I haven't offered either exhibit, yet."

Forsythe nodded. He said to Wilkins, "I have got to let the foundational questions be asked. When the exhibits are offered, then I am in a position to rule on objections. But," he reminded Reynolds, "be careful."

"Judge Moss," said Reynolds, standing back at the witness box, "let's start with the meeting you did attend. Which tape is that?"

"Exhibit 62."

"How do you know that?"

"It's marked with a label and the date. I recognize it," said Digger.

"Who was at that meeting?"

The question caused a murmur in the audience whose members were itching to find out which local executives of Whitaker Industries were going to be accused.

Digger took his time remembering all the names. "Randall McCoy was there. Some others from Duluth. Most were people I had known or knew of by reputation. There were two I had not met before. Orrin Rasmussen, Fred McCloskey, Charlie Hood, Bert Johnson and Harry Slater, I knew. A man named Hollis Fowler was there and also a man named Frank Vagelli. I had never heard of them before."

"Was anyone else there?"

"Yes, there was another man who was not one of the executives. I didn't know his name at the time, but he was the one who communicated their demands regarding the decision they wanted me to make. I now know his name was Frank Griswold."

"Judge, have you viewed this video tape, that is, what has been marked for identification as Exhibit 62?"

"I have."

"Does it have sound?"

"Yes."

"Based upon your viewing and listening to the tape, can you say whether it fairly and accurately reflects the meeting which you attended?"

"I can."

"Can you remember the meeting well enough to say whether it fairly and accurately reflects who was there, what they did and what they looked like, and what was said?"

"I do."

"All right, then, Judge," Reynolds braced himself to ask the critical question, "does Exhibit 62 fairly and accurately reflect the meeting, who was there, and what they did and said?"

"Yes, it does," answered Digger.

"Your Honor," said Reynolds, "defense offers Defendant's Exhibit 62 in evidence and we ask permission to publish it to the jury at this time."

"Mr. Wilkins?" said Forsythe, asking for the State's position. "Any objection to Defendant's 62?"

Reynolds had done to Wilkins what Wilkins had done to him earlier. Now it was Wilkins whose objection would be seen as keeping valuable information from the jury. The lawyers could argue the legal niceties of video tape evidence, possible editing and all that, but the jurors knew, and the audience knew that the tapes would speak for themselves. What better evidence could there be? Digger Moss said he was at a meeting and here it was on tape!

Wilkins was in a quandary. He certainly needed to object to preserve the record, but he did not want to alienate the jury, or the audience, come to that. But wait, there was one way he could get the reasons for his objections known to the jury and attack the credibility of the tape, even if Judge Forsythe let it in.

"Your Honor, may I *voir dire* the witness?"

"You may inquire for purposes of objection, yes," answered the judge.

"Mr. Moss," Wilkins began, "you didn't take this video tape, did you?"

"I beg your pardon?" said Digger.

"I mean, you did not operate the camera or the recording equipment that produced this tape, did you?" Wilkins walked over to Reynolds who was standing beside the defense table, took the tape from Reynolds' hand and held it in the air.

"No, I did not," answered Digger.

"Do you know who did?"

"Yes, I think so," said Digger.

"Who?"

"Objection, your Honor," said Reynolds. "Relevance. The witness has testified that to his own knowledge, it fairly and accurately reflects what it is supposed to be. Therefore, it doesn't matter who operated the equipment that produced it."

Forsythe thought for a moment and then nodded and said, "Sustained."

"How long have you known about this tape, Mr. Moss?" asked Wilkins, still holding the tape up in his left hand.

Only since Friday," said Digger, "three days."

"Since you didn't operate the camera or other equipment, you have no idea if this tape is the original or a copy. Is that true?"

"Yes, that's true."

"And you don't know, do you, Mr. Moss, if this tape has been edited or altered in any way from the original?"

"I don't know," agreed the witness.

"Your Honor, may we approach the bench?" asked Wilkins.

"Please come forward," answered Forsythe.

At the bench, Wilkins standing close beside Reynolds and the judge leaning in close to them, Wilkins whispered, "Judge, I think we've covered all the foundational questions. Now we need to see the tape before we can fully appreciate what objections might need to be made."

"Mike," said the judge, his voice low so the jurors would not overhear, "I know we are in the trial, and I don't want to disrupt your presentation, but since Gordon hasn't seen the evidence before, I'm certainly inclined to grant his request and take the time for an *in camera* viewing with the lawyers present."

Mike nodded. He would far rather just have the tape come in quickly, for its shock value on the jury, on the audience, and even on H. Gordon, but the judge was right, Wilkins certainly had a right to see it first.

As the lawyers retreated to counsel table, Judge Forsythe announced, "Ladies and gentlemen, we have some matters which we need to attend to outside the courtroom. We will recess for approximately thirty minutes. The bailiff will let you know when we are ready to continue."

The courthouse has several television and VCR sets on rolling metal stands or carts for use in the courtrooms. The bailiff brought one of these into the judge's chambers for the parties to view the videotape which was being offered into evidence.

The Case Against Digger Moss

Fifteen minutes later, still in chambers, the judge invited the lawyers to make their objections and arguments.

"Now Mr. Wilkins, you may proceed," he said.

"Thank you, your Honor," Wilkins acknowledged. "May I have a moment?" he asked, glancing at his notes.

"Certainly. Take your time."

Wilkins was obviously discomfited by the tape they had all just seen. It did show the Whitaker executives meeting in the boardroom of the Kitchi Gammi Club. It did show that Digger Moss was there! The tape was an overhead view, apparently from a ceiling mounted camera, but you could see the persons present, identify them, and clearly hear what they were saying. And what they said was good for the defense and bad for the prosecution. They made remarks that did acknowledge that they were behind a scheme to blackmail Moss into making a decision favorable to them. Wilkins even admired Moss when he basically told them to "shove it," said if they didn't deal with him, he would decide against them, and got up and walked out. Pretty gutsy, thought Wilkins.

But what was he to do about the tape? Wilkins was here to accomplish one thing and one thing only, convict James Digby Moss of First Degree Murder of a Duluth police officer. Nothing else mattered.

Outside the southeasterly facing windows of Judge Parker's chambers, the large United States flag stood straight out from its pole in the steady northeast wind off Lake Superior. Capable of reducing the downtown air temperature by as much as twenty or even thirty degrees in a few seconds when the wind shifted and came from off the lake, it seemed to be chilling Wilkins' case and his disposition just as quickly as he sat thinking what to do.

The tape, of course, did not deal with the real subject of the trial, the murder of Sergeant Greg Larson. Therefore, there was a genuine relevancy issue. There were the problems of possible editing or alteration. *And*, Moss *was dealing* with them! Wilkins made a note. Of course! If he was dealing with them at this meeting, for his own financial benefit, then he could have been just as corrupt before and decided killing Greg Larson was in his best interest! Wilkins smiled to himself. He could pull this out! He could turn the tape against Reynolds and Moss by pointing out that it showed Moss's real character and actually would have shown more to support the State's case if it hadn't probably been altered. Well, that was for cross examination of Moss and final argument to the jury, if the tape came into evidence. First things first.

"Your Honor," said Wilkins, finally, "clearly this witness doesn't know if the tape has been edited or altered in any way. We object on that ground and also on the ground that it contains statements by persons who are not parties to this case and are therefore hearsay. I am being deprived of the right to cross examine them."

"Your Honor," said Reynolds in response, "the statements made by persons on the tape are not hearsay or are admissible as exceptions to the hearsay rule. The statements made related to requesting or demanding a particular decision from Judge Moss are not offered to prove the truth of the statements, since they are not even statements of fact, but simply to prove that they said it. Therefore, such statements are not hearsay. Statements made regarding their involvement in the blackmail scheme Judge Moss describes would clearly be statements against interest and therefore admissible under that exception to hearsay in Rule 804 (b) (3). I can't call these witnesses to testify. They would be admitting a crime and would certainly refuse on the ground of self-incrimination. Therefore the statement against interest exception applies."

"Judge," Reynolds continued, "either way, the statements of the people on the tape are admissible and since the witness has confirmed its accuracy, it should be allowed in evidence."

Judge Forsythe pondered the arguments the lawyers had presented for several seconds. He took a rule book from the shelf behind Judge Parker's desk and examined it briefly. Then he spoke.

"After due consideration," the court reporter's fingers flew across the keys of her machine, "and in the exercise of discretion with which the trial court is vested in evidentiary matters, this Court believes that satisfactory foundation has been laid for the exhibit and that it does not include objectionable hearsay. Exhibit 62 is received in evidence. Mr. Reynolds, you may play it for the jury. Mr. Hackett, when you have moved the television equipment back to the courtroom, please bring the jury back to the courtroom."

"Judge?"

"Yes, Mr. Reynolds?"

"Perhaps we should talk about Exhibit No. 63, also. We will be offering that and would like to play it for the jury as well, at this time."

Nice try, thought Digger.

Bailiff Hackett and George, the law clerk, paused in the doorway where they were in the process of moving the TV and VCR back to the courtroom.

"Your Honor, I object!"

"Yes, Mr. Wilkins," interrupted the judge before Wilkins began a lengthy oration on the various grounds for excluding the tape. "Mr. Reynolds, the witness has testified that Exhibit 63 is a video tape of a meeting he did not attend. Therefore, he cannot, as far as I can see, lay any foundation for its accuracy or authenticity. Mr. Wilkins' objection is sustained as to Exhibit No. 63 on the state of the evidence at this time."

"Ladies and gentlemen," said Judge Forsythe from the bench, "defendant's Exhibit No. 62 has been received in evidence. Mr. Reynolds, as you have requested, you may play it for the jury."

"Your Honor," interrupted Wilkins, standing to address the Court, "may we have a standing objection to this exhibit based on relevance, lack of foundation, and possible alteration?"

Forsythe bit his lip. Wilkins was trying his patience. He had to let the jury know his arguments even though they were already on the record. He even looked directly at the jury when he said, "possible alteration." Well, you won't get a mistrial out of me unless its absolutely necessary, he thought. "You may," he muttered. "Mr. Reynolds?"

The television was wheeled in front of the jury. Reynolds had hired a local professional video firm to set up more equipment so the judge and audience could see and hear the tape. A set was put at the head of the aisle for audience viewing. A smaller set was placed on the bench for the judge. The television screens burst into life and the viewers were immediately in the boardroom of the Kitchi Gammi Club, watching Digger Moss, several prominent Duluth citizens and some other men most did not recognize. They saw Orrin Rasmussen, many in the courtroom recognizing his pure white hair, golden tan, and elegant appearance. They heard Harry Slater a very prominent Duluthian speak about the blackmail and the evidence they had on Judge Moss. They recognized Randall McCoy. They heard Digger Moss threaten to decide the civil case against them and watched the rather stunned reactions of McCoy and the others. The television screens switched to a snowy black and white picture and the sound became steady static noise. Reynolds touched the power button on the remote control and the screens went blank. The sound stopped.

The audience was shocked. What did this mean? Was Digger Moss telling the truth?

"Your Honor," Wilkins broke the stunned silence, as he moved out into the pit between counsel tables and the bench. He stood close to the jury rail facing the judge as though the jurors were his clients and he were speaking on their behalf. "We renew our objections on all the grounds stated, but especially relevance, your Honor. The charge here is that the defendant, James Digby Moss murdered Sergeant Gregory Larson. This tape has nothing to do with that issue. Therefore, it is irrelevant and inadmissible under Rule 402 of the Rules of Evidence. Move to strike."

All eyes turned to Judge Forsythe. The judge felt Wilkins' theatrics were out of order and done entirely for the benefit of the jury rather than for the purpose of actually persuading the judge, on issues already argued and ruled upon outside the jury's presence. Forsythe paused. Reynolds had not said anything. Then, trying very carefully not to appear to be suggesting anything about the weight to be given to the tape, he simply said, "The Court will abide by its earlier rulings for the reasons stated. The objection is overruled and the motion is denied."

Wilkins returned to counsel table and resumed his seat, entirely satisfied. By the time he was done, he thought, he'd make the tape look like an elaborate subterfuge by the defense designed to lead everyone away from the truth, that Moss was guilty of murder! His eyes met those of Digger Moss in the witness box. He held eye contact with Moss and smiled slightly at him in triumph.

"That son of a bitch!" Digger slammed a fist down on the holding cell table. "The arrogant, skinny little bastard stared at me and grinned, right in front of the jury!"

"Easy Digger," said Mike, "he's doing that on purpose. He wants exactly this reaction from you as he starts his cross-examination."

"Well, it's working! I can't stand the asshole!"

"Digger, we only have a few more minutes on the break. We need to decide what we do next. This is where we planned to finish, especially if both tapes came in. Even without the second tape, this is all we have. Next is cross-examination of you by Wilkins and then we rest. We don't have anything else."

"Do you think it's enough?" asked Digger.

"Digger, you know as much about it as I do. Reasonable doubt. That's what it's all about. The people in the courtroom and the people in the jury box were truly shocked by the tape. Unfortunately, it does not prove your innocence of murder. Wilkins is right. It only corroborates part of your story, but not your denial of the charges against you."

Judy Moss was not in the room. They asked her to stay with the family when the judge called the short recess. It was a good thing. She would not react well to the lack of confidence of these two men in their defense against the case against Digger Moss.

"So, what do we do?" Digger was calmed down from his ire and frustration with H. Gordon Wilkins. Now his tone was depressed and forlorn.

"Digger, my friend, I think we've done it," answered Mike, putting a hand on Digger's shoulder. "This is it. We can only do the best we can do."

"What about Wilkins' cross of me?"

"It'll be brutal, Digger." Then, knowing it was important to improve Digger's confidence and resolve, he said, "That's it! How you handle this cross will define how much the jury uses the tape and whether they believe you or Wilkins!" He knew it was risky to play with the emotions of a client who looked about to give up, but Digger was a fighter, a man who did not give up, and a man who faced problems head on. So, Mike went for the whole nine yards. "It's you against H. Gordon, Digger!" Mike repeated. "He's coming after you on cross. You go after him! Take the fight to him. Be confident. Don't protest your innocence, declare your innocence!"

Digger looked doubtful.

Mike finished. "Digger, he's going to come after you on cross. When he does, kick the shit out of him!"

For a moment, Digger Moss brightened. A look of determination was forming on his face. Then it waned as quickly as it had begun and he slumped in his chair. "I wish we had the other tape," he said.

"Well, we don't." That was all Mike could say. The deputy knocked on the door, opened it and announced, "The judge is ready. Time to go back."

Digger hung his head and stared at the carpet as he walked down the empty narrow hall toward the courtroom. He knew he had to hold his head up, look confident, and appear sincere in his denial of the murder charge. As he entered the courtroom, he tried his best and hoped that he did not appear to the audience and to the jury like he felt, beaten and dejected, the look many often associated with guilt.

As he seated himself, Hackett, the bailiff, brought him a small folded piece of paper. Digger was dumbfounded by what he saw when he opened it. The note said simply:

I'm here.
Milo Bracken

Digger folded the paper and gave it back to Hackett, whispering an instruction to give it to Mike Reynolds at the counsel table. When Reynolds opened it, his eyes widened and he looked up at Digger. He looked around at the people in the crowded courtroom.

Digger was frantically trying to silently communicate with Mike when the judge ascended the bench.

"All rise!" commanded Hackett.

"Please be seated, ladies and gentlemen," said Forsythe, seating himself.

"Mr. Reynolds, you may continue your direct examination of the defendant."

"Thank you, your Honor," said Mike rising from his counsel chair. "Before we finish direct examination, we have a witness to call out of order, with counsel's permission." He turned to H. Gordon Wilkins.

Wilkins concealed his surprise. What witness could they be calling now? No matter, defendant was against the ropes. Wilkins wanted his cross-examination of the defendant to be the last thing the jury heard in this trial. He would rather deal with this new witness out of order than to have it come later and interfere with the significance of his cross of Moss.

He stood. "Well, Judge, we don't have any idea who this witness is, or whether he is even qualified to testify, but as far as his being called out of order, we have no objection to that."

"Very well," said the judge. "Judge Moss, you may step down, temporarily. Mr. Reynolds, you may call the witness."

"Thank you, Judge." Mike waited until Digger walked across the pit area and seated himself at counsel table.

"Defense calls Mr. Milo Bracken," he announced.

The courtroom fell into utter stillness with Reynolds' calling of the witness. Who was he? The case had had considerable news coverage. But no one had heard the name, Bracken. Who was he and what did he have to do with the case? People looked around the courtroom, waiting for this mystery witness to stand and show himself.

Milo had not been in the courtroom, which was full. He had been in the fourth floor jury lounge with many others listening to the proceedings and had seen the tape on the television in the lounge. When his name was called he left the lounge and walked across the wide hallway toward the courtroom. One of the uniformed sheriff's deputies let him in.

The only one in the courtroom who recognized him when he entered the courtroom was Digger Moss. Digger's hopes soared as he watched the large, balding man walk slowly up the aisle. Was this man going to save him a second time?

Bracken wore tan slacks and an open green blazer, which had no chance of being buttoned across his massive paunch. His paisley necktie against a cream-colored, oxford cloth, button-down shirt was a remotely reasonable match to the trousers and jacket.

He stopped before the clerk who was standing with her hand raised.

"You do swear to tell the truth the whole truth and nothing but the truth, so help you, God?"

"I do," said he, turning to enter the witness box.

"Milo Bracken. B-R-A-C-K-E-N" said Milo, following the clerk's instructions after he wedged himself into the narrow witness chair.

"You may inquire," said the judge to Reynolds.

"Thank you, your Honor." Digger and Mike had the opportunity for a quick whispered conference at counsel table before the examination began. At Digger's insistence, Mike dispensed with the usual identification and background questions normally asked of a witness. "Mr. Bracken, what is your occupation?"

"Private investigator."

"Did you have a job in Duluth a while back?"

"I did."

"What did it involve?"

"Surveillance."

"Of anybody in particular?"

"Judge Moss." He nodded toward Digger.

"What kind of surveillance?" asked Reynolds.

"We had a van. We installed video and sound equipment so we could watch and listen to him. We sat in the van, watched and listened, and made recordings."

"Where?"

"His office," answered the witness, "here in the courthouse."

Both jury and audience were spellbound.

"By whom were you employed?"

"Man named Griswold."

"Did you keep this job, Mr. Bracken?" Reynolds asked.

"Nope."

"What happened?"

"Griswold fired me."

"What did you do after you were fired?"

"We surveilled him."

"What?"

"We turned the tables on him and we watched him."

"And did you make recordings?" asked Reynolds, as he prepared to get to the real point of all this.

"Yes."

"Your Honor, may I approach the witness?"

"You may."

"Mr. Bracken, I'm showing you what has been received in evidence as Exhibit No. 62. It is a video tape that we just showed to the jury a little while ago. Do you recognize it?"

Milo Bracken took the tape from Reynolds and examined it, turning it over in his hands.

"Yes, I do recognize it," he said.

"And what do you recognize it to be?" asked Reynolds.

"It's a tape of a meeting at the Kitchi Gammi Club of a bunch of the PowerPlus Battery people. It's the one when they met with Judge Moss," he added. "See, here's my label that tells what it is."

There it was. And now a simple clarifying question and on to phase two, thought Mike Reynolds.

"Did *you* make this tape recording?"

"Yes, and I made the label on the tape."

Now!

"Did you tape record any other meetings?"

H. Gordon Wilkins snapped forward, ready to pounce.

"You bet I did."

Reynolds left the witness box, returned to counsel table, picked up another tape, and said, "Your Honor, may I approach the witness again?"

"You may."

"Mr. Bracken, I am showing you what has been marked for identification as Defendant's Exhibit No. 63. Do you recognize it?"

Digger held his breath.

"I do," said Bracken, examining the tape.

"Mr. Bracken, without telling me anything about what was said on the tape, can you tell me what it is a tape recording of?"

"Yeah. It's another meeting of the Whitaker Industries, PowerPlus Battery people. Actually, it's the same meeting, right after Judge Moss left. I changed tapes right after he was gone."

"Why?"

"Why what?"

"Why did you change tapes?"

281

"Oh, because the counter showed we were coming to the end of a tape. With our equipment we can shift to another blank tape, while we are recording, so we don't lose anything. We just have to watch the counter. Actually, we don't even have to watch it. It beeps."

"So you changed tapes and you didn't miss anything?"

"That's right."

"Mr. Bracken, did you watch the meeting over your video equipment as it occurred?"

"Yes."

"And did you listen to what was said over your audio equipment as the meeting took place?"

"We did."

"Mr. Bracken," asked Reynolds, "does this tape fairly and accurately portray the meeting as you observed it?"

"It does," confirmed Bracken.

Bingo! thought Digger.

"Your Honor," said Reynolds, holding up the tape, "defense offers Exhibit 63 in evidence and requests that it be published to the jury."

"Mr. Wilkins?" asked the judge.

"We object, your Honor," said Wilkins. "Once again, there are significant questions of hearsay and alteration. We have no idea if the tape has been edited or altered."

"Your Honor, may I inquire of the witness for further foundation?" asked Reynolds.

"You may."

"Mr. Bracken, you have testified that Exhibit 63 is a fair and accurate representation of the meeting as you observed it yourself. Has this tape been edited or altered in any way?"

"No, it has not."

"Was your equipment shut off at any time during the meeting?"

"No, as I said, not even when I switched tapes."

"Then, Mr. Bracken, is this tape a full and complete recording of the meeting as it took place from the time you switched tapes for recording?"

"Yes."

"Judge, we'll offer that additional foundation."

"Defendant's Exhibit 63 is received in evidence," said Judge Forsythe. "The objection is overruled. The basis of the Court's ruling is the same as earlier stated on the record with respect to Exhibit 62. You may publish it to the jury."

The video equipment was still in place from the viewing just before the break. When Bracken was called to testify, Reynolds had declined the bailiff's offer to move the equipment. Reynolds wasted no time inserting the tape and turning it on.

The scene was the same. Digger Moss was gone. The executives of Whitaker Industries continued their meeting, discussing their meeting with Moss and the stand he had taken with them. The audience was jolted by hearing Hollis Fowler tell the others that they would eventually have to kill Judge Digger Moss.

Then it happened.

Harry Slater was speaking. Most people in the courtroom recognized the well-known local citizen. Everyone knew that Harry Slater had died when his Cadillac lost its brakes going down Second Avenue West.

At the bench, Judge Forsythe was watching his own private small screen. In his notebook, he made a note that, being deceased, Slater was an unavailable witness to which the statement against interest exception to hearsay clearly applied.

What Slater had to say would change the whole trial.

"Well, I for one, am not happy with this turn of events." Slater's voice floated out from the audio speakers. "Hollis Fowler is telling us we are going to have to kill Judge Moss! This has gone too far! Originally we were going to just blackmail Moss with some fabricated evidence about drugs. Then Griswold, here," he nodded toward the stocky, blond man in the corner, "thought we needed more."

Then he said what Digger and Mike had been waiting for.

"When we agreed to have Griswold kill Greg Larson and blame it on Judge Moss, we put ourselves in the horrible position we're in, now."

Reynolds stopped the tape. "Did you hear Harry Slater say that?" he asked Bracken.

"I sure did," Bracken answered.

The courtroom was in chaos. Judge Forsythe's attempts at control were to no avail. Finally, afraid he might break Judge Parker's gavel if he hit it any harder, he nodded to the uniformed deputies and bailiff Hackett. They moved around the room, ordering people to quiet down. They warned reporters talking on cell phones. Eventually, the room began to come to order. Forsythe was about to start striking the gavel again to finish the job when Reynolds yelled.

"Your Honor, may we approach the bench?" Reynolds called out over the noise of the onlookers.

"You may." The judge shouted back.

Reynolds hurried to the side of the bench away from the jury, followed by Wilkins who was, in turn, followed by his two young assistants. Judge Forsythe leaned over to hear them.

"What is it?" he asked.

"Judge," said Reynolds, "I have a motion to be made on the record, but I think it should be out of the hearing of the jury."

"I'm sure you do have a motion," the judge remarked. "We'll excuse the jury."

"But judge," sputtered Wilkins.

"Relax, Gordon," said the judge, keeping his voice low enough so the jury could not hear. It wasn't difficult, with the clamor in the courtroom. "We'll let the jury go to the jury room for a few minutes and hear what Mike has to say."

CHAPTER TWENTY-NINE

T he pandemonium in the courtroom began to settle as the trial participants and the audience watched to see what would happen next. The room became silent as excited onlookers watched the jurors file out and they realized something was about to happen. Mike Reynolds broke the silence.

"Your Honor," he began, standing at counsel table, "at this time defendant moves for a directed verdict of acquittal."

The crowd reacted with excitement at the thought that the trial would suddenly end, Digger Moss would be acquitted, and he would be free. It was, everyone thought, a wonderful ending to what had been a terribly perplexing problem. Digger Moss had been loved by some, revered by many and well respected by all. The events of the last few weeks had shattered their beliefs in a very troubling way. Now, it was certain, all would be returned to normal.

Then it happened. H. Gordon Wilkins rose to address the Court. His words were a shock to everyone in the courtroom.

"Your Honor," said Wilkins, "the State opposes the motion."

"What?" said an astonished Judge Forsythe, departing momentarily from the very formal manner of courtroom decorum to which he normally adhered.

"The State opposes the motion," repeated Wilkins. "I wish an opportunity to be heard, your Honor."

Bedlam returned to the courtroom. Only this time it was not the joyful reaction that had prevailed earlier. The crowd was upset and showed it. They were close to a serious disturbance. Judge Forsythe pounded the gavel on its clapper. Again. And again. Finally the crowd began to settle down.

"Order!" he shouted. "Order in the court!" The raised gavel in his right hand was ready to strike again. "Any further outbreaks and I will clear the courtroom." The bailiff moved to stand beside the bench, staring out at the crowd. Two uniformed deputies standing by the rear door, straightened to attention, hands poised above the nightsticks they wore on their belts.

The audience became quiet. Forsythe lowered the gavel. He glanced at the antique clock over the rear door. "It's a quarter past

eleven," he said. "Court will adjourn until this afternoon at one
o'clock. Arguments on the motion for directed verdict will be heard
at that time." He rose and exited the courtroom.

"**T**hat complete asshole!" Mike Reynolds was enraged, his jaw
set in a grimace, and his face flushed. "I can't believe he
didn't join in the motion!"

"I'm sorry, Judge," said Marilee Jackson, who had joined them in
the consultation room. "You know the County Attorney's office
would not oppose the motion."

"Thank you," Digger said, and added, with a slight smile, "That's
why you're not prosecuting."

Digger was not nearly as upset as the two lawyers. The video and
audio tape evidence had cleared him as far as he was concerned. No
matter what happened, he was sure people would know he was
innocent. People would believe him. Sitting next to him, Judy did not
seem as calm as Digger. She was relieved that the evidence showed
Digger did not do what he had been accused of, but she was confused
by what had just happened. She was not sure what would happen
next or what danger her Digger was in now. The reaction of lawyers
Reynolds and Jackson made her worried for Digger.

The clock reached one o'clock exactly as Judge Forsythe
entered the courtroom and the bailiff called for everyone to
rise. The courtroom was packed. The two deputies guarded the rear
door. The fourth floor jury lounge was also packed with interested
people listening to the proceedings over the speakers connected to the
courtroom sound system.

"The record should reflect," announced Forsythe from the bench,
"that the Court and counsel are in the courtroom out of the hearing of
the jury to consider the defendant's motion for a directed verdict of
acquittal. Mr. Reynolds, it's your motion. You may proceed."

Mike Reynolds glared at the gaunt features of the hawk-nosed
Wilkins who stared straight ahead ignoring Reynolds. "Your Honor,"
he said, "I believe my motion was self-evident from the recent

evidence. I defer to my esteemed colleague. I'm interested to hear what he could possibly have to say in response!"

Wilkins sat staring ahead giving no reaction.

"Very well, Mr. Reynolds," said the judge. "Mr. Wilkins?"

H. Gordon Wilkins straightened his slender frame and addressed the court. "Thank you, your Honor," he said. "The State opposes defendant's motion for acquittal. This recent evidence is being used as a deception to mask the evidence we have introduced to show that the defendant is guilty of murder beyond a reasonable doubt. This new evidence does not refute our evidence and acquittal cannot be ordered!"

Judge Forsythe listened carefully. The audience was spellbound as they had been before when Wilkins argued. Wilkins continued.

"Remember the tennis shoes? The defendant intentionally hid them, kept them from the police investigation. He lied to the police. He escaped from police custody! He did that while he was involved in the court system, his own court system!" Wilkins was nearly yelling now. "He covered up his knowledge about the murder of Sergeant Larson. Why?" Wilkins turned so he was speaking to the audience as well as the judge. He wished the jurors were in the box. "Why?" he continued, "I'll tell you why. Because he murdered Sergeant Gregory Larson! That's why!"

Mike Reynolds stood to speak. Judge Forsythe waved him back into his seat.

"The Court has heard the motion for acquittal and has seen the evidence on which it is based," said the judge. "The Court is satisfied that the evidence is compelling in favor of acquittal. Defendant's motion is granted. The Court directs a verdict of Not Guilty. The defendant is discharged."

Whatever order had been maintained in the courtroom before was completely lost. Reporters spoke on cell phones, again, although they were prohibited in the courtroom. People stood and milled about. Judy was hugging her husband. A smiling deputy came forward to remove the stun belt Digger wore.

"Just a minute deputy!" shouted Wilkins. "Your Honor!" he shouted over the din. "I have a Complaint and a Detention Order for your review and signature!"

"What's that?"

"Here judge," Wilkins hurried to the bench and handed the judge some papers.

Judge Forsythe glanced briefly at the document and grasped the gavel. He brought it down hard, sending a loud crack through the room, amplified by the bench microphone.

"Order!" he shouted. The crowd became suddenly silent. "The record should reflect that I have just been handed a Complaint which deserves our attention. I will ask the bailiff to make sufficient copies so we can all consider it. Please be seated," he said as he handed the bailiff the document.

In moments the bailiff was back, handing out copies to the lawyers. He gave one to Digger, looking at him apologetically.

"All right," said the judge, "the Court has been presented with a Complaint for determination of probable cause. I'll read aloud. You may follow along. It reads,

STATE OF MINNESOTA   DISTRICT COURT
COUNTY OF ST. LOUIS   SIXTH JUDICIAL DISTRICT
****

File No. _____

State of Minnesota,

             Plaintiff,

     vs   COMPLAINT

James Digby Moss,

           Defendant.
****

The Complainant, being duly sworn, makes complaint to the above-named Court and states that there is probable cause to believe that the Defendant committed the following offense(s). The Complainant states that the following facts establish PROBABLE CAUSE: ...

Forsythe read through the body of the Complaint which set forth in detail the investigation of the case against Digger Moss and his escape from custody. The charges were obstructing justice and escape, both charged as felonies.

The judge finished reading and looked at the lawyers on both sides.

"I don't believe this, Judge!" screamed Reynolds, waving his copy of the Complaint in the air.

"Your Honor, we intend to proceed," said Wilkins. "Mr. Moss," he accentuated the "Mr." emphasizing the absence of Digger's title as a Judge, "is to be held pending a Rule 5 hearing on these new charges. That need not occur for thirty-six hours."

"Mr. Wilkins," said Judge Forsythe, beginning to sound irritated, "if, and I repeat, *if* this Complaint is approved, we will hold the Rule 5 hearing right now, or as soon as the defendant and counsel are ready to proceed. The thirty-six hour rule is for the protection of the defendant, that he be brought before the Court within a reasonable time from arrest, *not* to give law enforcement the right to hold an accused for some particular period of time. *And*," he continued, "reasonable bail will be set as required by the Constitution."

"Judge, we'll ask that no bail be set or that bail be quite high," answered Wilkins. He sneered at Digger and Mike Reynolds and added, "Remember, this is the guy who escaped from this very courthouse!"

Forsythe winced at the thought of trying to determine proper bail on a judge who was charged with, among other things, Escape from Custody.

"Judge, I have duly submitted the Complaint for a probable cause determination and ask that you review and sign it now."

Forsythe was beginning to resent Wilkins' commanding tone, but he, Forsythe, was not the prosecutor. He did not decide whether charges were to be brought. The prosecutor did. He only decided on the facts presented whether there was probable cause to issue the Complaint. In this case the facts supported the charges, and the facts were facts which he knew to be true from the evidence in this case. The escape was part of the court's record. He sighed. How could he avoid approving the Complaint? But one thing was odd.

"Mr. Wilkins," he said, "normally a Complaint is signed by a law enforcement officer as complaining witness and also signed by a prosecuting attorney. In this case, I see you have signed in both places. Isn't that a little unusual?"

"Your Honor," Wilkins began to explain ...

"Judge, maybe I can explain." The familiar deep voice came from the second row of benches behind the counsel tables.

"Chief Morgan?" Forsythe recognized the big police chief.

"That's right, Judge. John Morgan. I am Chief of the Duluth Police Department. A few days ago one of Mr. Wilkins' assistants there brought us a Complaint that was drafted for signature by D.P.D." He winked at Digger. "We declined."

"You declined?" repeated the judge.

"We refused to sign it, Judge," said Morgan.

"Your Honor," interrupted Wilkins, "I can swear to the facts. Actually anyone in this room can swear to those facts. We have already proved them in this case except for the escape and that is a matter of court record."

"Your Honor!" Mike Reynolds was on his feet. "Chief Morgan says they came to him with this Complaint a few days ago." He pointed at the tall thin prosecutor. "He's been waiting with this in his briefcase, ready to spring it at any time! It's improper! It's ... unethical!"

Wilkins jerked in his seat at Reynolds' last choice of words. A lawyer simply didn't call another lawyer unethical in court. He would see that Reynolds paid for that remark.

Forsythe was perplexed. He didn't seem to have any choice. Reynolds had tried valiantly, but had not said anything that justified refusing the Complaint. Stalling for time to think, he swore in Wilkins as the complaining witness in a much more formal fashion than he would ordinarily do. He was taking no chances.

"Raise your right hand to be sworn."

Wilkins complied.

The courtroom clerk stood facing Wilkins. She raised her own hand and said, "You do swear that the testimony you give in this proceeding shall be the whole truth and nothing but the truth, so help you, God?"

"I do."

"Mr. Wilkins," said Judge Forsythe, reluctantly, "do you swear that the contents of this Complaint are true and correct to the ..."

"Just a minute, your Honor." A smooth soft-spoken voice came from the second row bench also, a few seats away from where Chief Morgan was sitting. "I might be able to help." Standing with his hands on the back of the front row bench was the St. Louis County Attorney, Thornton Pederson. Seated in front of him were two of his prosecutors, Marilee Jackson and Chief Prosecutor, Andrew Preston.

"Yes?" Judge Forsythe had not met Pederson.

"Judge," said Pederson, "my name is Thornton Pederson. I am the St. Louis County Attorney. The Chief Prosecutor, the Assistant Prosecutors, and I have met regarding these charges." He glanced down at Preston and Jackson seated in front of him. "Your Honor, we decline to prosecute these charges."

"Now just a minute," H. Gordon Wilkins started to say.

"Your Honor," interrupted Andrew Preston, whom Judge Forsythe *had* met, "as the Court is well aware, we have absolute discretion in determining whether to charge."

"But I am handling this case!" shouted Wilkins.

"Not any more," responded the soft voice of Pederson. His voice was soft, but easily heard in the courtroom because the crowd had become silent, waiting with collective bated breath to see what would happen.

A relieved Judge Andrew Forsythe, wrote "Withdrawn" in a heavy black pen across the face of the Complaint and set it aside. He looked at the lawyers and finally, at Digger before speaking.

"The proposed Complaint is withdrawn. By directed verdict, the defendant has been found Not Guilty by the Court." He stood and raised the gavel. "The defendant is discharged and these proceedings are adjourned." He cracked the gavel smartly against its clapper, turned, and left the room, leaving H. Gordon Wilkins standing and sputtering in the middle of the pit. But no one was listening to him, even his two young assistants who were busy gathering papers on the counsel table, their heads lowered, afraid to look at him.

As Digger Moss was receiving congratulations from his family and colleagues and trying to express his gratification to his attorney, he was approached by Assistant Chief Pelton and Officer Kathy Winslow of the Duluth Police Department.

"Congratulations, Judge," said Pelton. "I hope there are no hard feelings."

"None," said Digger. "You were doing your job, and a good one at that. I would not have wanted to be the judge on this case."

"Thanks for the understanding, your Honor. We do have a question."

"Yes?"

"This Bracken," said Pelton. "He seems to have disappeared right after he testified."

"Oh?" Digger smiled. "Is that so?"

"Yes. We will need to talk to him. His testimony suggests his actions were probably illegal and that he was part of this blackmail scheme against you."

"I imagine he's going far away," said Digger. "And I don't blame him. In fact, I wish him luck."

"I suppose you're right, Judge. I guess he did more good here today than he did bad when he was spying for the Whitaker people. I guess we won't worry too much about him."

He nodded to Officer Winslow as she turned to leave. "Thanks, Judge," she said as they left through the crowd.

"Thank you," Digger called after them. Good, he thought, the pressure was probably off of Milo Bracken. He hoped it stayed that way.

In the comfort of his own chambers, a free Digger Moss sat with his wife and the good friends that had stood by him throughout the ordeal.

Kate Riley opened a Diet Coke, kicked off her high heels and put her feet up on the adjacent chair at Digger's conference table. "Digger," she smiled broadly, "Jesus Christ, it's good to have you back. Now would you please get to work? I'm gettin' tired of covering your sorry ass, while you're off horsing around."

Judy smiled at the crudity of her close friend. Only Katy, she thought, could get away with that.

"Well, *excuse me!*" answered Digger. He felt wonderful, but he wondered when the reality of it all would hit him.

"Old 'Thorny' Pederson was wonderful," said Kate, laughing.

" *'Not any more,'* " she tried to mimic Pederson's soft spoken manner as she quoted him.

"The county attorney's office did save the day, that's for sure," said Mike Reynolds. "It makes you wonder what would have happen if they hadn't."

They all stared at him.

He answered their inquiring looks. "Well, think about it. Digger committed some crimes." He looked at each of them in turn. "And so did we."

"Okay, Party Pooper," said Kate Riley, "so what's your point?"

"Judge," Mike said to Kate, "there are some difficult issues here. Both of you, think about these questions your Honors:

"First, is it a crime for an innocent man to lie to the police to protect himself from prosecution?

"Second is it a crime for an innocent man to conceal evidence to protect himself from prosecution?

"And third, is it a crime for an innocent man to escape from pre-trial custody to protect himself from prosecution?"

"Of course those are crimes," said Digger, "They have to be."

"Then why isn't old 'Gordo' right?" asked Mike.

"What? That skinny prick?" sneered Kate.

"Exactly the one, Judge," answered Mike. "Why isn't he right? Why shouldn't Digger be prosecuted for his crimes. For that matter, why shouldn't we?"

"Shit!" said Judge Kathrine Megan Riley. "Those are legal issues I don't even want to think about."

The Honorable James Digby Moss silently nodded his agreement.

Milo put down the newspaper and smiled. He had read every word of the lengthy story about Digger's acquittal. Of course, before that he had heard all the news about it on CNN and several national network shows and the local Twin Cities news broadcasts.

The news had also been filled with the story of the attempted blackmail scheme by certain executives of the PowerPlus Battery

Dave Sullivan

Division of Whitaker Industries in Duluth. Each of the men involved had been arrested. Milo remembered each of their names from the Kitchi Gammi meeting. According to the news stories, Chief Prosecutor Andrew Preston and Assistant County Attorney Marilee Jackson were apparently not the slightest bit reluctant to prosecute each of them to the fullest extent of the law.

He went back to his packing. He didn't have much, but everything was going, either in his few traveling bags or in the trash. He would not be back.

CHAPTER THIRTY

At the judges meeting in Judge Parker's jury room, it was suggested that Digger spend a few days with his staff, his scheduling clerk, court reporter, and bailiff attending to mail, straightening his chambers, and trying to get his caseload and schedule in order. Then they said, Chief Judge Carrie Parker speaking for the Court, he should take off for a week or so, take Judy and go somewhere quiet, away from Duluth, and away from the courthouse. After that, of course, they expected him to be back, pulling his own weight, for a change.

And so it was done. Judy made arrangements for a week's stay at a cottage in Bay Harbor, Wisconsin, a tiny hillside town on Raspberry Bay, in the Apostle Islands National Lakeshore in Lake Superior. They planned to visit a friend and retired lawyer, Mike Reynolds' cousin, Jake Kingsley, and sail in the Apostles on his sailboat, the *Resolution*.

Digger sat at his desk going over accumulated mail and looking forward to the much needed vacation. His thoughts were interrupted by the ringing of the desk telephone.

"Hello?"

"Judge Moss?"

"Yes, this is he."

"Judge, Some lawyers are out here to see you. Frank Williams and Gerald Morton. Should I send them back?"

"Yes, go ahead."

"Hi, Judge."

It was Frank Williams, a long time business lawyer at Jeanetta & Bartlett, an established Duluth law firm. He stood in the open doorway of Digger's chambers.

"May we come in?"

Jerry Morton followed him in and accepted a seat from Digger. Morton was a Minneapolis corporate lawyer in one of the city's 300 lawyer law firms. He had a number of clients in the Duluth area and frequently did business with local lawyers here.

Morton began. "We're here, Judge, to discuss a case you have under advisement. One you probably don't want to even think about, but we think you'll like what we have to say."

Morton was right. These were the lawyers on the PowerPlus Battery case. He didn't want to think about that particular case.

"Judge, we've settled our case. We just need your signature on an agreement to judgment. As you know, the judgment is needed to resolve the other cases out there."

Great, thought Digger. "Hmmh," he muttered. "What's the settlement?"

They were the two principal lawyers on the case. Many other individual contract holders had their own lawyers, who put various pressures on Jerry Morton. He represented the contractee of Contract No. 1, and in more than just a sense - Digger speculated there were other fee arrangements involved - represented the entire class of people in the pyramid opposed to the planned two per cent increase to be paid by them to those higher on the pyramid. Frank Williams represented the company, which happened to be the holder of Contract No. 1.

Frank Williams spoke. "Judge, the parties have agreed to renegotiate the contracts and that has been done. Basically the additional payment of two per cent of gross sales back up the pyramid has been eliminated. Those contracts held by McCoy and the others who tried to blackmail you have been terminated because their actions specifically allow termination by the company because of the crimes they committed."

Jerry Morton continued. "That's right, Judge, and the value of those contracts in the future have been spread across the pyramid to all contract holders." Digger mildly wondered what kind of a fee that might generate for Morton from all those contractees he represented, directly or indirectly.

"We think the company has been very generous, here," said Williams. Morton nodded his agreement. "Whitaker Industries is an unusual company. It is family owned, but as a company it is like a family, itself. We can't begin to apologize to you for what some of our executives have done, but we can assure you that the company's structure is now such that such a thing will not happen again." Again Morton nodded his agreement.

"Sounds like everybody is happy," said Digger. "Even the little people are sharing in the wealth."

"That's exactly right, Judge," said Morton. Williams nodded his agreement.

"Do you have a Stipulation and Order?"

"We do, your Honor," said Williams, placing a sheaf of papers on the desk in front of Digger and offering him an expensive fountain pen for signing.

"**G**ood morning, Digger."

Digger removed his reading glasses and looked up from the brief on his desk to see Chief Judge Carrie Parker standing in the door to his chambers.

"Hi, Carrie," he said, pushing his chair back and coming around from behind his desk to greet her. "Come on in. May I get you some coffee?"

"Thanks, Digger, and yes, please," said Judge Parker, taking one of the comfortable upholstered chairs by the window.

Digger poured a cup of steaming black coffee for her and one for himself, joining her in the chairs by the window. "What's up?" he asked, smiling.

"I thought you'd like to know I signed the Complaints on the boys from Whitaker Industries," she said, holding her saucer in one hand and lifting the china cup to her lips with the other, her deep blue eyes looking over the cup, watching for his reaction.

Digger's expression immediately turned sober. He put his coffee down on the end table between them. "What are they charged with?" he asked. "Who is prosecuting?" Digger was anxious to know in one sense, but in another, he would prefer to never think about them again. But, of course, the latter was impossible. "Are they arrested?"

"They will be, Digger," she answered. "All five of them." Of the original eight, Slater, Fowler, and Vagelli were dead. That left Randall McCoy, Orrin Rasmussen, Bertram Johnson, Charles Hood, and Fred McCloskey.

"And the charges?"

"Andy Preston and Marilee Jackson are the prosecutors signing the Complaints. Chief Morgan, himself, brought them to me for signing off on probable cause. He signed them as the complaining witness."

"Morgan, himself?"

"That's right," she acknowledged. "The Complaints I signed requested warrants, so I expect there will be some arrests in the next day or two. Apparently Randall McCoy is nowhere to be found, but the police know where to pick up the other four, and Digger?"

"Yes?"

"They are all charged with murder." Her eyes fixed on his reaction. "They were all committing a felony by acting to blackmail you into making a decision in the civil case. Greg Larson's murder was a part of that, so, even though they didn't pull the trigger, it makes it murder for each of them."

Digger made no response. He had been dealing with the fact that his ordeal was over, dealing with it very well in fact. But this brought it all back. As he thought about how he felt, though, he realized he really didn't care what happened to the PowerPlus Battery executives who had brought him so much trouble and nearly ended his life. That realization suddenly gave him an enormous sense of well-being. He would not, he now knew, dwell on some need for retribution as so many did these days. He was fine. He was over it. He just didn't want to think about it a lot in the future.

"What are you smiling about, Digger?" asked Carrie Parker. "Going to enjoy a little payback?"

"Oh, it's nothing," said Digger. "Who will get the cases?" he asked, only mildly curious.

"Not you, Digger," she grinned. "No, I'm taking all of them. It'll be less disruptive to the Duluth calendars and caseloads. And you never know, some of them might get consolidated."

Carrie Parker rose from her seat. "Thanks for the coffee, Digger," she said. "I just thought you would like to know what was going on."

"Thanks, Carrie," he said, standing to watch her leave.

EPILOGUE

"**A**ll rise." District Court is now in session, the Honorable James Digby Moss presiding!"
It was Digger's first day back in court. He noticed Mike Reynolds seated in the back with some other lawyers. Digger did not recall that Mike was involved in any of the matters on the morning calendar. He saw Kate Riley slip into the courtroom as people resumed their seats.

After calling the first case, he invited the lawyer for the moving party to proceed to argue her motion. Instead both lawyers stood. Behind them, other lawyers waiting for later hearings also stood. The lawyer whom Digger had invited to argue her motion spoke.

"Judge, before I begin on behalf of the plaintiff in this case, I just wanted to say, that is, *we all* wanted to say, and I got the privilege, that it's wonderful to have you back, sir."

The lawyers standing around the room nodded.

"Welcome back, your Honor," someone said, and they began to clap.

Digger was overwhelmed by the display of respect and affection. As the clapping subsided and people were again seated, he spoke.

"Thank you, I'm not sure what to say," he stammered slightly, then continued. "I must say it is a pleasure and an honor to be back. It is much better to be up here in a black robe, than down there in a jail uniform!"

The crowd sat watching him.

"Well," he said, a little flustered, "thank you, again. Now we had better get to work. Ms. Fletcher, now you may proceed."

"Thank you, your Honor," she rose to stand at counsel table. "This is a case in which my client, the plaintiff, was injured in ..."

A few months later ...
Milo Bracken squeezed lemon juice onto the raw oyster, salted it, held up the half shell and used the small fork to lift it into his mouth. He followed the morsel with a bite of cracker and another swallow of Coor's Light. He sat at a booth alongside the window over

299

looking the boardwalk at John's Pass in Madeira Beach, Florida. Milo was satisfied that the Friendly Fisherman restaurant at John's Pass served the finest oysters and Grouper sandwiches anywhere. The boardwalk was a full story above the water in John's Pass. The drawbridge carrying Gulf Boulevard traffic over the pass itself was just a few yards away. It was the entrance from the Gulf of Mexico into Boca Ciega Bay.

Milo finished the last of "a dozen raw" and got up to leave. Outside he walked across Gulf Boulevard to the beach where it ended at John's Pass. He turned north and walked along the beach as had become his habit. In the few months since he had left Minnesota, his appearance had greatly changed. Besides the deep rich tan from the Suncoast sun, his hair was cut short, a rejection of the idea of any further attempt to cover the top of his balding head. He had lost several pounds and trimmed up his figure. The mid-level paunch was gone. His lifestyle changes had transformed him quicker than he expected. Instead of the big, sloppy loser he had been, he was tall, lean, muscular and good looking, a far cry from his former self.

Three brown pelicans floated in formation over the tops of the condo buildings lining the beach.

The life that money brought was not all bad, he had decided. Milo reflected on his current situation as he walked among the tourists and beachcombers, the afternoon sun beating down on them. He lived here in Madeira Beach in a beachfront condo he had purchased. His open, green and tan Jeep Wrangler was parked in the reserved parking space underneath the building. The oversized tires were totally unnecessary, but he liked them. The swimming pool was maintained at a steady 84 degrees. His daughter was visiting from Minneapolis. His ex-wife might even come down to visit. He had always regretted the pain he had caused her and the trouble he brought to their marriage.

From the three million dollars he got from Griswold, he gave Vince Turcotte a half million. Vince would not take more, although an even share was offered. In Florida, he purchased the condo for $100,000. The payment of his gambling debts, the Jeep, some furniture, a bicycle, and some other toys amounted to about $60,000. It had taken some time to develop an adequate cover story for the rest, $2.34 million, but eventually he had done so and had conservatively invested it at a return of 7% *per annum* which gave him a very comfortable annual income of more than $160,000.

A small brown stingray swam close to the water's edge. Several beach walkers had stopped to watch it.

Milo smiled to himself. With everything paid for and that income he had what he came for: comfort and security on the beach.

Milo turned off the beach at the Madeira Beach Holiday Inn. At the Tiki Bar near the beach, he ordered a Diet Coke on ice. He stopped to chat with Brad, the owner of the beach umbrella and cabana concession along Madeira Beach.

"The sting rays are interfering with people swimming, but they still want to be on the beach. My business is great!" He said to Milo. "Had over three hundred filled the other day."

Three hundred at fifteen bucks a day, thought Milo. This guy has a business that's a lot better than people realize. A well kept secret. He smiled. So, he guessed, was his ... a well kept secret.

Milo walked off the beach at the public parking lot next to the Holiday Inn on the south. He unlocked his bicycle from the palm tree where he had chained it earlier. He rode out of the parking lot, across Gulf Boulevard, and a block further on 153rd Avenue past Eckerds Drug, and the Wynn-Dixie store, to the mailbox in front of the Madeira Beach municipal office building. He checked the pick-up time listed on the front of the box and deposited a plain manila, insulated envelope in the U.S. Mail. Satisfied, he rode around the curving road to the Tom Stuart Causeway, back to Gulf Boulevard and turned south towards his beachfront condo.

A few days later ...
Digger Moss looked at the large plain manila envelope. He recognized all of the rest of the mail in his basket. He was in a hurry, trying to mentally catalog each piece of mail for later handling when he had time. But the unmarked envelope bothered him.

"They're ready, Judge," said his bailiff.

Digger Moss looked at the envelope. It had no return address. It was marked, *"PERSONAL AND CONFIDENTIAL."*

"Oh, God, no!" he whispered to himself.

"Judge?" The bailiff stood, waiting for direction.

"Tell the lawyers that I'll be just a moment," he said.

Unlike the envelopes he had received from the man he now knew as Frank Griswold, this one had been mailed, not delivered. It was post marked, "Madeira Beach, Florida." He carefully opened the envelope's sealed flap and shook out the contents. Nothing came out at first. There were no documents. There were no pictures or printed messages. The only thing in the envelope, with no accompanying letter or note, was a sea shell! About the size of a silver dollar, on the smooth inner side of the shell, Digger noticed some black markings. Two large dots with a curved line below them formed a happy face on the inside of the shell. Below the grinning face, a name was printed. It simply said, "MILO."

Digger smiled, slipped the shell into the pocket of his robe, and turned toward the courtroom.

"All rise ..."